BITE OF THE

LOTUS

Shane Briant

ISBN: 0-9578-8260-02
ISBN-13: 9780957882607

In memory of Coco our beloved Pig Dog, without whom I struggle for breath.

And for Wendy, without whom I would not be able to breathe at all.

ACKNOWLEDGMENTS

I would like to thank all those who kindly helped me with my research.
Rowan Barnsley for his limitless contacts.
The New South Wales Police Force, The Bomb Disposal Unit, Chris furze, Mike Holtly, Carmel Walton, Jack Curtis, Mike Hagan,Russell Oxford, Gary Simpson, Carl Robinson, Loc Tran, Peter Smith, Alan McKay, Tony Holmes, Ron Dunphy, Russ Properjohn, Nick Thompson, John Ferguson, Bon Senkewitz, Tony Caristo, Alex Postan, Andrew Stroken, Marsha Pearl of Communications Control Systems International New York, and Jeffrey Bloom.

Scott Citron of Scottcitrondesign, New York for the cover design.

Wendy Lycett-Briant for a wonderful edit.

1.

Challis Street. Sydney.
March 26th.

The thin girl opened the fridge door, reaching inside for the four-inch square cellophaned package. As her slender fingers hung momentarily in the chill air, she became aware of a muscle in her forearm as it fibrillated slightly. It spasmed for a couple of seconds then was still.

Bathed in the soft bluish neon light of the Kelvinator, the skin of her arm seemed to glow almost translucently, the baby hair beginning to stand up as it reacted to the change in temperature. The thermostat had been turned down low; the explosive had to remain malleable.

Her fingers closed round the yellow parcel. Lifting it out, she pushed the fridge door shut and crossed to the small kitchen table behind her.

Her slim forefinger pressed a vein in her right wrist as she felt for a pulse, aware that her heart rate was up. Fifty-two. She'd settle for that.

She crossed to the pantry and opened the cupboard, concentrating on the steady rhythm of her breathing. Slowly in, hold, then slowly out.

On the center shelf was a packet of breakfast cereal. She pulled it down, placing it on the table next to the yellow slices. She then moved into the tiny bedroom.

The room was cold, dank, and airless. Curtains were drawn across the single small window. A bare bulb in the bedside lamp provided the only light source.

In the top drawer of a small Taiwanese chest of drawers was a money belt. Returning to the kitchen, she spread it lengthways from left to right across the table.

A glance at the kitchen clock told her she had plenty of time. The call had come through just before 6 am. The plane was in the air. He was on board. The flight would take approximately eight hours - give or take an hour allowing for adverse weather and possible stacking at Mascot.

She closed her eyes, leaning back against the uncomfortable kitchen chair, her hands resting lightly on the edge of the table.

The images began to flow. She was crossing the busy street, entering the building. The elevator doors slid shut. There was upward movement. She was walking down the hall. The door was directly ahead. It opened and she was stepping inside, her finger on the switch.

A truck barreled down the road outside, interrupting her reverie.

The cereal box housed a length of coiled wire, a nine volt battery, a simple light switch, a small light bulb, and a three-inch silver cylinder, the thickness of half a pencil, from which two wires protruded.

She laid the components carefully on the table, just below the money belt; the loop of wire to the left, the switch and the tiny light bulb in the center, the cylinder to the right.

Her treasures seemed to have a life of their own. Sufficient explosive to reduce a human being to the smallest of tissue fragments. Enough to reduce a life to body vapor.

She was reminded of a line by Shelley – *From whence we come, to which we will return - commended to cold oblivion.*

A chill coursed down her back.

She stripped each of the four-inch slices of explosive from their individual plastic coatings, stacking them in two separate piles.

Unfolding the coiled wire, she laid it flat the full length of the vinyl belt, threading the wire through the customized eyeholes. The main bulk of the waistband contained three compartments, two the same size as the squares of explosive, designed to hold the Metabel snugly, a smaller one to accommodate the nine-volt battery. A hole in the belt to the left held the switching mechanism.

Her fingers worked surely and efficiently as they had done so many times in rehearsals. The wires were attached to the battery, the light bulb and the firing switch. In under a minute the circuit was complete, and ready to be tested.

She flicked the switch, enjoying the familiar pressure of the hard plastic lever on the thumb of her left hand. The light shone brightly. All set and ready to arm.

Disconnecting the wires from the light, she placed the bulb to one side, and reached for the three inch army issue detonator, the white lead wires distinguishing it from commercial issue. Inside was the central core bridge wire - the heat sensitive element that would set off the charge of PETN as the electricity coursed through it.

She gently lifted two slices of the yellow Metabel from the first compartment, placed the detonator between them, then pressed the sandwich together. Then she disconnected one wire from the small battery, and connected the twin white wires to the circuit. Finally she opened the flap of the first compartment and slipped the yellow material inside, then patted the Velcro shut.

Its twin, the second stack, was loaded into the compartment directly adjacent, and the second flap closed.

Finally she checked the firing switch. It was in the 'off' position.

She looked away for a second, clearing her mind of all thoughts, then looked back at the switch. It was as she had thought, clearly marked 'off'. Now was the time for the greatest care. She'd come this far. She'd choose the time, not fate.

A twist, and the last wire was secured to the battery.

Withdrawing her slender bony fingers from the belt, she slowly and deliberately unbuttoned her blouse, easing it off her shoulders. Naked to the waist, she walked back into the bedroom, halting before the mirror. Her torso was painfully thin, though the breasts were heavy, the nipples hardening in the chill of the room.

She ran her hands over her upper body, then up her slender neck and through her short tousled chestnut hair. She'd once been pretty. Or so they'd said.

It hardly mattered now.

She walked back to the kitchen and secured a wire to the arming.

Lifting the belt carefully by both ends, she wound it round her small waist, buckling the belt at the front.

3

It felt tight against her skin. It felt good. She was a living, breathing bomb.

She laughed aloud.

Hendrik Ohlson shifted from foot to foot in the forecourt of the Savoy Hotel. He felt uneasy. Something about her voice had disturbed him. Something he couldn't comprehend.

He scanned the crowds exiting the Royal Arcade on the opposite side of the street, but still there was no sign of her. The small photograph she'd given him was curled tightly in his right hand. A few feet away from him, the bell captain, a tall Maori, stood at his desk, busy with valet car dockets.

A van braked heavily as a motorbike courier snaked in and out of the rush hour traffic. Then the lights changed, and the crowds began to flood across the road towards him.

'Are you waiting for someone, sir. Can I call a cab for you?'

Ohlson jumped as the bell captain placed an arm on his shoulder. He stared at the hotel employee for a second before regaining his composure.

'Thanks, but I'm fine,' he replied. The man obviously wanted him out of the way, he thought bitterly. To hell with him, he'd stay there as long as he liked.

The street was like a wind tunnel, the blast swirling into the sweep of the hotel entrance.

Just then the cellular phone in his jacket pocket pulsed. He pulled it out.

'I'm across the street,' she said.

His eyes swept the crowds outside the arcade opposite. 'Where?'

'Is he inside?' There was a sharp edge to her voice. She sounded so different. Cold.

'Yes. Arrived ten minutes ago.'

'Did you get the room number?'

'One five zero one. Fifteenth floor.'

'Now listen very carefully.' She spoke slowly, without emotion. 'Leave now. Destroy the photo. You never spoke to me today. Do you understand?'

'I understand," the young man replied uneasily.

The line went dead.

As he pocketed the phone Ohlson could see the bell captain moving back in his direction, so he began to amble down the slip road that led to the street.

As he reached the pavement, he saw her crossing the road in a wave of pedestrians. Her eyes were on fire. Within seconds she was at the main doors of the hotel. A doorman held open the door for her, and she was inside.

She moved swiftly to the elevators. She'd mentally been here so many times before, imagining the sharp clicks of feet on the beige marble, the milling crowds, the smell of soft leather and carpets, the scents and brand new designer clothes. But in her imaginings there had been sweat and fear. Today each limb felt energized, as if powered by lithium batteries.

Today she felt better than she'd felt in a long time. Her skin was warm, and her pulse was as slow as a marathon runner's.

She halted before the bank of six elevators. With a soft ping the doors directly in front of her slid silently open.

Hers was empty. Pressing the fifteenth floor button, she willed it to continue its smooth ascent unchallenged to the fifteenth.

Five, six, seven, eight. Her eyes were set on the numbered lights above her head. Then she closed her eyes and began to mouth the words.

The faintest breeze caressed her face as the elevator doors slid aside. A glance left and right. The corridor was empty. Across the hallway the room numbers were listed with arrows.

Turning to her right, she walked slowly down the empty hall, checking the numbers on the doors. The air was thick with the pervasive scent of peace lilies - a floral centerpiece stood on a period oak refectory table opposite the double doors of a suite.

1501. 'The Stutton Room'.

The hallway was deadly quiet. She leaned her head towards the door, straining to hear conversation from within. There was no sound.

Her left hand slid inside her jacket, the fingers searching for the belt, the ball of her thumb making the lightest contact with the firing switch. Then she raised her right hand to the door.

'*Behold, I stand at the door and knock,*' she whispered.

Ohlson pushed his way through the crowds back into the hotel. He was concerned for her - she'd looked out of control.

As he did so, he stopped dead in his tracks. Through the glass he could see a man stepping from a cab outside. Ohlson's mind began to race. How was it possible?

The man brushed past him, the doorman skipping ahead of him to hold open the glass doors.

Ohlson swore silently as he pulled the cellular phone from his pocket and stabbed at the keys.

Venice's hand hung in the air for several seconds. The silence that had followed the sharp rap on the oak doors was an eerie contrast.

This was the last thing she'd anticipated. In her daydreams, everything had happened quickly. She'd knocked, she'd heard footsteps, the door had opened. Now she stood in the silence of the hallway and the cloying sweet smell of the lilies was beginning to sicken her.

She drew her hand back to knock again when a wave of uncontrollable apprehension surged through her body. What was happening? Why was there no response?

Her face felt stung by a million tiny red-hot needles, the skin on her back and chest suddenly wet with sweat. Her ears were buzzing.

The stench of the funereal lilies seemed like an invasive portentous canker.

Her left hand was now beginning to shake, the forefinger on the switch drifting dangerously left and right on the plastic.

As she opened her mouth to scream, the door in front of her clicked open.

A man stood before her. A totally unfamiliar face. She stared in bewilderment.

'Can I help you?' he asked kindly, a quizzical look playing on his friendly face.

The blood was roaring through the veins of her temples. The man's words were as indistinct and incomprehensible as a scream in a hurricane. She could vaguely make out the figures of others in the room. She lifted her finger from the firing switch.

Like an automaton, she took one step forward into the room. The man followed her inside, walking past her to the window to speak to a colleague who was sitting at a long glass conference table.

'I think you have the wrong room,' the shadowy second man said matter-of-factly.

She stood three feet inside the door, her breathing now coming in short sharp bursts, thinking at any second she would vomit.

It was then that she saw him.

He was sitting in an armchair by the window. The strong light behind him had made him a shadowy silhouette.

'Perhaps we should call security,' the silhouette said to one of his colleagues as he rose and stepped slightly closer, away from the backlit window.

As his features began to take shape, the hatred surged within her in an instant. Suddenly she was whole again.

But as she opened her mouth to speak her body froze. The eyes, the lips, the same build - maybe a few pounds less. He looked practically identical. But it was someone else!

Her entire body was now beginning to shake uncontrollably. It was someone else.

The three men stared open-mouthed at the young girl. The man by the table looked at his companions, completely nonplussed.

'Perhaps we should call someone?' he said softly. 'Our young friend here looks ill. I think she should see a doctor.'

The silence was broken abruptly by the shrill beep of her cellular phone.

Slowly she fumbled with her left hand, searching for the phone in her pants pocket. As her fingers closed round its base, she eased her right forefinger from the firing switch on her body belt.

The man by the table reached out for a phone to call security, as his companions continued to stare at the girl as she tugged at the phone, now snagged in her waist belt.

It was then that the aerial made contact with the lead wire.

No one in the room experienced another second of their lives as the blinding white sheet of light lit up the room and the blast ripped them to shreds.

2.

JFK Airport. New York.
March 26th.

It was twenty-eight degrees Fahrenheit and falling, the tarmac still wet from the mid-afternoon shower, reflecting the silver underbelly of the jet in a surreal Daliesque configuration. Vapor clouded the hood of the FMC parked at its side, drifting slowly upwards, mingling with the exhaust of the truck and the hoar-breath of the crew beneath the fuselage. The conveyor belt chugged and rippled unevenly as it rotated, devoid of luggage; the noise mixing with the roar of the engines from the runways and the whine of jets taxiing nearby. As ever, the air stank of Avgas, packaged air food, and stale humanity.

Yevgeny Poliakov looked down from his vantagepoint just inside the bulk cargo door at the rear of the Boeing 767. The shallow angled rotating conveyor belt reached just inside the twin skins of the hull. Molino stood at its base, looking away from the plane towards the baggage dock for the second wagon train of dollies carrying the last of the bags.

'Doc' Cheetham, the ramp supervisor, or Tarmac One as the coordinators were known, was pacing, slapping his gloved fists together trying to keep warm, trying vainly to alleviate his anxiety. From the moment a plane shut down to the moment it was pushed out he perpetually crisscrossed beneath, searching for the slightest hint of trouble – a belt breakdown, a glitch in the refueling, anything that might delay departure by one minute.

Poliakov watched as Cheetham switched his attention from the refuellers to eyeball the loaders, standing idle by the side of the FMC – the customized Ford vehicle that held the conveyor on its back. He could see him pulling out a handheld radio to call load control. He could almost lip-synch the motherfucker, *What the hell's going down? Our slot's 5.45. Come on guys, it's shift-ass time!* Well, he'd soon be well and truly up to his fat ears in shit. To hell with him - he'd never liked the miserable old man.

Poliakov sucked his teeth in satisfaction as he shifted his glance to the left engine pod. Sol Yeager, the ground engineer, was inspecting the inlet compressor blades; his green beanie pulled down well over his ears. Screw him too. Screw 'em all.

Two refuellers stood under the aircraft. A high-pressure hose, coupled to the underside of the aircraft, pumped in Avgas.

Molino looked up at the bulk cargo hold then deliberately ran two fingers round the rim of his Mets cap, curling his forefinger as he locked eyes with his partner. Poliakov nodded his head once. He understood. The second tractor was on its way and with it the armored truck.

Walking casually to the cab of the self-propelled high lifter parked by the forward cargo hold, Molino opened the driver's door and climbed in out of the chill. By the lifter's side another vehicle was hoisting the igloos – the panniers that contained the majority of the passenger bags – onto the flat top of the lifter, before they were taken up along the rollers into the hold.

At the base of the conveyor belt, a tractor towing four dollies drew to a halt. Cheetham barked orders at the other loaders, hustling them along.

Poliakov watched, motionless in the cargo doorway, as the men moved truculently forward, their arms wrapped round themselves as they fought to keep warm. He felt a warm glow of confidence. All was progressing smoothly. Nothing he and Molino hadn't foreseen. He hoped it would stay that way - he knew he had an awful lot to lose.

The silver Delta 767 had docked at bay 14 and shut down at 16.20. Originating from Boston, it was now in the process of being turned around double quick to become Delta flight 30 to Moscow. Normally the daily flight to Moscow originated out of JFK, but today was different - it had been grounded due to a hydraulic leak so an incoming flight had been re-scheduled. This had been an unforeseen stroke of luck. People would be hurried, and hurried people were careless.

To Poliakov's left the catering scissors truck had been locked on to the rear of the jet for more than fifteen minutes. Soon it'd be gone. To his right, Molino was sitting in the cab of the high lifter by the forward cargo hold, ready.

The two other members of Yevgeny's crew, Greer and Phipps, stood by the foremost dolly, heaving the late bags onto the belt. The majority was silvered trunks of varying sizes, numbered on the side from one to fifty. Each one was marked, 'Optical Equipment – Fragile'. The biggest, number 38, had the dimensions of a medium-sized trunk and an added sticker, *Heavy*.

Poliakov's focus was on the cream armored truck that was approaching from the airport building.

He checked his watch quickly. Five-twenty. They'd have to load fast.

As the armored truck drew to a halt, Cheetham strode to its side and the cab door swung open. A guard stepped down, slamming the door behind him. A pump action shotgun was carried lazily across his chest. He nodded off-handedly to Cheetham as he loped to the rear of the vehicle and banged on the metal. The rear door opened, and two more armed guards jumped down lightly.

As the silvered trunk numbered 38 was hefted onto the conveyor, Phipps shouted up at Poliakov. 'Hey, Yevvy! Look at this,' he said, pointing to the *Heavy* label. He then lifted one end of it with one hand to show off, then roared with laughter. Yevgeny grinned back, flexing his biceps. Phipps and Greer laughed loudly.

As Poliakov dragged the trunk off the conveyor, he looked across at the armored truck. The driver was backing it up, so the rear faced the conveyor belt.

The driver remained in his cab. The other three guards stood at the corners of the cream truck, looking around them unconcernedly while the loading of the late bags continued. They'd wait their turn. Their consignment would be the last on. As always.

Poliakov continued to haul the bags off the conveyor belt, stacking them in the hold. Each time he returned to the open cargo door, his eyes drifted past the waiting guards to the farthest dolly in the train.

As Greer shifted the final two bags, Poliakov spotted the cage. A fat Persian cat stared through the wire, wide-eyed with apprehension. Livestock was always the last to be loaded. Poliakov's shoulders relaxed. The cat was his comfort ticket. The cargo hold was normally kept at seven degrees Celsius. But if an animal was listed on the manifest, the pilot threw the switch in the cockpit from 'normal' to 'vent'. In vent mode the temperature rose to 18 degrees for the comfort of the animals. It also ventilated the hold, taking care of any unwanted smells.

As the cage reached the top of the conveyor belt, Poliakov checked his watch once more. Twenty-six minutes past five. Just about on schedule. Over the top of the cage he could see the two guards beginning to pull the white canvas sacks from the rear of the armored truck, dragging them to the belt and heaving them on. Poliakov knew exactly how much each of the fifty bags weighed. Eighty-eight pounds. Fifty bags. He began to feel the first signs of an adrenaline rush.

The driver and the third armed guard stood at the base of the belt, shotguns across their chests, while the other two sweated with the sacks.

An airport security vehicle cruised silently to a halt some twenty feet from the cream truck, the driver flashing his headlights. The third armed guard nodded in his direction then continued his lazy scanning of the perimeter. The security vehicle cruised on.

Poliakov hefted the first of the white sacks off the belt at the top, dragging it to the far side of the fuselage. As the others followed, he stacked them five abreast, five deep and two high. When the last was in place, he hooked up a vertical net of webbing that separated the bulk cargo from the aft freight container, clipping it to the rings in the ceiling and walls of the inner fuselage.

He paused for a few seconds. His chest was heaving with the exertion. He then secured another net over the stack of white canvas sacks. Finally, he secured the last of the remaining vertical nets, behind which were the late suitcases and the silver optical containers.

After one quick backward glance around the hold, Poliakov stood at the open door and called to one of the guards below, jumping down onto the front of the conveyor vehicle, one hand braced against the fuselage of the plane. The guard nodded perfunctorily, making a note on a clipboard as he moved forward toward the jet to check the inventory.

The guard was only a few feet away, when there was a harsh scraping sound several feet forward of the hold door, like chalk on a blackboard. Poliakov abruptly felt the shell of the plane shudder. He smiled inwardly as he saw the approaching guard's head whip round, his attention abruptly diverted from his checklist to the high lifter.

Instantly Sol Yeager was screaming something, waving his arms as he ran towards the lifter.

Molina had initially backed it away from the jet, and had then attempted a forward arc. But he'd failed to make the turn, striking the underside shell with the top right-hand corner of the vehicle, creasing the outer skin.

This was nightmare time for Yeager.

Poliakov quickly scanned the immediate vicinity of his cargo door. The driver and all three guards were looking open-mouthed towards Molina's truck. Yeager was shouting and swearing at Molina, while reaching up to examine the skin of the plane. Cheetham had vanished, but soon reappeared from the far side of the plane in animated conversation with the flight engineer. They looked as grim as hell.

Greer, Phipps and the other loaders had ambled over to the side of the high lifter to enjoy the show. Molina was now trying to back it up again. As it began to move, Yeager screamed wildly at Molina to stop.

Poliakov watched from his position on the side of the conveyor truck. Now was the moment.

In a single fluid movement, he jumped back into the bulk cargo hold, rolling under the black netting. He opened the top of number 38 and stepped inside, tucking his knees tight to his chest, pulling the lid shut with the customized handle on the inside of the lock.

Outside, Molina leapt from the cab of his FMC, flailing his arms in frustrated anger. The loaders laughed and the guards looked on curiously as Yeager fumed – as ground engineer, he was responsible for the serviceability of the aircraft, and he was now in major trouble.

Yeager and the flight engineer spent the following twelve minutes on a platform examining the damage to the skin of the hull, deciding whether the plane would still be serviceable. If the damage was limited to the outer skin surface, as was often the case with bird strikes during flight, then a quick spot repair might be effected with high speed tape, an extraordinarily tough silver plasticized tape which could withstand in-flight winds of up to six hundred knots.

Fifteen minutes later, the tape was in place. Yeager had signed off the repairs in the captain's technical log in the cockpit, the captain was calling the tower to confirm his slot time, while the co-pilot was feeding in the pre-stored navigational flight plan to Moscow. One by one the lights signifying open doors were changing from red to green as they were closed.

'Bulk cargo hold still open Mr. Yeager.'

'I'll see to it on the way out. Enjoy the trip Captain.'

'Will do, Mr. Yeager.'

Cheetham signed the forms on the guard's clipboard, then stepped up onto the side of the conveyor belt truck to reach the bulk cargo door. Behind him he could hear Yeager shouting something at him. He pulled the door closed and locked it into place, then jumped down onto the apron.

In the hold, curled up in his personalized silvered flight capsule, Yevgeny Poliakov tried to make himself as comfortable as possible. It was going to be a hard night's work – his only companions a Persian cat and two hundred and fifty million dollars in freshly minted uncirculated one hundred-dollar bills.

3.

Sydney.
March 26th.

Raymond Brancusi looked up as a shadow was cast across the Australian Bomb Data Center newsletter that lay on his desk. Through the window of the prefab his eyes locked briefly with Steve Gorman as the tall detective strode past outside with just the suggestion of a swagger. Gorman winked. Always the joker, Gorman. One of the spooks, the nickname given to members of the Technical Services Group. Spooks were a breed of their own, a secretive bunch. None of the other police sections had access to their small bunker. But if the National Crime Authority, the Independent Commission Against Corruption, or the Australian Security Intelligence Organization needed technical surveillance, the spooks were their men. They could wire a house within an hour – twenty minutes if pushed. After that, if anyone so much as farted inside, it was on tape.

Brancusi's eyes returned to the bulletin from St Louis. The bulk of new information usually came from the States. Today's selection was pretty run of the mill; letter bombs, diagrammed and photographed, together with sketches of construction and labeling for future reference; breakdowns on various American terrorist organizations – 'Christian Patriots', 'Freemen', 'Right Wing Loyalists', 'Guardians of Freedom' and the like. Nothing groundbreaking.

He looked up sharply as the door at the far end of the prefab slammed shut.

'Take a look at this, Ray. Page five, ' Schroeder snapped angrily, tossing the *Sydney Morning Herald* onto the corner of Brancusi's desk. Arty Schroeder had been his partner for several years. 'Miserable bastard. Strapped a device to the collar of a dog and let the mutt loose with the IED round its neck hoping some bastard would call a uniform and it'd take a cops legs off. Can you believe it? I'd have filth like that put down!' He walked to the corner of the prefab, to what passed for a small kitchen area. 'You want a coffee?' he called over his shoulder to Brancusi as he poured water into the head of the espresso machine.

The Bomb Unit was full strength at four. A branch of the Forensic Services Group, the squad worked in twin teams on twenty-four hour call. They were the full-time complement of the Bomb Disposal Unit. Schroeder and Brancusi were one team; Maier and Williams the other. Of course, there were another fifty or so fully bomb trained police who could be called on if the need arose, but it seldom did. There'd been meetings concerning the Olympics, at which a projected figure of a 150 full-time had been bandied around. Brancusi and Schroeder had suggested more than 200, but had been met with cold stares by their bosses. Everyone had his or her financial agenda.

'What time's your appointment with the shrink?' Schroeder asked, as he packed the Pavoni with Italian Dark Roast.

'Five-thirty. He's new. Hope he doesn't take himself too seriously.'

Brancusi was due for his annual 'psycho' that afternoon, the psychological review each member of the squad was given each year; one usually complemented by a physical. The psycho made good sense, bearing in mind some of the more stressful situations the squad was put through during the course of the year; disarming improvised exploding devices, often with only the scant protection of their sweaty thirty-five kilo Kevlar protective suits, pulling mangled babies from the burning shells of cars, or collecting body parts smaller than a roast dinner from the debris of buildings for identification.

Over the years some of the squad had coped better than others. None had cracked, though a few had moved on to other areas. To Brancusi and Schroeder, it was still a job; a corpse or limb was just that, part of a crime scene to be made safe. It was then a source of trace evidence to be carefully placed in a body bag to be tested for radiopaque and radiolucent material and explosive residue. But the images that always scarred their minds were the children and babies. They were the stuff of nightmares.

Brancusi was about to speak, when the sound of distant thunder was audible in the room. He looked up, locking eyes with Schroeder.

'CBD?' Schroeder asked. But he knew.

'Better finish your coffee Arty - I give that phone two minutes, max.'

'Could be something else,' Schroeder ventured.

'Could be,' Brancusi replied, not believing it. He drained the steaming espresso, his eyes on the phone.

'You'll miss the psycho.'

'Shame, hey?' Brancusi replied, smiling. This was when the adrenaline began to flow. If he was right, the radio call from VKG would come through in under a minute, and they'd be on their way to who the hell knew what. He began to do some squats, stretching his arms – who knew, he might be trapped in a Kevlar suit for hours, and he knew how much the muscles would ache.

As Brancusi's eyes drifted back to the phone, it rang. He picked up. 'Bomb Disposal Unit. Brancusi.'

Schroeder sat on the edge of his desk, blowing on the surface of his coffee, presenting a calm exterior as he listened to Brancusi's side of the conversation. Though he felt the same surge of adrenalin as his partner, action affected him differently. He thought of his boy. He always thought of Sammy as he went on a job. He knew Brancusi had nerves of steel, and often wished he were made of the same stuff, but it was always these first few minutes that unnerved him. It couldn't be called fear, just an apprehension at the prospect of some terrible scenario that lay ahead. That, and the thought he might never see Sammy again.

'Should be there in around fifteen minutes if we get lucky.' Brancusi replaced the phone. 'Let's get moving. It's the Savoy. Something big just went off on the fifteenth floor. Not gas. Sounds like a major IED to me. No fire yet. Area's being secured.'

Schroeder drove. No sirens. Policy, unless absolutely necessary - and post explosive situations were not so deemed. The Police Department preferred to keep the profile of the Bomb Disposal Unit as low as possible. Plain white truck, no insignia. Brancusi sat behind his partner, patching a line through to the Crime Scene Officer in Charge for information.

By the time the clean, white, four-cylinder turbo diesel Mercedes truck had turned right into Botany Road, Brancusi was already on the line talking strategy.

'Detective Senior Constable Brancusi. Bomb Squad. We're on the road.'

'Inspector Ross Pulman here. What's your ETA?'

'We'll be with you in around eight minutes.'

Schroeder pressed his foot down on the accelerator as he wove his way in and out of the rush-hour traffic.

'Will the area be clear by then?' Brancusi continued.

'Couldn't be a worse time of day. Getting ambulances through isn't going to be easy, but the hotel's practically evacuated already. Staff has been pretty efficient. Last civilians are coming out now. We'll draw the lines three blocks in all directions.' Pulman spoke very quickly and concisely. He knew Brancusi needed to know as much as possible now so as to cut down the chat on arrival. 'There's a hell of a lot of debris, glass and so on for hundreds of yards.'

'Any fire?'

'The fire boys were keen as hell to go on up. I gave them the okay with the proviso - no flames, no entry. I know how you guys feel about the brigade tramping through the crime scene screwing up the evidence.'

'Casualties?' he continued.

'Down here, plenty. None deceased. Up there, we don't know. That's why I gave the boys the go ahead. The Fire Chief took one quick look up on the fifteenth. Said that was enough for him. If there's anyone up there, they're part of the debris.' Brancusi could hear the ambulance sirens and a good deal of shouting in the background as he waited for Pulman to continue.

'Epicenter is the fifteenth floor - conference room directly adjacent to the lift.'

'How many were in there?'

'No one knows. But it's the smallest meeting room they have, thank God. Accommodates up to twenty. Every window on the floor is out, plus most on up to the seventeenth. Same two floors down. Damage across the street's pretty bad too, but mostly cosmetic. There's some pretty dense smoke coming out of the windows facing the epicenter.'

'But no evidence of flames?'

'Not as yet. I've sent a man across the road with some binos to keep an eye out for flames. If he sees any, I won't be able to hold off the fire boys. Sorry.'

'I'll need a detailed list of everything that should be in the conference room, sir. That means all furniture, any electrical equipment, decoration - the whole box and dice. I'll need that before we go in. That'll give me some idea of what *shouldn't* be there.'

'Already organized. It'll be on hand when you arrive.'

Schroeder stood hard on the brakes to avoid a flat bed truck that had right of way at the intersection of King Street. He slapped the horn as his truck snaked through behind it, hurtling down George Street - they were a matter of minutes away now and he wasn't stopping for anyone.

'Getting suited up,' Brancusi called to Schroeder as he replaced the receiver and made his way towards the back of the truck to where the Kevlar equipment was hung.

The truck lurched suddenly to the left, then to the right, then straightened out. At the police tape across George Street, Schroeder stood on the brakes. The road ahead was littered with debris; broken glass, branches of trees and smallish pieces of twisted metal from damaged vehicles. Up further, police and ambulance personnel were attending to the injured. Some were on stretchers, others still lying on the pavement, or in the road being attended to by medics. Splashes of blood were everywhere.

A uniformed policeman ran across the road, pulling aside the tape. Schroeder again stepped on the gas, accelerating down to the corner of Grosvenor Street, at the same time shooting a glance up at the side of the Savoy for signs of smoke and flame.

'We'll leave Woody. He'll be useless unless we set the controls up on the fifteenth, can't operate him from down here. We take the Little Rat - what do you say?' Brancusi shouted. Schroeder nodded.

Woody was the robotic disarming device shackled to the center of the truck behind the driving seat. The twin-tracked vehicle was controlled from the console behind the driver's seat. The robot looked like a baby tank, with a cut down twelve-gauge shotgun that ran along the center and two video cameras mounted on the front. For many initial bomb screenings, Woody was invaluable. But he weighed plenty, and the logistics of taking him up fifteen weren't appealing. Besides, there'd be real problems receiving the signal back in the truck from that far away, and that'd mean having to disassemble a good deal of the controlling hardware, and hike it up to the crime scene. The Little Rat, on the other hand, was perfect for a job like this if they encountered an IED. A miniature Woody, the Little Rat was state of the art new issue, much smaller, lower, and a breeze to operate.

Schroeder stopped the truck and set the handbrake. Brancusi was already suited – his helmet in his left hand. He pulled open a compartment to the left, reaching inside for the breathing apparatus.

The BA gear was usually a must in these situations, not only because of the presence of smoke, but on account of airborne particles. Normally these dispersed with open blasted windows in approximately thirty minutes. But in a contained area dispersal took longer – maybe hours. With the possibility of vaporized body tissue hanging in the air, BA gear was invaluable – especially in the modern era of HIV. However, it was a question of choices – it was either the Kevlar protective suit, or the BA gear together with a lightweight protective suit. You couldn't wear both. So Brancusi's initial choice on seeing the windows blown was to err on the side of caution and go for the suit – the possibility of a secondary explosion outweighed the danger of smoke and airborne particles.

Pulman strode up to the truck as Brancusi stepped out.

'Inspector Pulman, Incident Commander. The details of the room,' he said, handing Brancusi the list itemized by the hotel management. Brancusi's eyes scanned the diagram as he did his best to memorize each item together with its place in the floor plan of the conference room.

'Still no fire?' Brancusi had to shout over the noise of the media chopper overhead.

'No,' Pulman replied.

'Secondary?'

Pulman's face was momentarily a blank. Brancusi estimated his superior to be in his early thirties – pretty damn young to have pulled his rank. He shot a glance at Schroeder, who was now out of the truck and standing behind Pulman carrying the BA gear in case one or both of the team changed their minds and decided to use them. Schroeder grinned as he dropped the equipment beside Brancusi, and returned to the truck for the Little Rat.

'Excuse my asking, sir. Have you attended a bomb incident before? You may be unfamiliar with some of the procedure.'

'No, Senior Constable Brancusi, I haven't.' There was the slightest edge to Pulman's voice. He clearly didn't enjoy being lectured by a junior, though he was very much aware of the chain of command in these situations, and right now it was one based on expertise rather than rank.

'Right. Well, the Bomb Unit is now taking control. Has there been any secondary explosion?'

'No.'

'Okay. My partner and I are going up right now. My partner will take up a position two floors below the blast floor. From there he'll be in radio contact with each of us.'

Schroeder reappeared from the truck with the small robot, placing it beside the other gear.

'I want this entire street completely evacuated,' Brancusi continued at speed. 'If you have to move those injured in the streets faster than the medics would wish, do it. No one is to go inside the building or stand in the street inside the tapes until Senior Constable Schroeder or myself say so. If that means the use of reasonable force, so be it. The Fire Brigade is an exception. Okay?'

Pulman nodded.

'Please reposition the tapes two hundred meters from the farthest piece of wreckage. Set another cordon a hundred feet further back. That's for the general public. All exterior wreckage will have to be sifted for bomb fragments. Also any human tissue - if there *are* casualties. Police and emergency vehicles can operate within the two cordons. As soon as we give the all clear for secondaries, we can shrink the distances, but not till then.'

Schroeder looked upwards to the news helicopter, then locked eyes with Brancusi as he handed him an attaché case of tools and X-ray gear.

'And get rid of the chopper,' Brancusi continued. 'If there's a secondary explosion on the roof it could blast in all directions, including upwards. Could well bring it down, as could the vacuum created afterwards.

'When Constable Schroeder and I come out, and have declared the area safe, the conference room will be classified a 'crime scene'. Then we'll officially be in 'post blast situation'. Up to that moment my partner and I call the shots. I'll need to talk to the Crime Scene Examiner then - not before. Please have a team of people ready to extract any casualties. All to wear BA gear.' Brancusi shot a quick look at Schroeder. 'Let's go?'

'Let's do it,' Schroeder replied. They strode forward towards the Savoy, walking as fast as their heavy awkward suits allowed.

The climb up towards the fifteenth floor was hell, though both men were extremely fit. At the thirteenth floor, Schroeder pushed open the fire door and put down the robot in the corridor, unloading the radio equipment.

Brancusi placed all the gear he would not need immediately next to Schroeder's.

'Okay, I'm going up,' said Brancusi, picking up the tool bag, attaché case, and the X-ray camera in his left hand, while he adjusted the chin support of the helmet which housed the microphone with his right.

Schroeder nodded at his partner. 'Brancusi's going in now, sir,' he told Pulman on the radio. He then slapped Brancusi lightly on the leg as his partner disappeared through the fire door.

At the fourteenth floor Brancusi began to encounter severe smoke haze. It was to be expected, even though smoke usually traveled upwards unless escape was possible through a window or door.

As he reached the fifteenth floor, Brancusi stopped and looked down the hallway. The elevator bank was just visible through the smoke, half way down. The entire hallway was littered with fragments of wood, glass and green vegetable matter. A gaping hole in the wall allowed daylight to shine through the smoke haze into the hallway. Brancusi presumed this to be the entrance to the conference room - the double doors must have fragmented completely as the blast radiated in all directions within the room. Opposite the door were the shredded remnants of a heavy refectory table on which could well have stood an arrangement of flowers – this accounted for the vegetable matter, though it was always possible it had come in through the windows. As far as he could estimate, the hotel had not suffered any significant structural damage. This was a good sign for the structure, not so good for anyone inside at the time of the explosion - if a blast was in any way contained it had the effect of magnifying the damage inside.

'On the fifteenth. In the hallway. Structure looks good. Lot of debris. No fire visible.'

As he walked slowly forward, he felt the walls with his gloved hands. They were cool and there was no evidence of outwards buckling. He looked upwards at the ceiling, though the heavy smoke made vision difficult.

He paused as he reached an opening which once had been the double doors of the conference room, placing the tool bag, the attaché case, and the X-ray camera on the blackened and debris-strewn carpet just outside. If he encountered anything dubious he'd ask Schroeder to bring up the Little Rat to render it safe with the help of the disrupter. It was either that or 'hand entry' with tools such as scalpels or screwdrivers. This was a last resort since it was inherently the most hazardous.

'Going in,' said Brancusi.

'Roger,' Brancusi heard in his headset, followed by the faint relay of information to Pulman.

Brancusi moved forward, edging round the splintered doorway. He looked inside.

The large room, even through the smoke, looked like a charnel house. The initial blast had blown out every window into the street below, including the wooden frames. The walls appeared to have contained the blast. There was some minor evidence of a buckling of the ceiling a couple of feet inside the doors as the blast radiated upwards, but it was insignificant. The vacuum caused by the massive surge of air out through the windows had dragged plaster and brickwork from the outside of the building. It was strewn everywhere. There had been a massive amount of secondary fragmentation as the furniture was blown to pieces the size of matchsticks. But worst of all was the color of the room. Blood and tissue covered the floor, walls and ceiling – in some cases in splatters a foot wide, in others sprayed as with a garden hose.

'Looks bad. Casualties. Blood, tissue everywhere. No movement. Moving forward.'

'Roger.'

Brancusi took one step inside the room and scanned from left to right in sweeps of not more than a foot at a time, mentally attempting to checklist what he saw with what had been on the list given to him by Pulman. It was damned hard, as very little was where it should have been. It was scarcely recognizable as furniture anyway. It was made doubly hard by the smoke, which continued to swirl towards the open windows.

His eyes suddenly locked onto what was now clearly identifiable as a human torso. It was to his right, up against the wall that backed onto the hallway. At a guess, Brancusi judged it to be female, but he could easily have been wrong – size wasn't everything. The legs were missing, possibly blasted through the window, possibly in smaller pieces somewhere within the room, possibly vaporized entirely. The torso from the waist to the middle face had been entirely de-gloved of skin. The amount of body tissue at chest height again confirmed Brancusi's suspicions that it was a female. The configuration of the peel-back was a clue to the location of the device. Significant de-gloving, a peeling effect as the blast radiated, usually followed the direction of the radiation of a blast. This suggested the explosive material had detonated at a level below the decedent, though not necessarily directly below. Here, however, it looked very much as though this were the case, bearing in mind the vaporization of the legs.

'Victim one. Deceased. Could be female. Moving on.'

He continued to scan the room. The immediate priority was to declare the room safe – there was no time to dwell on dead bodies. Was there a secondary device? If so, where?

Not much was still in one piece. A couple of feet from the torso lay what initially looked like the tube of a television.

As he moved along the right hand wall, Brancusi became aware of various other body parts, but his concentration remained focussed on electrical equipment or any evidence of explosives.

'Plenty of tissue fragments. We're looking at more bodies.'

'Roger.'

Then a driver's license caught his eye. It was half hidden by a section of indeterminate human flesh. He bent down and lifted it to his visor. It appeared completely untouched, not even an abrasion. Since it was flat, thin, plastic, and normally carried in a back pocket, unless it burned it was hard to damage. The photograph was slightly obscured by a smudge of fresh blood. As he studied the print on the upper left portion closely he froze. 'Christ Almighty,' he mouthed.

'Please repeat.'

Brancusi stared at the picture. This was the driver's license of Maynard Buchanan - one of the biggest industrial construction entrepreneurs in Australia. This wasn't going to please the bosses. If this man had been blown away, the shit was really going to hit the fan.

'Forget it, moving on.'

Brancusi replaced the license exactly where he'd found it. It was paramount that nothing whatsoever be disturbed prior to photogrammetry, the three dimensional photography that recorded the crime scene. He then continued to edge his way down the right hand wall, steadying himself with a gloved hand as he carefully swept only as much of the debris from the floor to allow him to move forward.

Against the far wall he caught sight of what initially looked like the crumpled form of another victim. An arm and a leg were missing, and the body appeared to have caught the full effect of the secondary fragmentation of the glass table that had stood in the center of the room. Most of the clothing had been stripped from the body, and hundreds of shards of the thick glass were embedded in his head and body.

'Victim two. Deceased. Male.'

Maybe the body was Buchanan? It was impossible to tell. That would be the task of the pathologist.

Still no evidence of the bomb – and more importantly, any possible secondary.

Brancusi shifted his weight off the wall and began to slowly edge across the center of the room. Five feet across, and three from the doorway, he came to what must have been the epicenter of the explosion. A three-foot hole had been blasted through the floor. He looked down. He could see clear through to the suite below. The outer rim of the hole sloped downwards. A glance above confirmed his suspicion. There was a convex blast pattern in the ceiling. Fortunately the ceiling had held.

'Blast epicenter. Blown through downwards. Ceiling's held. Structure still good.'

As he looked up from the gaping hole in the floor, something near the far wall caught his eye.

'Moving to the far wall. Possible IED. Checking it out.'
'Roger.'

A small section of what had undoubtedly once been the keyboard of a laptop computer lay under a pile of splintered glass. Brancusi crouched down beside it.

Brancusi examined the keyboard closely with a plastic lens. No telltale yellow or black explosive residue. It was highly unlikely that this was the source of the explosion; it would have been completely fragmented. Nor did it seem to be a secondary. He ran the lens along each inch of it, but there was no evidence of attachments, either electrical or explosive.

'Computer. Not live,' said Brancusi straightening.
'Roger.'

As he continued to move forward, a third body soon became visible, half hidden beneath debris.

'Victim three. Deceased.'
'Roger. Three dead. Confirm.'
'Roger.'

This body still retained all its limbs and a fair amount of clothing. Even bearing in mind the black discoloration of the skin by the blast, it was apparent that the body was Asian. It was too light to be Negro, though part Negro was a possibility.

As he reached the far left-hand side of the back wall, he saw yet another body. All limbs were still attached, but the torso had sustained major damage from flying glass fragments.

'Make that four. Victim four. Male. Deceased.'
'Roger.'

Brancusi moved back to the right, re-tracing his steps round the room. As he did so, he noticed something to the right-hand side of the Asian victim. It looked as though a small box had become lodged beneath the victim at waist level.

'Checking out small opaque box. Plastic. Inch-and-a-half thickness, four inches square.'
'Roger.'

Brancusi moved forwards to examine it, leaning practically to floor level so he could study the box. Thirty seconds later, he rose.

'Computer disk storage box. No presence of explosive.'
'Roger.'

Just over an hour after entry, both Brancusi and Schroeder emerged from the building, removing their headgear as they walked slowly towards Pulman. Brancusi had rechecked every piece of electrical equipment in the conference room, every possible hiding place for further explosive charges, and had come up empty-handed. The victims lay where they had died.

The chopper had long since gone, and the streets in the immediate vicinity were as quiet as the grave. A large group of press had gathered behind the secondary incident tapeline. All four major television networks had camera teams present. Photographers were snapping shots of Brancusi and Schroeder in their Kevlar suits as they threaded their way carefully round the glass and debris towards Pulman at the Forward Command Post. These shots always sold a lot of papers. Not as good as a tight close-up of a policeman carrying the body of a dead child – that was gold dust.

'The conference room is now safe, as far as we are able to tell, sir. There are no secondary IEDs inside the conference room itself. I can't vouch for any other room in the hotel. I'm sure you have that in hand, sir. Casualties number four. As far as we can initially tell, there are three males and one female. All deceased. Amongst the debris was a driving license in the name of Maynard Buchanan. Whether or not he is one of the victims depends on what initial ID the pathologist finds possible.'

Pulman looked outwardly calm, but the telltale swallow told Brancusi that he was fully aware of the ramifications once the media caught a whiff that a prominent celebrity had bought it. They'd lap it up.

'There's no significant structural damage. It's mostly cosmetic,' Brancusi continued swiftly. 'Better get the engineers in as soon as possible. They're to stay out of the conference room till I say so. Are the pathologist and Crime Scene Investigator ready to go in?'

'They're standing by just over there,' Pulman replied, pointing to a police incident truck that had just pulled up next to the Savoy. Brancusi caught the eye of a short fat man who smiled across at him, waving cheerily. Brancusi raised a hand in recognition.

'Good,' Brancusi continued, redirecting his look back to Pulman. 'Better get the usual team up there. BA gear's no longer necessary. Smoke and airborne particles will be out through the windows by the time they get up there. Protective clothing and masks is all we need.'

He began to walk to the bomb truck, then stopped and turned back to Pulman. 'Please post men at each end of the hallway of the fifteenth – don't want any media poking their noses in. Oh, and just one more thing, sir. No one without a specific designated function is to go near the crime scene. That is regardless of rank I'm afraid, sir.'

'I hear what you're saying, Brancusi,' Pulman replied easily. He had a newfound respect for the bomb boys. He was glad it had been someone else's job to go in, risking their lives as they sifted through the human debris. 'Good work,' he added.

'Thank you, sir,' Schroeder interjected at Brancusi's elbow as he placed an arm round his partner's shoulders and steered him back to the truck to change.

The stench in the conference room was getting worse by the minute as the technicians continued to record the state of the room before the bodies were removed. This was a vital stage of what would later become a full investigation.

The video unit was filming and the photogrammetry was in progress. Ultimately, three-dimensional slides of every inch of the crime scene would be available to calculate precise angles and distances. As Schroeder and Brancusi stepped back into the room, the pathologist, Eric Grompard, was standing in the doorway talking to Detective Sergeant Robbins, the Crime Scene Investigator.

'Evening lads. Just when you least expect it, eh? Months of peace and quiet with no loonies about, then kaboom!' Grompard made an expansive theatrical gesture with his arms as he blew out his cheeks. 'Well, keeps you young boys busy, I suppose.'

Eric Grompard was a stumpy, jovial man in his early sixties; a man not looking forward to retirement. He'd worked with Brancusi and Schroeder many times, and they shared a great deal of respect for each other. In his book there was no point in mooning round with a long face. Those who were dead were dead. Now there was a job to be done. Those responsible were to be tracked down so that the living could continue to live.

'Evening Eric,' said Brancusi. 'Could take you a few hours, this one.'

Grompard looked round the room, sighing good-naturedly. 'Well, it looks like it might well be dinner on the run tonight until I finish this human jigsaw. Bits all over the shop.' Slowly his expression changed to one of compassion. 'Poor bastards,' he murmured. There was a moment of silence. Then his mood was once more jovial as he turned to Schroeder. 'Give me a clue, eh? What do you both reckon?'

'Practically impossible to tell until we've got everything tagged and have a chance to look at trace evidence, but it'd have to be plastic of some kind, Semtex maybe, possibly C4, Metabel - if there's still any of that around. The residue will soon tell us. As to whether anyone here brought it in or whether it was a disguised IED - that's debatable.

'Looks as though it exploded three feet inside the doorway. The body of the female was blown backwards towards the inner wall, and the others blown towards the windows.'

'You mean it's possible the female brought it in?' Robbins asked.

'Could have. It's pure speculation,' Brancusi replied.

As he spoke, one of the video camera team joined them as his two assistants began to pack up their equipment. 'We're done, sir,' he said to Robbins.

Robbins turned to Grompard and the bomb team. 'Your turn, lads.'

'Right you are,' Grompard said with enthusiasm. 'Time to examine, bag and tag. Let's get busy.'

'Let's get *lucky*,' Brancusi replied. 'Oh by the way, Eric,' he added, pointing to the body closest to where he'd found the driving license. 'There's a small surprise over there. May be someone famous. Not giving any clues unless you ask.'

Grompard smiled. It was a challenge. Maintaining an emotional distance was the only way to retain sanity. 'I'll let you know as soon as I'm stumped,' he replied. Grompard was undoubtedly the best pathologist in Australia. He wouldn't need any clues.

As Brancusi and Schroeder began their painstaking task of sifting the debris, Brancusi called out. 'My bet the body in the far corner is Asian. If we find anything that suggests he's not local, we'd better give immigration a bell so they can look at his visa and get Interpol to get moving on the DVI.' The Disaster Victim Identification system correlated by Interpol was invaluable when the physical damage was great, as in plane crash or bomb scenarios. Dental records, scars, tattoos, surgical implants – all were in the computer for cross-reference. It was always worth a check.

Thirteen hours later they called it a day. The bodies and body parts had all been videoed, photographed, examined, tagged, bagged and removed for detailed radiography to locate and identify radiopaque material, the residue which might yield trace evidence. Grompard still looked quite fresh, the others not so. The room was then sealed for the night, and a guard stationed outside. Investigations would continue possibly for several days until every minute piece of metal, wood and fabric had been tagged and sent down to the warehouse where they'd be worked on for weeks, possibly months.

'You want to come back to my place for a bite to eat?' Schroeder asked Brancusi, as they reached the truck. "Aly will be happy to fix us something.'

'Maybe next time,' Brancusi replied. Though he'd never have admitted it to either Schroeder or Grompard, he felt sick as a dog. Maybe the job was getting to him after all. Better reschedule the 'psycho', he thought dryly.

4.

The skies above Moscow.
May 27th. 10.40 am.

Poliakov leant back against a bulkhead and closed his eyes. It was only the second time he'd taken time out from his work since the Boeing had leveled out and he'd twisted the handle in the lid of the silver trunk, stepping from his hiding place.

It had been tougher work than he'd anticipated - perhaps the toughest of his life. For seven and a half hours he'd sweated with the bags. He'd pulled them down, one by one, cutting the wires that secured the throat, then emptying the contents on the floor of the plane. He'd then opened up each of the fifty silvered cases marked 'Optical Equipment' and switched the contents – bundles of newspaper cut to shape for bundles of one hundred-dollar bills. Finally he'd withdrawn pieces of wire from his overalls, similar in thickness to the wires the Union Constitution Bank always used, threading the surprisingly nondescript manila tags through them, twisting the wires tight with pliers.

It was all so simple. Hard work, but simple.

Now only one bag remained. His watch told him he had approximately seventy-five minutes left before the plane began its descent into Sheremetyevo airport.

He snapped the wire, pulling the tag from the end. Then closing his eyes tightly, he reached into the bag between his legs and drew out a fat bundle of bills, still in its Federal Reserve wrapper. He held it to his nose and inhaled deeply. Christ, it smelt so sweet!

For a second or two he was tempted to slip just one bundle into his overalls. Almost at once his eyes snapped open and the moment was gone. That'd be madness.

The way he saw it, he was now taking the most calculated risk of his life. When Khamovnikakh was told of the switch – that would be a good time to be either dead or invisible. Poliakov was suddenly aware of the muscles in his sphincter.

They'd all made plans; Molina, Grasby at the Union Constitution Bank, and himself. His personal cut was to be twenty-two pounds weight of fresh one hundred-dollar bills. One million US dollars. That'd be plenty of seed money for the lifestyle he had in mind in Costa Rica. If he couldn't make a success of his life with that much, he *deserved* to be found by the Russian.

The plane hit a patch of turbulence, and the Persian cat shrieked with alarm. Poliakov laughed and blew the animal a kiss, then switched the contents of the last suitcase with the bundles of bills, securing the last wire round the neck of the bag. Lifting the final white canvas sack into place, he replaced the suitcase next to the others. They all bore a Prague address.

At 10.55 am, Delta 30 touched down at Sheremetyevo airport, Moscow.

Less than five minutes later, the bulk cargo door was opened and two men in army fatigues and black beanies jumped into the hold. They made straight for the white sacks, pulling them towards the opening of the plane, tossing them roughly out onto the tarmac to four more army fatigued Russians who stood by two waiting armored trucks. All had semi-automatic weapons slung round their backs.

They didn't check the wires, they never did. Five times a week for the past two years Delta 30 had docked at the same time. Each time the routine had been the same. Pull out the sacks, check the number against the manifest, stick 'em in the trucks, get 'em to the banks. Simple.

Fifteen minutes later the men and the sacks were gone. Regular Russian baggage handlers were now inside the hold. Eighty-three bags, and one cat in a cage. Fifty numbered silver cases for transshipment to Bay 23. Private flight to Prague. Twenty bags, transshipment to Iberia, Bay 20; thirteen bags, plus the animal, to the customs hall.

As the containers, the animal cage and the thirteen suitcases made their way directly to the customs area, the twenty bags headed left to Bay 20, while the fifty numbered optical cases were trucked in the opposite direction, across to Bay 23 where a Gulfstream jetliner was parked.

As the luggage carts came to a halt, from within his trunk Poliakov could just make out someone on the apron giving instructions in Russian to the loaders. He couldn't make out the exact words. Then he heard the carts being unhooked, and there was silence.

Ten minutes later Poliakov heard approaching footsteps. Three men, he judged. Metal clanked on metal as the carts were re-hooked to a towing vehicle and the snake of carts was off again.

This time the journey took less than three minutes.

Poliakov held his breath as the men manhandled his trunk up some narrow steps. A few moments later it was dropped carelessly, and someone sat atop of it. Whoever it was seemed to be tapping lightly at the locks. If he was sending Morse code, he was out of luck, thought Poliakov.

At 11.34 Poliakov could just make out the captain in the cockpit calling Sheremetyevo Tower for clearance to taxi. In less than five minutes the 727 was lifting into the gray skies over Moscow, heading east.

Poliakov felt the plane level out and he began to breathe easier. Finally he could relax. Reaching up with his left hand for the inner handle, he twisted to the right and pushed. But to his surprise the lid stuck fast. As he attempted to twist his body so he could bring his shoulder up against the lid, he heard muffled voices. He called out, but there was no reply.

A few moments later he heard footsteps approaching. Two men. He called out once more, but again there was no response. Straining to listen, he could just make out the sound of whispered voices.

Suddenly alarmed, Poliakov pushed violently against the lid, but since he was lying flat he couldn't get sufficient leverage to budge it. Throwing caution to the wind, he shouted as loudly as he could manage, but his lungs were so constricted the volume didn't amount to much.

It was then he heard the sound of casters, and felt the rear of his trunk being lifted. There was a short period of silence, then he became aware of the sound of a rope being slung beneath the trunk and it was lifted onto a trolley.

Abruptly he felt the plane shudder as though the pilot had put on the speed brakes. The plane's nose dipped suddenly forward. Three minutes later he felt the nose pitch up again. They'd descended a considerable distance.

Poliakov continued screaming his lungs out, but he was fighting a losing battle inside his coffin, pushing upwards with his shoulder, vainly attempting to contort his body to apply extra leverage. One of the men outside the trunk whispered something indiscernible and his companion laughed. Poliakov screamed again and again, but they were oblivious to him, continuing to chat to each other.

Ten minutes later the screams became less frequent as Poliakov's exhaustion set in, yet they were perhaps more piercing than ever.

A third man with a high-pitched voice barked out an order in a language Poliakov had never heard before, and he heard the unmistakable sound of the rear passenger door being manually cranked open. The roar of the slipstream thundered through the plane as the air began to rush in. It was then that Poliakov felt a tidal wave of abject terror. His sphincter was pulsing uncontrollably; his breath came in short bursts. He knew he'd made the biggest mistake of his life.

A few minutes later he felt his coffin sliding backwards towards the meter and a half opening that was the gateway to oblivion.

As the trunk dropped lazily through the clouds, Poliakov felt a searing needle pain in his chest as a massive coronary mercifully cut short a terrible death.

Molina never made it to Lima. He never even made his flight. A short-bladed knife ripped into his back as he left his apartment in Queens. He died instantly on his doorstep. George Grasby made it as far as Fiji. There he climbed into an airport taxi and gave the name of his hotel to an Indian driver. Twenty minutes later, on the coast road to Suva, the driver stopped the car and shot him twice through the left eye.

5.

Central Business District. Sydney.
May 13th.

The rain pounded on the glass window of McCann's office in the Priory Life Assurance building on Bridge Street with the force of a fire hose. A small wiry middle-aged businessman sat neatly on the edge of his Bentwood chair facing McCann; his hands resting carefully over each other on his lap as he gave his full attention to his financial adviser. McCann spoke slowly and easily, his voice filled with quiet assurance. Roberts was his last client of the day. He'd be glad to see the last of this annoying little man.

Because of the pressure of work, lunch had been limited to two pints of draught Guinness and a beef damper at the Fortune of War in the Rocks. Now a certain degree of lethargy was beginning to set in, though none showed on his face.

It was his first day back in the office after fifteen days at sea on the L'Échapper Belle, the forty-one foot Formosa 41 ketch that was the focus of practically every spare minute of his life. The musty smell of his office was a sharp contrast to the thirty-five knot winds he'd encountered on the final haul into Sydney less than thirty-six hours ago. It was always difficult to adjust to the pace of life back in the world of normal people.

A shaft of lightning arrowed down through the storm outside the window, and McCann paused momentarily, his thoughts drifting back to England.

It was at times like this that he missed the windswept moors of Cornwall, where he'd spent his childhood. Also the rain, the cold, the dirt, and innate vitality that was London, to him the capital of capitals, the city of his early adult years.

Nostalgia wasn't a feeling he was prone to very often. He'd moved to Australia two years ago, and it was everything he'd hoped for; a great climate, an easy lifestyle, money wasn't difficult to earn, the women were beautiful, and the wines as good as any in the world. But most importantly, Sydney provided the perfect jumping off point for L'Echapper Belle, the true love of his life.

McCann stood six one and weighed the same as he had at twenty – two hundred pounds exactly. From his shoulders to his waist he was one solid block of muscle. He was now in his late forties. His hair was pepper and salt on dark brown. The skin round his dark brown friendly eyes was creased with well-defined laughter lines, as were the areas at the corners of his mouth. His nose was straight, with a small turn up at the end that gave him a slightly puckish quality in keeping with his innate sense of fun.

McCann's clients looked across the table and saw an amiable, soft-spoken, polite life assurance salesman. The last thing they would have imagined would have been that their financial advisor worked no more than three months a year as such. The irony was that if he had chosen to work full time in life assurance, he'd have earned far more than the thousand dollars or so a day he earned doing his more private commercial work – using the experience that he'd learned while an SAS Captain in the United Kingdom.

His military training had begun in the Territorial Army, then continued at Aldershot with the Parachute Regiment where he'd been immediately marked out as special material and had soon undergone the full Hereford SAS selection procedure. While most hardened soldiers found this a truly testing course, to McCann it was an exhilarating experience – a time when he came to terms with himself, a time he discovered his true métier.

He'd served all over the world with his regiment, One Para, finding action in Northern Ireland, Central Africa, and finally the Falklands, where he won several medals.

His first tour with the 22nd SAS had seen him stationed mainly in the Middle East. The second tour, 'on invitation', had taken him to various parts of Africa.

During that time, the 'spooks' at Vauxhall Cross, the headquarters of the Secret Intelligence Service, more often referred to as MI6, had unofficially 'borrowed' him on two occasions, utilizing his specialist capabilities in deep penetration and hostage recovery. His regiment had on both occasions made it clear to him that the choice to take 'leave', and work for the men at Vauxhall Cross, was his alone to make. Although the SAS didn't take too kindly to their men being 'borrowed', it was often politically unavoidable, and pressure from the highest echelons of government was often brought to bear on the regiment at such times.

McCann had been only too willing to help on both occasions. So, on his retirement from One Para in 1985 he had made it known to the SIS that he'd be happy to 'do the odd job for them', as the need arose.

They'd taken him up on his offer on many occasions. He'd worked in Central Africa, Panama, Chechnya, Kosovo, and most notably in the Gulf, where he'd been sent into Iraq well before the expiry of Bush's deadline to the Iraqis to leave Kuwait.

Naturally he had all the personal skills expected of a man with his SAS background – self-defense, unarmed combat, weapons use, and self-sufficiency. But his particular skill was to be able to control, train and operate a group of men who were as skilled as he was. So it was a natural progression for him to drift from the action itself to the area of consultancy. If a company wanted to set up its own security system, or a minor political party in Central Africa needed its own cadre to protect its senior people, McCann would go in, establish a training scheme, and teach them about weapons use and self defense.

At home, in a small safe, McCann had a 'black book'. If twenty people were needed at short notice, he'd make a few calls and they'd be ready to leave home within a couple of days. They worked for McCann because they respected him; and in many cases they had previously worked with him while on active service.

As well as the purely commercial side of his consultancy, McCann chose to continue to accommodate the British Secret Intelligence Service, as and when they called on him to perform some 'unofficial business'. This was the product of an ingrained sense of nationalism. In return, Matthew Hutton at Vauxhall Bridge had arranged his residency in Australia.

McCann was just one of a significant number of 'unofficials' all over the world, men who were actually part-time soldiers, on call at any moment, but never appeared as such officially anywhere. If a four-man team were required somewhere on foreign sovereign soil, men like McCann would be called upon. A hostage situation, or a job requiring some element of violence against a so-called 'ally' that could not be seen as the work of the United Kingdom – men like McCann would be contacted; a closet army performing the backdoor dirty tricks of governments around the world. If they perished or disappeared, one didn't read or hear about it. McCann and his fellow unofficials knew and appreciated the risk. They were well paid, but that was not their *raison d'être*. It was the pure adrenalin rush they experienced that counted.

A couple of close colleagues at the office had a vague idea of McCann's other world. It was no dark secret. After all, he was no spy. However, they never knew the scale of what he was up to. He'd done jobs that he felt he could talk about, such as working as Sheik Yamani's security advisor. Back in the mid eighties, all photographs of Yamani had McCann hovering somewhere in the background. He never looked like a staffer, always like a companion.

His eyes had none of the cold stare of the psychopathic killer; there was softness there. There had been many circumstances when McCann had had to pull the trigger, either as part of the job, officially when he was with the SAS, or unofficially, when protecting people like Yamani. McCann never enjoyed killing, but in the arena of professional global violence it was kill or be killed. That had been his world.

McCann now rented an old timber house on McCarr's Creek Road, forty minutes north of Sydney, a home which provided the perfect anchorage for his boat. The house was small and in pretty bad repair. By contrast, the ketch, the boathouse and the jetty were immaculate. McCann made sure of that.

The majority of the money he earned was channeled straight into the boat. She was his wife with expensive tastes, and he denied her nothing.

His love life was adequate and uncomplicated. With his craggy good looks he was never short of a partner, yet he most times preferred his own company rather than embroil himself in a shallow relationship that often led to a difficult and emotional parting of the ways. He liked to keep himself free to sail off into the sunset on a whim, or jump a plane as and when the call came through from London.

A distinct rap on the desk brought McCann sharply back to reality. He quickly tried to gather his thoughts as he stared into the stern eyes of his client. Roberts looked annoyed. McCann leant forward.

'To summarize, Mr. Roberts. What we have here is a double strategy. On the one hand we have the personal pension...'

He was about to continue when the telephone rang. A further look of aggravation colored Robert's face. 'Would you excuse me for just one minute?' McCann asked with an easy charm as he picked up the phone, though it was apparent from Robert's expression that he minded very much.

He swivelled his seat to one side. 'McCann speaking.'

'Leo McCann?' It was the voice of a woman.

'Yes.'

'I'd like to see you as soon as possible.' The voice had an assertive edge of confidence. McCann fancied that when this woman spoke, she took it as a matter of course that others would listen. He was not among such people.

'I'm afraid I'm with a client at present, then I'm off home. Perhaps I could call you back tomorrow morning,' he said. He was damned if he was going to spend another minute in his office, particularly with a woman who evidently treated everyone as servants. 'You didn't mention a name,' he added as an afterthought.

'No, I didn't. I apologize. I'm afraid tomorrow's out of the question. I've taken a considerable amount of time to find you, Mr. McCann. I must see you immediately.' The words came quickly, as though the caller were in danger of missing a plane. 'If it's a question of money – ' she continued, but was cut short by McCann.

'It's not,' he replied sharply. He could see Roberts out of the corner of his eye. He'd begun to fidget, and his face was as dark as the storm clouds outside the window. Yet, boring as the man was, his business year in year out was worth having. Besides, McCann was beginning to find his caller annoying.

'Much as I would like to help you, I'm afraid I can't.' He paused. There were several beats of silence. 'Look, I still don't know your name.'

'A name that would probably mean something to you is Hutton.'

Matthew? She now had his full attention.

'Hold on a second – *your* name is Hutton?' He replied after a couple of seconds. Perhaps he'd misunderstood her.

'No. My name is Buchanan. You seemed about to cut me off, so I felt I had to grab your attention.'

'I see. Straight to the point.'

'Look, Mr. McCann. This is a matter of some urgency, and Matthew intimated that you'd give me at least five minutes of your time if I called. As a courtesy to him. If that's the case, and it's not too inconvenient, perhaps we could meet for a drink at the Regent. Shall we say the Club bar in half an hour?'

'As a courtesy to Matthew, yes. Though it's by no means convenient,' replied McCann. If she was going to be rude so would he. 'The Regent at – ' he paused to glance at his watch. 'Six-fifteen. Please don't be late.'

'I am never late,' she replied evenly.

The line went dead. He would have preferred to have been the first to ring off, in view of her abrupt manner, but she had beaten him to it.

'If it is not too much trouble, Mr. McCann, perhaps I could take the superannuation details with me. It'll give me time to come to a decision.' Roberts spoke slowly and crisply. He hadn't enjoyed the interruption, and was making a point.

'I have them all right here, Mr. Roberts,' McCann replied, as he picked a folder from a tray to the left of his desk. 'If you've any questions that require an urgent answer, please don't hesitate to call me at home. The number's on my card.' McCann seldom gave out his home number, but right now Roberts required a little mollification. Besides, he was rarely off the boat at weekends, so his client wouldn't be able to reach him, even if he tried.

It seemed to have the desired affect. Robert's face softened as he rose.

'I'll call you on Monday then, Mr. McCann,' Roberts said as they shook hands.

'I'll look forward to it,' McCann replied. He'd actually do nothing of the kind.

As the door closed behind his client, McCann returned to his desk and reached for the phone, dialing an international number. It rang a couple of times, then an answering machine clicked in.

'Matthew Hutton here. I'm unavailable for a couple of hours. If it's urgent, call Henry. I'll be back at eight. Leave a message if you really have to.'

McCann debated as to whether to do so or not. Matthew was seldom unreachable. But to give him his due, it was only just before 7.25 am in London.

'It's McCann. Expect you're up to some naughtiness or other. I'll call you back later this morning. Who the hell's Buchanan, you old bastard? Ciao.'

McCann replaced the phone and opened a desk drawer, reaching in for the fifth of Stoli he kept there for his usual end of day shot. He drained the remnants of cold coffee that stood in a cup on his desk, pouring in just under two fingers' of the vodka. Though it was the last thing he felt like, he'd have to see Buchanan. As a favor to Matthew.

6.

The Regent Club bar was busy. McCann quickly scanned the room as he entered from the foyer.

Buchanan. The name had been buzzing around his head ever since he'd put down the receiver. Though it wasn't an uncommon name, the more he recalled her tone, the authority and self-assurance in the voice, the more convinced he was that she wasn't *a* Buchanan, she was *the* Buchanan. At least, her father had been, before his death. Now she was arguably the richest woman in Australia. What the hell did she want with him that was so urgent? And what was her connection to Matthew? What on earth had possessed Matthew to put her on to him anyway?

He took a seat at the bar, glancing up at the Deco clock above the bar as he did so. It was a minute before six-fifteen. He'd wait five minutes, he determined, not a second longer. Signaling the barman, he ordered a beer, shifting in his seat so he could keep an eye on the door.

As the minute hand reached the first quarter she walked in.

She stood five ten and walked with an unstudied easy grace, her wide shoulders held back and her chin held high. She wore a tobacco brown silk hunting jacket, beige jodhpurs, a simple white shirt, and lace-up ankle boots. No jewelry. Her raven hair was shortish, two inches above the shoulders in a style reminiscent of fifties Chanel. If a finishing school in Switzerland had been responsible for her deportment, they deserved every penny her father had lavished on her, McCann thought, as she threaded her way through the tables without the slightest hint of affectation.

As she reached the bar she held out a hand. McCann had not anticipated that her smile would be so instantly warm, friendly, genuine, and appealing. Judging by her laconic tone earlier on the phone, he'd mentally attuned his mind to confrontation and friction.

'It's very good of you to see me at such short notice. I'm Rosalind Buchanan.' Her voice betrayed her emotions. Although the smile was still manifest, it was evident to McCann that she was deeply troubled.

'Leo McCann. Shall we find a table?' he asked.

'No. A seat at the bar's fine, thanks,' she replied, sitting up on a chromed stool.

'Can I get you a drink, Miss Buchanan?'

'No thank you, Mr. McCann, not just at present,' she replied, placing a small Italian leather purse on the bar top, and tilting her head back, allowing her hair to fall gently away from her cheeks. The smile was now gone, and the furrowed brows evinced her anxiety. McCann signaled the waiter, ordering a bottle of Perrier for good measure.

'How do you know Matthew?' McCann began after a few seconds pause. He was intrigued, not only by the Hutton connection, but also by the woman herself.

'Our family and the Hutton's have been close for ages. My grandfather was a friend of Matthew's father. They were both army men, so you can see the bond goes back a long time. We often stayed down at Marlow with the Huttons when we were in England. I was a child then. So when I needed some sound advice recently, I knew I could rely on Matthew.'

'I was very sorry to hear about your father.' There was an awkward moment of silence. Rosalind averted her eyes.

'Excuse me, but I am correct that Maynard Buchanan was your father?' McCann continued.

'I'm sorry, Mr. McCann. I must appear to be behaving in a strange fashion. Yes, Maynard was my father.' Her words had a hesitation, as though she were afraid she might cry at any second. 'Thank you for your sympathy,' she replied simply.

There was an uncomfortable silence. It was as if the mention of her father's death had instantly sucked the life from her soul. She dipped her head to mask her emotion and her hair fell either side of her face like a black cloak of privacy. She then looked up to face McCann.

Her face was really quite perfect in a classically beautiful way. A straight sharply defined fringe crossed her forehead an inch above her equally well-defined eyebrows. She wore little or no make-up, just the merest suspicion around the eyes. She didn't need it, McCann judged; her skin was flawless and seemingly untouched by the ravages of the Australian sun. Her black hair positively shone under the halogen spotlights that hung above the bar. McCann could see she was fighting to control her emotions.

Then quite suddenly she lifted her head and stared at a point in the air a few inches above his head, and breathed in deeply. As she began to speak, the veil of sadness lifted and her voice took on a distinctly stronger vocal timbre.

'You'll have to excuse my telephone manner. I'm told it's less than perfect. I hate phones, always have. So I spend as little time on them as possible. I get to the point quickly and try not to dwell on niceties.'

'That much was apparent,' McCann replied good-naturedly, attempting to put her at ease.

'How English. You're the masters of the understatement,' she said with a wry look. '*Rude bitch* was probably what sprang to your mind at the time.'

McCann smiled. 'So how exactly do I come into the equation. I'm pretty sure you haven't come to me for financial advice.'

She looked away suddenly. 'I'm sorry. Do you think we could walk somewhere? I just can't seem to concentrate in a hotel bar.'

'Of course,' he replied.

'Really? You're not too pushed for time? I won't keep you long.'

The rain had ceased, but the gutters were rivers. The setting sun reflected off the glistening paving stones as they walked across George Street towards Sydney Cove.

'Matthew suggested you might not be too busy right now, that you might be free to work for me for a while,' she began, testing the waters. 'Should you wish to, naturally.'

This remark, right out of left field, took McCann completely by surprise. Matthew had said what? That he was for hire?

'Well, I'm afraid I have to tell you right now that Matt had no right to make such a statement. As it happens I'm up to my eyeballs.'

'But not in work you enjoy,' she continued tentatively. 'Am I right there?'

He cast her a sidelong glance. 'How much did Matt tell you of my background?'

'Very little. But I rely on Matthew's judgment. My father always did, and I don't see why I should break with tradition. I've always found Matthew to be one of the few men you could trust with your life, if that's not being too theatrical. Bearing his work in mind, I imagine that others think so to.' She turned her head and met his eyes for the first time since they had left the hotel. 'My grandfather was with the OSS during the Second World War, so as you can imagine I am aware of Matthew's role in intelligence.' The OSS was the Intelligence arm of the US army, and the forerunner of the CIA.

They walked on in silence for a while across the grass of First Fleet Park. McCann studied her closely. She appeared to be marshalling her thoughts, not quite knowing how to put her case to him.

'And how did Matt think I might be able to help you, Miss Buchanan.'

To his surprise, she seemed quite happy with his formality. He'd been sure she'd invite him to call her by her Christian name.

Just as surprisingly, she stopped quite abruptly and turned to face him. 'It has been nearly seven weeks since my father died. Seven weeks and still no one has been able to unearth the slightest motive for the bombing.' Her voice was low and controlled, but it belied the intensity of the emotions that lay just beneath the surface. 'I must know why. I must have a reason. It's not because I have a need to see those responsible punished; that's another matter, one for others. But I must have a *reason*.'

She looked away towards the Opera House, and her jaw set in determination. 'I would like you to help me find an answer.' McCann noticed the smallest suggestion of a tear. She immediately touched the side of her eye with the thumb of her hand as if to remove a speck of dirt.

'Miss Buchanan,' McCann began simply. 'I am not a private investigator. I can't imagine why Matt should have thought I could have been in any way useful to you. Nevertheless, I can empathize absolutely with the pain you're suffering - '

She cut him short, still staring dead ahead out into the harbor. 'Can you, Mr. McCann?' Her voice trailed off.

For one brief second McCann was sorely tempted to reply. For one moment he felt a sudden surge of annoyance. How was it that those who had lost a wife, husband, father or mother, supposed that others were complete strangers to suffering. He had seen good men die of hypothermia in the desert, watched men struggle across mountain ranges dragging broken limbs behind them, watched men tortured to death, powerless to help them, seen the beseeching eyes of war ravaged children as he carried them to safety, seen the corpses of babies and old men in shallow graves in Bosnia. Yes, he believed he did have at least some idea of the pain she was suffering.

'It's been forty-eight days since my father was murdered. In that time the authorities have achieved nothing. I turned to Matthew for help. He argued it was a civil matter. But after I'd brow-beaten him for a while, he suggested that if anyone could make a few fresh waves, it might be you. And there was the added bonus that you were 'on site', as he put it.'

Their eyes locked briefly, then she smiled. 'Nevertheless, he warned me how you'd react.'

'Why didn't Matt call me first, I wonder?'

'He tried. I was with him. Said you were most likely at sea.'

McCann nodded. It was probably true. And what was he making such a fuss about anyway. Matt had hardly compromised his security – this wasn't the Cold War any more.

The sails of the Opera House turned a pale pink as the sun set behind them.

'Just last night I saw a documentary on Kuwait,' she continued in a softer tone, gazing out across the water, a fresh breeze dancing her hair over her cheeks. 'An Arab woman was talking about her husband. They'd been married only three months when the Iraqis invaded. He walked out the door to buy food, and she never saw him again. I can see her now, holding up a photograph for the camera. It could have been a photo of anyone, but to this tragic woman it was her love. *That was five years ago*, she said. Then she added, *I have to know. Perhaps it is better that I know he is dead, but it is the knowledge that is paramount.*' She turned her head slightly towards McCann. 'That's it, you see. I have to know, and you are my only chance. No one else will do.'

McCann could see a fierce determination in her eyes. She meant it. Then her expression softened.

'Perhaps I appear a bit crazy?' She leant forwards, willing him to say otherwise. He just smiled his assent.

'The past few weeks have made me mad.' She placed a hand on McCann's arm. 'Will you help me?'

'I'm not a PI, Miss Buchanan.'

'You're a man who can provide answers. At present all I have are questions.'

'And because Matt thinks I'm *it*, you want to hire me?'

'I've no one else.'

'You say the nicest things, Miss Buchanan.'

'I didn't mean it that way.'

'Sure. Look, I've been a soldier most of my life. Quite why Matt should intimate I'm some kind of Phillip Marlowe is a mystery.'

'He obviously has a higher opinion of you than you do of yourself.' She paused briefly. 'Look, my father was blown to pieces together with three others, and all they can tell me is that, to the best of their knowledge, they think that the girl who killed my father was carrying the explosives when she went in, strapped to her waist. I desperately need to know why she did what she did. Can you understand that? I can't get on with my life till I do. I owe it to dad.' Her expression changed slightly, as if embarrassed at her childlike choice of words. 'My father deserves it.'

She gave an involuntary shudder. The last rays of the sun were fast fading the far side of the Harbor Bridge behind them, and the breeze had whipped itself up into something more approaching a squall.

'You look cold,' McCann said. 'Perhaps we should discuss this somewhere warmer. How about something to eat?'

'I'd like that. Look, please let this be my treat. It's the least I can do - you've been kind enough to drop everything to see me. Can I cook you something at my home? It's not far, and I don't feel much like a busy restaurant right now. Since my father died, I haven't been out much. Do you mind dreadfully? I actually *can* cook quite reasonably.'

'That would be fine. Do you have a car?'

'No. At least, yes. But not today. I came in a taxi.'

McCann swung the car off New South Head Road into Wolseley Road, Point Piper – possibly the best address in Sydney. Buchanan's millions had been well spent, but then Maynard Buchanan and his father Frank had rarely made an inept financial move, so what had he expected?

'Matthew tells me that you have a virtual love affair with your boat.'

'L'Échapper Belle? Yes. I suppose that's not far from the truth.'

'And the name?'

'It means – '

'I know what it means,' she interrupted, 'I was curious as to why you named her.'

'I called her "Narrow Escape" because I bought her just after my return from overseas a few years ago. That was the first time I'd come seriously close to journey's end, as they say. I'd come face to face with the Grim Reaper, trapped in a small cavity, under hundreds of tons of rubble, and it changed me. Gave me a fresh appetite for space.'

'Where was this?'

'Somalia. Nothing terribly exciting. I was sent in to bring out someone important to Matt's people. No one could reach him, and he wasn't a popular lad politically with General Adeed at the time. I found him around the same time as a Buccaneer fighter turned up. Problem was, the pilot didn't know we were down the road – bombed the shit out of us. Excuse my language.'

'Did you get him out?'

'Not in mint condition, no, but he's walking around now so -' His voice trailed off as he remembered a good friend who was still fit enough to play polo at Smith's Lawn, despite the loss of a leg.

Rosalind wound down the window of McCann's old Volkswagen, and indicated a house with her forefinger. 'On the left. Look for the avocado tree.'

There was no number. The house spoke for itself. The massive avocado tree stood to the left of the wide electric gates, the only concession to modernity.

Built in the late 1920's, Sheerbrooke was a family residence of quite exceptional beauty. An architectural thoroughbred, it was every inch the classic Australian family home.

As McCann nosed the VW Beetle into the driveway, Rosalind pulled a remote from her purse, pressed the button, and the gates swung open with surprising speed.

The bleached blue shuttered façade of the house stood behind a semi-formal garden; a mélange of cypress and topiaried hedges.

'It's beautiful,' said McCann, as she opened the wide doors, stepping into the entrance hall with its high domed ceiling.

'Don't think I don't appreciate it,' she replied, looking over her shoulder and smiling as she strode down the hall. 'May I call you Leo? Can't be calling each other Mr. McCann and Miss Buchanan all night, can we?'

'Call me Leo, by all means.'

'It's been our home for three generations. I love it with a passion. I feel secure here. I don't entertain. I'm going to keep it all to myself. Maybe I'm selfish, I don't care.' She flicked a light switch. 'Look, I've got to organize dinner and change. Won't be more than a few minutes. Help yourself to a drink; the strong stuff's in the living room straight ahead. Champagne, wine, and beer if you want it, are in the fridge in the kitchen. You'll find that on the left. Make yourself at home.' So saying, she ran up the left hand side of the double staircase that swept up either side of the hall to the first floor.

McCann stepped down one step into the main reception room. It was two cricket pitches at least in width, and one-and-a-half in length. Despite the polished wood floor, it felt warm and comfortable. Antique faded Persian rugs were scattered randomly. Two vast sofas on which several Great Danes could easily have stretched out, faced each other in the center of the room either side of a Georgian coffee table, on which were scattered copies of *Vogue*, *The New Yorker*, *The Economist*, the *Wall Street Journal*, and other financial magazines. The picture windows and French doors at the far end looked out onto the gardens, the pool, the private jetty and the harbor. There was no sign of a boat.

McCann helped himself to a whisky and ambled round the room, studying the paintings that hung from the picture rails. Contemporary art had always been one of his passions.

Some artists were familiar, others not. Above the sideboard was an early eighties Susan Norrie, with her characteristic pink brooding sensual theme. To the left, a couple of Margaret Prestons, and a theatrical portrait by Herbert Badham. Either side of the steps to the hall were two Boyds – late forties, McCann judged by the religious themes. Above the fireplace was a pastoral piece by Grüner, cattle in the soft light at dawn.

'Do you eat red meat?' Rosalind called from the hall.

'All my life,' replied McCann.

'Good. It's Charelais.'

A few moments later, she walked through into the living room, a folder in her hand. She stopped behind McCann, as he studied the landscape. She'd changed into an outsized white sweatshirt and baggy jeans.

'Daddy loved the Grüner. It reminded him of his childhood. He grew up in the Hunter Valley. We have a property there – a small vineyard. I haven't visited since my father was killed, the memories are still too painful.'

McCann looked from the painting to Rosalind. A shadow clouded her features for a brief moment, then she caught his eye, and it was gone.

'Let's sit out on the verandah. I'll just get some wine from the fridge and join you,' she said, snapping on the spotlights.

The house faced north-west towards the Opera House. McCann strolled out through the French doors and stood beside the pool, looking out at the skyline as he waited for Rosalind. For a moment the skyline of the city looked in the darkness like a magnificently bejeweled theatrical cyclorama specially commissioned for the house. It was the skyline real estate agents dream of.

McCann crouched, letting his fingers play in the water of the pool. The last thing he wanted right now was to begin a new career as an investigator. He didn't need the aggravation. But Matt was part of this particular equation, and his friend would be the last person to saddle him with someone he didn't think deserved a fair hearing. He'd hear her out, then make a decision. He owed Matt that much.

'I brought two wine glasses, but you're more than welcome to stick to Scotch,' she said as she placed the decanter, together with a bottle of white on the glass table. As she did so, the folder she'd been clutching under her right arm fell from her grasp.

'Shit!'

'Don't worry, I'll get it,' said McCann quickly as he slipped the papers back into their sleeve.

'Even getting these few documents together has been like drawing teeth. Damn bureaucrats don't like sharing a thing, let alone parting with details of their investigations.'

McCann flipped through the contents of the folder as she poured the wine. 'This all concerns the bombing?'

'Yes. It's just somewhere to start from. God knows, it's precious little.'

McCann held up a hand. 'Hold on one moment. Start? What do you mean start? I can't remember having agreed to anything.'

'I'm sorry,' Rosalind began, with a halfway decent impression of genuine surprise. 'I really thought you'd kind of agreed to help me.'

McCann stared at her, giving nothing away.

'Please help me, Leo. Just name your price.'

'I can't be bought Rosalind, even by a Buchanan.'

'I apologize,' she interjected quickly, 'I shouldn't have put it so clumsily.'

He looked at her. Unlike a few moments earlier, she now looked genuinely contrite.

'Your father was killed in March?'

'The 26th. I was in Los Angeles at the primary with Bradley Radcliffe, Theodore Radcliffe's son.'

'The Republican front-runner?'

'The same. We were celebrating his win in the primary when I was told what had happened. Everything was really confused that night. Apparently they'd been trying to reach me for hours, but all the lines to the Biltmore were blocked with calls of congratulations, and by the press.'

'Who had been trying to call you? The authorities?'

'No. Ian Mackintosh. He is - was - my father's right hand. He wanted to break the news to me personally, but was ultimately forced to fax me from Sydney. I was on the plane thirty minutes later.'

'The company jet?'

'Not ours. It was in Europe somewhere at the time. Theo arranged a plane.'

'Radcliffe's plane?'

'It wasn't his plane - it was a friend's. The Radcliffes, contrary to what you might think, aren't that wildly rich. They made their money out of law, not oil.'

'Practically the same thing in terms of reward,' McCann interjected, more to himself than to make a point.

'Most of their money's gone into two campaigns for Congress, and one for the Senate. The last one bit off a large portion of the Radcliffe fortune. The Presidential race is seeing to the rest. So you can see there's not much left for private jets. Does that answer your question?' There seemed to McCann to be just a hint of annoyance.

'Just to go back a bit. Why was your father's jet in Europe?'

'I've no idea. I don't really see it's that important.' She studied McCann, confused. 'I'm afraid I don't see your point.'

'Your father's personal jet was in Europe, whilst he was in Sydney. It doesn't make much sense,' he replied, shrugging.

'The Buchanan jet is available to all directors,' she replied.

'I see,' McCann replied, deciding to let the matter drop. It was hardly significant, anyway.

'It wasn't till I was in the air that I was able to speak to Ian and get some idea of what had happened; though God knows he knew little enough himself, except that dad was dead.

'At Mascot there were police and media everywhere. Same thing here. Couldn't even get into Wolseley Road - the traffic was backed up to Double Bay. When they caught sight of me, the press went bananas, sticking cameras in my face.' Her eyes were flashing with anger.

'Does it say in here who was dealing with the case? The officer in charge at the time?'

'Yes, you'll find it itemized. Can't remember his name right now.'

'When did you first speak to him?'

'As soon as I got home. He was good enough to come out here. I saw him briefly again the following day.'

'What exactly did he say?'

'He told me the nuts and bolts of what had happened. Not in great detail. It was more of a duty call than anything else. Bear in mind of course, that at that time I probably knew practically as much as the police did, thanks to Ian. The only thing they were certain about was that they had four bodies in the Glebe morgue: dad, Andrew Horan, dad's oldest friend, a girl, and an unidentified Asian.'

'Did they ask you to identify your father?'

'I offered; they didn't ask. They'd asked Ian for the telephone number of dad's dentist. It was then – ' She broke off as she looked down, took a deep breath, then resumed. 'It was then that I realized how bad his injuries must have been.'

'The dental records tallied with the body of your father?' continued McCann evenly. It seemed better just to carry on clinically with the questions.

'Yes.' She looked up. Suddenly she was again all business. 'If you're even for a second thinking that there's been some mistake and dad's still alive, forget it. It was my one hope that the whole thing might have been some terrible mix-up, and that dad would suddenly walk in. That's why I asked Richard Barthwaite, our dentist, to make absolutely certain of the findings. He's one of the best and an old family friend.'

'And he concurred with the pathologist?'

She nodded. 'Mind you, I had to wait till the next morning. That wasn't fun. Apparently they take forever to examine the victims.'

'When were they able to tell you what happened.'

'Look, they still know zilch.' There was a hint of anger, coupled with a good deal of frustration in her voice. 'It's a Task Force matter now. The decision was made practically within the hour to form one. A man called Torrance is heading it. He met with me shortly afterwards. Treated me like a child - or how a man like him would treat a woman. It amounts to the same thing.' Her voice was becoming increasingly bitter. 'The sum of their investigations then was about as it stands today. Unless they're about to break the case wide open, and there's a conspiracy to keep the fact from me.' She stopped speaking for a second, aware that her voice had risen to almost a shout. 'Anyway, all they'll share with me is the same old thing – that they know nothing more than that the plastic explosive was brought into the conference room by a young girl called Venice Messon.'

She stood and began to pace round the pool, her hands on her hips, looking up at the stars, her face a picture of frustration. 'I mean, Christ almighty, it took them two days to ID the girl!'

McCann didn't feel like acting out the devil's advocate, though to give the pathologist and the detectives their due, it might not have been the easiest task to identify anyone when a belt packed with plastic explosive had torn her body to shreds. It had been in all the papers.

'And the other two?'

She walked back to the chairs and sat, as she tried again to calm down. 'Dad and Andrew had been friends all their lives. They actually both went to Scots College. Educated together, played rugby together, dated the same girl once for a while. Then they died together.' She paused to refill McCann's glass. Hers was untouched.

'He was a lovely man, Andrew. One of nature's gentlemen, if you can stomach that sort of old-fashioned aphorism.'

'And the other victim?'

'No one knows.'

'That's what they told you?'

She looked up, trying to interpret McCann's thoughts. 'Well, maybe you're right, and perhaps I'm being naïve to believe them, but at this stage I do.'

'Perhaps he was a business contact?'

'Nobody in our company knew of anyone that dad was scheduled to meet that morning. But then no one knew what he and Andrew were doing at the Savoy that morning anyway. There was nothing in dad's diary.'

'Your father's secretary had no idea?'

'He didn't have one. Barbara left six weeks ago to get married. Dad said he was too busy to interview anyone till after the float.'

'Buchanan was going public?' McCann said with surprise. The stock market had always interested him. He was surprised to have missed word that Buchanan Construction was about to be traded.

'Still is. In the fullness of time. Can't proceed right now obviously.'

They sat in silence for a few moments. Then Rosalind stood. 'You must be hungry,' she said without any particular enthusiasm. 'I'll get us some dinner. Sorry, I wasn't thinking.'

As she turned to leave, McCann called out to her. 'Just a thought, but would anyone have anything to gain by obstructing the public issue?'

'You mean would anyone kill my father to stop it?'

'Yes, I suppose that's what I mean. Would they have enough to lose to make them that desperate?'

'Absolutely not. If anything, they'd have more to lose if it didn't go ahead.'

'Just a thought,' McCann replied.

'What makes me mad as hell, is that no one wants to tell me anything. It's as if I have no right to know. *Your father's dead. So sorry, Miss Buchanan. Best to put it behind you because all investigations are our business, and you'll just have to read about it in the papers, as and when we find out anything.*' She sucked in air through clenched teeth. 'But I just won't lie down and take it. And that's where you come in. At least I hope you'll agree to. They'll talk to you because Matthew's promised to put on a bit of pressure from London.'

'Let's get back to the Asian,' McCann continued. 'If he were in a conference room with Horan and your father, it would be a reasonably safe bet to assume he had some business with the company. Who's been running the company since your father was killed? Just give me the broad strokes, I can find out the details later.'

'It's all in the notes I've given you, but basically Buchanan Construction's still a private company. Nominally I'm running it myself, but in reality our two Group Managing Directors, Ian Mackintosh and Bob Zeltis. I'm learning the hands-on stuff as fast as I can. Right now I'm just a construction academic. At least that's how I think of myself. I've got the business degrees; I just need the practical experience.'

'You think you can run Buchanan Construction yourself?'

'Damned right I do. Bob and Ian respect my judgment. They think I've got what it takes.' She smiled, 'You seem surprised.'

'Not at all. But the paparazzi have a habit of giving the impression that you played hard in New York and London.'

'I also worked hard. Harvard Business College and the London School of Economics in London. Yes, I did play hard too. Why not? I was young, still am. Twenty-seven next Tuesday. I was having some fun. You see any harm there?'

'Absolutely not. But the press don't tend to list your academic achievements, only the gossip about the lifestyle.'

'I wouldn't have picked you for a reader of the *National Enquirer*.'

McCann didn't rise to her jibe – he could see from her expression she was teasing him. Anyway, it seemed to have broken her anxiety.

'If your escort's the future President's son, you're going to have to get used to the limelight.'

'Hey, hold on,' she said half laughing as she moved off into the house. 'The Republican convention's still a long way off.'

'Just one more thing before dinner. Zeltis and Mackintosh; they had no knowledge of the Asian, or his purpose in the conference room?'

'No. They checked further down the line to Ellery Travis, CEO, Buchanan Construction Asia, but again nothing.'

'Could be just a personal acquaintance I suppose. But that's unlikely with Horan present as well. That suggests a business connection to one or both of them.'

Just then a phone rang in the living room, and Rosalind excused herself. 'Excuse me a moment. Help yourself to anything you want.'

It was quite dark now, and surprisingly still and quiet after the pounding rain of the afternoon and the high winds of the early evening.

A couple of pelicans turned into the wind at the end of the jetty and dropped down into the shallows, skidding to an inelegant halt on the surface of the water. McCann knew he'd have to ask some difficult personal questions concerning her father sometime or other, and he hoped she didn't have too thin a skin.

'Dinner's almost ready,' Rosalind called from inside. 'You want to eat out there, or in the kitchen?'

'Here's just fine,' McCann replied.

Rosalind was true to her word about her culinary skills. The steaks were as good as she'd promised. A thick charcoal crust of herbs and olive tapenade; pink succulent tender beef inside. Between them on the glass table was a simple salad of rocket lettuce, sun-dried tomatoes and chèvre.

'Of course the damned press had a field day when the police released their statement,' Rosalind continued, as though the conversation from ten minutes ago had been continuous. 'My father, Andrew the prominent banker, and an unknown Asian blown to bits by a young girl on a suicide mission? You can imagine the reaction of the press! They didn't miss a trick.'

'Which brings me to my next question,' McCann began. But before he could continue, she leant forwards in her chair.

'Was my father having an affair with her? Am I right?'

'More or less,' McCann conceded, glad that she'd taken the initiative.

'Not as far as I know. Very young girls were never his predilection. Anyway, I'm sure I would have known. We were very close. Maybe she had ties with Andrew. It's hardly likely, but who knows? I could hardly have asked his wife – she's over sixty, and close to a nervous breakdown. Maybe the girl was bonking the Asian. Which brings us to the most crucial question. Who the hell did she mean to kill? Was it dad, Andrew or the Asian?'

'Or all of them? Maybe none. You see, it's just conceivable she didn't give a damn *who* was in the room. She could have been psychotic, even an anarchist. What do the police think?'

'How the hell should I know?' she replied, then smiled. 'Sorry. I must appear very rude in my manner. It's just that I've had lawyers trying to elicit the smallest germ of information - and the police either know nothing, or they know plenty and they're not saying. Either way, the ball's in your court now. If you agree to do this for me, that is.'

She stared challengingly at McCann. He stared back. Only a couple of hours ago he would have dismissed the idea out of hand. Yet here he was giving it serious thought. And why? Maybe because he admired her guts and determination. She deserved support. She had a good deal of the right stuff. Added to which he owed Matt a favor or two, so why not bend a little?

'What would your fee be?' she asked, after a few moments.

'The money's immaterial.'

'First time I've ever heard that.'

'Well, you just heard it now.'

'So what can I offer you?'

'A new mast for L'Echapper Belle.'

'Agreed.'

'And a complete refit.'

'Agreed.'

'You clearly don't know how much that costs,' McCann said, grinning.

'The money's immaterial. Wait a minute, I heard that somewhere before.' She held out a hand and McCann shook it.

'Deal?'

'Partners,' McCann replied. 'Plus expenses of course. And we do things my way. You don't like what I do, you can tell me and I'll listen. Then you can walk away if you disagree with my judgment.'

'Is that the end of the small print, Leo?'

'There is no small print. It's a simple contract - I call the shots.'

'Not on your life. Together we call the shots. Together.'

'You sounds like your future father-in-law's campaign slogan.'

'You read the papers carefully.'

'Some things tend to stick. Look, in the field, I always call the shots. That's the way it's always been. Not going to change now. Afterwards, we discuss matters.'

'Okay,' she said grudgingly, but not without a hint of a smile. 'But you report back to me.'

'That's what I just said. And we pool all information each day. Okay? It's important we both have a full set of facts to cross-reference.'

'Makes sense. A team. You're Schwartzkopf, I'm Powell.' Although she smiled, McCann could see she meant it. She was tough. He'd have to bear that in mind.

'And please don't marry me off just yet. We're not even officially engaged.'

7.

May 14th.

The following morning at the Priory, McCann crammed five days work into a few hours, tying up loose ends that would free him up temporarily to work for Rosalind Buchanan.

At midday he told Rita, the secretary he shared with two others, that he would be 'away' for a short while. She should refer urgent matters to Neale Frank in the next office until further notice. If anything vital transpired, she could leave a message on his home phone and he'd check the voice mail. The news of his imminent departure came as little surprise to Rita.

'Of on holiday again, Mr. McCann?' she replied cryptically. She had some idea that his 'holidays' had little to do with sun-drenched beaches, but she kept her thoughts to herself.

A couple of hours later, McCann walked up the steps of the Monmouth Center.

The meeting with the Task Force Commander had been arranged for 2.30 p.m. by Chief Superintendent Torrance's incident room co-ordinator. She'd been brisk, yet polite. Nevertheless, McCann smelt conflict in the wind. Torrance had failed to return his initial call, and it had taken three calls to confirm the meeting.

The Task Force headquarters were on the fourth floor, at the back of the building. There was no reference to the police presence on the directory in the foyer, nor was there was any security in evidence as he stepped from the lift.

The corridor was empty. McCann made a random choice and turned left. The rooms on either side all had their doors ajar. No one bothered to look up as he passed. Some were sitting at desks staring at computer screens; others were leaning back in chairs talking animatedly with colleagues.

At the end of the corridor, McCann glanced to his right into a small office. The room was empty, a steaming cup of coffee on a cluttered desk the only evidence of recent occupation.

To his left was a room by far the largest on the floor, with six workstations. Four were occupied; three by women. Pinned to the wall by the door was a sheet of paper on which was computer-printed, *Task Force Acorn*. One corner of the room was partitioned off. Through the plexi-glass McCann could see the figure he'd often seen on the news; an obese man of around forty-five, two hundred and eighty pounds, bald head, and walrus moustache. He was talking on the telephone, sitting back in an ample chair set well back from the confines of the desk, the belt of his pants unbuckled, allowing his stomach full freedom. As McCann studied him, Torrance lifted his head slightly from his notes, and their eyes met for an instant. The Chief Super then looked away. Even at a distance, McCann detected what he initially interpreted as the briefest flash of antipathy.

'May I help you?' asked an uniformed policewoman who sat at a desk just inside the door. The voice was familiar. It was the crisp efficient voice on the phone that had arranged the meeting.

'My name's Leo McCann. I have an appointment with Chief Superintendent Leonard Torrance at 2.30.'

She glanced down at a diary. 'Yes, he's expecting you. He's on the phone right now. Would you mind waiting in the meeting room? It's just over there.' She indicated a room to her right. 'I'm sure he won't keep you long. If you'd like a coffee, perhaps you could help yourself.'

The meeting room was as shabby as the other rooms on the floor. An oversized oval desk, ten chairs, barren walls that wore the scars of the previous tenant's picture frames, and a slim, cheaply veneered chipboard side table that ran half the length of one wall on which were the coffee fixings.

On the wall farthest from the door was a whiteboard, divided into sections, each of which was designated to one of the team. There were ten members in all; three detective sergeants, five detective senior constables, and two detective constables first class. The seven women were the most senior. Beside each name were notes such as dates, appointments, names, and priorities. These varied from person to person.

'Sorry to have kept you waiting Mr. McCann,' a voice behind him said pleasantly.

McCann turned. Torrance had put on his jacket. It hung round his vast bulk like a crumpled cloak. He'd thought to buckle up his belt, but had failed to zip his fly quite up to the top. It hardly mattered since his paunch practically hid the first three inches of his pants. He carried a manila folder in one hand, and a small brown paper bag in the other.

'It's good of you to take the time to see me, Chief Superintendent.'

Torrance smiled. His lack of response spoke volumes, yet the man seemed to have a good-natured aura about him. The eyes smiled gently yet clearly studied him closely. 'If you knew me better, you'd know I very rarely take time out to do favors. Personal ones, that is. I'm pretty single minded when it comes to my work.'

'I've heard.'

'Oh yes?'

'Just articles and so on.'

Torrance remained silent, his eyes probing, assessing, judging. 'The Kremmer case,' McCann added by way of explanation. The trial had fed the tabloids for most of the previous summer.

'The Kremmer case... yes,' replied Torrance. 'Did anyone offer you a tea or coffee?'

'They did, thank you.'

'I don't take it myself. I prefer bottled water. Keep a stock of it in my private little area out there,' he said gesturing. 'Take a seat. I'm afraid I can't stay long.'

The Chief Superintendent pulled out a chair, easing himself into it with the reticence of a bather unsure of the temperature of the ocean; perhaps equally uncertain whether the chair would take his weight.

'So you're the pal of Matthew Hutton?' said Torrance.

'That's right.' McCann met the Chief Super's steady gaze. 'You know each other?'

'Never heard of him till yesterday. Good man to have on your side I gather. A fair bit of pull and influence in the most sensitive of areas.' He paused momentarily to gauge any reaction. There was none from McCann, who in turn waited for Torrance to continue; he wasn't about to discuss Matthew's background.

'And what's the connection with Miss Buchanan?'

'Whose? Mine or Matthew's?'

'Mr. Hutton's.'

'Miss Buchanan's father was a buddy of Matthew's, apparently for some time.'

'Well, that was a bit of luck as far as Miss Buchanan is concerned?'

'I don't follow you Mr. Torrance.'

'Care for a toffee, McCann?' he said with a smile, holding out the paper bag he'd pulled from his trouser pocket. 'Quite forgotten I had them with me. Very flavorsome.'

'Thanks,' McCann replied. 'Not right now, maybe later.'

Torrance shrugged as he popped one in his mouth. 'Put it this way, I don't take kindly to interference from outside. And that means by anybody. The State Commander knows that, and respects my reasons. As, incidentally does the Assistant Commissioner. We work bloody hard here, and we come up with the goods. But our files are for us alone, we don't share. Not with the press, not with outsiders, and not with you, Mr. McCann. The integrity of the investigation's paramount. Sorry.' He suddenly and unexpectedly smiled, looking McCann straight in the eye with an expression that seemed to tell him the ball was now in McCann's court.

'I've basically been an army man most of my life, Chief Superintendent. Never cared much for interference by civilians. I can understand you wouldn't take kindly to people poking their noses into your investigation?'

There was a long beat, as McCann held Torrance's stare.

'If you don't mind my asking. Your accent. Leeds?' McCann ventured eventually.

Torrance cocked his head to one side for a second, chuckled, then stuck his hands in his trouser pockets.

'Pudsey, but you're within a few miles.'

'Spent six months in that neck of the woods twenty odd years ago. Training. Explosives course.'

'You wouldn't be trying to butter me up by any chance, Mr. McCann? Because there's no need. You see, there's one person I *would* do a favor for. And his name is Mike Dodds. Looked after me when my dad was killed. Your pal Mr. Hutton must have gone to some trouble identifying the one person I'd cross a continent on all fours for. But then, I expect he moves in the right circles to do the odd bit of research, eh?' He paused again and stared with raised eyebrows. McCann pretended to look confused. Torrance then switched his glance down to the bag of sweets.

'Sure I can't interest you in a cream toffee? Stick to the teeth a bit, but well worth the inconvenience.'

'No thanks.'

Torrance twisted the paper bag closed. 'Mike tells me Hutton's a major player at Vauxhall Bridge. Or is it Thames House?' He seemed to be enjoying his mental fly-fishing, though it was apparent to McCann that Torrance knew quite well the general thrust of Matthew's intelligence work with the SIS. Torrance's eyes twinkled with amusement as he observed McCann's reticence to comment.

'Matthew Hutton's basically an army man, Mr. Torrance.'

'Was once, yes. If rank's your only guideline, he still is. But it's life's light and shade that's always intrigued me. And there's a man of shadows if ever there was one. Military intelligence would be closer to the mark, don't you think? Which makes me wonder a bit about *your* credentials.' Torrance produced a roll of peppermints from inside his jacket - as if by magic. 'No offence intended, Mr. McCann. I'm afraid I was just seeing how tight you were with a confidence. Important to make such a judgment before I let you sift among all my 'stuff' for want of a better word. You appear to be tighter than most. I can see you prefer to keep things close to your chest. That's good. Maybe you'd prefer a peppermint?'

'Thank you,' McCann said leaning forward and taking one.

'Anyway, somehow Miss Buchanan's pal Hutton is in turn a good pal of Mike Dodds, and Mike's asked me to spare you some time. So spare you some time, I shall. You've got an hour,' he said, helping himself to another peppermint. 'Less the time you've had already. I'd estimate that would be forty-eight more minutes. We'll call it fifty,' he added magnanimously. He pushed his chair back, slackening his pants belt a couple of inches. 'So ask away.'

'It's been just under two months since the bombing – '

'Forty-nine days to be precise.'

'Are you any closer to identifying the girl's motive?'

'Well, that may quite possibly prove a red herring, in that a nihilist would have had *no* motive.'

'Which breed would you be more inclined to believe she was? A nihilist, terrorist or random anarchist?'

'Well, a terrorist or anarchist would have some sort of motive, albeit a political rather than a personal one.'

'If you had to hazard a guess?'

'I've never done such a thing. Conjecture is a luxury I allow myself very rarely, and then only based on solid evidence. Databased analysis - that's the key. Hazard a guess? Never. Certainly not at this stage. Deduction based on fact is one thing, supposition quite another. Guessing is for no-hopers.'

He threaded his fingers together, the thumbs circling each other like Thai boxers. 'But if I were a man prone to making swift decisions, I'd say that although all the evidence we've built up so far points to a profile of Miss Messon as a terrorist, most of her psychological profile doesn't back it up.' Torrance closed his eyes briefly, as if he had a picture of the girl in his mind. 'Just a feeling, that's all,' he continued with a twinkle in his eye. 'But don't you ever quote me.'

McCann returned his smile. He couldn't help liking the man. Torrance had an attractive, self-effacing sense of humor.

'So you think there may be a personal angle associated with one of the men who died?'

Torrance held up a finger. 'Didn't say that, McCann. You can't have been listening. I said if I *were* a man prone to hunches and the like, *then* I might think along those lines. But that's not my style - I prefer to narrow the angles until I know *all* the answers.

'Let's put it another way, McCann. A young girl walks into a hotel with enough ex-army issue plastic explosive to take out half a supermarket, and blows herself to bits. That really doesn't fit too well with someone with a personal axe to grind, unless she wasn't in control of her faculties, and didn't care who else was caught in the crossfire. Explosions tend to be indiscriminate as far as casualties go.'

'Maybe she didn't care,' suggested McCann.

'Maybe she didn't. Maybe she had a grudge against all three. And possibly everyone on the floors above and below.' Torrance grinned at McCann. 'Personally, I don't much care for 'maybes'; they waste a lot of time. I get on with piecing together what I know for a fact. But I suggest you look at the sheets in Detective Sergeant Blackwood's office. She's been collating the information on Venice Messon.'

'What about the Asian victim. Has he been identified?'

'No. Thought we'd fingered him for a while early on, but that proved a cul de sac.'

'When was that?'

'A few weeks ago.'

'He wasn't who you thought he was?'

'Sadly, no.'

'What do we know about him then?'

'Very little. Surprisingly so, as a matter of fact. The body wasn't as badly damaged as the others. Blast killed him, together with a fragment of glass that penetrated the left eyeball and lodged in the brain.' As with most policemen, surgeons, and doctors, Torrance's tone was as impersonal as a mechanic discussing a minor carburetor problem with a customer. 'Plenty of small fragmentary damage to the face, but not enough to make identification impossible. The point is, we still have no idea from whence this Mr. Asia came.'

'You released a statement to the effect that you thought he was of Vietnamese extraction.'

'Yes, that much is reasonably certain. Don't ask me how we can be so definite as to rule out Laotian, Cambodian and Thai, but it's possible. Ivor Kantor, a Professor of Ethnology, suggested our dead man's a Cham. They're a minority group of less than a hundred thousand in Vietnam. There's more than a dash of Indian in the Cham physiognomy. Kantor says it's unmistakable to an expert.'

'Can't be too many Chams in Australia?'

'Very few,' Torrance answered, slipping another file across the table. 'Here's the Mr. Asia file. Have a look at it, then chat with Detective Roberts – he's been trying to nail him down since the bombing. Shares an office with Detective Sergeant Blackwood.' He reached into his pocket, withdrawing another toffee. 'There was no means of identification on his body, no wallet so no credit cards, money, business cards. Nothing in the clothes, most of which were expensively tailored, but with no tags. Shoes were expensive. But no one walks around town without some money or the means to get some; and that means a credit card of some kind. In my experience that suggests a man with something to hide. And that interests me. You see, it was the girl who was supposed to be the bad guy, not one of the victims.

'So we had him tidied up facially by our mortician, then photographed, and the proofs cosmetically airbrushed. Then for good measure an artist made us up a composite of the damaged left eye and surrounds, which were laid onto the photo.'

'No luck?'

'Drew a blank everywhere – the Vietnamese community, Immigration, newspapers, TV, the lot.'

'What about DVI?' asked McCann, referring to Interpol's common identification system.

'Nothing's shown up yet,' Torrance replied.

'Did the Immigration boys rule out the possibility that he was a foreign national?'

'Up to a point. I asked them to run a check on all Vietnamese, Cambodian, Laotian and Thai nationals whose visas were granted before the date of the explosion, and were still outstanding. In other words those who hadn't yet exited the country. As you might expect it came to a good many. Some had good reason to still be here, others didn't. They then tracked back with the photo we'd given them, and it was sent to all the consulates and embassies in each of our targeted countries to cross-check with the photos in their records. Even allowing that chummy might not look his best dead and cosmetically enhanced, none matched.'

'So it looks more likely he's one of ours, an Australian?'

'Look, McCann, he could be a German national, or a Bolivian. To cross check every visa issued in the past seven to ten months would take forever. Look at it this way. Take a visa issued in Vienna. It doesn't say *"bearer looks more like a Cham than an Austrian, but believe me, he actually is an Austrian!"* Get my point?'

McCann nodded, smiling.

'If he's an Australian citizen, then he kept his profile as low as the bottom rung in an Olympic limbo competition,' Torrance continued. 'Task Force Oak's run him through all their files. They deal with Asian crime in New South Wales. So far they've come up with nothing - on their computers, or out on the street. And they've been asking plenty of questions I can tell you. Would you like a glass of water?'

'Thanks no,' replied McCann.

'Another mint?'

'No, thank you.'

'We checked his fingerprints and sent them to Interpol. Nothing, so no criminal record. No record at the Roads and Traffic Authority, so he didn't drive. Dental records drew a complete blank. Referred them to Interpol. Nothing. Faxed them to Jakarta, Singapore, Hong Kong, Kuala Lumpur. You name it. Those that had the courtesy to reply were negative. Hanoi didn't even acknowledge our request. Not much two-way co-operation in that neck of the woods. Curious, in view of the fact we were possibly trying to give them back one of their nationals.'

'They've probably been handed back enough nationals in the form of refugees to last them a lifetime,' observed McCann.

Torrance continued as if he hadn't heard. 'Mind you, the teeth were in pretty good shape. Quite a lot of fancy bridge work; so if he *was* Vietnamese, he must have been worth a quid or two. We X-rayed the body for fractures that might show up something in the Department of Health records. Again zip. We circulated his snapshot to every likely Asian society, group, and friendly society in Australia, and it's been published in every state in newspapers, and seen on most TV stations.'

'Have you tried the intelligence services?'

'Yep. Gave ASIO all we had on him. They handed it on to their counterparts at Langley and in Whitehall. That's when we thought for a while we'd nailed him.'

'The Americans, or the British?'

'Langley. They faxed back that they had a match with a guy they hadn't come across since the fall of Saigon. Guy called Tran. Made a fortune, much to the chagrin of the CIA, selling off the military hardware they left behind when they pulled out of Saigon in a hurry. A strategic intelligence pal of mine in the ASIO office in North Sydney told me that his contact at Langley had told him off the record they'd spent four years trying to 'waste' the fellow, as they so nicely put it, but he'd always been one step ahead of them. By the mid-eighties the CIA had lost interest. Tran was taken off the hot list and they left him alone. They hadn't heard of him since - at least till they got the transmission of the photo from our intelligence boys,' Torrance paused.

'But it wasn't Tran?'

'No. We checked very thoroughly through the Embassy in Hanoi to be absolutely sure. He's alive and kicking. Reliably informed by our diplomatic staff that he's turned over a new leaf. Very highly placed in political circles there. I asked the Embassy to check, and they did. The long and short of it is that he's alive, but our particular chum is frozen on a steel tray at the Glebe morgue.'

'Have you been able to link the girl to either Horan or Buchanan?'

Torrance's answer was to peel two more folders from the pile in front of him and slide them across. 'The thicker one's Buchanan, the other's Horan. And the answer is no, try as we may. Horan never was a ladies man. Buchanan could have been if he'd tried - heaven knows he had the looks - but he doesn't appear to have taken advantage of them for many years. His life would seem to be an open book. Mind you, I've always found there's always the odd few pages stuck together somewhere or other, and those are the ones that yield fruit.'

Over Torrance's shoulder McCann saw the face of the female co-ordinator appear round the side of the door.

'Sorry to interrupt, sir.'

Torrance looked round.

'Call from Commander Barrett. Thought you'd like to take it in your office, sir.'

The chair groaned under his weight as Torrance stood. The Chief buttoned his jacket over his gut. McCann couldn't help staring at him. How a man with such an ordered meticulous mind could walk around looking such a complete shambles staggered him.

'Thank you, Lou. Tell him I'll be right there.' Torrance turned to McCann. 'I know I said I'd give you an hour, but I'm afraid I'll have to leave you for a while. Why not take the time to read the files I've given you, then if you have any further questions, feel free to chat to any of the team. If you want to make notes from the files, feel free to do so, because when you leave, the originals stay. Understood?'

'Very good of you,' replied McCann.

'Before you go, pop into my area and say goodbye. Have a glass of my spring water. It's Snowy River stuff. Delicious.' Torrance pushed back his chair and left the room.

'She died just a couple of weeks short of her twenty-first,' the detective said.

Detective Maggie Blackwood scrolled through the pages on her computer screen. Her office was down the corridor from the meeting room; a cramped room she shared with a very small man with delicate features and intelligent eyes. Maggie introduced him merely as Kieron. It must have been the Detective Roberts that Torrance had mentioned. As McCann had entered, the young man had looked up briefly from his own screen and nodded. A less observant man than McCann might have missed the most transient of polite smiles.

'Though motive is still a mystery, her upbringing would have had any child psychologist's alarm bells ringing. Have you met her father?'

'I thought it wiser to check in here before I called him.'

'Good move. He's one very angry fellow.'

'Probably has good reason to be.'

Maggie screwed up her face, swinging round in her typist's chair to face McCann. Her aura had the energy of an express train. 'Not too sure about that. I mean it's probably not his fault his wife pissed off and left him; though middle-aged men should really think twice before they marry bimbos half their age. But if you're a single dad and you ignore your only child all her life, what's going to happen? She's hardly likely to grow up into a balanced kid.'

'I suppose not. What sort of schooling did she have?'

'First class. But if you ask me, packing her off to boarding school was just an excuse as far as Messon was concerned. Intuition tells me that as soon as Mrs. Messon packed her bags, it wasn't long before hubby realized he couldn't cope with the child on his own. Venice was eight when mum scooted off without a word. Must have been crushing for the girl. Even Messon concedes it broke his daughter's spirit - and remember, he'd be the least likely to exaggerate the bond Venice had with her mother, bearing in mind his hostility towards the woman. So when I say it was a bit of a smokescreen to send her to a fine boarding school, it was just that. It made him feel noble, spending so much money on her education. Cost him a fortune, but it got her out of his hair. Only had to deal with her for the holidays.'

She paused for a microsecond to draw enough breath to fill her lungs. 'Mind you, he was hardly up to that task either. 'Old man Messon was too old to bond with her for one thing; she was a young kid of the eighties, he was a relic from the fifties. Don't think he could find any middle ground. They were like life forms from different solar systems; that's how one of her teachers put it. I drove out to her old school, spoke to the principal for a couple of hours. Quite illuminating, bearing in mind Messon's side of things.

'A private education away from home doesn't necessarily breed disturbed children.'

'No, it doesn't. In Venice's case she was outstanding as far as her studies were concerned. But the shrinks put a different slant on things. Our advisory psychologist says that given the absence of a mother, together with her somewhat estranged relationship with her father, she'd be a prime candidate for acute introspection, withdrawing into the sanctuary of her studies. Which is exactly what she did. The plus side was she became a major achiever. Remarkable Higher School Certificate results. Had her pick of universities, but decided to do a graphic design course at Billy Blue. That didn't exactly please her father, which was very possibly the rationale behind her choice.'

'What about boyfriends?'

'Still trying to find one when she killed herself. At school she was a loner. And at home she mixed mostly - that's when she mixed at all - with girls older than herself. I tell you, I've tried to track down anyone who might qualify as a friend, without much success.'

'So she didn't have a boyfriend?'

'Had she ever had a physical relationship? Not as far as we can tell. No clues at the postmortem. The lower torso was blown away with the legs. All we know is that Messon senior assures us that she was a virgin prior to going to London. But then, he was so out of touch with his daughter - how would he know? Nevertheless, he's adamant that the closest she came to sex was a close platonic friendship with a boy called Hendrik Ohlson, and that's going back almost two years. Incidentally,

Ohlson was ID'd at the Savoy the morning of the bombing.'

'He was involved in the bombing?'

'No. We've no evidence to support that theory. We interviewed him quite thoroughly. He volunteered the information.'

'But you said he was identified.'

'Yes, he was. That came to light later.'

'Then in my book he was smart to come forward before the finger was pointed.'

'I had a session with him myself,' Blackwood continued. 'As far as the sex angle is concerned, he told me candidly he'd have been happy to take it further, but she didn't want to.'

'You think the "sex factor", for want of a better expression, is important?'

'In cases of this kind, it's one of the first things we look into. Serial killers, drive-by killings, deranged people who kill their children then top themselves. Quite often there's a deep-seated sexual resentment lurking somewhere.'

'Was she living at home while she was studying at Billy Blue?'

'Yes. But I don't think she saw much of her father. Most of the time he was at Bankstown Airport making love to his flying sex substitute.'

'Who told you that?'

'Hendrik Ohlson.'

'Single engine plane?'

'No. Big bugger. A DC3. Actually, the military version, the C-47.'

'Do you know if Messon senior often took her up in it?'

'No. She was terrified of flying, which again didn't help their relationship. Ironic really. He lived for the plane, and there was his daughter practically puking with terror at the mere mention of a joy flight. Then out of the blue she decides she wants to study in London.'

'When was this?'

'April '96. Did a real number on dad. Said she needed to get away; wanted to study design in London - would he come up with the cash. Well, he wasn't exactly strapped for funds, though most of his money for years had been funneled into his plane rather than directed towards his daughter. Maybe he thought he could assuage his guilt by agreeing, who knows? Anyway, he did agree, and off she went.'

'How long prior to the bombing did she get back?'

'Immigration control logged her back November 16 last year. That's four and a bit months before she blew herself up.'

'Did she actually study in London?'

'No. She wrote to Messon saying she'd changed her mind. Didn't say what she was up to, but she kept in touch every few weeks by post from London.'

'Do you have her old London address?'

'Yes, it's in the file. North London - Highgate.'

McCann flipped through the pages of the file Torrance had given him. 'Any trace on the origin of the explosive?'

'We're liaising with Special Branch on the Metabel. You're an army man aren't you, Mr. McCann.'

'Does it show?'

She laughed lightly. 'This morning's briefing. The boss told us you were coming.'

'He's a thorough man,' said McCann

'Sure is. Like to think I'll get to his standard someday,' she said stabbing at the keys to bring up another file. 'Anyway, you'll be familiar with Metabel. Ex-army. No longer standard issue, though the federal guys say there's still quite a lot around, both militarily, and socially in the hands of certain harebrained civilian paramilitary organizations.'

She speed-read off the screen. 'Comes in plastic sleeves, sheets three feet by two, prolonged exposure causes – ' Her voice trailed off. 'Hey, you'll know all this. But the answer to your question is no, we haven't been able to isolate its origin. The Federal Police couldn't believe the silence that followed the bombing. No one claimed responsibility, no one said a damned thing. So if you hold to the theory that she was a terrorist, what was the point? And if she wasn't, then who was she after?'

She swiveled away from the screen and looked at McCann. 'So you see, we're still basically at square one, though the AFP can't wait to attribute the blame to one of the paramilitary groups they've got their eye on.

'Naturally, when the girl blew herself up at the Savoy, and the politicians began sharpening their knives, the weirdos all went to ground - disappeared.'

'Are there many paramilitary groups in this country?'

'Nothing like the States. America gives new meaning to the word "paramilitary".'

'What do they call themselves over here?'

'The Guardian Militia is one group, then there are the Confederate Boys over in Perth. There are others. Pretty impressive names for groups of unimpressive right-wing racist thugs. Special Branch and the Federal boys have been keeping an eye on them for years. By and large they've never done much more than play bush war games. No political agenda, you see. Quite a few of them are ex-vets who enjoy shooting up the bush at weekends. Plus a lot of the good ol' boys who like the feel of an Armalite in their hands. Well, that's what the AFP thought up till the Savoy incident – then it became a different matter. Suddenly they were keen as mustard to pick up the crazies and have a chat." She took a subliminal intake of breath. 'Then the week after the bombing, when they'd come up with a connection– '

'What connection?' McCann interrupted.

'I'll get to that. Anyway, the AFP started pushing SACPAV for permission to send in a team to round up the Guardian Militia, and see if they could find an explosives match. But by that time it was too late. They'd just melted into the mist as if they never existed.'

SACPAV was the Standing Advisory Committee for the Protection Against Violence. For any gung-ho police action it was necessary to get their clearance before you could wheel out the SWAT teams. Especially if you wanted to bring in the army in the form of the SAS.

'But what was the connection that linked the Guardian Militia to the Savoy?'

'Patience, McCann,' she chided. 'We'd shown the girl's photo pretty much all over Sydney, Melbourne, the Gold Coast, Surfers and Brisbane. Needed to know where she'd been since she came back from overseas. A few days down the line an informant belonging to the Drug Enforcement Agency in the Cross here in Sydney recognized her. They showed him a book of AFP mugshots, the one concerning paramilitary organizations. He picked out someone he said Venice Messon had been living with. Man calling himself Ritz. Ex-army, fought in 'Nam. Charged in '95 for having explosives in his possession – stolen from an army store. But by the time we went to pick him up, he'd disappeared.

'What's the word on the street?'

'No one's talking. The AFP is convinced Ritz is their man - that he found the plastic for her, and that she's a member of the Guardian Militia. I must say it seems the most logical explanation. Mind you, it doesn't really matter what the AFP think - this is *our* baby now, they merely advise.'

'Did you manage to establish that Venice had been living with Ritz?'

'There were some woman's things in his rooms. Can't say for sure that they belonged to Venice, or how long they'd been there.'

McCann stared into space, his mind filled with conflicting thoughts. Why had the Guardian Militia not claimed responsibility? If Venice was doing their work, then they'd had a major success? Why weren't they crowing?

'Any other questions? Everything we have on Mr. Asia's there in the files.' She seemed suddenly anxious to get back to work.

McCann quickly scanned the pages in the folder. 'Did you inform Messon senior of the results of his daughter's autopsy?'

'That was the Chief Super's decision. No, he didn't.'

'But Messon did know his daughter was a junkie - surely?'

'Apparently not. He says she looked quite normal last time he saw her - before she left for London. She didn't contact him between her return to Australia and her death.'

'You believe him?'

'No reason not to.'

'Don't you think he had a right to know she was HIV?' he added, reading the report from the folder.

She turned to face McCann and stared hard at him. 'No, Mr. McCann, I don't. You think it's going to make him feel a whole lot better to know his daughter was dying anyway?'

'If it were me, I'd like to know everything. Maybe I'd be able to understand things a little better.'

'At the moment, no one understands a damn thing - so we thought we'd spare him that particular piece of information.'

'Is it usual to test for AIDS?'

'Only as a precautionary measure for the bomb boys. There was a hell of a lot of airborne tissue the day of the bombing.'

'She was merely HIV positive? Nothing more?'

'Correct.'

'Is there a full list of evidence taken from the crime scene?'

'Yes, there is. But the boss made a decision not to include it in the files he gave you. You can ask him for it but he won't give it to you. It's one of the things he keeps close to his chest.'

'Which overseas agencies are you working with?'

'Well, as I said, we're liaising with the Federal Police because of the possible terrorist aspect, tracking movements of target group members in and out of the country. Special Branch are involved, as usual, since it was a bombing. They can quite often target groups of a paramilitary nature operating in Australia, and can liaise with foreign agencies around the world.' She began to chew on a pencil, tapping the desktop with her other hand. 'Who else? Interpol. Langley to a limited degree - they'll usually toss us some info if we ask nicely. Same with MI6. ASIO help us as well.'

McCann was about to ask another question when Blackwood held up a hand. 'Got to get back to work. Sorry,' she said, swiveling back to the screen.

That seemed to be that.

McCann spent two hours in the meeting room taking extensive notes from the files Torrance had given him.

Torrance popped his head round the door just before five-thirty. His jaw was working hard. McCann was surprised the man had any toffees left.

'I'm off home for my dinner. Stay in touch, will you, McCann. If you come across anything we ought to know, do the right thing, eh?'

'I will indeed,' replied McCann. 'I've made a few notes as you can see. I'll leave the originals with Detective Blackwood.'

As Torrance walked to the door, McCann called after him. 'Just one more thing, Chief Superintendent.'

Torrance turned.

'The evidence sheet. Any chance I can see it?'

Torrance gave McCann an old-fashioned look, crossed with a wry grin. 'It was worth a try, eh McCann? I know *I* would have asked. But no. There's no chance of that whatsoever. Sorry, but I won't take the chance of the media releasing that information till I'm ready.'

'Mind if I have a word with the Bomb Squad?'

Torrance thought for a moment. 'No, I don't see why not. But you'll need a letter of authority. I'll do it now and leave it on my desk. Pick it up on the way out.'

'You're a very gracious man, Chief Superintendent. I hope in return I can be useful to you.'

Torrance merely smiled good-naturedly as he picked at his teeth with his forefinger. 'Damned toffee. Sticks to the teeth no matter how careful you are,' he said, then left the room.

As soon as he was outside the building, McCann called the contact number listed in the file for Hendrik Ohlson. A woman who identified herself at once as Ohlson's mother answered the phone. Her son was in New Zealand, she said - a family matter. He was not expected back till Sunday night.

McCann felt a rush of disappointment. He would have liked to have seen the young man right then.

He was about to ask for an address when the line went dead. He redialed the number several times but the phone wasn't answered.

8.

May 14th

The corpulent banker sat facing Rosalind, perched on the edge of the Chesterfield like a toad on a lily. 'Andrew's irreplaceable - no two ways about it. He came to us from Hoare as your father most probably told you. Headhunted actually. Thirty-one years ago. Been with us ever since. As a matter of fact, I was looking forward to handing the chairmanship over to Andrew in a couple of years.'

Though an eighth generation Australian, Rupert Gerson looked every inch the stereotypical Swiss banker; square bifocals, gray double-breasted Gieves and Hawkes suit, Turnbull and Asser starched white shirt, and understated gray and white spotted tie. His manner was smooth and reserved. His thin lips were curled into a smile of sorts, one usually reserved for children. Over the years his and Rosalind's paths had crossed many times, though usually it had been on social rather than business occasions, since Buchanan Construction had always chosen to bank with a more mainstream institution, the Commonwealth Bank.

'Such a terrible waste of such a fine man. Senseless violence is such a part of day to day life these days.' Gerson made a face, the kind he clearly imagined accompanied sad disapproval. 'Your father and I grew up in another world altogether. I wish we could return to those days - the personal touch has become so lost in time I can scarcely remember what it was like to deal with a business associate I could call a friend. Most of what I do nowadays is handled electronically, and the majority of my decisions are made alone. Sad state of affairs. But, I suppose one must endeavor to move with the times.'

There was a soft knock on the door, and a middle-aged matronly woman entered, carrying a tray of coffee. She placed it on the Edwardian coffee table that separated Gerson from Rosalind.

Gerson smiled with all the genuine warmth of Saddam Hussein greeting his generals, then removed his spectacles, holding them up to the light as he searched for some tiny blemish or spec of dust that might have escaped his notice the last time he'd checked them three minutes previously.

'Thank you Margaret,' he called towards the departing figure of his secretary as she closed the door softly behind her. He then leant forward, replacing his glasses. 'How do you take it, Rosalind? Black with no sugar, judging by your figure.'

Rosalind smiled politely at the unoriginal pleasantry. She'd expected somewhat more from a man of Gerson's intelligence. 'That would be fine, thank you.'

'Anyway, to get back to our previous discussion, I can well see that you would like to get to the bottom of it all - that is, if there's more to this matter than a senseless terrorist attack. However, if you ask me,' he paused for effect, obviously a studied mannerism he frequently used in boardroom meetings, 'I see no bogeyman - no hidden agenda, as they're so fond of saying nowadays. From what I gathered from the detective who came to see me three weeks ago, the police have not been able to establish the slightest personal link between the girl and Andrew. Not at the time of the bombing, and not since I should imagine. He was just tragically in the wrong place at the wrong time. As was, I hasten to add, your dear father.'

Gerson passed Rosalind her coffee.

'I think we must always be wary of taking things entirely on their face value, Rupert,' she replied. 'It's just too easy to conclude the bomb attack was a senseless act of violence. Events are seldom completely irrational. It's just that we sometimes don't see beneath the surface to their real significance.'

'You think the girl had some deeper motive of which we are unaware; one the police have missed - one we might do well to investigate further?' It was plain from his tone, tinged as it was with the barest hint of patronage, that Rupert Gerson didn't believe one existed. 'If so, it presupposes some personal involvement with at least one of the deceased surely? Have you any reason to believe that your father knew the girl, or had had any dealings with her?'

'None whatsoever. But I can't rule out the possibility that he might have met her at some time in the past, but have been unaware of the fact; or that the girl might have had a grudge against the company rather than my father. If her own father had been retrenched or fired she may have felt that the company acted in bad faith.'

'Have you looked into that scenario?'

'It's in hand naturally. So far we've drawn a blank. As you know, Maynard was a very honorable man. He dealt plainly with people. I can't envisage any personal grudge she could have harbored against the company that would have driven her to those lengths.'

'I agree. But wouldn't that logic also apply to Andrew?'

'Quite obviously, yes.'

'You see,' Gerson continued after some moment's thought, 'fundamentally we have to remember that this was in the nature of a suicide bombing. She chose to die along with the others.' Once more he leant forwards in the sofa and polished his spotless glasses. 'Without a personal connection we have no motive. And that in turn leaves us with an act of senseless anarchy - an angle I believe the authorities are pursuing at present'

Rosalind was beginning to become tense – Gerson so loved to hear himself speak. 'The Asian who died. Could he have been an associate of Andrew's?' she continued.

'Not as far as we know,' Gerson replied. 'He was not a client of ours. I checked with Duncan. The police asked the same question as a matter of course.' He paused to sip his coffee. 'Incidentally, Duncan McKinley has taken over Andrew's portfolio. Have you two met?'

'No, we haven't.'

'I'm sure you will. Hasn't been with us long. English. Nice fellow.' He replaced his cup on the table. 'Of course there's no reason to jump to the conclusion that it was in fact a business meeting taking place when the bomb exploded. As you're well aware, your father and Andrew had been close friends since school days. As for the unknown Asian, he could have been there for purely personal reasons. I suppose it's possible the three of them had some personal business, unconnected with our bank. I take it you've checked with your own people on that score?' Gerson raised his eyebrows for confirmation.

'Yes. None that we are aware of.'

'I see.'

Gerson leant back, prodding his bifocals firmly back onto the bridge of his nose.

'Might I ask whether Andrew had any portfolios at the time that one might call sensitive?'

Gerson paused for a fraction of a second, then laughed lightly. He hadn't found the question so amusing when the police had asked it. 'Dear girl,' he said dismissively. 'If you're for a moment thinking that there was any link between Andrew's and your father's death and this bank, I think you may be drifting into the realms of fantasy. I very much doubt that the girl was an assassin paid to kill Andrew over some web of intrigue he may have uncovered at the Australian Pacific,' Gerson said, somewhat tartly.

'I didn't suggest that. I merely asked whether Andrew was engaged in any matters that an independent observer might have considered 'sensitive',' Rosalind prodded relentlessly.

Gerson looked blank. 'I fail to see your point, Rosalind. I count *all* banking details sensitive; that's the very nature of our business. However, I do not believe any of Andrew's work would have led to the intervention of an assassin. Does that satisfy you?'

Rosalind noticed Gerson was beginning to look uncomfortable, so she went after him like a terrier. 'I agree it's highly unlikely,' she replied crisply – she didn't much care for Gerson's patronizing tone. 'However, since I haven't the slightest notion of what Andrew was engaged in at the time of his death, it's hard to say. I'd imagine that if he'd uncovered a link between the

Australian Pacific and organized crime, I might be forgiven for thinking that his sudden death was more than chance.'

Gerson looked shell-shocked. He was quite unused to straight talk of this nature, especially from a woman young enough to be his daughter. He was used to businessmen of the top echelon treating him with the deference he felt to be his due. The dual references to the Australian Pacific and organized crime in the one sentence left him momentarily stunned.

He was about to speak, when Rosalind placed a hand on his arm and smiled her most engaging smile. 'Naturally, I am not for a second suggesting this to be the case. But there are many things it's possible to miss simply because they appear equally ludicrous.'

Less than mollified, Gerson nevertheless returned her smile, albeit weakly. 'One might just as easily conjecture that the girl was being thought-controlled by little men from Mars.'

Gerson relaxed back into the sofa and chuckled at his little joke.

'Seriously,' he continued, his composure back in place, 'I fail to see that any of Andrew's work would have been of the slightest interest to the girl. They were just the usual merchant banking procedures. Anyway, for goodness sake, she was a teenager, wasn't she?'

'Twenty, I'm told. I am twenty-six.' Her message was loud and clear. She could see her words had hit the mark – Gerson looked distinctly embarrassed.

'Believe me, Rosalind, if I thought for one second that a detailed analysis of Andrew's work would shed light on anything that might be relevant, I would give the authorities access to Andrew's papers. However, I don't believe they would, and as I'm sure you're aware, to allow you access to Andrew's papers is out of the question for the usual obvious reasons of banking confidentiality. However, please take it as read that I have gone through them most carefully, and have found not any mention of Triads, the Mafia or Colombian drug cartels.' He waved his short fat arms in the air. This was obviously the cue for laughter, but Rosalind was not in the mood. A look of disappointment crossed Gerson's face briefly, then he took out a handkerchief and mopped his brow to cover his discomfiture.

'Have you popped in to see Whitey?' Gerson asked, as Rosalind sipped her coffee in silence.

Imogen Whitehead had been Horan's personal private secretary for the best part of thirty years. She gave new meaning to the word 'treasure'.

'I'd planned to, on my way out. I spoke to her at the funeral of course. Since then we've been in touch by telephone a couple of times. She appears to be coping reasonably well.'

'Yes, she's shown great strength of character. She and Andrew were very close you know. She organized him with a vengeance. Fine grasp of procedure too, as a matter of fact. Mind you, you would expect that after more than thirty years in banking - fifteen or so as Andrew's right arm. But a remarkable woman nonetheless. We'll be very sad to see her leave.'

Rosalind raised her eyebrows. This was news to her. When she'd last spoken to Whitey, there'd been no talk of leaving. 'She's offered her resignation?'

'Sadly yes. She told me her heart just wasn't in it any more. They worked so much as a team, traveled abroad and so on. When Andrew died – '

'Andrew was *killed*, Rupert!' Rosalind interjected sharply, her words as sharp as razors. 'I do wish people would stop saying Andrew and my father died. It was murder. That girl blew them to bits!'

Gerson gaped. No one had shouted at him in years, and he didn't care for it.

Rosalind ran a hand over her lips. 'I'm sorry Rupert, I'm still very much on edge. I apologize.'

'I quite understand,' Gerson replied stonily, though his thin lips betrayed the fact that understanding was one thing, compassion another. 'Where was I? Oh yes, Whitey's resignation. It was as if she'd lost a brother. However, she told me that without Andrew it wouldn't be the same working here; that it might be the right time to think about retirement. I had to agree with her. I doubt she'd easily adapt to working with our younger men.

Take Duncan, for example. New breed of banker. Fine brain, but talks a different language to Andrew. Computer technocrat.'

Gerson looked at his wristwatch. It was evident that he had more pressing matters to deal with than discussing the personal vagaries of his staff. 'Goodness, is that really the time? Forgive me if I sound rude, but I have a board meeting in ten minutes or so.'

'Of course.' Rosalind stood, holding out a hand to Gerson. 'It's good of you to have spared me the time. I appreciate it.'

'Not at all Rosalind, not at all. It's been delightful to see you again. Let's hope you can put this matter to rest as soon as possible, to your own satisfaction anyway. If there's anything else I can help you with, do give me a call.'

Gerson walked her to the door, placing an avuncular arm around her shoulder.

'Whitey's still in her corner office?' Rosalind asked. 'Next to Andrew's?'

'Indeed. Do pop in. I know she'll be delighted to see you.'

As a child Rosalind had visited Andrew at the Australian Pacific so many times with her father that she'd always looked on Whitey as a mother figure. She knocked lightly on her office door, turned the handle, and poked her head round the door as she'd done so often when little.

Whitey was, as always, half hidden by stacks of paperwork, puffing on a cigarette. She looked up over her spectacles, and her face at once lit up. 'Gracious me, it's that scalawag Rosie again,' she said sternly, then chuckled. 'Come in. You look as if you're playing peekaboo.'

'I've just been in to see the headmaster.'

'Not much fun, eh?'

'Not a barrel of laughs, no.'

'I'd have been very disappointed if you hadn't popped your head round the door. Can I offer you a coffee?'

'Just had some, thanks,' she replied drawing up a seat. 'Let's not beat around the bush,' she continued with a grin, 'Rupert told me strictly in confidence that you were thinking of packing it in. I can't believe it's true - it'd be the end of a banking era.'

Whitey smiled. 'It's very sweet of you to put it that way. But it's true I'm afraid. The office has a very empty feel to it without Andrew buzzing in and out with memos and transcripts, forever fussing about where he could have left his car keys. Besides, I think maybe it's time to think of Kerry. He needs me more than ever now.'

Kerry and Whitey had been childhood sweethearts and had celebrated their forty-fifth wedding anniversary the previous year. The tragedy was that with the onset of the third stage of Alzheimer's disease, Kerry was now only able to recognize his wife during his increasingly rare moments of lucidity. Whitey had cared for him for more than ten years without a word of protest or self-pity; a devout Christian, she saw it as a part of a life that had been sent to test her.

'His doctor suggested it was time for a nursing home, but I won't hear of it. Most of the time he's an old grumble-guts, and hasn't the first idea who the interfering old woman is trying to force him to eat his Cornflakes. There are other times of course when he's still his old self, and we can spend some precious time together as we did in the past. If I weren't for these few moments, he'd have no reason for carrying on. Neither would I.'

Abruptly her face brightened. 'But enough of my woes. How are you coping with your new challenges?'

'Still learning, Whitey. Still learning.'

'You'll be doing that till the day you die. But Ian and Bob are both good men. Don't be afraid to take their advice when you feel a bit lost, and occasionally lean on them.'

Whitey's capacity to remember names and figures was legendary. How she could instantly access the Christian names of both of her fellow directors at Buchanan Construction was quite astonishing to Rosalind.

'You look busy as ever,' Rosalind said, to break the silence.

'Yes, I suppose I am. At least it must look that way. It's boring old hack work actually; not my kettle of fish at all. Not in the least bit testing,' she said, prodding the stack of papers on her desk, and flicking the ash from her cigarette into a glass ashtray.

'I was informed last week that the building has been designated a smoke-free environment,' she continued. 'I think that was the last straw; that and having to work for someone other than Andrew. It finally made up my mind to leave.'

'I believe Duncan McKinley has taken over Andrew's portfolio. I haven't met him. What's he like?'

Whitey grinned wryly. 'You haven't had that pleasure? Well, how to begin? He's young and abrasive. English. Arrogant. Good lateral thinker. Not my type, really. We're not on the same wavelength. I function on instincts, and he works strictly with figures - a product of the electronic age. Doesn't care to delegate; thinks he can do it all alone and in a hurry.' She stubbed her cigarette out and immediately lit another. 'You know me too well Rosie to imagine I'd be content to go back to performing the duties of a secretary. And that's how Duncan views my usefulness. Good Lord, I haven't been a secretary for twenty years. Andrew and I were a team. Obviously, he made the decisions - the broad strokes were invariably his - but I like to think he valued my advice. Heeded it on many occasions, too.

'I haven't been in this business all these years without having learnt a thing or two. Half the fun has always been doing a bit of financial weeding for him. I could spot the shysters right off. Andrew was never much good at that - he had to work on all the details before he drew the same conclusion. He used to tease me, saying I had an eagle's eye for a sound deal, and a bloodhound's nose for scoundrels.

'Now all that's come to an end, and I'm damned if I'll end up a glorified personal typist for the likes of Duncan McKinley.'

Whitey puffed away like fury on her cigarette. Rosalind had never seen her so agitated. Most probably still the legacy of Andrew's death, together with the burden of Kerry and her own failing health.

'Maybe now *is* the right time to deal yourself out and relax,' Rosalind said, attempting to comfort her.

'Relaxation's never been my thing. Don't think I've spent more than five minutes on a beach my entire life. More fun trekking across Costa Rica; riding in those filthy South American trains with Andrew when we dealt with the Government there in the fifties. Give me a North Sea oilrig any day to the Riviera.' She laughed gently, then her face set. She looked from her cigarette to Rosalind, was about to speak, then took another puff on her cigarette. 'To hell with them, if I want to smoke I bloody well will. They don't have to come into my warren, do they!'

Rosalind placed a hand on Whitey's arm. She could see her dear friend was desperately trying to mask her unhappiness. 'Whitey, I've got a great idea. Why don't you come and work with me? I need an old hand like you, and you could arrange the times to suit yourself.'

Whitey seemed deeply touched by the offer. 'You're such a dear girl, Rosie, but I think not. I'm all played out financially. Maybe the heart's not in it any more.'

'Well, the offer's there. Think about it.'

Whitey ruffled Rosalind's hair in a motherly fashion, but said nothing.

Rosalind stood. 'Well, I suppose I should be going. Any time you feel a bit blue, give me a call. Lunch, dinner, anything at all.'

'Sounds like a Cole Porter lyric,' Whitey replied, with a chuckle of amusement.

Rosalind was on the point of closing the door behind her when she heard Whitey call out.

'Rosie! Just a moment.'

Rosalind ducked her head back around the door childishly - as she'd done when she'd arrived, but this time Whitey wasn't smiling. Her expression was an amalgam of unhappiness, concern, and hesitation. She opened her mouth to speak, then once again appeared to think better of it. Her hand reached for her cigarettes, her eyes locked on Rosalind's. 'Please stay in touch, won't you Rosie,' she said quietly. 'You're family.'

Then she brightened visibly. 'By the way, young lady. It's your birthday next week isn't it?'

Rosalind laughed. 'Yes. Tuesday. Same steel trap memory.'

'Yes... well, I suppose I have to function for the two of us now that dear old Kerry's lost his marbles. Poor old sod.'

9.

May 15th

McCann had left five messages for Messon on his answering machine, but Venice's father clearly had no intention of returning his calls. In many ways it was understandable. Perhaps to Messon, MaCann was just another journalist sniffing round. What had Detective Blackwood said? That Messon was 'a very angry man'. Well, that was just too bad. Sure, his daughter was dead. But she'd taken innocent people along with her. As her father, Messon was probably beginning to feel his share of the burden of responsibility, and it hurt.

A small Cessna buzzed over the top of McCann's VW Beetle as he turned into Marion Street. The entrance to Bankstown Airport was fifty meters down the road.

For want of anywhere better, McCann began his search for Messon at the Royal Aero Club.

The average age of members present in the club bar that morning was around sixty. They were all familiar with Messon, yet judging by their reactions to the mention of his name, he wasn't the most popular character around. No one had seen him for days. However, they were all fully aware of his newfound notoriety.

'Don't suppose I'd feel much like sticking my head out the front door if I'd fathered a daughter like that,' offered an elderly gentleman who'd overheard McCann's enquiry at the bar. 'She was an evil creature. That's my view anyway, for what it's worth. Actually, you won't find too many here with a good word for Alan either. Don't know why - I quite like him myself. Can't blame the man for the sins of the daughter. She was an adult after all, for heaven's sake? Real truth is, no one here cares for a man who prefers his own company to that of club members.'

'Could you tell me where he keeps the plane?'

'The old warbird? Sure. The back of Dakota Air. Turn left out of here and follow the road round to the right.' He lifted his gin, held out a weathered hand richly decorated with liver spots and introduced himself. 'Hugh Rathbourne.'

'Leo McCann.'

'How d'you do, Leo. Care for a drink?'

'No time right now, thanks Hugh. Got to track down Alan Messon.'

'Well, you won't find him here at the club. Was a time, you wouldn't find him anywhere else. He was a real 'black hander' – loved to tinker with the old girl. If he wasn't taking her up, he was inside the engine cowls.'

Rathbourne cleared his throat, then drained his gin.

'Tell you what, I'll show you the aircraft m'self if you like. Take you round there, it's not far. What d'you say?'

'If you have time, I'd be grateful, Hugh.'

Rathbourne walked slowly with the aid of a stick. Every so often the stiff breeze lifted the few remaining strands of snow-white hair from his head, tossed them around, then let them drop. The sky suggested a southerly buster was on its way. That, or something worse.

'Not a bad old stick, Alan,' Rathbourne shouted as a Hughes chopper packed with businessmen buzzed overhead towards a landing pad.

'Not the most sociable chap you'd ever meet. Not what you'd call 'clubby'. But like any sherry worth drinking, he got better with knowing. That and the passage of time.'

'Were you close friends?'

Rathbourne chuckled. 'Nah! Couldn't ever get close to Alan. Wasn't in his nature. We were friends though - you could say that. I liked him a lot. Tough bugger, tough as they come. He'd flown everything he could get his hands on by the time he was seventeen. Joined the USAF aged nineteen, and qualified as a C-47 pilot within the year. Now that's what I call tough. And single-minded.' He was clearly impressed. 'The C-47's the military version of the DC3, you know,' he added as an afterthought.

A dull rumbling in the distance was a sinister presentiment of bad weather.

'He grew up in California. Flying crop dusters by the time he was fourteen.' Rathbourne winked. 'Lied about his age, I fancy. Can't help liking his style, though. Told me he always loved the C-47's best. Been flying the buggers all over the world. Korea, Vietnam, New Guinea - you name it. Probably spent more time in 'em than you've spent driving cars.' He raised the end of his cane and pointed. 'Over there, that's where he keeps her. In among the old wrecks that never see the inside of a cloud. Know why he keeps it there?'

'Tell me.'

'Alan's a solo man. Doesn't care for company in the cockpit. Problem lies in the damn civil aviation rules. Bloody bureaucrats stuck their noses in and said you could only fly C-47's with another fully endorsed pilot. So what did old Messon do? Well, what would you do? Think about it.'

But McCann was still mentally occupied trying to recall the information about Messon in the file Torrance had shown him. *Age, sixty-five. No criminal record. Retired from the U.S. Air Force aged forty in 1975. Joined Indonesia's Garuda Air as a commercial 747 pilot until retiring, aged fifty-five, in 1989.*

'There she is. She's a real beauty, wouldn't you say? Mind you, she bloody well should be. The man's spent a fortune on her.'

Rathbourne walked McCann round the front of the aircraft, coming to a halt directly under the nose that hung twenty feet above him. She was painted in lizard camouflage, her VH number signifying that she was in fact a civilian aircraft. Her old military registration marks and squadron insignias were painted on the tail rudder.

Above them, the giant twin row Pratt & Whitney engines hung from the wings. Two thirds of the way down the fuselage was the double opening cargo door peculiar to the C-47, allowing motor vehicles to be carried if necessary.

'How much work's he put in on her?'

'Told me he found her on a small strip outside Darwin. Scarcely serviceable, so he says. Had to put her down twice in the desert on the way down here. She's registered as a warbird, an historic airplane. Means Alan doesn't have to meet all the strict civil standards. They're a pain in the neck. Think he said she originally came from Laos, but I'm not too sure.'

'What would you pay for one of these?'

'Maybe two hundred thousand in bad shape. I'd say Alan's spent another three hundred just in the last five years or so. Lot of warbirds around, you know; Mig-15s, 17s, 19s, Sabres, the odd Vampire - that sort of thing. Got to be able to afford the upkeep, mind you. Costs a fortune in fuel just to take 'em for a joy ride.'

McCann backed a few feet to peer up at the cockpit window. As he did so, there was a sharp angry call from behind him. 'And who the hell might you be?'

McCann turned.

Striding towards him across the asphalt was a slim wiry man with short white hair wearing flight overalls and carrying a cap. He looked mad as hell. McCann was about to reply, when Rathbourne beat him to it.

'Morning, Alan. Just showing this pal of yours the warbird. Knew you wouldn't mind.'

Alan Messon could barely mask his fury. '*Did* you now? Well, you couldn't have been more wrong. I *do* mind. I mind very much. And this man's no bloody pal of mine. Don't know the bastard from Adam.'

Messon approached menacingly, his fists bunched at his sides, and stood a foot or so from McCann and Rathbourne, finally placing his balled hands on his hips as a gesture of confrontation.

'Don't be so bloody testy, Alan,' Rathbourne said after a beat. 'You don't own the tarmac. What are you going to do, fight a man who's young enough to be your son, and strong enough to knock you down?'

McCann held out a hand. 'Sorry if I've upset you, Mr. Messon. I'm Leo McCann. You *are* Alan Messon?'

'What's it to you? Are you someone else that wants to make my life a misery? Go on, surprise me. Tell me you're not a journalist, or some other media bastard?'

'I'm neither a journalist, nor media, Mr. Messon. '

'Oh no? Just an enthusiast, eh? Sure.'

'I am a friend of Rosalind Buchanan. Her father was – '

Messon waved a hand angrily. 'Believe me, Mr. McCann. I do know who her father was by now. What do you want? Are you her lawyer?'

'No, I'm not. I just hoped you'd spare me a few minutes.'

Messon stared at McCann, inched forward and looked him in the eye. 'Clear off, McCann.'

Rathbourne tapped his cane on the asphalt in a nervous fashion. 'Well, I'll leave you two to it. Maybe see you in the bar later, Alan.' He looked across at McCann. 'Goodbye, Leo. Nice meeting you.'

Rathbourne shuffled off, leaving the other two standing toe to toe.

'The only place I can escape you people is up there.' Messon said finally, pointing skywards at the threatening clouds. 'Over a month now, and my house is still surrounded by news hounds. I expect any minute the bastards will be out here.'

'Mr. Messon. I'm only asking for a few minutes of your time. I know it's hard, but please show some compassion for Miss Buchanan. I know she does for you.'

Messon looked up at the gathering storm, the muscles in his jaw working hard.

'Weather looks filthy,' he said. 'If we don't get moving right now, they'll keep us on the ground forever.' He strode past McCann to the plane's double doors calling over his shoulder. 'You coming?'

'Why not?' McCann replied.

Messon had opened the left hand cargo door, pulled the aluminum steps from their slots on the door seal, hooked them to the fuselage and was up and inside the aircraft with an agility that belied his years. By the time McCann had caught up with him and had swung his head inside the fuselage, Messon was already at the cockpit door.

'Do you know anything about aircraft?' Messon shouted, as he walked back towards McCann, dragging behind him what looked to be a life-sized rag doll dressed in a blue uniform.

'A little.'

'Well, see if you can squeeze into my first officer's jacket, McCann. Then close the aft door,' said Messon holding out the stuffed dummy towards McCann. It was dressed in an engineer's jacket and hat. 'Hal, this is Mr. McCann,' he said by way of introduction to the dummy as he returned to the cockpit. 'He's fully endorsed,' he shouted to McCann. 'Now you are too.'

A crude face had been painted on Hal, complete with handlebar moustache. It had all the finesse of a kindergarten project, but would probably have fooled the tower at two hundred feet. 'Get a shift on, weather's closing by the second,' Messon roared from inside the cockpit.

McCann stripped Hal of his jacket and put it on. The engineer's hat was more of a problem since it was a good size and a half too small. McCann wrenched the sides apart until he heard the thread give, then jammed it on his head.

Securing the double doors, McCann looked back up the interior of the aircraft. The C-47 had seven rectangular cabin windows on the right hand side and six on the left. There were small circular rifle grommets in the center of each. Beneath these were the twenty-eight extended troop seats, the safety belts buckled neatly on the metal. In short, the aircraft looked as though it had just been rolled out of the factory.

McCann stepped through the cockpit door and sat in the right hand seat. Messon was already strapped in, his headset on, scanning the instruments and switches, checking they were set properly. As McCann strapped himself into the co-pilot's seat, he studied Messon. The old guy had calmed down significantly, his eyes flicking from instrument to instrument, checking the pressure, the circuit breakers, the fuel cocks.

Messon started the port engine first, setting the revs a couple of hundred above idle to warm them. He then turned on the radio and nav' gear so he could tune in to the Automatic Terminal Information Service, otherwise known as ATIS, which gave runway directions, radio frequencies, aerodrome weather information, and wind direction. McCann could see the smallest flicker of a smile cross Messon's face as he listened. Probably the weather report, McCann judged ruefully.

'Ever flown underwater, McCann?' he shouted gesturing to McCann to use his headset.

As McCann placed it over his ears, he just caught Messon calling for an airways clearance. Quite what the old man had in mind for him was debatable. Whatever it was, he knew he'd have to initially humor him.

The first few drops of rain were spotting the windshield. Maybe Messon thought he could scare him? Yes, that was most probably it. A quick glance through the windscreen confirmed it. The horizon was as black as a coal seam. Patches of dark gray cumulo-nimbus cloud with anvil tops hung in huge cauliflower formations where the upper winds had sheared them off like razors.

'Charlie Delta Oscar taxiing for Camden. Received, Delta,' Messon called into the radio as he taxied to the run-up bay, going through his final pre-take-off checks.

The aircraft was now at the holding point on the left of runway two nine. Messon checked the final approach area was clear of aircraft.

'Charlie Delta Oscar, ready.'

'Charlie Delta Oscar, you're cleared for take-off,' the tower replied.

Messon glanced briefly across at McCann, attempting to judge his demeanor, then pushed the throttle forwards to take-off power. The rev counter displayed just under two thousand seven hundred as the warbird began to gain speed. The tail gradually lifted off the ground and within seconds the plane was roaring along horizontally to the runway.

The frame of the large airplane shuddered as it gained speed, the sound of the engines deafening inside the cockpit despite the headsets. Messon pushed the stick further forward.

'The quicker you get tail up, the less drag you have, and the sooner you're in a flying attitude,' Messon shouted. 'Accelerate, then ease the stick back and lift off, pull up the gear and accelerate faster. Pretty damn simple, eh?'

The air turbulence as they made their gradual climb was initially not as severe as McCann had anticipated. At three hundred and fifty feet they hit the bottom of the rain cloud. It was like flying into a bowl of custard at close to a hundred and twenty knots. Messon engaged the wipers, which vainly tried to shift the water sideways.

There was now practically no visual sensation of movement, just the palpable proof supplied by the vibration, plus the deafening noise of the engines; that and the rainstorm smashing against the windscreen. It was as if the aircraft was being held stationary in the grip of a giant's hand. At night it would have been another matter. The landing lights reflecting on the wall of rainwater that pounded into the windscreen would have been terrifying evidence of the hundred and twenty knots of forward speed.

Messon's expression was almost beatific as he expertly guided the aircraft up through the rain clouds, oblivious to the thundering of the raindrops on the Plexiglas windows.

Then they were through the first layer of clouds.

The light was failing fast. McCann shot a look across to his left at Messon, then back out front. Directly ahead was another sheer blanket of wicked looking gray-black cloud. In the side window McCann could see Messon's reflection, calm as a sleeping child, his eyes now closed, drawing a series of deep breaths. Even blind, the old guy was doing a terrific job keeping the wings level in the ferocious turbulence, the plane bucking up and down, occasionally hit sideways as air currents kicked the aircraft in every direction as it gained altitude.

'It's the only place I feel absolutely safe,' Messon shouted over the roar of the rain as the buffeting continued, 'I expect you think that strange. Most people prefer the security of a warm bed. I like to be up here with my finger on the trigger. Preferably alone,' he added opening his eyes for perhaps the first time in thirty seconds. 'Most of the time I don't *need* to see,' he added by way of explanation. 'I can feel her through the stick.' McCann knew the old man was lying. If you kept your eyes shut for longer than fifteen or so seconds you could easily become severely disorientated - McCann knew that. But Messon was obviously trying to scare him, so, what the hell, he'd play along.

A sudden pocket of heavy turbulence hit the underside of the C-47, jamming them upwards. Messon responded within a fraction of a second, deliberately accentuating the discomfort by pushing the stick hard forwards, throwing them both up in their straps.

Messon's eyes bored into McCann's as he tried to gauge the younger man's reaction - his fear threshold.

'Know what a "Jesus book" is, McCann?'

'Collection of prayers for weather such as this?' he answered returning Messon's easy smile. If Messon was going to play silly buggers, let him.

'Way back, it was supposed to be the pilot's best friend, a notebook or diary we all used to keep in the war. List of mileages, compass bearings, average still-air flight times, radio frequencies, whatever was relevant to the country you were in. We all added whatever we reckoned was useful, based on personal experiences. Handy when you couldn't get maps and suddenly had to take off into the blue.'

'What about it?' McCann shouted.

'Well, I've got my Jesus book of life right here,' he said, tapping his forehead. I make additions up here in the clouds, where people leave me alone.'

McCann stared at the old man. There was a fierce intensity in his eyes, bordering on the manic. That, mixed with an aura of terrible despair. For the first time it occurred to McCann that Messon might be contemplating topping himself - taking him along for the ride. He knew he had to try to lighten the old man's mood.

'What's her name,' McCann shouted, looking around the cockpit.

The ploy seemed to pay off. At the mention of his pride and joy, Messon brightened visibly. 'She's called Effie. Short for Freedom Express. Understand? FE.'

McCann nodded, smiling.

'Think that's trite?' said Messon challengingly, his eyes narrowing.

'Not at all,' McCann answered equably.

'Don't you love a challenge, McCann?' The non sequitur came out of nowhere. 'I know I do. You can throw any weather at me, and I'll lap it up. I know Effie can take it, and so can I. Brings me back to the good old days, flying through the monsoons in New Guinea. By Christ, *that* was living; not the living death of suburban Sydney.'

They were back in the thick of the blanket gray cloud, jumping up and down thirty feet or so every few seconds, occasionally thrown fifty feet to the side. McCann looked at Messon's hands on the controls. They looked relaxed - no white showing on the knuckles. Messon was in control and loving it. McCann stared straight forward, aware of the old man's eyes on him. He could see Messon was enjoying the power he had over his younger companion, waiting for his nerve to break. Each time the turbulence showed the slightest sign of abating for more than two seconds, the old boy would give the rudders a good kick, sending the aircraft lurching to one side. At other times he'd quietly wind on a bit of nose-down trim, hold against it, then quite suddenly ease his hands off the controls so that the nose pitched down bone-jarringly hard until he'd finally grab back the controls and ease back out of it. It was fine for Messon; he could anticipate the jarring variations of height and side movement. For McCann each shock came out of the blue and Messon knew it.

'So you came to ask a few questions, eh,' Messon shouted mockingly. 'Take as long as you like. Bankstown's a training airport. Providing we stay out of controlled airspace, we can stay up here forever. Air Service might pester us for a position, but who cares? So, ask away. I'm all ears.'

McCann considered his options as the roller-coaster ride continued unabated. Messon looked almost dangerously out of control emotionally. This was hardly the time or place to wander into precarious psychological territory. It could well drive him over the edge. Perhaps he'd be better advised to humor the man now, and ask questions on the ground later.

An arrow of lightning knifed down across the nose of the C-47. The fuselage shone bright ghost silver for a second, then they were back in the yellow gray custard, as if in cotton wool limbo, the water crushing relentlessly against the Plexiglas.

'I'm just a friend of Rosalind Buchanan. The death of her father almost destroyed her. She thought you might be able to help each other.'

Messon sat in stony silence, his eyes again closed.

'Perhaps we should talk about it later,' McCann added after a few moments.

Abruptly the entire aircraft shook to the rivets as a huge thunderclap enveloped the entire sky for a hundred feet in all directions. McCann started sharply, suddenly straining against the straps, momentarily taken by surprise by the intensity of the thunderclap. Messon hadn't moved a muscle. His eyes were the smallest slits as he smiled. He'd enjoyed McCann's startled expression.

'I was in a Sabre once, in heavy cloud with no radar in New Guinea,' Messon began reflectively. 'It was the thunderstorm season, pretty much the same conditions as now. Couldn't focus on the instruments, we were shaking so badly. Worried about structural strength of the airplane because of the way we were being thrown around. Thought at any moment we'd get struck by lightning - not that I gave a toss about that. But back then, in those airplanes, there was bugger all in the way of navigation equipment that worked in that kind of weather; radio compasses pointed at the nearest thunderstorm, that kind of thing.' He paused, then turned to McCann, a kind of removed madness in his eyes.

'It was a beautiful time, flying on the edge, looking right into the pit of chaos, knowing you could beat the odds. Flying right into hell and out the other side.'

Another two swords of lightning slashed the gray-black cloud that engulfed them, followed by another crash of thunder.

'Flying at two thousand feet through the monsoon is like flying underwater. The windshields look as if they're keeping out a solid mass, not just rainfall. The noise of the hail smashing into the outer skin is like automatic fire. Turbulence topples the aircraft's artificial horizon - you have to gauge the altitude more by the airspeed VSI and the turn-and-balance indicator.'

Messon seemed to McCann to be rambling as the C–47 staggered forward into the eye of the storm. Hammered by the wind and rain, it was losing speed. But Messon looked quite relaxed as he stared before him into a world of nostalgia.

McCann knew he had to snap the man out of his reverie soon or they were history. Perhaps confrontation was the answer.

'Alan! You can't blame yourself for your daughter's death. The best we can do is try to understand.'

Messon blinked as he mentally raced back through time from his jet pilot youth to present day reality. Then he gradually pushed forward on the controls, deliberately pitching the nose down.

This was the reality of McCann's worst fears, as he began to rise up and up in his seat, experiencing the less than pleasant negative G feeling. He knew what Messon was up to. Perhaps the old man thought he'd fooled him into thinking he was in an air pocket.

As McCann opened his mouth to speak, Messon corrected the controls and – wham! – they were dashed back violently into their seats, and Messon was trimming out, kicking the rudder pedals.

To stay silent was not the answer. McCann knew that. He tried again. 'Both of you have suffered a similar terrible loss.'

'I doubt very much whether Rosalind Buchanan would see it quite that way,' Messon snapped. 'The world seems to view my daughter as a monster. They treated me as if I was a criminal. The police, the press, the media – even my neighbors.'

'Miss Buchanan needs to understand why her father died before she's able to come to terms with life again.'

Another head-splitting crash of thunder burst right above them like a howitzer shell, the white flash of lightning blinding in its intensity. An air pocket beneath and to one side sent the aircraft falling and sliding to the left like a stone. Somehow Messon held the controls firm and Effie evened out of a twisting dive and came up steady and level again.

'It's not so easy to come to terms with the fact that your little girl is a murderer, McCann,' Messon continued, for the first time sounding a trifle unnerved by the force of the storm. 'However, the girl that walked into that hotel room was not my daughter.'

McCann said nothing, hoping Messon would continue. The old man sounded as if he were back on the planet for the time being, flying the aircraft in a straight line again rather than diving her to the ground.

'It took them less than an hour to find me. They came with their cameras, their insincere platitudes, their easy manner, and camped on my doorstep. They knocked on my door, and when I asked them to go away they pressed past me and invaded my house. They said they wanted a snapshot. Can you imagine? The blood of my little girl was still wet on the walls of that hotel, and they were asking for a photograph! It is *they* who are the monsters, not Venice!'

Though his face was set in anger, tears were rolling down Messon's cheeks.

'Let's put down and talk. What do you say, Alan. Put Effie down.'

'For God's sake, I'm doing my level best to come to terms with the tragic death of my only child,' Messon continued again, off an another emotional tangent, 'and you have the hide to track me down and trick me into a conversation, lecturing me about compassion!'

Lightning scythed through the darkness again and again, the aircraft vibrating dangerously as the thunder crashed around them with the force of a cannon.

Messon's whole fragile body was now shaking with emotion as he gripped the controls ever more firmly, pushing the nose of the aircraft down to a perilously steep angle. The rain had turned to hail the consistency of gravel. McCann could see clearly from their angle of descent that they were losing altitude dangerously fast.

'Alan!' McCann screamed, at the same time grabbing Messon's right arm firmly. 'Pull the nose up, man!'

'I haven't got the strength to help others come to terms with their grief,' Messon screamed back at him in a delirium, taking his right hand off the controls so as to shake free from McCann's grasp.

'Pull up! For God's sake PULL UP!' roared McCann, but Messon was drowning in self-pity as he again pushed the stick forward.

Effie was now beginning to judder, her aerodynamics instinctively trying to pull her out to safety.

'For heaven's sake, look at me!' Messon screamed. 'I'm an old man! What do you all want with me? I just can't take any more.'

Quickly McCann unclipped his harness and lunged across at Messon, slapping his face, then holding the old man's head in both his hands.

'Alan Messon. You are no murderer. Do not follow your daughter's lead. She was driven by despair to do what she did. You *cannot* do the same,' McCann said looking deep into Messon's eyes.

The next twenty seconds seemed an eternity. The aircraft began to angle more sharply downwards and the airspeed increased dramatically. The wind and hail smacked into the windscreen like thousands of miniature hammers.

Then something seemed to give in Messon's eyes – a moment of sudden comprehension. He began to fight with the stick to bring Effie back up, but he no longer had the strength. McCann threw himself onto the metal floor of the aircraft, crouching beside Messon, grabbing hold of Messon's wrists, wrenching the stick back.

Very gradually, the nose began to come up, and the vibration eased slightly. As the aircraft leveled out Messon took a very deep breath and turned to McCann.

'You can take your hands off now, McCann. I've got her. Get back in your seat. I'll take her down.'

The instant McCann relaxed his grip on the stick, a lightning strike hit the nose of the C-47 with an ear-splitting crash and white flash, vaporizing a hole the size of a golf ball in the nose of the aircraft a couple of feet directly in front of Messon's seat.

The blinding light was so vivid, that both Messon and McCann were temporarily blinded. McCann opened his mouth to shout something at Messon, but was immediately thrown violently sideways against the co-pilot's seat, cracking his head hard against a metal stanchion.

A few seconds later McCann regained consciousness. Completely disorientated, he became aware of Messon shouting at him through the smoke-filled cockpit.

'GET BACK IN YOUR SEAT! STRAP YOURSELF IN TIGHT, FOR CHRIST'S SAKE.'

McCann pulled himself into the co-pilot's seat and fastened the seat belt as tightly as he could, shooting a quick look at Messon. The man showed no fear, just intense concentration. The wild look of desolation he'd worn only seconds before was gone.

'You all right, McCann?' Messon shouted.

A small trail of blood from a gash on McCann's right temple was running into his eye. He wiped it with his hand. 'Guess, so,' he replied.

'Good. Look, don't worry,' Messon began, as he fought for control of the aircraft. 'Bit hairy, nothing more. No need to panic. No problem. No electrics, that's all.'

McCann could see the old man was attempting to humor him - he'd never flown an aircraft larger than a Tiger Moth, but he knew that flying a C-47 without any electrical system in a storm as severe as this was more than "a bit hairy". It presented a very major problem.

'Both generators have failed – the batteries don't appear to be supplying power!' Messon called out to McCann.

The only instruments Messon could now rely on were the airspeed indicator, the altimeter, the VSI, and the turn and balance indicator.

Now was the time to see just how good the old man was, thought McCann, there was nothing he could do to help. He was in God's and Messon's hands now.

'Have to go see where we are, old heart,' Messon said, pushing the stick forward hard. 'Knew where I was when we were hit, but no way of knowing now. Got to get under the cloud. Okay?' Messon shouted, obviously trying to calm McCann. 'Going down to take a look see! Just hang on, eh?' he shouted.

Effie began to dive steeply at close to a forty-five degree angle, the smoke in the cockpit becoming more intense.

'What do you reckon's the cloud base?' McCann called to Messon.

'Fucked if I know! Let's hope to Christ it's above two hundred!'

Messon's face was alive with the thrill of the danger. Here at last was a real challenge, and McCann could see he was loving it.

The seconds ticked by, as time seemed to stand still. They plunged earthwards, and the clouds raced by in a blur of gray and yellow, the rain still pounding on the Plexiglas like machine-gun fire.

McCann stared dead ahead, willing the cloud to break, then shot Messon another look. He knew they were seconds from impacting into the ground at this rate of descent, yet the old man had nerves of steel, his hands gripping the stick firmly, his eyes dancing in their sockets as he waited for the break in the cloud.

As McCann saw the arrow on the altimeter sink below three hundred feet, he closed his eyes and began to pray. Immediately, he was punched upwards in his seat as Messon violently brought up the nose. They were through!

'SHIT!' Messon exploded as he slammed on full right aileron and gave Effie a massive boot of right rudder. 'MOVE! MOVE! MOVE!' the old man screamed as the massive radio antenna of station 2RN suddenly raced at them out of the mist and rain, dead ahead. They were closing at close to a hundred and eighty knots and an impact at around two hundred and sixty feet looked inescapable.

'COME ON, EFFIE! RIGHT GIRL! RIGHT!' Messon screamed as the aircraft responded agonizingly slowly, swinging to the right.

In a flash the radio antenna was past. The left wingtip had cleared the guy wires by about ten feet.

'GOOD GIRL! YES!' Messon shouted as he leveled out, his eyes riveted to the contours of the ground ahead. 'That's where the old Jesus Book comes in handy, McCann. Had a feeling that metal sonofabitch was around here somewhere!'

McCann was breathing hard, yet Messon was actually chuckling. The old boy had nerves of reinforced concrete. They'd escaped death by fractions of seconds and a very few feet.

'Know where I am now. Taking her in. Think we've probably had enough up here. Agreed?'

McCann reached across and touched Messon's shoulder. 'Thanks,' he shouted. 'Just take us home, eh?'

The old man smiled. 'Will do.'

Messon slept in the pilot's seat for just under two hours. He'd brought Effie back to Bankstown, landing the C-47 in deadly windsheer conditions with the assurance a Phantom instructor would have demonstrated returning to the deck of an aircraft carrier in a dead calm.

A few seconds after he'd killed the engines, Messon's head fell forward on his chest and he was asleep. His face was that of a man every ounce of whose energy had been sucked out of his soul by an emotional vacuum cleaner.

McCann sat to his left. He'd decided to wait till Messon awoke to make sure the old fellow got home safely. In the volatile psychological state Messon was in today, he shouldn't be left alone. And it appeared he had few friends - he'd shut them all out.

It was ten past nine when Messon opened his eyes and looked around him, momentarily startled to find himself still at the controls of his plane. McCann placed a hand on his arm, and reassured Messon that all was well.

McCann offered to drive him home, and the tired old man accepted gratefully. He offered no apology for his actions in the plane, but McCann could see he was too unwell even to think about his aberrant behavior. Messon took McCann's arm as they walked to the car park.

The members stood at the club window looking down at them. Presumably someone had filled them in with the gossip in the tower. McCann asked Messon how he felt, and he replied that with the exception of a headache and exhaustion, he felt *pretty well all right*. Messon gave his home address to McCann, closing his eyes the moment the car moved off.

Half an hour later they crossed Gladesville Bridge and turned right towards Drummoyne.

It was then that Messon broke the silence. 'I can't believe I lost control like that,' he said, his eyes still closed, the evidence of tears once more at their corners.

'It's over, Alan. We're safe. It doesn't bear thinking about. Better to concentrate on the future.'

'The future, yes,' Messon answered as though the concept was incomprehensible.

'And don't forget, as it turned out, you saved both our lives.'

'After contemplating throwing them away?'

McCann turned into a small street looking out onto Hen and Chicken Bay, checking the numbers of the houses. A solidly middle-class street. Unpretentious. Inexpensive. Small houses with well cared for gardens out front. So what had Messon done with his money? Spent it all on Effie presumably. He could identify with that – most of his own money was lavished on his ketch.

Messon's house was without doubt the best in the street; 1950s red double-brick bungalow with small metal-framed windows. The garden was an unexpected delight. Messon obviously knew a thing or two when it came to roses; the front yard was filled with every conceivable variety.

A man in shirtsleeves stood in the road, a camera slung over his shoulder. McCann eyeballed him. The young man got the message and moved off down the street.

'Come in, Leo,' Messon said as he summoned the energy to get out of the car. 'Least I can do is give you a drink. Can't make up for what I did, but there you are.'

It was a good excuse to make sure Messon was able to take care of himself. 'Thanks Alan, I will. A stiff one. Not every day I ride with a stunt pilot.' McCann smiled and Alan returned the gesture.

'Thanks, Leo,' he said quietly, placing his hand on the back of McCann's. He then opened the passenger door. On his way through the garden Messon stopped to pick a white rose, pulled the house keys from his pocket, then opened the front door.

Inside the drawing room Messon walked to the window, placing the rose beneath a silver photo frame on the desk.

'Will you excuse me a moment? I shan't be long. The drinks are over there,' he said pointing to the sideboard. There's a toilet down the hall if you need one.'

While he waited, McCann wandered round the room. It was simple and uncluttered. Most of the wall space was devoted to books. The furniture was fifties functional; beige lounge suite, coffee table, and a rattan carpet that probably shared the same birth date as Ronald Reagan.

There were three photos on the desk, one in a silver frame, the other two framed in wood. One was of Messon and a child, presumably his daughter. Messon was laughing; Venice standing beside him, displaying a toothy grin. They weren't holding hands. The second photograph was a faded sepia snap of a DC3, in the midst of jungle vegetation, possibly taken in New Guinea; maybe Indochina. Messon's face was clearly visible through the cockpit window. He looked to be in his late thirties, and was again laughing as he saluted the camera. The largest photo, the one in the silver frame, was a full length shot of Venice, aged about twelve. She proudly held what looked like a diploma of some sort in her hand. She looked every inch the model child, the academic achiever. Her hair was caught in a ponytail, her clothes neat and conservative. It was here that Messon had placed the rose.

'I am a very foolish fond old man, nothing more, nothing less,' Messon said, as he reappeared from down the hall. He'd washed, changed and combed his hair. 'I've been so consumed with rage since Venice died. Rage at God, fate, society, human nature, justice - everything you can imagine. And ultimately a rage against Venice, for what she did. Now the rage is directed inward. Today I think I snapped, and I'm deeply sorry to have involved you in such a tawdry adventure. Had you not been with me, perhaps events might have turned out very differently. I dread to think.'

'Then don't.' McCann handed Messon his glass. 'To Effie,' he toasted.

'Yes, to Effie, bless her.' Messon smiled ruefully.

'Did Venice enjoy flying with you?'

'Quite the contrary. Scared to death of the plane. My fault again. I took her up on her eighth birthday, thought it would be the treat to end all treats. Unfortunately we hit a bit of bad weather. Nothing like today - just a bit bumpy. Poor Venice started screaming, so I took her down at once. I promise you, it was no big deal. Anyway I thought the best thing was to get her up again quick as possible, but she wouldn't come. It became a thing with her. She said she could see me dead at the controls. Kid's stuff. Nightmares, nothing more.'

He picked up the silver frame, wiping a smudge from the side as he smiled down at the photo of his dead child. 'My daughter was a poet, you know. Very fine, though few knew it. She chose to become a graphic designer, but there's not much romance in that, to my mind.'

'This was Venice at school?' McCann said indicating the photo of Venice with the diploma.

'University,' Messon replied, then noticed McCann's look of surprise. 'I know, she never looked her age. She's actually seventeen in the photo.'

'She was beautiful.'

'Yes, she was beautiful,' Messon repeated in little more than a murmur. 'Before they murdered her.'

'Who? What are you saying, Alan?' McCann prompted.

'It wasn't my daughter that walked into that hotel. Something happened to change the girl in that photograph into the woman whose photo was published in the papers. Someone is responsible. Someone murdered her spirit. When I find that person, he will die.' It was a calm statement of fact. Cold and to the point. He meant it, though quite how this broken man intended to make good his promise was another matter.

Then his shoulders sagged. 'I don't know. Perhaps I'm to blame more than anyone,' he continued. 'The moment she was gone, it became so clear I'd failed her as a father, as well as a friend. Isn't that always the way? I am one of her murderers. I've been found guilty too.

'I was never a real father to her. We were never very close. I suppose it's part of my nature to retain an emotional distance from others, even my own blood. I've always been like that, my father before me. Called him 'sir', and never gave it a second thought. Then I made the cardinal error of marrying a woman scarcely more than a child, and before I knew it Venice was on the way. Didn't really give the matter much thought – just seemed like the thing to do. When I wasn't flying jumbos, I was selfishly spending every spare moment on Effie, quite oblivious to the fact I was driving a wedge between my family and myself.'

'Your wife is dead?'

'As far as I'm concerned she is. Though I believe she enjoys a more than comfortable life somewhere up north. Can't remember where exactly,' Messon answered bitterly. 'She walked away when Venice was eight. Found richer pastures, together with a fancier man. Not too difficult a task, I suppose, not when you look at me. I think I'd lost sight of the fact that she was almost twenty years my junior when we married. Didn't matter then. She enjoyed scooting around the skies. But the novelty inevitably wore off, together with her romantic vision of me as the fearless aviator. She did have the good manners to leave me a note. Didn't extend the same courtesy to Venice.'

'Did they stay in touch?'

'No. She didn't call for six months, and by that time Venice said she didn't want to know. Of course I knew she *did*; she desperately wanted her mother's love, but she refused to admit it. She felt utterly rejected.'

Messon faltered, scratching the side of his face in an embarrassed fashion.

'You'll have to forgive me, I'm rambling. Funny thing being alone; there's no one to share your thoughts with, and that's remarkably frustrating. I mean, there's always a jumble of confused thoughts in my brain - but to voice them, now there's the catharsis.

'You'd think that Margot's desertion would have driven Venice closer to me, but the reverse seemed to be the case. I retreated into myself, and Venice did the same. I suppose I imagined that providing the best education and a good home would be sufficient. I never thought about the healing qualities of human warmth. That's the real tragedy.'

'Margot knows of Venice's death?'

'Oh yes. Gave a few well chosen grieving interviews to the media. Did very nicely financially out of it I'd imagine,' he said, rubbing his forefinger and thumb together. 'Then rang to tell me it was all my fault, that it had been due to my bad influence; that she'd always known *the girl would turn out badly*, as she so sensitively put it'.

It was time to ask the specifics; Messon seemed ready to talk about his daughter.

'As far as you were aware, did Venice know either Mr. Buchanan or Mr. Horan?'

Messon's face was a blank mask as he gazed abstractedly at the ceiling. Then his eyes flicked towards McCann.

'Did Venice know the people who died? To your knowledge, that is?' he repeated.

'I'm afraid I've no idea,' Messon replied simply. Then he smiled thinly. 'I don't seem to know too much about my daughter, do I? You see I hadn't seen her for more than a year when she died. Last time I did see her, she told me she needed her own *space*.' He accentuated the word with distaste. 'It's the modern way of saying, "I don't want to be with you any more", isn't it?' He laughed emptily. 'I could see she no longer needed me. I thought, now it's Venice's turn to desert me; first the mother, now the daughter. As usual, I'm afraid I only considered my own feelings.'

'Where did she go?'

'London. Said she wanted to study. Soon changed her mind when she got there. Just a ruse to squeeze cash out of me, I suppose,' Messon continued. 'Didn't give me an address. Just told me she was living somewhere in Highgate. Sent me postcards every now and then. What was I to do? Go there and search her out?

'I must admit I was a trifle bitter. But if she needed her *space*, then she was welcome to it. That's what I remember thinking. And if she wanted to come back, that was fine with me too. Of course she never did. Not to me personally, anyway.'

'Did she have any close friends here in Sydney?'

'A few as a child. Not many. Hendrik Ohlson was one I remember. Nice boy. Good family. Norwegian immigrants.'

Hendrik Ohlson again. One more pointer towards Ohlson and he was flying to Christchurch - no question.

'She left for London just before her nineteenth birthday. I'm sure her circle of friends would have changed since then. Judging by that terrible photograph the police showed me - the one that appeared in the gutter press - I'd say it changed radically.'

McCann remembered the photograph well. The headline in *The Telegraph* the day following the explosion had been, 'Mask of Death'. The photo beneath was of a very different Venice Messon to the innocent seventeen-year-old in the silver frame on the desk. Here was a wild street girl, the cheeks sunken, the hair disheveled, a feral look in the eyes. This would most probably have been the Polaroid supplied by the Drug Enforcement Agency informer - possibly taken by the man who called himself "Ritz".

Messon looked as if he'd talked himself out. His head hung over his chest, the full glass in his bony hand untouched. A dull rumble sounded miles away. The last vestiges of the storm. The room was silent.

McCann was anxious to tread as carefully as was humanly possible, but if any headway was to be made there were things that had to be said - questions that had to be asked. Messon would have to deal with the facts sometime, now was as good a time as any. At least the man was presently not alone. He had a friend of sorts beside him.

'Alan, I know Venice hadn't been living at home for quite a while. Would you mind terribly if I saw her room?'

Messon shrugged. 'There's very little to see. It's been a long time. But yes, of course. I'll show you.'

Venice's bedroom was small, clean and bright. Messon hadn't lied; there was little to see. A double bed on which there were two teddy bears; one small, one large. A child's school desk on which were several children's picture books, a school bag of crayons with her name embossed on the side, a stack of postcards, and a roll of red ribbon. The walls were bare, the marks of sticky tape evidence of posters that had at one time been important.

'Pictures of movie stars?' McCann asked, directing Messon's attention to the faded patches on the wall.

'Not at all. You could never have called Venice an obvious child. She never paid much attention to pop stars and all the stuff that appeals to the average youngster nowadays. She lived in her own fantasy world.' He ran his hands over the wall, as if by touching the faded patches of wallpaper he could bring back memories of Venice's childhood.

'Maps of Indochina, portraits of Manchu rulers, scenes depicting the fables of the past. She loved that sort of thing.'

'She took them with her when she left?'

'I suppose so, I don't know. I didn't take them down myself.'

Messon pointed at a spot on the wall, smiling. 'This one I remember. It was a depiction of the Hung Sisters' triumphant coronation.' He looked back at McCann. 'I don't suppose that means much to you?'

McCann shook his head.

'They led a rebellion against the Chinese in around AD 40. The rulers had executed the husband of one of the sisters for insurrection, so the sisters rallied tribal support, eventually forcing the Chinese to flee. Immediately the sisters proclaimed themselves queens. Unfortunately the Chinese counterattacked. Rather than be taken prisoner, the sisters threw themselves in the Hat Giang River.'

He paused as he studied the empty space on the wall. 'Venice loved those kind of stories. Larger than life stuff. Theatrical. Every now and then I'd read them to her. A good way to teach children history, though the one I just mentioned was possibly a bit on the violent side.' He shrugged, adding, 'That's life though, isn't it?'

'The Hat Giang River's in China?'

'No, Funan, as it was then; what was ultimately to become Vietnam. I suppose you could say the Hungs were the first Queens of Vietnam. Vietnam didn't exist as such before then. Strictly speaking, Funan was just the southern part. Later on, Funan was absorbed into the kingdom of Champa. That was the stuff of the best stories; Champa. Pirates that raided along the entire Indochinese coast; the Viets to the north, and the Khmers to the west.'

'Venice loved history?'

'As a child yes. Hence all the posters. Mostly Indochina. Maybe because I flew there for so many years and she'd seen all my photographs. You've never been to Vietnam?'

'Never.'

'When you do go, don't miss the Cham museum in Da Nang. They have a wonderful collection of sculpture.'

Cham. That word again. According to Torrance, Professor Kantor had said the Asian in the Savoy had been a Cham. It was the most tenuous of links. Nevertheless...

McCann picked up the postcards, flipping through them picture side up. They were all tourist shots of London and the Home Counties of England.

'She sent me those from England. They're my last link to her.'

'She never telephoned?'

'No. Perhaps she was saving money,' he said defensively, though quite clearly he didn't believe it. 'I couldn't call her because she never gave me the number.'

'Tell me to mind my own business if you like, but may I look at what she wrote?'

'Go ahead. There's nothing personal.' It was clear from the tone how much Messon had wished there *had* been "something personal".

McCann shuffled slowly through them. They each began, *"Father"*, and ended, *"love from Venice"*. Each had the simple details of day-to-day life away from home.

McCann put them down where he'd found them.

A fly began to buzz behind the yellow curtains, disturbing his concentration. There was something about the cards that nagged at him, though he couldn't put his finger on what exactly. Messon was sitting on the bed, running his hand in a smoothing action over the pink candlewick bedspread, tracing the concave contours of where his daughter had once slept. *'Thou art lost and gone forever, dreadful sorry, Clementine – '* he hummed abstractedly to himself.

'Alan. Earlier when you said she wasn't your daughter, you meant she was changed in some way - not herself?'

'I actually struck one of them,' he muttered, as though unaware of anyone in the room but himself. 'A journo. Never done a thing like that in my life, but I was driven to it.' Then he caught sight of McCann, adding. 'Said he'd sue me for common assault. Big heart, that man. But it didn't take them long to find their snapshot. It wasn't the daughter I knew.'

'What exactly do you mean, Alan?'

'It was the face of despair. God knows where they dragged it up from.'

'I believe the police released the shot.'

'Well, they had no right to do so.'

'Perhaps not, but they were pursuing their investigation.'

'Investigation! She died, didn't she? Blown to pieces! What was there to investigate, for God's sake?'

'The reason why.'

There was no answer to that. They both knew that was their common quest.

'Oh Lord, if I could only know.' Messon touched McCann's arm. 'Leo. Will you help me? I know you're doing this, asking questions, for Miss Buchanan, but *I* need to know as desperately as that poor girl does. I can't die until I *do* have a reason for such a terrible waste. Please promise you'll tell me when you find the answers - if you ever do so.'

'I'll let you know, Alan. That's a promise,' McCann answered. The old man had a right to know.

As they left the bedroom, McCann stopped dead in his tracks. The dates on the postcards. That was what had nagged him

'I'll be right with you, Alan,' McCann called after Messon, as he returned to the desk and the cards. He shuffled quickly through to the third. *'Father'*, it read, *'Not a great deal to report. I went down to Worthing in a friend of mine's car. The weather's been smashing. Really surprising. I'm told it always rains at Wimbledon. Queued for tickets yesterday, but couldn't get in. Had to go home and watch play on television. I walk a lot in Regent's Park now that the flowers are out. It's beautiful. See you soon. Love from Venice.'*

McCann checked the postmark for the second time. June 10th. That was what had nagged at him earlier. Each of the nine postcards had been franked on the 10th of the month exactly - a coincidence in itself, but it was the card in his hand that was the clincher. How could Venice have queued for Wimbledon on the ninth of June when the tournament hadn't begun till the 26th? The answer was simple. Someone had posted the cards for her. Someone had done so because Venice had not able to do so herself. Because she'd been out of the country at the time. The question was, where was she?

10.

May 15th

Rosalind had just opened the door of her car when she heard the cell phone bleep in her handbag. She quickly leant across the driving seat and placed it in the cradle near the gear lever, locking in the lead.

'Yes?'

'Rosie? It's Whitey. Look I hope I'm not being a nuisance, but are you anywhere close by?'

'Just round the corner, as it happens,' Rosalind replied. It was a lie, but she'd have driven from Melbourne if Whitey had needed her.

'Do you think you could just spare me a couple of minutes, there's something I'd like to discuss with you.'

'Of course,' she replied at once.

'I make it sound so important. It isn't really. Just something that I'd like to run by a friend. Kerry is in one of his rather difficult moods, you see. Otherwise I'd have a one way conversation with the old bugger and leave it at that but – '

Rosalind cut her short. 'I'll be with you in about ten minutes, okay?'

'Bless you, dear. I'll get the ice, and make sure we've got enough gin.'

Whitey lived in a small yet charming terrace house in Birchgrove, facing out across Snail's Bay. As Rosalind drew up in Wharf Road, she could see the front door open wide. Whitey was visible a few feet inside the hallway, supporting the thin frame of her husband as they shuffled towards the living room.

As Rosalind closed the car door, she could plainly hear Kerry shouting obscenities at his wife.

'Blast you woman! I wish to garden a little longer. I have no inclination to sit indoors. In the good old days Mr. Butterworth would have understood.'

As she turned right into the living room she caught sight of Rosalind at the front door. 'Come in, dear, and close the door. I won't be a moment.' She disappeared for a second, then came back out into the hallway. 'Kerry's being a menace today,' she said, pushing a wisp of hair back from her forehead. 'But never mind. Come with me while I get some ice. It's taken me all this time to get the old darling out of the garden. Problem is, I can't leave him out there on his own. He'd probably take off to God knows where.'

A couple of minutes later Kerry had fixed the gins and they were sitting in the living room. Kerry held his drink firmly with both bony hands; he'd already accounted for at least two-thirds.

'No one gives a damn these days. Now, Brian Butterworth was a nice man,' Kerry muttered from the comfort of the armchair - one which held the best view of the bay. '*Butterfingers* we all called him. Green fingers for the gardener, eh?' He laughed shortly, then his face immediately set in anger as he stared at his wife.

'No idea who all these people are,' Whitey said in a whispered aside. 'He makes them up. The gin will cheer him up; nearly always does the trick. I think I should tell the doctors. Far better medicine than all the pills they force me to give the old bugger.' She looked across at Kerry's angry glare, and smiled. The depth of her love was etched in every wrinkle of her face.

'So how can I help? Anything specific, or is this just a comforting chat?' Rosalind was once again aware that her old friend was lost in thought. 'Not smoking today?' she continued lightly. 'Scarcely believable.'

'Been feeling a bit under the weather the past day or so, but nothing to worry about. As long as I keep up the blood sugar level, and don't drink too many gins.' She laughed, and toasted Rosalind. Then her expression changed.

'I don't know if I should even be asking for your help on this one, but these days I'm on my own with my thoughts all day, and in the evening I'm alone again. Of course Kerry's here, but he can't understand much. The lucid periods are getting shorter.'

'Does Betty still look after him during the day?'

'Yes, God bless her. And he adores her. I think he believes he's actually married to *her*, and that *I'm* the home help.' Rosalind opened her mouth to speak, but

Whitey held up a hand. 'No need to feel sorry for me. I'm quite used to it now. But it's the time I have to think that's the worst thing. And what *is* on my mind is what's driving me nuts.'

'If it's to do with business, you know I'd never repeat a word.'

'Dear girl, that goes without saying,' she said, holding up a hand. 'I know you'd be the soul of discretion. But in my thirty years in banking I've always lived by the principles of confidentiality; acutely aware of my fiduciary responsibilities, boring and old fashioned as that may sound nowadays. But it's darned difficult to throw them to the wind overnight. I'd just love to natter to an old pal - just to talk it out, so to speak. Share my frustrations. Does that sound reasonable to you, dear?'

'Absolutely.'

Rosalind stirred the ice round her glass with her finger. 'Well, natter away.'

'Well, you remember when you called me a couple of days after Andrew's memorial service, you asked whether I knew of any business appointment he might have had on the day he died?' Whitey continued.

'I do.'

'And I told you there was nothing in his appointments book. I assumed it was a personal matter between your father and Andrew?'

'Yes.'

'Well, I feel a bit guilty now that I didn't share one or two things with you then.'

'About what?' Rosalind began, but was cut short.

'It's all gone,' Kerry barked out suddenly. 'They always kept the glasses fully charged at the club, let me tell you.' He stared stoically through the window into the twilight.

'I'll get you a refill in just a moment, darling,' Whitey cooed. 'Be a little patient.'

Kerry put down his glass on the table beside him, crossing his arms in frustration.

'Kerry's never been a member of any club, anywhere in the world,' she whispered to Rosalind, 'Delusions of grandeur, I'm afraid. But where was I? Oh yes. As the days passed and I began to put all Andrew's affairs in order, I began to think it was possible that everyone in that hotel room might have had a common purpose.'

For no apparent reason, Whitey abruptly stopped talking and began sipping her gin. 'Yes,' Rosalind prompted.

'Look, before I carry on I want to explain that the reason I'm asking for your advice as a friend is that I'm at present faced with a dilemma that has nothing to do with either your father or yourself. It basically boils down to whether or not to make it my business to take further some of the things that Andrew turned up during the course of his work; specifically his work during the three months prior to his death.'

'Take them further? In what way?'

'After Andrew's death I went through all his papers in minute detail. However, when I brought the final analysis to the attention of McKinley, he just took the report from me, together with all Andrew's files, said they were now part of his personal portfolio, and that he'd see to the matter himself.'

'He didn't?'

'No action has yet been taken on the part of the Board, so I can only presume he has yet to do so, or has decided not to proceed further.'

'That's his prerogative, surely?'

'It is, yes. But in my opinion, to ignore Andrew's findings borders on the irresponsible.'

'Go above his head.'

'To Rupert Gerson? I suppose I could. I've never been put in that situation before, but now that I'm leaving I really should do just that.'

'Look, hang on a minute. I don't need specifics; you'd probably prefer to keep those to yourself. But are we talking some kind of misdealing? Or to put it more bluntly, fraud?'

Whitey laughed. 'Don't be so dramatic. Nothing so cut and dried, exciting or sensational. Perhaps I should fill you in with some of the basics. Without them you won't have the first idea what I'm talking about.'

'Can't wait.'

'And neither can I,' snapped Kerry from the corner. 'Been here for well over an hour now. Where's my gin? Better get it m'self, I suppose?'

'Stay where you are, Kerry. I'll fetch it right now.'

Whitey shuffled off into the kitchen, while Kerry stared at Rosalind.

'And who exactly may you be,' he began in a friendly tone. 'You're a fine looking girl.' Kerry had known Rosalind since childhood.

'Rosie Buchanan. Delighted to meet you, sir.'

'Don't worry, the drinks are coming,' he added with a reassuring grin.

Whitey returned with Kerry's refill, then sat. 'Right then. I'll tell you what I know,' she began.

Rosalind held up a hand. 'Before you start, do you mind if I make notes. They'll just be for me I promise. It's an awful habit, but I think better if I'm doodling.'

'All right, dear, but remember, this is not for publication. The Australian Pacific could end up in a load of trouble if the financial press got wind of what I am about to tell you.'

'Spit it out, Whitey,' Rosalind chided jokingly, pulling a small notepad from her handbag.

'Here goes.' Whitey took a deep breath. 'Two months before he died, Andrew was instructed by Rupert Gerson to head up a special internal audit. The terms of reference were wide, and no one, besides myself as Andrew's personal private secretary was to know Andrew was conducting it.'

'An audit of the affairs of the Australian Pacific here in Sydney?'

'Heavens, no. The concern was for our DTC in Hong Kong, Aust-Pac Finance. DTC means Deposit Taking Company as I'm sure you know. Basically it's our merchant banking arm in Hong Kong. Well, in '95 it showed it had turned a '94 profit of $78 million into a deficit of $120. There was little concern here initially because it had been the product of the financial climate that had affected the entire Hong Kong community – property values that continued to slump.

'As far as the Hong Kong market was concerned, since we at the Australian Pacific Investment Bank were the parent company, and a prestigious bank to boot, no alarm bells were ringing. But back here in Australia it was a different matter. It began to disturb Gerson, and that's why he asked Andrew to investigate the exact extent of the Bank's exposure, impressing on him to use as much discretion and subtlety as possible. What he feared the most was a Barings-style scandal. The last thing he wanted was to be obliged to keelhaul the bank's managing director in Hong Kong, a difficult and arrogant man called Greville. Not before he was sure of his facts, anyway. That might have left Gerson with a lot of egg on his face.'

'Hence Andrew's secret internal audit?'

'Exactly. You see Gerson was terrified that Aust-Pac Finance had loaned considerably more than they were admitting to, through a tangled web of property companies. So Andrew and I scooted off to Hong Kong for a look-see.'

'Greville was presumably unaware of Andrew's real purpose.'

'Needless to say. Andrew was pretty diplomatic about the whole thing. Had to be. Greville treated us regally; took us to all the usual places. We dined at the Peak, lunched in his box at Happy Valley for the races, went to Macao for the weekend, gambling.

'Anyway, little by little it became apparent to Andrew that the extent of the Australian Pacific's exposure was huge. We were the parent bank. Why, he asked himself, had loans been sanctioned, for such obviously high-risk investments? And why loaned to companies buying Hong Kong property?'

'How does dad feature in all this?'

'He doesn't. Just be patient for a minute.' She wagged a finger. 'Your job is to listen to an old fool, and eventually tell me what I should do about it all.'

'Right,' Rosalind replied, like a scolded child.

'The more Andrew looked into the loans that Greville had authorized, the more he wondered why the investment had not been made in the Special Economic Zones in China. They would have been a much better investment bet. In the Zones, foreign investment, even a hundred per cent foreign owned plants, were, and still are, welcomed with tax and tariff concessions, soft loans, exchange-control waivers and assurances of low wages. You see, property values in Hong Kong had quadrupled between 1978 and 1981 because the Hong Kong banking system at that time was swimming in liquidity and foreign banks were rushing to participate in the rapid growth of the Pacific area. But the bubble had burst with the fall of the Chung family. It was then that it had become evident to the world that property values were hugely puffed up beyond their real value, and that the majority of property deals were inter-company and false book profits had been the result.'

'So why choose a time like this to grant loans to companies wishing to buy into Hong Kong property?'

'Exactly! It didn't make financial sense, either for the recipients of the loans, or for us, since it was the Australian Pacific that would be exposed ultimately should the companies be unable to service the loans. The worst scenario, needless to say, would have been if those companies had gone under.' She paused just long enough to light a cigarette.

Rosalind could see her hand was shaking as she blew out the match.

Kerry turned and eyed her through slits. 'Dirty habit,' he growled, then sipped his gin.

'Does all this make sense to you?' Whitey continued as if she hadn't heard him. 'I hope I'm not getting too detailed and confusing.'

'Not at all. But what was Andrew's gut reaction? Did he feel the specter of financial manipulation of funds?'

'Andrew was never a man to jump to conclusions of corruption and skullduggery. He always gave people the benefit of the doubt. But the possibility of kickbacks was beginning to become evident, and the more research he did outside the offices of Aust-Pac Finance with financial analysts, the more concerned he became. His doubts were only reinforced by local market tittle-tattle. Hong Kong has to be one of the most gossip-ridden cities of the world, you know. The Chinese love nothing better than to bad-mouth each other, especially the old guard, of which Greville was undoubtedly one. That was one thing Andrew took pains to point out to me – that Greville was one of the least-liked people in the city, and by that token would be a prime target for malevolent tittle-tattle.'

'Andrew thought Greville was perhaps the victim of ill-intentioned rumor?'

'It was always possible. Andrew's only real option was to attempt to sort out the structure of the loans, and how they'd been disbursed. More importantly, whether the companies had a sound financial base, and if the money had been properly invested.'

'What about the question of kickbacks?'

'Well, this is always very shaky ground. It's the easiest thing in the world to arrange for the transfer of money from one account to another. Kickbacks can be disguised in many different ways. For instance, as consultation fees. Another way is to grant discretionary overdraft facilities at far below par interest rates. These loans needn't be repaid for many years, while the principal can be invested in high yielding stock. The list of scams is endless. Also, you have to remember that Greville is a rich man in his own right. The addition of a couple of million dollars to one or another of his accounts, offshore most likely, would have signified little. It's not as if the man suddenly bought a new house, motor launch or a Lamborghini. Besides, if it were a kickback, he'd make sure the funds were wired to an offshore numbered account so no one could follow the trail.'

'So who were the recipients of Greville's loans?'

'Here again Andrew encountered problems. The intention was that he was to work without the directors of Aust-Pac Finance being aware of his interest, so he could hardly ask too many direct questions. He had to do a fair bit of financial digging. It was the people behind the companies that Andrew was after. Ascertaining the companies involved was routine. The names won't mean much to you.'

'Try me.'

'Pac Seng Investment Limited. Mean anything?'

'Afraid not.'

'Doesn't surprise me. Of course it wouldn't. Didn't mean a thing to me either. Just a mid-sized company.

'Anyway, it was during that time I began to wonder whether a bit of financial juggling might be going on. If this was the case, the whole scenario mightn't have been too bad, though we'd still have ended up with a loss, albeit small enough to write-off without too much trouble.'

'Explain.'

'I'll give you a simple example. Suppose my company had bought a lot of property in Hong Kong during the boom years, and had got stuck with it. I wouldn't want to sell it at a huge loss, would I? And who the hell would buy it at a premium anyway? No one. So what do I do? I arrange for someone to negotiate a reasonably soft loan from a buddy at a merchant bank, to be taken up by another of my companies run by a nominee or associate. What happens? My buddy gets a kickback for his trouble, the secondary company buys my property at a good profit, and the selling company records that profit in its books. Plus, the paper value of the property in question has risen rather than fallen.'

'Was that what happened?'

'Well, we began to unravel the web of subsidiary companies, to find out who was the driving force behind the loans. But the more we untangled, the worse it looked. We could soon see that our exposure was huge, and could well be massive.'

'Wouldn't this have been the time to confront Greville? In the nicest way possible I mean.'

'Andrew couldn't without checking back with Gerson for authority to do so. Plus if we had been on to something hot, then Greville would have been ideally placed to cover his tracks pronto before we had the ammunition to sink him.'

'But who was getting the money? Who was the ultimate beneficiary of all this?'

'That's who we were after,' said Whitey animatedly. 'But the difficulty in finance has always been in revealing the man behind the mask. For example, if a loan is granted to a holding company, it's more than likely that behind the holding company is a private company, one that owns more than fifty per cent of its shareholding, effectively controlling it. Behind this private company, more often than not in Hong Kong, is a nominee company, which owns the private company lock, stock and barrel. And who is the mystery nominee? That's the hard one. Hong Kong attitudes are very accommodating when it comes to the anonymity of nominees.'

'But it would have been a matter of record who applied for the loan?'

'Of course, but who was the ultimate recipient and why was the money used in this way? And the vital question, when it comes to even suggesting that Greville was authorizing loans for purposes unconnected with proper banking procedures, was who ultimately benefited by the whole affair? If we knew that, we might be able to find out whether Greville took kickbacks. Difficult but not impossible.'

'How long were you in Hong Kong?'

'Ten days. During that time Andrew worked like a beaver. He'd built up a lot of connections in Hong Kong over the years, and they didn't let him down. As things began to gel a bit, Andrew became more anxious. From the information he was getting day by day from his sources, Andrew was more and more concerned that the loan company, Pac Seng, was siphoning off funds from monies it had been loaned by Aust-Pac Finance to give to offshore companies, while maintaining fraudulent profit statements on its books. And now it was beginning to look as though Greville was about to authorize further loans to an anonymous offshore investment company so that it could bid for, and take control of, one of the Pac Seng's profitable subsidiary insurance companies. This would have shifted control offshore, beyond the reach of Hong Kong fiscal authorities, and thereby our control. This would have spelt disaster.

'The final crunch came during the course of a boardroom meeting at which Andrew was present, when it was suggested that Aust-Pac Finance grant yet a further loan to another offshore company, Meridian-Zenith, owned by an Englishman, Sir Henry Trevor. Andrew said nothing at the time, but as soon as the meeting was over he got to work. And what did he find? Sir Henry was no more than a nominee Executive Director of the offshore company, and that it was in fact controlled and owned – '

'By the nominee company behind the original loan company – Pac Seng?' Rosalind cut in.

'Good girl. On the button. After a lot of digging and detective work it transpired that Pac Seng wanted to sell some hugely valuable assets and needed Aust-Pac Finance to grant a loan. This way they could move assets out of Hong Kong offshore to a Channel Islands tax haven where Sir Henry's company was incorporated.

'As soon as he was reasonably sure of his facts, Andrew took up the subject of the imminent loan with Greville, saying, diplomatically as ever, that he thought it a most unwise move. He told Greville that if he continued with the loan, it would be against his express advice and authority, and that he would feel bound to bring the matter, together with 'other practices' to the attention of the chairman of Australian Pacific on his return to Sydney.'

'And how did Greville react to this?'

'Andrew told me that night that Greville had seemed very composed, replying that it was Andrew's prerogative to refer back to Gerson, but that until he was personally relieved of his job by his chairman, he would continue to operate as he thought fit. He added rather pointedly that it was Gerson to whom he answered, not Andrew - though he would make Andrew's comment a matter of record.'

'And then you returned to Sydney?'

'We did. Andrew and I went through all his notes both on the plane back and for two days afterwards. He continued to work on his notes from home. The following day he was killed.'

'Let's be clear about this. Are you saying you think Andrew was killed to silence him?'

Whitey stubbed out her cigarette, saying nothing.

'Whitey?' Rosalind prompted gently.

'No, not really,' she said, though it was clear to Rosalind she wasn't even convincing herself. 'The reason I was reticent to share all this with you weeks ago was because I was afraid you'd think I was being too theatrical. After all, men of Greville's caliber do not go around killing their fellow bankers merely because, during the course of an audit, sensitive areas of mismanagement have come to light.'

'History has confirmed time and time again that's *exactly* what they do,' replied Rosalind.

'Besides, Andrew and your father were killed by a deranged girl, not an assassin.'

'We don't know that, Whitey. We know little or nothing about her.'

The silence of the room was interrupted only by the sound of Kerry running his finger round the rim of his glass.

'Besides,' Rosalind continued, 'Rupert Gerson may have been recently fed a line by McKinley. How much do you know of his background?'

'Nothing really.'

'Have you discussed the Hong Kong findings with Gerson?'

'That's what I've been vacillating about. I didn't know whether I should.'

'What's your opinion of Greville? Do you think he's involved in anything serious enough to consider taking matters into his own hands?'

'No, I don't. What we had was circumstantial. We had few solid facts. Greville wouldn't have *needed* to kill Andrew. He'd be far better off covering his tracks. He'd have ample time to do so while the waters were well and truly muddied.'

Whitey's logic as usual was cool and reasoned.

'Does McKinley know Greville?'

'Professionally they know of each other; they'd have to. No idea whether they've ever actually met.'

'So what is your point, Whitey? You said earlier that you had an idea everyone in that room might have had a common purpose. What did you mean by that?'

'Well, it struck me that the unidentified man was an Asian. So it said in the papers, anyway. He could well have been someone Andrew had dug up in Hong Kong who was prepared to do the dirty on Greville.'

'Then why should my father have been there?'

'I know. It's a bit like a jigsaw where all the bits fit together snugly, but as a whole the picture is an abstract. Perhaps Andrew wanted your father to give an opinion.'

They sat in silence for a while. Kerry was dozing in his chair, his glass held like a vice in his bony fingers.

'Well, what advice can I give you, Whitey? That was your initial request, wasn't it?'

Whitey's expression softened as she leant across the desk. 'It was. And I'm very sorry if I'm being too difficult. It's just been such a frustrating time recently, not knowing how I should proceed.'

'Gerson knows of all this?'

'I don't know the extent of his knowledge, no. Andrew had a short meeting with him as soon as we got back from Hong Kong. He didn't tell me the reaction though. Professional etiquette; a courtesy to Gerson till he made his move. But I'd hazard a guess that Gerson was mightily taken aback by the bank's position in all this, not to mention the financial exposure. I'd imagine right now he'd be doing his utmost to keep the tightest wraps on this whole affair until he has a chance to balance our position. Even then, it's difficult for him to take disciplinary action without harming the reputation of the bank. As far as I'm concerned, since Andrew never told me exactly what he said to Gerson, I can only surmise that Andrew told him everything, and that Gerson knows the full extent of our findings.'

'So Gerson has all the details?'

'No. Andrew didn't have time to commit all the details to paper; that was to be my job. I'd imagine he told Rupert a full report, together with all the details, would be on his desk in a matter of hours. I'd already started work on it, you see. It was practically finished the morning of the explosion. But the thing that gives me sleepless nights is that maybe he didn't tell Gerson everything. Maybe he just gave him the big picture, telling him to expect the full report later.'

'And Duncan McKinley took possession of it before it reached Gerson?'

'As I said earlier, McKinley took all the papers I was working on, including Andrew's report, so it's quite possible he never gave them to Gerson. I told McKinley I was going to schedule a meeting with Gerson to appraise him of my own version of events, but he told me that the report was now his responsibility. I just instinctively did what I was told. Now I feel angry as hell at his attitude. And Greville is still heading up Aust-Pac Finance in Hong Kong.'

Whitey laid her spectacles down on the desk, ran a hand through her hair, and took a deep breath.

'So do I walk into our chairman's office and calmly ask him what the hell's going on? Or do I just say it's none of my business, and let them get on with it? You see, I really want to do the right thing by the bank. I owe it to the shareholders. Plus it's been the major focal point of my life. I'd hate to see all Andrew's work go down the drain in a massive banking scandal, when looking back in a few years time I'll know there was something I could've done to stop it.'

They sat in silence for several minutes. There didn't seem any easy decision to make. If Whitey couldn't think of one, it most probably didn't exist.

'I'd like to go back to Hong Kong,' Whitey said eventually, breaking the silence. 'Maybe that's the answer. Do some further digging on my own. I'd dearly like to find out who's behind all these shell companies and subsidiaries, and how involved Greville and Sir Henry Trevor are. If they're crooks, I'd like to bring it all out in the open. Thing is, I don't have the nerve. Does that sound spineless?'

'Not at all Whitey. You've got enough on your plate.'

'I'd like to do it for Andrew, to finish where he left off. But I just feel too old and feeble. And it's Kerry that deserves my time, not the bank.'

From the corner there was a sudden shout as Kerry woke from a dream. He quickly scanned the room to get his bearings, his eyes settling eventually on Rosalind. 'I say, it's Rosie, isn't it?' he said sleepily. 'Good lord, haven't seen you for ages. How's your dear father.'

Rosalind rose and walked over to the frail man, who smiled up at her, reaching out a hand. She held it firmly. 'He's fine, Kerry, just fine.'

11.

May 16th

McCann found the atmosphere within the Buchanan Construction building was subdued. It was as if every member of the staff had suffered a deep personal loss. It was clear that Maynard Buchanan had been a much admired man.

The Chairman's suite on the penthouse floor of the massive building in Milson's Point had not been touched since the day of the explosion. The police had requested a detailed examination of Maynard Buchanan's papers within days of the tragedy. On behalf of the company, Ian Mackintosh had agreed to this. Five days later they'd given Rosalind the all clear to see to her father's affairs. Since that time, only she had entered the rooms.

She sat at her father's desk, turning the pages of his diary as she'd done so many times during the last few weeks while McCann stood by the window overlooking Luna Park, reading Buchanan Construction's Annual Report. It was a couple of minutes before the 8.30 am meeting arranged with Buchanan's Group Managing Directors, Macintosh and Zeltis.

The Commander telephone beeped. 'Miss Buchanan? Both Mr. Mackintosh and Mr. Zeltis are in the board room when it's convenient to you.'

'Thank you Leila. Please tell them I'll be right down.'

The boardroom was on the floor below Maynard Buchanan's offices. Mackintosh and Zeltis were seated when Rosalind and McCann entered. They rose.

'Good morning Ian. Bob. I'd like you to meet Leo McCann. He's going to be working for me personally, investigating my father's death.'

McCann shook hands with both men. Zeltis had a friendly look about him, Mackintosh a less open and outwardly more ambitious demeanor.

'Leo hasn't had a chance yet to learn too much about the company structure, so I thought you should meet. I'm sure there are a good many things he'll want to ask you.'

Mackintosh gestured towards the coffee tray. Rosalind shook her head, then made her way towards the huge board room table. McCann was curious as to where Rosalind would choose to sit. Mackintosh and Zeltis were now effectively running the company, though at present neither had any official status to do so. Rosalind had stated her intention of taking the reigns herself, and once probate was granted she would own the vast bulk of the shares. The top job was hers if she wanted it.

'Perhaps you could give Leo a thumbnail sketch of our operations Ian, just to get us going,' she said, sitting halfway down the long boardroom table beneath the portrait of her grandfather. Zeltis sat to her left, Mackintosh and McCann opposite. Maynard's usual seat at the head of the table remained empty. It was a good move. McCann watched for a reaction. There was none. One up for her diplomacy, thought McCann.

'Buchanan Construction is a privately owned company consisting of three major business units. Technologies, Construction, and Construction–Asia,' began Mackintosh.

It was immediately clear to McCann that Mackintosh was a practiced speaker. The question was, how to cut the verbosity short without offending him.

'The Technologies unit provides engineering, manufacturing, construction and maintenance in power generation, materials handling, process equipment and environmental remediation throughout Australia and Asia.'

McCann held up a hand. Ian stopped speaking immediately.

'Was there something you wanted to ask, Leo?' Mackintosh's tone was friendly enough.

'Sorry to halt the flow, Ian. I just thought before you went much further into the business detail, I'd point out that what really interests me is any unusual turn of events that may have occurred recently. So, the broader the strokes, the better.'

'Understood,' Mackintosh replied, then blithely continued his prepared speech. 'The second unit, Construction, is our largest. Internationally competitive engineering, building, fabrication and operation. We have a long history of achievement in the petrochemical, power, process and building industries.' He paused to look for affirmation at McCann, whose expression was impassive. Mackintosh swept on.

'The third unit is Construction Asia. Main office in Kuala Lumpur, with subsidiary offices in Thailand, Indonesia and Loas. That's Ellery Travis' new domain.'

'How long has he been with Buchanan?' asked McCann.

'One month,' replied Mackintosh.

'Does the company have an office in Vietnam?'

'Not as yet. We're considering some infrastructure projects near Hai Phong at present. Perhaps I should say Maynard was doing so, prior to his death. I've no doubt that negotiations will continue shortly, and should they be successful, we'd seriously think of premises in Hanoi.'

'Had Maynard visited Vietnam during the course of the negotiations?'

'He was there just before Christmas. Meetings with the Vietnamese Minister of Foreign Trade, and one of the AusAID people. The project there would be funded by foreign aid, you understand. The Australian Government has yet to make a decision.'

'But at present you have no projects outstanding in Vietnam?'

'No firm contracts, no.'

It was Rosalind's turn to interrupt Mackintosh's flow. 'If you feel like calling a spade a spade, Leo, go ahead. I think I know what's on your mind. I know Ian won't be offended.'

'It's the Asian who died alongside Maynard that concerns me, Ian. Who was he? At present he's unidentified. The police have referred the matter to Interpol, Immigration - everyone. Yet he was in the Savoy with Maynard and Mr. Horan, and died there. Unless he'd broken into the room, and was being confronted by them both as the girl entered, it stands to reason he had some valid reason to be there, and that either Maynard or Horan, or both, knew him.'

'Seems logical,' Zeltis offered, his first contribution.

'Yet Rosalind tells me there is no record at Horan's bank of any projected meeting between Horan and this mystery man on the 26th.'

'Nevertheless, Horan must have had countless Asian contacts,' Zeltis continued.

'The Australian Pacific has been in touch with them all, bar a couple in Japan who wouldn't be relevant,' Rosalind explained. 'All are still alive and kicking. We're after someone Maynard met, knew, or had dealings with, who is no longer alive. The detectives at Task Force Acorn think he may be a Vietnamese.'

They sat in silence for a few moments.

'Perhaps it's best if we all give some thought to his identity. Meanwhile, would you all mind if I just throw a few unconnected thoughts at you?' McCann directed his question to them all.

'Go ahead', said Rosalind. 'That's the whole reason I called this morning's meeting.'

Another good turn of phrase, thought McCann. It was Rosalind who had called the meeting. She called the shots. And why not? She owned seventy per cent of the share capital.

'Firstly, Miss Buchanan told me that only a short while ago there was a move towards a public share issue, a listing on the Stock Exchange.'

'Just over a month ago, yes,' Mackintosh replied.

'But the company didn't proceed with it?'

'No.'

'Might I ask why? It may not be relevant - I'm not very familiar with the intricacies of going public - but what was the reason for the move in the first place?' McCann in fact had more than a layman's knowledge of such things; he just wanted to see how Mackintosh would spell it out.

Mackintosh looked across at Zeltis, indicating to him that probably he was best placed to field that question.

'Well, it all goes back to a difficult situation we found ourselves in Malaysia last year. We'd bid for and secured the contract to build a petrochemical plant to manufacture PTA; it's one of the chemicals used to manufacture video film in the plastics industry. It was situated just outside Telok Anson on the coast.'

'Worth approximately?' McCann interjected.

'Approximately two hundred and ninety eight million US dollars.'

'Quite major.'

'Not as far as petrochemicals plants go. We've built much bigger. They can cost up to a billion. But Telok Anson is on the coast; handy for bringing in raw materials through a berth facility.' Zeltis reached for his coffee. To McCann's eye he looked slightly reluctant to tell his tale.

'There was a problem?' McCann prodded.

'A very major one. Our project manager was a man called Palmer. Immensely talented, outstanding record. In view of the prestigious nature of the contract, Maynard went out to KL to sign the contract. Thereafter, Christopher Palmer was left in charge, naturally reporting through a structure. Strictly speaking it should have been through the country manager, who at that time was myself. But I had been recalled to Sydney, so Palmer made the day-to-day decisions himself, subject to regular updates to the Chief Executive Officer - Maynard.'

'What went wrong?' asked McCann. Zeltis was taking forever to get to the nitty-gritty.

'Without the collusion of the bank syndicates in Malaysia who had organized the loans for the project, and the government cooperation, it would not have been possible.'

McCann held up a hand. 'What would not have been possible?'

'Misappropriation of funds. You see, somehow Palmer managed to alter the initial letters of credit to offshore companies in Hong Kong – ones that turned out to be his own shell companies – so that he could take draw-downs himself.'

'Steal the money?'

'That's a clearer way of putting it, yes. You see, one should only take what we refer to as 'draw-downs' of cash on the basis of goods delivered. The project was about fifteen per cent through when it ground to a halt. Palmer had siphoned off the great bulk of the cash, and there was nothing to pay for the goods.'

'How was it possible to get away with such an obvious maneuver? Surely the Malaysian banks would have smelled a rat or two before things got out of control?'

'They did, but it turned out that certain governmental ministers I'm not at liberty to name vouched for Palmer each time the banks showed any signs of concern. Now, of course, the ministers deny ever having done so. And as I mentioned earlier, there was also a good deal of insider bank collusion – that's my view anyway.'

'So what was the end result?'

'We were out of pocket over a hundred and eighty-five million. Added to which, we were left with a great deal of egg on our faces. It wouldn't have looked too good to the business community if they'd got wind of our situation. So Maynard made a decision to attempt as much of a cover-up of our vulnerable situation as was possible until alternate financing was possible. This was a hard ask, since it could have taken weeks, and we were fully contracted to building the plant.'

'Nevertheless, Maynard found the money?'

'He did. He was remarkable. Had the whole thing arranged in forty-eight hours. How he did it is beyond me. I can tell you that re-financing such large sums at such short notice is not easy – banks tend to view with suspicion any projects that have fallen down, especially where inter-company fraud is concerned.'

'Who came to the rescue?'

'The Union Constitution Bank. The deal was brokered out of Hong Kong. The Jensen Rollason Partnership. Maynard was referred to the company by Theodore Radcliffe's son, Bradley.'

McCann shot a quick glance at Rosalind. From her expression, he guessed Zeltis' information regarding her boyfriend had come as news to her, and she was embarrassed that she hadn't been aware of it.

'The Union Constitution re-financed the loan?'

'Well, they were the *lead* bank. They put together a worldwide syndicate of three other banks who offered the loan.'

'And they were?'

Zeltis looked temporarily flummoxed. 'Our dealings were with the Union Constitution Bank. The other three would have wired the money to New York via CHIPS. It's operated by the New York Clearing House Association. International dollar transfers usually move through CHIPS. It's an inter-bank payment system.'

'So we don't know who they were? Or where the money originated?'

'I'm sure it's a matter of record, Leo,' replied Zeltis awkwardly. Something about McCann's line of thought was bothering him, because it had set his own mind thinking along similar lines, and he didn't care to think about what the answers might be. Where had the bulk of the loan capital come from? 'It didn't much matter at the time,' Zeltis continued. 'What was vital was that the loan was guaranteed fast. I'm sure Maynard knew all the minor details – after all, he secured the loan, not myself.'

McCann nodded his head, surprised at Zeltis's lack of detailed knowledge of such an important transaction. 'Perhaps you could research the details for me, Bob. I'm sure the Union Constitution would be happy to tell you the origin of the money?'

'They would indeed. I'll get onto it today.'

'Thanks, Bob,' McCann continued. 'But, to get briefly back to my initial question regarding the public issue, how does this Palmer fraud tie in with that?'

'Perhaps I could answer that one, Bob.' Now Ian took over.

Zeltis nodded.

'We have a major expansion program. We're growing at a prodigious rate. Maynard always took the long-term view; anticipating world needs so as to place our company for long-term investment in core Asian markets. To that end we'd planned to go public. Our lawyer had completed our prospectus, passed by the Stock Exchange Authority and the Australian Securities Commission, but it was yet to be audited. Then, kaboom, Palmer places us in a very invidious position. Here we are trying to keep our embarrassment to ourselves, yet about to be scrutinized in detail by investors from all over the world. It just wasn't on.'

'So you pulled out?'

'Maynard pulled the plug. With the greatest diplomacy. Said he'd found alternative funding for all our current projects, and would re-think the public issue at a later stage.'

'The business community bought it?'

'No need to be so surprised. Though a withdrawal of a prospectus doesn't happen too often, it could well be construed as a sign of strength – that Buchanan Construction didn't need to go public. Alternatively, that Maynard preferred to retain absolute private control.'

There was another moment of silence. Zeltis seemed relieved that the discussion of the Malaysian affair was over, an episode he hadn't relished raking over again. He felt to some degree responsible for having hired Palmer in the first place, though his credentials had been impeccable and thoroughly vetted. Mackintosh looked expectantly at McCann, happy to be of further use. Rosalind had knitted brows, looking deep in thought, as if something said had given her cause for concern.

'Can you think of anything else that occurred during the last few months that either of you would regard as out of the ordinary?' continued McCann. 'Something that might cause a person, possibly an employee or a business associate, to feel legitimate cause to hold a grudge against Mr. Buchanan? An episode that might have made Maynard an enemy?'

The response of the two men was quick.

'Maynard Buchanan was not a man to make enemies. He was a straightforward man of great principle – a rare commodity in today's world,' Mackintosh stated quietly.

'Don't make him sound so dull, Ian,' Zeltis interjected 'He had a fine madness, as they often say, and had a great sense of humor.'

'Absolutely true,' chipped in Mackintosh. 'Added to which he was well loved and respected by all his staff. He was one of the best friends a man could wish for. I'll miss him greatly. But to reiterate, no, I don't believe he had an enemy that would have wished to take his life.'

'I hope Miss Buchanan won't take offence if I ask this last question, but if I'm to do my job effectively for her I'm afraid I must. Were either of you aware of any liaison between Maynard Buchanan and anyone on staff, or of any casual gossip that was floating around the building concerning his sex life?'

Rosalind didn't move a muscle.

'Maynard would never have considered a personal relationship with a member of the staff,' said Mackintosh. 'Or with a business associate outside this building. He would have been the first to say it wasn't good business practice.'

'What about outside of the business community? Were any tongues wagging?'

'If they were, they wouldn't have wagged within my earshot.' Mackintosh replied crisply. 'Possibly in the mail room. I'm afraid I can't help you there.'

'I think Leo is trying to determine whether my father might conceivably have been having an affair with the young woman who died,' Rosalind stated carefully, with some dignity. 'That he might have had a proclivity towards very young girls. Am I right, Leo?'

'I have to ask,' McCann replied.

'Not as far as I am aware, Leo,' said Zeltis. 'Unless I am an exceptionally poor judge of character, I would say this was not the case.'

'I agree Bob,' added Mackintosh. 'I'm not saying he became a monk after your mother's tragic death. Sure he'd had the odd affair, and I'm pretty sure you were well aware of the last one, Rosalind. But that was four years ago.' She nodded. He continued. 'This girl was barely out of her teens wasn't she?'

'Twenty.'

'Then it's out of the question.'

That seemed to be the end of that line of conjecture, so McCann changed tack. 'What happened to Palmer and the money?'

'Vanished,' said Zeltis stonily.

'That seems hardly possible these days,' McCann countered. 'Short of living in the Amazon basin, or an Indonesian island, I'd say it's practically impossible to get lost.'

'I tend to agree with you,' said Mackintosh. 'Nowadays everyone has at least half a page of computer space on file somewhere. Anyone worth a toss has maybe five. Depends on how much you're worth, or how much trouble you can be to various world authorities.'

'Okay, so where is he?' asked Rosalind.

'Dead, I'd say,' said McCann bluntly. 'Anyone who thinks they can steal that amount of money and walk away is stupid. Someone will take it away from him soon enough. Only way is to make damned sure no one knows you've got it. Problem then is how to spend the stuff. No, he either worked alone and it was taken from him, or he was working for someone else and they cut him out of the deal.'

'That has to be pure supposition. With that amount of money you can buy a good deal of privacy, surely,' Rosalind argued.

'You can for a while, yes. But not in any civilized part of the world.'

'Not everyone wants to live in Europe or America, Leo.'

'I'm not saying he can't be living in a Third World country, protected by his cash. That's possible for a while, but not long. I'm just giving an opinion.'

'Fair enough,' she replied, then turned to Zeltis. 'But couldn't they trace the money, Bob?'

'They traced it to Hong Kong. He banked it in Kuala Lumpur, where it was wired to the Hong Kong Mutual Mercantile Bank, credited to Silvan Mining, a shell company. From there it went through a complicated system of 'layering', as it's called, passing the money through a number of transactions to confuse the trail. Ultimately our investigations ended up in the Caymans. That's where we think the money ended up, we just can't prove it. Certainly can't get it back.'

'And that was the end of the line?'

'We think it ended up in a fiduciary account,' Zeltis said by way of explanation to McCann. 'The bank acts as a trustee. All the dealings are done in the bank's name, so the name of the holder is separated from the account itself.'

'Point is,' Mackintosh cut in, 'we were dealing with Malaysia originally, then Hong Kong, and ultimately the Caymans. Malaysians are notorious for their lack of financial transaction records, and the Hong Kong authorities at the time had no reason to distrust Palmer until the money was moved out from there. Later on they admitted they'd smelt a rat then, but weren't in a position to do anything at the time. Besides, whom were they going to tell? The Caymans we all know are completely unregulated, and have some of the toughest secrecy laws in the banking world to protect financial data. They reveal nothing unless it suits them and the price is right. Had the money passed through the States, then AUSTRAC would have been able to liaise with FinCEN and get their computers humming.'

'Just exactly who are they?'

'Very simply AUSTRAC is the Australian Transaction Reports and Analysis Center. It's a federal agency for recording and analyzing financial data. They take a hard look at any large cash transactions, international wire transfers and suspicious transactions. The computer has a state-of-the-art software program known as ScreenIT, a knowledge-based system that automatically processes information in ways that are set up to emulate human experts. From what I'm told it's so accurate at automatically detecting major unusual transactions, it's freakish. AUSTRAC's equivalent in the States is FinCEN. Their ScreenIT is called FAIS, short for Financial Artificial Intelligence System. FinCEN's part of the U.S. Treasury Department, set up in 1990. It analyses any criminal financing in the States.'

'Do they liaise with Malaysia?'

'They can ask for assistance from any foreign country. In fact AUSTRAC did ask, but there's no Malaysian equivalent of American and Australian statute law requiring banks to file cash transaction reports, so tracking Palmer and our money was a nightmare, and ultimately fruitless.'

'How did the police know Palmer went to Hong Kong?'

'They covered all the bases. Hong Kong was one of them. Immigration found an entry record but no exit. That's why we say he vanished there.'

'Maybe he has friends in Beijing?' Rosalind suggested. 'Some well placed bribes there, and he'd be home free. All he'd have to do is wire the money from the Caymans to China. I doubt if they'd be too particular about its origin.'

It was true, she had a point, McCann conceded to himself. But how long a man who had deposited more than a hundred million U.S. dollars in a Chinese Bank could hang on to it was another matter. Personally, he wouldn't have fancied Palmer's chances.

The meeting lasted only a few more minutes. Try as he might, McCann couldn't think of any fresh avenues of inquiry. It was clear to him that Zeltis hadn't much enjoyed the session. Maybe because he'd been asked some difficult questions and hadn't demonstrated he was up to the task of answering them. Mackintosh by contrast had seemed in control from beginning to end, and this had quite probably irked his fellow Group Managing Director.

'Bob's a good man, Leo,' said Rosalind later in her office. 'I know he didn't perform too well just now, but he's as tough a negotiator as they come. Wall Street tough. Ian's more City of London Stock Exchange smooth, a quiet achiever. Both get results. I think you rattled Bob with the questions concerning the loan. I'm surprised he didn't have the answers. His brain's a mainframe of financial detail.'

She pressed a button on the telephone in her office. 'Leila? Could you send in some coffee please?'

'Of course, Miss Buchanan,' came the instant reply.

'So, what do you think our tack should be, Leo? Where to start?'

'I told you when we first met, I'm no PI. You insisted, so I'm just running on instinct right now.'

'And what does it tell you?'

'It tells me we're skirting the real issue. The girl. Why was she there? Who did she know? What was going through her head? Did she have a motive? Was she acting alone?'

There was a knock on the door, and a conservatively dressed woman of about thirty-something entered with a tray of plunger coffee. Rosalind thanked her, and she left.

'I'm going down to South Sydney to see the Bomb Disposal Unit.'

'What can I do?'

'Find Palmer,' said McCann.

'Oh yeah. I get the easy job. Find Palmer. The police have found it impossible but – '

'They don't have your kind of resources. Spend money. You've got plenty, they haven't.'

'You mean offer a reward.'

'That's exactly what I mean. Big time advertising campaign in Hong Kong. You tell me you're serious about getting answers. Well, prove it. They're as venal as sin over there. Appeal to their basest instincts.'

'I wouldn't have picked you for a racist, Leo,' Rosalind murmured. It wasn't a reproach, more a point of interest.

'I'm not. I have been to Hong Kong, though. And you'll have to offer them more than the usual thirty pieces of silver.'

'Okay. Sure. The money means nothing. I'll take a full page in the *South China Morning Post* and the *Sin Tao*.'

'Television?'

'You usually have to buy airtime ahead. I'll see.' She began to make notes. 'What exactly should I say? 'Have you seen this man?' That kind of thing?'

'Just a photograph of Palmer – most recent. His name in bold across the top. Underneath the word 'Where?' Under that the reward and a phone number. Better make the reward big, and you'd better expect a whole heap of crank calls, so engage extra staff and get the phone people in to hook up some dedicated lines for the number.'

'What makes you so interested in Palmer?'

'I don't know. He could have nothing to do with your father's death, but a criminal fraud of that magnitude so close to the bombing is worth looking into. Maynard's dead, so is Andrew Horan, a prominent banker. Palmer is missing, as is one hundred and eighty-five million dollars. See what I mean?'

'Maybe,' she replied.

The speaker phone interrupted them. 'Excuse me, Miss Buchanan. I have Rupert Gerson on the line. He insists it's very urgent. Shall I tell him you're in a meeting?'

'No, please put him on Leila.'

'Good morning, Rupert,' she said placing her hands on the desk, leaning forward over the phone.

'Rosalind. I'm relieved to have caught you. I'm afraid something rather terrible has happened to Whitey. She's in hospital in a coma. They tell me she's not expected to live.'

The blood drained from Rosalind's face. McCann was afraid she might collapse, so he quickly moved to her side.

'What happened,' she asked quickly.

'The reason I called is because of Kerry. As far as I could see, you and Maynard were the closest thing to a family Whitey had, and right now there's no one to look after Kerry, apart from the home help of course.'

'Please tell me what happened,' Rosalind repeated in a stronger tone.

'I don't mean to pass the buck, but – '

She flicked the speaker phone switch, snatching up the receiver. 'For pity's sake, Rupert! Answer my question. What has happened to Whitey?'

'The home help found her this morning when she came to look after Kerry for the day. She found Whitey collapsed in the kitchen. You knew she was a diabetic, I suppose?' he added as an afterthought.

'Of course.'

'Well, from what I can gather, it appears she accidentally overdosed on her insulin. They think she possibly forgot she'd taken the stuff, and gave herself a second dose. She then went into a hyperglycemic coma.'

'Where is she?'

'The Royal Prince Alfred Hospital.'

'Thank you for contacting me, Rupert,' Rosalind said quickly. 'I'll see to Kerry, leave that with me.'

She turned to McCann, her eyes burning with anger. 'Someone did this to Whitey, take my word for it.'

'Did what,' asked McCann.

'Someone tried to kill her. I know it.'

McCann drove Rosalind to the Royal Prince Alfred Hospital. Whitey was in a private room at the rear of the building. She had not regained consciousness.

Rosalind sat with Whitey for a while, then joined McCann and the attending physician, Toby Wiseman, in a consulting room two floors down.

'I wish I could be more optimistic, Miss Buchanan. However, it's probably more useful to tell you what you can reasonably expect. We have to wait and see. The amount of brain damage is unclear at present. I spoke to her doctor very shortly after her admission. You were aware she had diabetes mellitus?'

'Yes.'

Rosalind had her arms folded in front of her in an attempt to control her nerves, but McCann could see her whole body was trembling.

'Late-onset diabetes – she developed it twelve years or so ago,' Wiseman continued. 'She'd been treating herself. Forty-two units in the morning, twelve units at night. Of course this could vary a bit depending on the morning sugar test.'

'Could this explain her condition?' McCann asked.

'That she made an error with the sugar test, and injected a bit too much? No, I think not. It would require a quite substantial dose to cause this much damage. No, I would say she simply forgot she'd injected, and did so again within a very short time.'

'Rubbish,' Rosalind said shortly.

To give the man his due, Wiseman didn't take obvious offence – he was probably used to distraught relatives.

'I have attended cases exactly such as this before, I assure you Miss Buchanan. It is not so uncommon,' he replied equably.

'She would not have made such a mistake, Mr. Wiseman. She has the sharpest mind of anyone I know. She can carry pages of figures in her head for weeks. She could certainly remember what she did a few minutes ago.'

'Long term memory's one thing, short term quite another. To put it simply, she's over sixty, and her doctor informs me she'd been to see him two days ago, complaining of incontinence, fatigue and a lack of appetite; all of which are symptoms of high blood sugar.

If she'd become disorientated in the early hours of this morning, I can see just such a thing happening.'

'How much insulin was in her body, doctor?' McCann asked calmly to balance Rosalind's abrasive manner.

'It's difficult to estimate precisely. A blood test revealed a very large dose indeed.'

'But could you quantify it, Mr. Wiseman,' Rosalind insisted.

'We had no means of knowing how long Miss Whitehead had been unconscious. Insulin dissipates within the system, so an accurate measurement to within a few units is practically impossible. If she had died, it would have been a different matter.'

'Shame, eh,' Rosalind muttered.

'However, the police informed us they had found Miss Whitehead lying in the kitchen,' the doctor continued, despite her rudeness. 'On the sink was her medical bag, in which she kept her Isophane. Beside it was a used needle. Upstairs in the bathroom was another used needle. The inference seems clear to me.'

'It may be to you, doctor. Not to me. With respect, I know her personally, you don't. Were there bruises on her body?'

'Bruises where?' Wiseman replied, confused.

'Just bruises, doctor!'

'Please, Miss Buchanan, though I appreciate you're under some strain, I would ask you to lower your voice.'

'I think Miss Buchanan is intimating that there might have been visible signs of a struggle if someone else had injected the insulin against her will.'

'If recent bruising had become apparent during Mrs. Whitehead's examination, they would have been noted. However, I was there, and there were none that I could see.'

'You weren't looking for any, were you doctor.'

'I had no reason to, Miss Buchanan, I was too busy saving her life. Something I achieved – against all probability.'

'Tell me, will she live?' McCann interposed evenly. He could see the doctor was at the end of his rope. He didn't deserve to be at the wrong end of Rosalind's tension a minute longer.

The doctor took his eyes off Rosalind, where they'd been locked for over a minute.

'Mrs. Whitehead's condition is now reasonably stable. The tachycardia is under control, but as I said earlier the coma is another matter.

'It's possible she double-injected.'

It was McCann who broke the silence as they drove in Rosalind's car from the hospital to Birchgrove.

'Bullshit. She didn't double inject. She's not a stupid old woman. It's Kerry who's suffering from Alzheimer's, not Whitey!' McCann could see she was on an emotional knife edge.

'So someone injected her with a massive dose of insulin against her will?'

'Right.'

'And what was she doing while they stuck in the needle? If she was asleep, you'd think she'd wake up. And if awake, she'd protest. Yet there were no obvious bruises.'

Rosalind's head snapped round to face McCann.

'Leo, my life was turned over and emptied of everything when my father was murdered. Before that, I was a pretty normal person. Spoilt rotten, I expect – but normal nonetheless. I was happy - even contemplating marriage and children. Within a few seconds of Ian's call all that changed.'

She took a breath and continued at an ever-increasing intensity. 'Let's just recap for a moment. Remember two days ago? I told you that Whitey had called me, asking for my help, telling me she had some information she thought was relevant to daddy's death. She was frightened, right? Actually, scared is a better way to put it, though she wouldn't have admitted it. Scared because it appeared Andrew Horan had uncovered what looked very much like a major financial conspiracy. Remember?'

'That's what you told me, yes.'

'Yet this morning I'm asked to believe that a woman who had a brain as fast, if not faster, than the average personal computer injected herself by accident with a lethal dose of insulin? That's bullshit! I don't buy it! So *you* better tell me how they did it to her!'

McCann turned the car into Wharf Road, Rosalind's words echoing round the car. Betty was at the door to meet them.

'It's quite terrible. Tell me at once, Miss Buchanan, how is Mrs. Whitehead?'

'She'll be fine, Betty. Let's go inside. Have you said anything to Kerry yet?'

'Nothing. Thought it best not to. He's in the back garden on his hands and knees amongst the weeds.'

Inside the drawing room Betty offered them coffee which they both declined.

'You found Whitey this morning?'

'That's right. I arrived at 8.30. I went to the kitchen to make Kerry a hot drink, and she was lying there. I called the ambulance at once.'

McCann rose. 'I think I'll see how Kerry is.'

Kerry craned his head up as McCann approached and began to speak in a theatrical tone. '*Tis an unweeded garden, that grows to seed. Things rank and gross in nature possess it merely.*'

'You have a fine garden, Kerry. Do you look after it all by yourself?'

'That's "Hamlet". The Dane's not referring to gardens, you know. He's speaking metaphorically. But I'd say a man such as yourself would know that.'

McCann watched as Kerry pulled out large clumps of lavender, tossing them onto the path.

'Are you certain you should be doing that, Kerry. They look so fine.'

He gave an impatient shrug. 'Weeds. All weeds. Now if you don't mind, I'm a bit rushed this morning so I've no time for idle chit-chat.'

McCann squatted down beside the old man. Kerry looked anxious and apprehensive, sliding him furtive looks.

'Whitey's going to be away for a few days. Betty'll be here to look after you during the day, and another woman will be living-in for a while. That's what Rosalind has arranged. I hope it's convenient.'

The old man's reaction was startling. 'Please don't let them take me,' Kerry whispered suddenly, his eyes filling with tears. 'Don't let them put me in a dreadful home. I'm not stupid, you know.'

McCann put an arm round Kerry's shoulders. He was clearly terrified about being taken into care. 'Take it easy, Kerry. It's all right. You can stay here. No one's going to force you into a nursing home. We're all here to help you.'

Quite abruptly Kerry stood, hugging McCann to him in desperation, burying his head into the younger man's shoulder as sobs racked his body. '*O let me not be mad, not mad, sweet heaven! Keep me in temper; I would not be mad,*'

McCann held Kerry's thin frame and they rocked together for a few moments on the garden path. McCann could feel the tension flow from the old man as he held him. Then just as suddenly, Kerry struggled to free himself as a Siamese cat would, suddenly tired of being petted. He wiped his eyes on the sleeve of his shirt as he gazed out into the bay.

'It's a terrible thing you know when the fog clears, and you drift back through the soft mists of ignorance, towards the clear air of sanity. There, one is faced with terror. The terrible mirror of dementia.' The words were tinged with no self-pity. It was a statement of fact. He looked back towards the house, and his eyes glazed again. 'Poor thing,' he added sadly.

Suddenly McCann was listening hard. Kerry was no longer raving, he was trying to tell him something.

'Who's a poor thing, Kerry?'

'They came for her, and they'll come for me.'

'Who?' McCann coaxed gently.

'I was waiting for my tea,' Kerry replied, oblivious to the question. 'Tea first thing, always the same. The staff took for ever to come, so I thought I'd make my own.'

Kerry dropped onto his knees and renewed his attack on the lavender.

'They came for her?' McCann whispered into the old man's ear. 'Who came for her?'

'Mr. Butterworth, I expect,' Kerry replied, looking around furtively for imagined spies. 'He's a dancer, you know. Came with a partner.'

'There were two men in the house this morning? Before Betty arrived?'

'Men don't dance together!' Kerry exploded. 'Whatever will you suggest next. A lady. Before Betty arrived. Yes, of course! They danced with Whitey for a while. Round and round. I watched them but they didn't see me. She became tired after a bit and had to lie down. Went to sleep in the kitchen! When they left, I made my tea myself. Had to.' He turned to McCann, smiling again, then lashed out at the lavender.

'Please excuse me one minute, Kerry. I have a call to make.'

McCann stood pulling the card that Torrance had given him from his wallet and dialing the number.

'May I speak to Detective Superintendent Torrance please? My names Leo McCann.'

Thirty seconds later Torrance was on the line.

'What can I do for you today, Mr. McCann. I have to tell you I'm really up to my eyes at the moment.'

'I think I may have something important for you. Something needs to be done at once, and I can't set the wheels rolling myself.'

'You sound excited, Mr. McCann.'

'Please give me one minute of your time.'

'A minute, then.'

'Mrs. Whitehead was Andrew Horan's personal private secretary. She shared a confidence two days ago with Rosalind Buchanan to the effect that Horan had uncovered some financial hanky-panky at the Australian Pacific Investment Bank. She was frightened. A couple of hours ago she was admitted to the RPA in a coma. Insulin overdose. The doctors think it was self-administered accidentally. I know to the contrary.'

'Know or believe?' Torrance attempted.

'Believe - but please allow me my minute. I'll tell you why I'm so sure later. I believe she was visited very early this morning, and injected with a paralyzing drug. She was then given a lethal dose of Actrapid or some similar fast acting, fast dissipating, insulin.'

'Quite a hypothesis. So what do you ask of me?' Torrance stated quickly.

'Not a great deal. It's just something that I can't insist on, and something that might either confirm or deny my conjecture. Please bring pressure to bear on the hospital to test Imogen Whitehead for the presence of tubocurarine in her system.'

'Jesus, McCann, how the hell do you spell – '

'It's a synthetic form of Curare. Mention that, then they'll know what you mean. But you'll have to act quickly or it'll be through her system before they can get a blood sample.'

'I'll do what I can, McCann. Hope you're not going to make me look too foolish.'

'And most importantly, make them check for puncture marks. Won't be easy, she's been using insulin for years. Use your imagination. Someone held her and gave her a shot. I'd bet my boat on it. Check any muscle tissue, possibly the buttocks. Tears in her nightdress, maybe.'

'I'll be in touch, McCann.'

As he put the receiver down, he noticed Rosalind standing by the door watching him.

'You heard?'

'Yes, I did. Was it something that Kerry told you?' she said calmly.

'Something like that, yes.'

'What's Curare?'

'If you want to stick someone with a needle of insulin, you have to be sure they won't react, shout or scream for help while the drug takes effect. Unless you're prepared to tie them down, or fight them until the drug takes over, and that would leave marks, bruises etc.'

'How long does it take for insulin shock to set in?'

'I've no idea. But I can't imagine it happens immediately. I wish I'd asked Wiseman. I'll call him later.'

'So how did they do it?' asked Rosalind.

'My guess is that they surprised her – Kerry's been talking of a man and a woman. While the man held her for no longer than a couple of seconds, the woman gave her a shot of a muscle relaxant. It takes effect almost immediately, causing paralysis. Doesn't effect the consciousness though. Whitey would still have been in terror, but quite unable to move. Then they gave her the shot of Actrapid, the fast acting insulin, and they kept giving her the tubocurarine till the insulin kicked in.'

'But what's Curare exactly?'

'A poison made from plants by the South American Indians that paralyses the motor nerves. Tubocurarine is the synthetic counterpart they use during surgery today.'

'What makes you so sure of this?'

'Look, I'm not. And Kerry may just be talking nonsense. But you're sure she would never have self-injected in error. Right?'

'Right.'

'And if someone broke into her house and threatened her, she'd have struggled, wouldn't she?'

'She would. No doubt of that, she's a tough old bird.'

'Okay. Remember you asked Wiseman if there were any bruises, and he said he hadn't seen any?'

'Of course I do.'

'Well, I've used this stuff before. The Tubocurarine. When I was in the search and rescue business. Invaluable if we had to pull someone out of harm's way fast. We'd stick him with half a milligram of the stuff and carry him out. No struggle, no muss, no fuss.'

'Does it kill?'

'That's not what we used it for. But it can, yes. Unfortunately, I have a feeling that it breaks down so quickly in the body we may have missed it already.'

'Then let's hope Torrance isn't too late.'

12.

May 16th

'I have a man here named Leo McCann. He has a letter of authority, but I just thought I'd double check, sir.' Brancusi listened for a few seconds, before adding. 'Right. Thank you, sir.'

Brancusi replaced the receiver. 'No need to take offence, Mr. McCann. 'I like to check. Don't trust any signatures at face value these days. These are very sophisticated times.'

'No offence taken, Mr. Brancusi.'

'Ray.'

'Ray, it is.'

McCann sat opposite Brancusi in the Zetland Bomb Squad prefab. He'd hoped the atmosphere was going to be informal, rather than 'interview by the rule book'.

'Chief Superintendent Torrance has asked me to share my stuff with you, so what can I interest you in?' Brancusi leant back in his chair, putting his feet up on the desk. McCann leant forward. This was a step in the right direction.

'Could I look through the photographs?'

'Sure. I thought you'd seen them.'

'I have. At Task Force Acorn. But if I could go through them again with you, I might see something I missed the first time. It's often the case.'

'You were in the job once?'

'Not the force. The army. Intelligence. My experience has told me that one man sees one thing, another something else entirely. Together they see things they'd both miss individually.'

'Okay, why not? But I've been looking at the bastards for days already,' said Brancusi standing. 'Follow me.'

Brancusi led the way to a room at the far end of the main area.

Inside, the walls were covered with cork boards. Some carried photographs of the burnt-out shells of cars, others damaged buildings. On the wall facing the door was a five-foot-square board on which were fixed photographs of the Savoy Hotel bombing. They were pinned up in sequence, mirroring the path Brancusi had taken round the room from right to left when he'd initially gone in looking for secondary explosive devices.

'There's no doubt the girl was carrying the explosive?' McCann asked, scanning the first few snaps.

'None whatsoever. The lower torso was vaporized. This, together with the upward degloving of the upper body skin was the clearest indication of explosives carried around the waist.' He turned to McCann, who'd put on his reading glasses and was studying the photos from a distance of only a few inches. 'Are you familiar with my terminology, Mr. McCann?'

'Leo. And yes, I am.'

'Sure. Leo.'

'Looking at these photographs, it'd be a pretty safe bet to assume that she could have seen everyone in the room when she detonated.'

'I'd say so. Nowhere for anyone to hide. She could see them all.'

'So she either wanted them *all* dead, or she didn't much care one way or the other *who* died?'

'Looks that way.'

McCann nudged still closer to the photos.

'I use a magnifying glass to look at the detail. Like to borrow it?' Brancusi offered, reaching in to a drawer and pulling one out.

'Thanks, I would,' McCann replied, taking it from him.

'One thing, while I think of it. You just said, as if it were a fact, that she'd pulled the plug on the device. I happen to think it's possible she didn't.'

'Didn't detonate the device herself?'

'That's right.'

Brancusi took a pencil from his inside pocket and tapped one of the photos.

'See here. We now know the explosive was in a belt round her waist. We know this from tissue and explosive residue samples taken from the upper torso, some deeply embedded. Also fiber samples of the belt.'

'How was the device triggered?'

'Hold on, I'll get to that. But first the blast pattern. The epicenter was three feet into the room from the doorway. The female's here.' He tapped the photo. 'You can see the torso on its back, the face up, as if she's been thrown up and backwards by the blast. The hole in the floor in this photo,' he said pointing to the one on the right, 'is approximately three feet across.' Then Brancusi tapped a spot on the following picture, which was detail of the area round the hole. 'See that?'

McCann focused on the exact spot Brancusi was highlighting. He could see what appeared to be a small fused lump of metal and plastic. 'What is it?'

'Cellular phone. We were able to take partial prints. We also checked with Mobilenet. It's her phone. Now look over here.' He moved a couple of feet to his right, directing McCann's attention to some detailed photographs of wires and metal fragments.

'This is what's left of the girl's belt. This is part of the wiring, and this a fragment of the detonator.'

'Military.'

'That's right. You'd know them well as an army man – silver with white leads. Now this here.' He tapped again with the pencil. 'This is what we believe to be a tiny fragment of the bridge wire. And here,' he said, now some real excitement in his voice, 'here we have the remains of the triggering switch.'

McCann stared through the magnifying glass, but could hardly confirm the twisted fragment of metal as anything remotely resembling a trigger or switch. 'That's a switch?'

'I've seen plenty. That's a switch, and it's in the "off" position. Believe me, Leo. It's definitely off,' he finished triumphantly.

'If she never pulled the switch – '

'An accident,' Brancusi cut in quickly. 'She didn't mean to kill them. See the cellular phone in this picture here? There's scarcely any of it left. Now look really closely here. Maybe I only think I can see it because I've had it analyzed by the lab boys. But the final cut is the fact that the aerial of the phone is fused to the triggering switch. Somehow it made contact, and up she went.'

'What are you saying? That she had a belt full of plastic round her waist for the fun of it, or that she changed her mind about detonating it, but that it went up by accident anyway?'

'The latter. Torrance says we have insufficient detailed evidence to prove the phone made the circuit complete, and strictly speaking that's accurate. I just happen to believe that's what happened.'

McCann was silent.

'Maybe the phone set off the explosive before she had time to do it herself,' Brancusi suggested.

'Or maybe she entered the room, and something she saw made her change her mind, but the explosive went up anyway through sheer bad luck.' McCann said, walking back to the first series of photos and beginning to re-examine them.

'You found no secondaries?'

'None.'

'Anything in the room that shouldn't have been there?'

'Surprisingly few personal effects. No briefcases at all - one might have expected at least one among three businessmen. The remains of a personal computer.'

'Where is it? Which photo?' McCann interrupted, searching for the relevant snap.

'Here.'

'Who's was it?'

'Still unconfirmed. It was a Macintosh Powerbook G4.'

'Horan's?'

'He owned one. Doesn't mean it's his though. Look, you can see there's not much of the bloody thing left. The case is fragmented all over the place. What we're left with is a part of the keyboard, a fragment of the motherboard, and the floppy drive mechanism.'

'Serial number?'

'Blown away with the back of the case.'

'Have the tech boys given it a thorough going over?'

'Of course. None of the data's recoverable.'

'Floppy drive?'

'There's a disk in there, but it's completely fused to the shell.'

Under the photo of the shattered remnants of the computer were detailed photos of the sides and top. One of them was of particular interest to McCann. On careful examination he could just see a flash of blue within the floppy drive.

'Doesn't look so bad to me.'

'The disk? Not from the outside, but believe me it's pulp inside.'

'Anything else of interest?'

'Only a plastic computer disk container. Empty.'

155

'Did you find the disks somewhere?'

'No. There were none in the room. We looked, I can tell you. We sifted every damn piece of shrapnel in there. Could have been blown out the windows, or sucked out as the vacuum kicked in, but I don't see it happening. Besides we sifted all the debris outside as a matter of course.'

'Didn't that strike you as odd? A computer with a disk in the drive, and a container that was empty? Why would anyone carry an empty container?'

Brancusi shrugged.

'Where exactly was it found?'

'Under the Asian fellow. Well, jammed halfway under his body. Doesn't mean it's his, though. You've got to remember the force of the blast.' He pointed to another photo. 'It's here.'

McCann looked. It was a clear plastic box with the lid peeled back. As Brancusi had stated, it was empty.

'How come it's not as badly damaged as the computer?'

'Could be any number of reasons. Maybe something sheltered it from the blast. For instance, if it was in one of the victim's pockets, and that pocket was facing away from the epicenter, it might be thrown across the room as the jacket shredded, but remain reasonably intact.'

McCann was about to turn away, when something in the photo caught his eye. He looked even more closely through the magnifying glass at a spot between the empty box and the elbow of the Asian. The dead man's side and arm were drenched in blood, and there were three quite distinct pools of blood on the carpet by his side. Just to the left of the edge of the pool closest to the man's knee, was what appeared on first examination to be a smudge.

'Look at this, Ray. What do you make of this?' He took Brancusi's pencil, placing the lead tip exactly on the smudge. Brancusi examined it for a few seconds.

'A smudge of blood, that's all. It's sprayed all over the room. What's so special about that bit?'

'Look again. The blood has formed in a pool from the lower abdomen of the victim. Then something has been placed on top of the blood, thereby smudging it.'

'Maybe something fell on the blood; dislodged minutes later as the debris settled.'

'I don't think so, Ray. I'd lay a bet that is the smallest portion of a shoeprint.'

Brancusi looked at McCann, then to the photo, then back to McCann. He was puzzled as hell.

'I was the first person in there, Leo. And I sure as hell didn't tread in any obvious pools of blood. Nor did I move any debris.'

'I take your word for it, Ray.'

McCann looked again at the smudge, surprised that no one had seen it – more importantly, that no one had interpreted it correctly. He'd tracked a man across the Brecons in Wales during paratroop training as a young man with less than there was in the photo to go on.

Brancusi was still staring at the photo. 'I'll give Noddy a call. He'll check it out.'

'If you would, Ray. I'll leave it to you to call Torrance. Better coming from you than an outsider like me poking his nose in, eh?'

'Understood.'

'One more thing you might look into. Get Noddy to take a very close look at the computer. See if it looks as if any attempt was made to extract the floppy.'

'They'll probably have taken it apart themselves by now.'

McCann interrupted. 'No, I mean by someone else, either immediately before you checked out the conference room, or later in the evidence room.'

Brancusi looked puzzled. 'Before?'

'That's right,' replied McCann.

The traffic was murder. The sun was now beating down and it was as if the population of Sydney had decided to take the day off work and enjoy the glorious autumn weather. McCann was stopped halfway up Grovesnor Street, a cement truck blocking both lanes up ahead.

He pulled his phone from his pocket, punching in Rosalind's private line. Two rings and he was through.

'McCann here. I've just finished a meeting with the bomb guy, Brancusi. He's got some pretty radical ideas.'

'Like?'

'He thinks the detonation was an accident. The girl had a phone on her. Brancusi's theory is that it rang while the aerial was in contact with the lead wires of the detonator, and it thereby completed the circuit. End of story.'

'She turned herself into a walking time bomb, yet your bomb man says she didn't mean it? Bullshit!'

'Hold on. He's thinking she maybe changed her mind, that's all.'

'Maybe the short circuit changed it for her.'

'Yeah, that's possible too.'

The car ahead moved an inch forward and the driver behind leant on the horn. McCann ignored him.

'Two things I should tell you,' McCann continued 'First, I'd bet a lot of money there was someone in the conference room nosing around just after the blast.'

'Doing what, for Christ's sake?'

'That's what we've got to work on. Let's remember that whoever it was must have entered and left within seconds of the blast. You'd think anyone within a mile of the place would have run like shit in the opposite direction, yet this man, or woman, moves directly towards the blast site and walks in.'

'What makes you think there *was* such a person?'

'A smudged footprint the police missed.'

'It's definite?'

'No, but I'd bet on it.'

'Could whoever it was have been trying to help the injured?'

'Doesn't look that way. Only one print that I could see. The guy's being really careful, making damned sure he doesn't advertise his presence. Then he walks out without a word to anyone. No, he's not there to help.'

'How long did this person have to search the conference room before the police cleared the hotel?'

'Minutes. Ten at the most.'

'So what was he doing there?'

'He wanted something.'

'Wanted to see if those inside were alive or dead?'

'Perhaps. Or knew they were dead. He wanted something they had.'

'I don't follow your line of thought, Leo.'

'The Asian was found without any identification. The others both had wallets, but the Asian didn't. As yet Torrance has no idea why.'

'So?'

'Suppose our mystery guy was on his way up anyway to join the meeting, and missed the explosion by seconds. He at once realizes no one inside could have survived, but doesn't want the authorities to identify one of the bodies.'

'Christ that's a long shot,' replied Rosalind.

'Well, someone was in there, if I'm right about the print. Someone entered seconds after the blast and told no one he was there. He's our link to Mr. Asia. We need to find him.'

The traffic began to move. McCann engaged the gears.

'Got to go.'

'Where to?'

'The Savoy. I need to talk to the doorman.'

'Speak to you later.'

'Sure, later.'

It took McCann half an hour to reach the Savoy Hotel. As the doorman opened the door of the car, McCann slipped a twenty into his hand.

'Look, I'll just be ten minutes. Can you park it close?'

'Sure, no problem, sir.'

'Just one thing. Do you happen to know who was on duty the day of the bombing, March 26th?'

The doorman looked at him with a hint of wariness. 'You're a journalist?'

'No, I'm not. I'm a lawyer acting for the daughter of one of the victims. I was hoping you could spare a couple of minutes.'

'Sure, I can. But I wasn't on. Ted was. He's off-duty. You can have a chat with Mory, the bell captain, though, he's over there. He was on.'

McCann thanked him, slipping him another twenty for good measure.

The man that the doorman had indicated was at his desk to the right of the doors. He looked Maori. He was tall, handsome, around thirty, every inch the professional. He looked up as McCann approached.

'Excuse me, is your name Mory?'

'Yes, sir.'

'Mine's McCann,' he began, holding out his hand, two fifties in the palm. Mory extended his, and like a magic trick the money changed hands. His eyes never left McCann's – he never looked down; it was as if he could judge the denominations by weight.

'Good morning, sir. What can I do for you?'

'Your colleague over there tells me you were on duty the day of the explosion.'

Mory didn't have any of the reticence of his partner. 'That's right. I told the police all I know. Took a long, long time.'

'Can you spare me a couple of minutes?'

'Now?'

'Sure.'

'May have to leave you every so often. Can't just stop working.'

'I understand.'

'Start asking.'

'The police details state there was a young man standing around just minutes before the explosion. He and the dead girl talked as she entered. That's right?'

'No, they didn't talk. More like he tried to say 'hi' to her. Looked as though she ignored him. He'd been hanging around for several minutes. I'd already tried to shake him off. Didn't look good to have a downbeat kid like him hanging around.'

'Did you talk to him?'

'Yes I did, sir. Asked him if I could help him. He said something like he was fine. But he knew what was on my mind, so he moved on.'

'Did you hear what he said to the girl?'

'No, sir.'

'Did it look to you as if they'd just bumped into each other, or do you think they'd planned to meet?'

'Hell, I can't tell. Plenty people in and out here all the time.' He thought for a moment or two, then shrugged. 'Just casual, I guess.'

That's what the police thought too. Just casual. Maybe it was. McCann pulled out the head shot of Mr. Asia that Torrance had given him, passing it to the bell captain.

'Do you recognize this man? He was one of the victims.'

'Holy Jesus! This a dead guy?' Mory looked genuinely shocked.

'That's right.'

He stared at the photo for a few seconds, then stared up at McCann. 'Hell, you get off showing people photos of dead guys?' he said quietly. 'Jesus, that's one sorry thing to do.'

'I apologize, Mory,' McCann said peeling off another fifty, passing it to him. A second later it had found its new home in Mory's trouser pocket.

'Yeah I seen this guy.'

This was news to McCann. There was no record of the doorman having said he'd seen Mr. Asia before the explosion. Why hadn't the police shown the photo to Mory before now?

'When did you see him?' McCann asked.

'Came in a cab.'

'Remember the cab company?'

Mory laughed. 'Give us a break.'

'Okay. Was he alone?'

'Yeah.'

'How come you remember him?'

'Reminded me of someone I knew from way back.'

He took a closer look at the police photograph. 'That's one of the guys that died? No shit?'

'Yes.'

'Don't see how that's possible,' said Mory almost to himself.

'Why not?'

'Well, as I recall, the place blew just a couple of seconds after he went inside. Don't see how he could have gotten to the fifteenth floor in that time. Suppose it's possible. Must have been. The guy's dead, ain't he?'

'Yes, he's dead,' McCann replied.

He had to be, didn't he? That's what everyone kept telling him.

That evening, McCann rang Hendrik Ohlson's home on and off for two straight hours. Just after 10 o'clock the phone was picked up. It was the same woman he'd spoken to before.

'Yes?' She sounded very angry.

'Is that Mrs. Ohlson?' McCann answered.

'Do you realize what time it is? How dare you bother me this time of night.'

'I apologize, Mrs. Ohlson. It is a matter of some urgency. I have to speak to your son. It's a police matter. Do you have a contact number in New Zealand by any chance?'

'Yes I do. And I have no intention of giving it to you, or anyone else, for that matter. Just leave us alone.'

McCann was about to continue but, as before, Mrs. Ohlson just hung up.

Sunday. He'd just have to wait till Sunday.

13.

May 17th

Mrs. Horan looked a broken reed, a ghostlike figure that had given up the will to live. She sat in a greenish Paisley armchair opposite McCann in the drawing room of the Vaucluse Federation home she'd shared with her husband all her adult life. Her hands were resting on her knees, the legs together, the hem of her dress perhaps an inch above her ankles. Her face was drawn with the legacy of a terrible grieving process. She was fifty-eight, yet looked ten years older.

'I know I'm not being a big help, Mr. McCann.' Her Scots accent was as thick as the atmosphere.

'Please call me Leo, Nora.' McCann smiled, trying to bring a little warmth into the winter of Mrs. Horan's world.

She looked a little flustered as she returned his smile. 'Leo. Of course. How silly, I just couldn't remember.' She fidgeted with the cuff of her cardigan. 'Are you certain I can't fetch you a whisky? Andrew loved one in the evening. The single malts were his favorites. I've never taken alcohol myself. I'm a Presbyterian.'

'Maybe I will change my mind. A whisky would be great. Thank you, Nora.'

'Have you any news of Whitey?'

'Nothing fresh, I'm afraid.'

'It's been a terrible time. For us all. My personal Armageddon,' said Mrs. Horan absently as she poured McCann his drink at the sideboard, dropping two cubes of ice in the glass, and topping it up with soda. McCann watched the ritual slaying of the twelve-year-old Scotch with equanimity.

'So you wouldn't have said Andrew appeared unduly worried on his return from Hong Kong.'

'No. Not worried. He took things in his stride. He was a very forthright man, you know. It took a lot to make him break his stride. Funny really. I believe in an afterlife, yet I fear my own mortality. He was agnostic, yet feared nothing.'

'Whitey told Rosalind that Andrew continued working on his paperwork at home on his return from Hong Kong.'

'Yes, he was always very thorough. He did confide in me that he felt he hadn't come up with the goods; felt he'd let Rupert down.'

'In what way?'

'Oh, I don't know,' she replied, looking down into her lap.

McCann did his best not to show his frustration at her whimsy. He wished she'd concentrate.

'Did he discuss his work with you?'

'Very rarely.'

'On this occasion?' he probed. It was like negotiating a Christmas present from Scrooge.

'Not really,' she replied.

'I'm sorry? Not really? You mean he *did* say something?'

'He used to mutter a bit if things weren't going too well. Then again, if things *were* going well, he'd talk aloud to himself in his office. He was a very logical man and I suppose it helped him to talk things through.' Her eyes suddenly twinkled with amusement. 'Like counting out aloud when you're shopping,' she said, smiling broadly at McCann, who returned her smile, without the slightest idea what on earth she was talking about. 'I remember him repeating, *The wheel is come full circle* several times the night he came back from Hong Kong,' she continued. 'The reason I remember his phrase that night is because *King Lear* is my favorite play. I'd just called him in to dinner and he looked unusually jolly. I was glad because he'd seemed so frustrated all evening.'

'What do you think he meant by the quotation?'

'I didn't ask, I'm afraid,' she said fiddling once again with her cardigan. Though McCann felt for the unhappy woman, the conversation was becoming unbelievably frustrating.

'Andrew used a computer?'

'Yes. The police asked me. A Macintosh "Wall Street" Powerbook G3, I believe. Carried it everywhere. They told me it was destroyed.'

'I wonder if I might have a look at Andrew's study. I promise to be careful to avoid anything too personal.'

'Oh that's all right. Don't be silly. Please go ahead. It's down the corridor; first door on the left.'

Books covered the walls of the small room. In a corner stood a set of golf clubs, together with an ancient cricket bat that the banker might have used as a child. The walls were covered with photographs of Andrew, his friends, and several well-known sporting figures. On the smallish desk were two figurines of elephants, a lamp, an antique clock, and an ink blotter.

McCann walked behind the desk, listening for sounds in the hallway. To search Horan's private papers was a blatant invasion of privacy, but there was no alternative.

He'd only promised to avoid anything *too* personal. Well, he'd have to see if he came across any, wouldn't he?

The house was silent, except for the occasional knocking of the hot water pipes.

He reached down, opening the desk drawers one by one. He knew exactly what he was looking for.

Closing the bottom left drawer, he began opening those on the right hand side. He was about to close the second drawer, when a silvered cardboard box caught his eye. It had been slightly crushed by the weight of a stapler.

McCann lifted it out. It was a box of Verbatim three-and a-half-inch micro disks. Inside were six diskettes. Lying alongside them were the color coded identification stickers. Boxes of this kind usually contained ten disks. Six remained, so four had been used. Where were they? Had Torrance searched Horan's desk, and asked himself the same question? Had they once occupied the empty plastic box found under the body of the dead Asian?

He pulled the identification papers from the box and unfolded them, looking for a blue edge. It was missing.

Mrs. Horan was back in the security of her Paisley armchair as McCann re-entered, her face set in resigned despair.

'I haven't been so very helpful, have I?'

'On the contrary, Mrs. Horan, you've been a great help.'

That seemed to cheer her up. 'Have I? I'm so glad.'

McCann held out his business card, which she took. 'If there's anything that comes to mind, something you may remember Andrew having said on his return from Hong Kong; or if there's anything I can do for you personally, please give me a call.'

She thanked him, walking him to the door.

McCann was about to back out of Mrs. Horan's driveway, when his phone trilled.

'McCann here.'

'Len Torrance. Glad I caught you. I thought you'd better know that Miss Whitehead died an hour ago. I was about to call Miss Buchanan, then I felt it might be better coming from a friend. She's had a bucket full of tragedy already.'

'What's the official cause of death?'

'Can't say officially yet. Autopsy's in progress. Heart gave out.'

'Did you act on my call earlier?'

'I certainly did. Believe me, if there's anything to find, Eric Grompard's your man.'

'I hope so,' McCann replied. 'Thanks for calling.'

'I'll let you know if he comes up with anything. Keep in touch, eh?' Torrance seemed genuinely grateful for McCann's help.

'I will. Thanks for calling,' McCann replied.

Torrance rang off. McCann sat in the car for a few moments. A couple of weeks ago, he'd been bringing L'Echapper Belle into Sydney, beating hard into the wind without a care in the world, blissfully unaware of young girls who strapped plastic explosives to their waists; and multi-million dollar petrochemical frauds. Now Imogen Whitehead was dead, injected with a lethal dose of drugs in the security of her own home. In many ways, compared to these events, a search and destroy mission in Northern Iraq was chopped liver.

He pulled out his cell phone and punched in Rosalind's number.

14.

May 17th.

The evening was still and humid. Unusually so for this time of year. McCann slapped at his ankle; the mosquitoes had been as big as dragonflies this year. In the creek they never gave up, regardless of the seasons. He looked down at the smudge of blood and swore.

On his way through the kitchen he picked up a can of bug spray from the Welsh dresser, and a bottle of Corona from the fridge.

In the bedroom he pulled off his shirt, stepped out of his Levis, and sat on the bed in his boxer shorts, spraying his arms, neck legs and feet. Then he reached for the phone. As he'd expected Task Force Acorn was still on-line even though it was past six-thirty.

'Leo McCann here. Could you put me through to Mr. Torrance?'

'Evening, Mr. McCann. It's Maggie Blackwood. He's just stepped out of his office. I'll see if I can catch him for you.' She sounded quite happy to hear from him.

'Hold on, he's just come in.'

'Evening, McCann.' Torrance sounded as though he'd hit the toffees again; a good deal of smacking of the lips was going on. 'Just got in from Glebe. They finished the autopsy twenty minutes ago. They measured the exact amount of insulin present in her body when she was admitted to hospital, but can't be exact about how much was pumped into her – if that *was* what happened.'

'But it looks that way? What does Grompard think?' McCann was excited.

'Well, you were pretty much on the button looking for puncture marks. Two in the left buttock. One looks as though the needle was dragged as it entered, which would tie in with a scenario that she initially pulled away from her attacker as the needle entered. The second mark's clean as a whistle. Grompard was pleased as punch when he found it.'

'What did they pump her with?'

'No trace of anything. Could have broken down before they took the sample. Grompard says tubocurarine's constituents are normally present in the body anyway, so unless a blood test is taken immediately, and unusually high levels of the constituents are found, it would be impossible to tell it had been injected. He also found very superficial bruising on both upper arms.'

'As if someone had held her quite firmly while another injected her?'

'Give me a break, McCann. Just hold your horses, eh? It could have been Kerry holding on to her two days before, for heaven's sake.'

'Could have been, but it wasn't. She was murdered because they didn't know how much she knew, and were afraid she knew as much as Horan. The irony is that she didn't, and they didn't have to kill her.'

'Hold on a damn minute, McCann. Who the hell are *they*, eh? Don't run off at a tangent. Your whole scenario is still purely speculative.'

'The puncture marks are speculative?' McCann shouted incredulously. 'Come on, diabetics don't inject themselves in the bum as far as I'm aware. And the bruises?' McCann listened for reaction but all he could hear at the other end was Torrance masticating. 'Now add that to the conversation she had with Rosalind Buchanan the day before she died.' Chew, chew, chew. 'Look, I know you're not naturally prone to conjecture, but just this once can't you arrive at a conclusion based on the balance of probabilities? The facts are self-evident!'

The silence the other end of the line was palpable. 'And what about Kerry?' added McCann regardless, 'What about his account of the two people who came to the house?'

'McCann,' Torrance began calmly, 'I interviewed Kerry Whitehead myself only a couple of hours after his wife was admitted to hospital, and he made absolutely no mention of anyone *dancing* with his wife in the wee small hours of the morning. Now, before you say anything, let me just say I'm not for a moment suggesting that he was making it up. But what I *am* saying is that the man is in the final stages of Alzheimer's, and I will not give his statement any more credence than someone telling me he's seen fairies at the bottom of his garden. Maybe you caught him in a lucid period, maybe not. That's debatable.'

McCann cut in. 'Wait a minute, let's get this straight. Do you agree there's some evidence of foul play involved in Whitey's death.'

'On the balance of probabilities, perhaps,' Torrance said grudgingly. 'But I like to take things step by step. You're already talking of conspiracies and hired assassins. You probably already have a list of suspects.'

'Maybe.'

'Well, slow down, eh? Hell's bells, you seem to think I'm ignoring the obvious conclusions. I do *not* do that – ever. I hear what you're saying, and I can see the lines along which you're thinking. But I will not leap to conclusions based purely on circumstantial evidence. In the meantime, I've ordered a house to house in Wharf Road in case anyone saw the couple – that is, if they ever existed.'

'They did. Maybe no one saw them. But they did.'

Torrance ignored the remark, as his manner suddenly changed, together with a new thought. 'Which brings us to another matter. I wish you wouldn't take me for a complete ass. If you want to ask me a favor, please ask me yourself. I've been quite accommodating up till now, haven't I?'

McCann was confused. 'Very. What have I done?'

'If you wanted the lab boys to check the entire crime scene photogrammetry for footprints we might have missed the first time, why not ask me? It's a very expensive procedure, and I have to authorize it. I know bloody well it's you who put the idea in Brancusi's head.'

'Sorry, sir,' McCann replied in a adequately chastened tone.

'As it happens on this occasion, you've no call to be. In fact I'm very grateful indeed.'

Immediately McCann knew what he was talking about.

'The footprint?'

'The footprint. The lab boys worked back from the original neg, coupled with the video from the photogrammetry. There's no doubt it was a partial of a size nine European shoe print. From the configuration of the debris and the smudged blood, they're almost certain it was made by someone's entry after the explosion.'

'No other signs of prints?'

'Several minors. Three more near the Asian, one by the computer, and one by the girl. They're so small, you'd have to be looking for them specifically to notice them. That's why I'm grateful. You've got a very lateral mind, Mr. McCann. What made you look for it?'

'Just a hunch,' McCann lied, ribbing the Yorkshireman. He hadn't looked for it, the shoe print had just leapt from the photo and bit him.

McCann waited for a reply. There was none – just the sound of a toffee wrapper being untwisted. 'Just one more thing you might find interesting,' McCann said, after a few moments.

'Oh yes?' Torrance answered guardedly.

'I called Verbatim, a company that makes computer diskettes. You recall that there was an empty plastic container found at the scene of the explosion?'

'Naturally.'

'And the remains of a disk was still embedded in the shell of the personal computer?'

'Yes, it's all on the sheet I showed you, McCann. What's your point.'

'My point's this. When I visited Horan's house, his wife showed me Andrew's study. In his desk I found a pack of Verbatim computer disks. There were six inside, unused. That left four unaccounted for. If we'd found three in the plastic case, and one in the computer it would pretty well have proved what we already believed – that the computer was Horan's. But the plastic case was empty. My hypothesis is that Horan indeed took three disks into the room with him in a plastic box, and that they were stolen by the man with the size nine European shoe print. The same man would have taken the disk from the computer, but he couldn't prise it loose.'

Torrance was silent for a good ten seconds, then he replied. 'Pure conjecture.'

'Of course. But there's just one more thing. I asked the people at Verbatim if the color coded stickers put on the disks were always manufactured in the same sequence. They told me that they were. The fourth from the end is colored blue, which leads me to think that the three disks in the box were used before the one in the computer – the blue one. This means the disk in the computer contained Horan's most current work. That's why I suggested you look for signs of any attempt to prise the disk from the housing.'

'Brancusi asked the guys to take a look, but there was too much damage to the computer. Besides, the disk was fused inside the machine.'

'*We* know that, Chief Superintendent, but maybe he didn't. Still doesn't, I'd imagine.'

'You mean we could play on his interest there?'

'Worth thinking about, no?'

'Indeed. Look, I have to go, McCann. Thanks for your insight with regard to the disks, and for breaking the news of Miss Whitehead to the Buchanan girl. Appreciated. I mean that. Give me a call if there's anything more I can do for you.'

More to the point, what I can do for you, thought McCann as Torrance rang off. He then dialed London. A few seconds later he was through.

'Matthew Hutton, please. Section C-5. My name's McCann.'

'Please hold the line.'

McCann watched Cyclops, the resident one-eyed rainbow lorikeet, as she made slow progress down a limb of the closest tree towards the bedroom verandah, her head skewed to the right, presenting the good eye to the house. The bird was either uncertain of the correct time, or had the patience of Job. When he was home, McCann never failed to feed her at sun-up and sunset. Now it was quite dark and well past dinner time. Too bad, she'd have to wait.

Suddenly Hutton was on the line.

'Leo! How are you! Good to hear from you.'

'Likewise, Matthew. Where the hell have you been? I've been trying to reach you for days.'

'Yes, well, we had a few problems here over the last week. Won't go into too much detail obviously. Let's just say I had a short vacation in East Timor.'

'Very nice. Lots of dark skinned beauties under the palm trees?'

'Lot of palm trees, yes.' Hutton cleared his throat. Possibly his personal private secretary, the redoubtable Miss Macarthy was within earshot.

'Tell me, did Rosie Buchanan ever get in touch with you?'

'She did indeed. Gather you told her I was a gun for hire?'

'Come on, Leo. I was doing you a favor, lad. She's the most beautiful girl I've ever laid eyes on. Known her since she was a child. Knew you'd help.'

'Look, that's no problem. I'm happy to do *you* a favor.' It was important to make it clear who was doing whom a favor. Matthew was a tricky bastard. He'd borrow a pound, then ask for it back the next time he saw you. 'Your part of the deal is to open a few doors for me, as and when it becomes necessary. Okay?'

'Sure thing. What can I do?'

'Nothing too devious. Can you run a name past Latimer? Tell him I need to know UK entry and exit details of a girl called Venice Messon for April to November 1996. Australian passport. My guess would be she didn't stick around in the UK too long. Probably made for East Asia. I know it means involving the Thames House people. See how you feel.'

McCann could hear Hutton mulling it over. His office was in the Vauxhall Bridge building, the home of MI6. The kind of information McCann was after would necessarily involve the assistance of the Security Service, MI5. They operated out of the Thames House building across the river at Millbank. There was nothing worse than calling in a favor over a small search matter, which meant owing one to the Thames House boys. 'I'll see what I can do, Leo. Might ask a pal of mine to help me out there unofficially. When do you need the info?'

'ASAP.'

'Naturally. All right, Leo, I'll get onto it. And keep your fingers off young Rosie. She's too good for you, old boy.'

McCann laughed. There was a beep on the phone - Call Waiting.

'That's all you want right now?'

'Well, it would be a real help if you could follow through a bit. Find out where she finished up.'

'I'll do what I can,' Hutton replied.

'Better go, Matt, I've got someone waiting on the line.'

Suddenly Hutton was gone, and Rosalind was talking at fifty to the dozen.

'Leo. Chen just called me from Hong Kong. He put the ads in the papers. He thinks he's onto the real thing. The phones have been ringing hot since the papers hit the street. He followed up on any that looked possibles, without success till today.'

Richard Chen was the PI Rosalind had engaged through the Hong Kong office to field the reward calls. He had a good track record as a financial investigator.

'Steady, Rosalind, you're talking too fast. Slow down. What makes him think this call's it? Is it from Palmer himself?'

'No. Unfortunately it's not. Chen says the word is that Palmer's history.'

'So who's the caller?'

'A Chinese. Says he's acting for Palmer's boyfriend.'

'Did you know he had one?'

'We knew he was gay, yes. His friend was a young Englishman called Boydell. Chen rang to check the name. The Chinese guy says his client's scared to death. All he wants is some pocket money and a ticket to South America.'

'What do *we* get?'

'He says his client knows plenty. Chen wanted to interview him personally. I told him to wait till you got there – that you'd do it. Didn't please him much. But he sounds pretty sure of his source. The informant told Chen that if we were disappointed, we didn't have to pay.'

'Confident bastard.'

'Yes, he is. Which made Chen think he's straight up.'

Rosalind sounded pumped.

As McCann heard her draw breath, he knew what the words would be. 'So when do we leave? First plane out is a Cathay flight first thing tomorrow.'

McCann cut in. '*We* don't leave at all. *I* leave. That's what you hired me to do. So it's *me* that leaves, not *us*. Later I tell you what went down.'

Suddenly the excitement evaporated. 'I don't know why I even suggested that. I can't leave anyway. Bradley's flying out tomorrow. Told me I deserved some moral support at Whitey's cremation; it's the day after tomorrow in Bellevue Hill. I think he's right. I need a shoulder.'

'Yes, it's good of him to come. Shame he couldn't have come weeks ago when you really needed him.' The moment he'd spoken, he wished he'd kept his mouth shut. It was none of his business whether or not Bradley Radcliffe should take time off from the campaign trail to look after a fiancée whose father had been blown into the middle of next year. Of course, Rosalind and Bradley weren't yet officially engaged.

'He couldn't have left before the California primary. Theo relies on him,' she answered after a beat. She did a good job of justifying Bradley's priorities, but judging by the tenor of her voice, she didn't succeed in even convincing herself.

'You'll leave tomorrow?' It sounded more like a command, yet was carefully couched as a question.

'When I've had a chance to speak to Chen,' McCann replied, picking up the spirit of her last remark. 'I'm not about to jump a plane just on his say-so. But if it looks good, then it'd be worthwhile. Give me all your contact numbers, phone and fax.'

'Yes. Hold on, I'll find them.' She read the numbers down the line, adding, 'By the way, stay at the Peninsula.'

McCann smiled. He had every intention of staying at the Peninsula, the grand old lady of Hong Kong hotels, possibly one of the finest hotels in the world. It wasn't often he was on an unlimited expense account. If she wanted him over there, she'd have to push out the carpet. Still, it was nice of her to offer, rather than merely pay the bill.

'Thanks, Rosalind, I will.'

'Introduce yourself to the general manager. His name is Robert Bao. Daddy and I were there quite a lot. He'll do anything for you.'

'I'm sure he will.' General managers generally were kindness itself and quite unstinting when it came to ingratiating themselves on their mega-rich patrons.

'Now would you get off the line so I can ring Chen,' McCann added sharply.

'I'll call you.'

'I know you will.'

'Is there a shred of anything you haven't shared with me since this afternoon, Leo?'

'No. Not the slightest DNA particle. See you,' McCann said finally, putting the phone down.

Cyclops was now standing on the window ledge, her beak pressed to the glass, the eye wide as a saucer.

'Jesus, give me a break. You'll get fed, trust me.' The bird remained motionless in a frozen gesture of hunger. Had he been able to point to his beak, she would have done so.

McCann leant forward, looking at the numbers he'd scribbled on the corner of the *Sydney Morning Herald*, and began to dial. Hong Kong was three hours behind Sydney. With luck, Chen would be in his office.

One ring later an Oriental voice sang down the line. 'Good afternoon. Richard Chen Associates. May I help you?'

'May I speak with Mr. Chen please? My name is McCann. I am an associate of Rosalind Buchanan.'

'Oh, yes. Please wait. I tell him straight now,' the girl said.

Rosalind was clearly held in great esteem, presumably because she was overpaying Richard Chen hugely.

'Mr. McCann? Richard Chen speaking.' Chen's voice was urbane to the ultimate degree. 'Miss Buchanan told me to expect a call from you. Did she explain the details?'

'Yes, she did. You think the Chinese informant is genuine? That he has something to sell?'

'All he is selling is a guaranteed meeting with Mr. Boydell. It is with Mr. Boydell that we must come to terms; and I have yet to speak to him. Naturally the informant, a Mr. Liu, will not divulge Mr. Boydell's whereabouts until he is paid. A minor sum of ten thousand Hong Kong dollars. Besides, he informs me that Mr. Boydell is so concerned for his own safety he will only speak directly to you at a place of his choosing. This rendezvous will be disclosed to you when you and Mr. Liu meet.'

'We know nothing of Palmer?'

'Nothing from Mr. Liu, to be sure. As I mentioned to Miss Buchanan, it is common gossip here that Mr. Palmer is no longer with us.'

'You mean dead? Murdered?'

'I'd say so,' Chen answered, a trifle patronizingly.

'Let me get this quite straight, Mr. Chen,' McCann began, rising to Chen's hint of rudeness, 'There is as yet no proof that either Liu or Boydell have anything to sell whatsoever. If that's the case, why are you so anxious for me to fly out?'

'Because, Mr. McCann, there can *be* no proof of the contents of a conversation that has yet to take place. However, I would suggest to you that Mr. Boydell has a wonderful tale to tell. At least, that's what Mr. Liu assures me. Boydell has made it plain to him that for fifty thousand Hong Kong dollars, plus a ticket to Buenos Aires, he will name those responsible for the fix he and Mr. Palmer found themselves in when they arrived in Hong Kong. However, Boydell feels his life to be at risk; hence his circumspection.'

It was beginning to look as if Richard Chen knew his business.

'Have arrangements been put in place for payment by Miss Buchanan?' McCann inquired.

'They have. She told me she'd wire the money at the opening of business tomorrow. You'll be at the Peninsula?'

'Is there anywhere else?' McCann replied with more than a hint of sarcasm – he couldn't help himself, Chen's tone was so rich in snobbery.

'I checked simply because Miss Buchanan informed me to that effect; I didn't take it for granted, Mr. McCann.'

Immediately McCann regretted his brusqueness.

'I made a provisional reservation as a matter of courtesy,' Chen said politely, to rub salt into the wound.

'Very good of you, Mr. Chen. I'll call you as soon as I get in.'

'May I suggest the 10 am Qantas flight in the morning? The arrival time here is just after 5 p.m. I shall have a limousine waiting for you. When Mr. Liu calls back, I shall inform him that a meeting with Mr. Boydell in the early evening would be convenient. Have a pleasant flight, Mr. McCann.'

'Thank you, Mr. Chen,' McCann replied thoroughly chastened. 'You've been most helpful.'

'Not at all. Miss Buchanan asked me to fill in the boring travel details for you – the dots and dashes, so to speak. I'm happy to oblige.' Chen could have been taking tea with the Queen Mother.

As Chen rang off, the phone rang again.

'Mr. McCann?'

'Speaking.' Who the hell was this now?

'Meg Poole, Mr. McCann. St James Travel. Your seat is confirmed on flight QF 27 to Hong Kong. Departure time is 10 am. Arrival in Hong Kong 5.05 P.M.. Your first class ticket, together with all necessary documentation will be waiting at the international check-in at Mascot airport. Just present some identification. I have your address, Mr. McCann. Would you like me to arrange a car to take you from your home to the airport?'

'Why not.'

'A car will be at your home at 7.45 am if that's convenient, Mr. McCann.'

'Thank you very much Miss - ' he hesitated.

'Poole. I handle the Buchanan account. If there's anything else I can assist with, please don't hesitate to let me know.'

Perhaps someone to cook him breakfast, McCann mused as he put the phone down. Hell, Rosalind didn't leave much to chance.

15.

Hong Kong
May 18th.

McCann cleared customs at Kai Tak airport Hong Kong and walked through into the concourse. Up ahead stood a Japanese chauffeur with the physique of a sumo wrestler holding a card that read *Mr. McCann*. He was tightly squeezed into a dark blue suit, with a chauffeur's hat one size too small balanced on his head. The giant was scanning the crowd, looking concerned that he might miss his important client.

'That's me,' McCann said, pointing to the sign.

'Great. This the only bag, sir?' the Japanese replied in an unexpected thick Bronx accent.

'Right. Just the one.'

'Cool,' the giant replied, picking it off the cart with the ease a woman would lift a hand bag. 'Mr. Chen's in the limo, sir. My name is Huey.' He held out a hand the size of a joint of beef. 'If you'd just follow me, Mr. McCann,' he added, leading the way out towards the street.

The black stretch Mercedes was parked directly outside the terminal in a strict tow-away zone. Two policemen stood by it. Neither had it in mind to hand out a ticket. Maybe this said something about Chen. Huey opened the rear passenger door and McCann stepped into air-conditioned comfort.

Seated in the corner was a small elegant figure of a man, wearing a black silk Mao suit and highly polished black English Lobb lightweight brogues. His neatly manicured hands were folded on his lap. He lifted one a half inch in a brief gesture of greeting as McCann sat.

'Good afternoon, Mr. McCann. I am Richard Chen. I trust you had a comfortable trip.' He tapped on the thick glass that separated them from Huey. The car pulled out sharply, joining the heavy airport traffic.

'Thank you, Mr. Chen. I had a great trip. Can't fail to in First Class. I've spent most of my life in the back of the bus. Either that or hooked up to a parachute line.'

Chen looked puzzled.

'I served with One Para,' McCann said by way of explanation. Chen's expression did not alter. 'Parachute Regiment,' McCann added for clarity.

'I see,' Chen replied, attempting a smile.

'What time's the meeting with Liu scheduled?'

'Seven o'clock. In Stanley. Are you familiar with Hong Kong Island, Mr. McCann?'

'I've visited quite a few times.'

'Liu wants to meet at Stanley Market. Presumably because there'll still be plenty of tourists about. I'd say he's being cautious.'

Chen pulled two pristine white envelopes from a slim black hide attaché case that lay beside him on the leather seat, passing them to McCann. 'The smaller is for Mr. Liu, the larger one for Mr. Boydell - should you think he deserves it. That's your call. I suggest we drive immediately to Stanley. You can meet with Mr. Liu and set up a rendezvous with Boydell. Hopefully you'll have sufficient time between meetings to check in at the Peninsula. How does that sound?'

'Sounds fine.'

'I thought I'd accompany you over to Stanley and see how things pan out. Who knows, I might conceivably be of some use to you. However, if you'd prefer to be alone - '

McCann cut him short. 'Absolutely not Mr. Chen. My thanks.'

Chen adjusted his cuffs.

There was a moment of silence as the Mercedes dipped into the approaches to the Eastern Harbor tunnel that linked Yau Tong on the mainland to Hong Kong Island.

'You've only spoken to Liu, not to Boydell. Am I right?' McCann enquired.

'Correct.'

'Had you ever heard of the man before?'

'Mr. Liu? Never.'

'Do you think he's a criminal identity of some kind?'

'If he were, I would have heard of him, Mr. McCann. After all, that's my business. My opinion is that it was simply his good fortune that Mr. Boydell needed a conduit to reply to the advertisement published in the newspaper. Mr. Liu was handy, and could be bought.'

'When you told Miss Buchanan the word on the street was that Palmer had been killed, who were your sources? The Hong Kong Police? Informants? General gossip?'

'I have quite a network of informants, as you'd imagine. They're a motley bunch. We heard about Palmer naturally, much in the same way as Nicholas Leeson when Barings Bank got themselves into trouble. Word quickly spread that Palmer was here, but no one ever actually sighted him. One of our leading local 'characters' - you call them 'identities' in Australia - Yun Kwok, swore he'd seen Palmer gambling at Macau, but it was never confirmed. Logically though, it's somewhat unlikely that a man on the run would show up at a casino, putting himself in the spotlight, don't you think?' The question was purely rhetorical. Chen returned to looking idly out the window.

They again sat in silence for a while as the Mercedes swept past Happy Valley Racecourse, and down again into the Aberdeen tunnel that burrowed under the center of the island. The car surfaced again at the tollgates near Wong Chuk Hang to the south west.

McCann studied the slim man as he stared at the bare walls of the tunnel, his eyes dancing with just a touch of resentment. Chen was possibly annoyed that Rosalind had sent her own man to handle the meeting with Boydell. Too bad – he'd have to learn to live with it.

McCann's thoughts turned to Palmer. Was he indeed dead, as everyone supposed? Could he have been a key element in the death of Buchanan and Horan? Only if one believed the girl had been acting on behalf of a third party. Some player or players could well have put a contract on Horan, fearful that the banker's investigations could turn nasty. And Maynard Buchanan? He was in a position to identify the powers behind Palmer in the Malaysia Petrochemical deal. But time and time again he came back to square one; there was no way McCann saw Venice as a kamikaze assassin, acting for a third party. So why did she do it?

The Mercedes flashed down the coast road, past the brilliant blue waters of Repulse Bay, highlighted by the pale lipstick smudgeslicks of the sun setting over Middle Island out to sea.

'How will Liu know me?' he asked Chen.

'There's a small café at the far end of the market. On the corner. As I remember, at the opposite side of the lane sits a wonderfully noble Korean masseur, whom I would recommend to you, had you the time. Sit facing him and drink red wine. Liu will introduce himself.'

The car made a sharp hairpin right hand turn into Stanley Village Road, then accelerated down towards Stanley. Two small Chinese children scurried to safety.

Huey pulled over to the side of the road.

'We'll drop you off here. The market begins over there,' said Chen, indicating Market Road. 'We'll stay here. If you need any help, feel free to give Huey a call – he's not averse to the occasional spot of fisticuffs, and I like to keep him up to scratch when occasion allows.' Chen smiled wickedly. Possibly the man did have a sense of humor after all, thought McCann, albeit a cruel one.

Considering the time of the evening, it was surprising how many tourists still packed the market streets, edging slowly along past the stalls. McCann squeezed in among them, joining the conveyor belt of shoppers.

The configuration of the shops and stalls had changed quite radically since he last visited five years ago, but the merchandise was the same – silk ties, pajamas and shirts, cotton T-shirts, cashmere jumpers, Chinese wooden carvings, and therapeutic metal Happy Balls.

At the end of the pedestrian arcade the street veered left. On the corner was a café, across from which a Korean was busying his long fingers on the shoulders of a female tourist of about fifty. Both had their eyes closed; she was in massage heaven, he in Nirvana.

McCann sat across from them and ordered a red wine, scanning the crowds as they shuffled past. A glance at his watch told him it was a minute past seven.

At 7.20 p.m. McCann was beginning to feel that perhaps there had been a misunderstanding about the time of the meeting. The Chinese go-between, Mr. Liu, would hardly pass up the opportunity of such easy money. Then he noticed a shopkeeper to the left of the Korean cast a sidelong look in his direction.

As their eyes locked, the Chinese smiled, called to a woman at the back of his shop, then walked across to McCann, pulling out a chair and sitting at the table.

'I, Mr. Liu. So sorry keep waiting. You McCann, I know,' whispered Liu, grinning and nodding his head in an obsequious manner. 'Want make sure, you alone. Please understand, McCann.'

'I understand, Mr. Liu.'

'Maybe not, McCann. I take care for my friend. He greatly concerned. Full of fear, my friend.' His face creased again as though this was somehow a cause for amusement. 'Many looking for my friend.'

'Why is that, Mr. Liu?'

'That you must ask my friend. But I can say he has big tale to tell. That is what I say your man Chen.' His expression became abruptly serious. 'You have money for me?'

McCann withdrew the smaller white envelope from his inside jacket pocket, placed it on the table, covering it with the flat of his hand. Liu stared at it, unconsciously wetting his bottom lip with his tongue.

'I would like to meet with your friend tonight, Mr. Liu.'

Liu dragged his eyes from the money. 'Of course. I understand. That is why I here. You know Lamma Island, McCann?'

With the passing of each second, McCann found the servile grinning Liu increasingly obnoxious. 'I haven't been there.'

'You take ferry from Pier One. Not Star Ferry, McCann. Pier One to right of Hong Kong/Macau ferry terminal. You know?'

'Sheung Wan?'

Liu's eyes creased to the merest slits. 'Very good, McCann, in Sheung Wan district. You know Hong Kong very good!'

'Please just tell me the details, Mr. Liu,' McCann cut in.

'Of course, McCann. Take ferry to Lamma. North End, please. Yung Shue Wan, not Sok Kwu Wan. When arriving at Lamma please to walk all way round to right, past all restaurants. There is café called Wing Lok at far end. Very private, very small. Please to eat there. My friend will find you.'

'What time, Mr. Liu?'

'Ten o'clock tonight. This is good?'

'Yes, that's fine,' McCann answered, handing Liu the envelope containing his thirty pieces of silver. 'This money is for you,' McCann said leaning over the table so his nose was less than an inch from Liu's. 'Now let's get something very clear, Mr. Liu. If Mr. Boydell is not where you say he'll be tonight, I'll be a very angry man. Do you understand me? I come see you, quick-smart.'

Liu stood, nodded obeisance without a hint of a smile, then hurried back across the street to the sanctuary of his shop.

'Ten o'clock Lamma Island. Café called the Wing Lok,' said McCann as he climbed back into the Mercedes. He immediately wished he'd kept his mouth shut. Who was to tell whether Chen would sell the information to someone else?

'Would you care for Huey to accompany you tonight?'

'Thank you, Mr. Chen, I think not. I can handle myself.'

'As you wish,' Chen replied affably, then rapped on the glass partition. At once Huey fired up the Mercedes.

Rosalind had left messages at the Peninsula on the half hour ever since five-thirty. McCann estimated the next call would come through in approximately twenty minutes – time enough for a shower and change of clothes. Sure enough, on the half hour the phone rang.

Rosalind wanted to know every detail of the last two hours of McCann's life. He told her frankly that if this was the way she intended doing business, she'd have to find another investigator. She didn't apologize, but merely asked the location of the rendezvous, making him promise to call her on his return to the hotel, regardless of the time.

McCann walked to the Star Ferry along Salisbury Road, Kowloon. A ten minute ferry ride later, he was at the Star Ferry terminal in the Central District of Hong Kong Island. From there it was a short walk to Pier One.

The wind was now blowing quite hard, and the harbor was showing quite a chop. McCann turned up the collar of his jacket. He hadn't expected to feel chilled, the evening had been quite still as he'd left the hotel.

The ferry was rising and falling two to three feet on a building swell as he boarded. Rush hour was long since over, and the old ferry was practically deserted. The wooden seats gently vibrated with the throbbing of the huge diesel engines below.

A seaman walked the length of the side of the ferry that faced the wind, pulling down plastic window shields as spots of rain began to hammer into the side of the boat. He then moved to the other side.

McCann descended the small companionway to the deck below. Behind a small polished wood bar, a weather-beaten old Chinese was selling tea, coffee, chips and soup. A polished metal urn steamed and wheezed to his right. It looked as decrepit as its owner. McCann pointed at the tin of Yunan tea leaves, handed the old man some change, then took the cup of black tea back upstairs, sitting on the rear bench of the boat, a position that gave him a clear view of everyone on his deck.

He checked his watch, it was just before nine. He'd made good time. The crossing to Lamma would take maybe forty minutes.

He looked around at his fellow passengers. A young Chinese couple were cuddling each other a few rows in front. To the right an old man slept, his chin tucked snugly into a scarf. Up forward a group of young Chinese students were laughing and ribbing each other as they drank beers and ate chips. To their right a young European girl chatted happily into her phone, peeling a tangerine dexterously with her free hand.

A horn sounded three times and one of the crew walked to the landing lines either side of the wooden companionway. He freed the ropes, the bridge was drawn back by two wharfies, and the ferry began to ease backwards into the choppy waters of the harbor.

The rain had become distinctly heavy. As McCann settled back to wait out the journey, he was reminded of his nightmare flight with Messon above Bankstown airport.

As the ferry veered to port out of Victoria Harbor, passing between Little Green Island and Kennedy Town on the top western edge of Hong Kong Island, a southerly wind hit the boat head on, sending the bows pitching and tossing eight to ten feet with the swell.

The sea lanes were busy as ever. Every few minutes another vessel would loom out of the darkness; either a ferry making the return trip, a freighter, or a dredger, their prows digging deep into the waves, sending up walls of white water that practically obscured their bows entirely. The European girl he'd seen earlier was now at the stern of the ferry leaning out over the water, her hands hanging at her sides. There was no evidence of the phone, or the tangerine. The other commuters were taking the weather in their stride.

The landing pier stretched a good hundred and fifty yards out from the small village township. Promontories to the north and south sheltered Yung Shue Wan. As the ferry approached the small harbor, the swell abated noticeably. The rain, however, was still knifing down.

McCann looked through the plastic weather-shields of the ferry at the lights of the small fishing village, blurred by the rain. He wished he'd brought a coat.

In the water to the left of the jetty various expensive amphibious toys were moored; spanking new powerboats, slim-hulled speedboats, and fancy launches belonging to the rich. McCann held the lapels of his jacket together, and walked briskly down the long wharf.

Where was Boydell right now, he wondered? Did he live on the island? Or had he taken an earlier ferry? He could have come in a water taxi, though how he intended to leave was another matter. Possibly they'd travel together; the last ferry back to Hong Kong Island was scheduled for 11 p.m.

At the end of the jetty the promenade curved in a semi-circle to the right for half a mile. Various seafood restaurants were situated on either side, their tables and chairs under canvas awnings, the sides protected from the rain by transparent plastic sheeting. Business looked reasonably brisk, despite the bad weather. The patrons were an even balance of eastern and western. All looked affluent. Maybe Lamma Island was commuter heaven for those who couldn't afford the heady prices of The Peak, Wan Chai and Central.

McCann paused as he reached the end of the semi-circle. The road had narrowed from a wide pedestrian walkway flanked on either side by the restaurants, to a narrow pathway sided by cheap homes on one side and the water on the other. Ahead the lane continued for twenty yards, lit by small lamps set into the walls of houses. It then turned left. Here there were no street lights. McCann stared into the darkness; there didn't seem to be any more restaurants or shops ahead.

He walked back a few yards, entered a bar and asked the barman for directions to the Wing Lok café. A young man in an open-necked shirt seated at a nearby table looked up. He was wearing a pin-stripe suit. Beside him was a beautiful Chinese girl, her hair styled in a Gigi cut.

'Right at the end, down the laneway. Stick to the dumplings is my advice. Fish's never too fresh at the Lok. They say old man Kwok's too mean to buy fresh every day. Why don't you eat here? It's frightfully good.'

The beautiful girl at his elbow held out her arms and laughed. Her teeth were white as the cliffs of Dover and her body dangerously perfect.

'Thanks, but I'm meeting someone,' McCann replied, backing out into the street.

Two minutes later he'd found the Wing Lok. The rain had abated, and the half moon was now intermittently visible though breaks in the clouds. It was without doubt the least welcoming restaurant he'd encountered on the Island. Three white metal tables, each complete with two metal chairs, stood by the pathway opposite the door of the café. In the center of each table was an umbrella. A single lamp threw down an inadequate light from the café wall.

McCann stepped through the multi-colored plastic streamer curtain into the café. An elderly Chinese couple was sitting at a table eating white noodles and a whole steamed fish. They were obviously not privy to the local gossip. Behind the bar stood an old Chinese woman smoking a cigarette and chewing something. Despite her empty café, she didn't seem thrilled to see a new customer.

'We closed,' she said, flicking the ash of her cigarette into a full saucer of butts on the bar top.

'I'm meeting a friend here. Perhaps I could order a beer?'

'Beer, yes please,' she replied chewing leisurely. 'Noodles when you want. Fish gone today. All gone. So sorry.' Her expression and tone of voice didn't carry the apparent sincerity of her words. 'Local beer?'

'Local's fine.'

The woman popped the top off a fat bottle of Chinese beer, and slid it across the bar to him. It wasn't accompanied by a glass.

McCann carried it out to the sidewalk, and sat at one of the tables, brushing the rainwater off the seat of the chair. The clouds had thinned dramatically, and the moon shone like an off-white beacon, casting deep shadows across the cobbled laneway.

He'd drunk three-quarters of the bottle when he heard a muffled voice emanate from the shadows to his left. He turned, shading his eyes with his hand from the glare of the moon.

'Boydell? Is that you?' McCann called lightly into the darkness.

In lieu of a reply, a young man of maybe twenty-eight pulled himself up over the seawall. He was dressed in a dark parka and jeans. His fair hair was tousled, and judging by the face dimly lit by the street lamp, the young man looked haggard and full of fear. The eyes were darting left and right. He was breathing hard.

'You're alone?' Boydell said in a hoarse whisper, shifting continuously from leg to leg.

'I'm alone. Sit down. Relax.'

'Easy for you to say,' Boydell said as he sat, dragging the chair round so his back was to the sea wall. 'They're not coming for you.

'Who are *they*?'

'You brought the money?'

McCann pulled the thick white envelope from his pocket, holding it up for Boydell to see. 'It's all there,' he said. He then placed a small tape recorder on the table between them.

The young man eyed the envelope for a second or two, then locked eyes with McCann. 'You tell me to relax,' Boydell said with a hollow laugh. 'You don't know these people.'

'Where's Christopher Palmer?'

'Chris is dead,' Boydell replied simply without emotion, staring out to sea. He then returned his glance to McCann. 'Do I sound cold? Perhaps I do. Fighting for your life is a numbing process. At first I wanted to die too.' He stared hard at McCann. 'I loved Chris. I loved him with all my heart.' He reached across the table, taking hold of McCann's beer bottle, draining the remains. 'I was in the apartment when they killed him. I'd gone to the loo. They can't have realized I was in there – the light bulb had blown in the bathroom. When I'd finished, I heard them, then caught sight of them in the living room. One of them had a cushion over Chris' head while the other was stabbing him with long strokes of a thin bladed knife.' Boydell swallowed hard as he replaced the bottle awkwardly on the table. It tipped over and rolled towards the lip of the table, where McCann caught it. Boydell was oblivious – he was back in the dark recesses of the bathroom watching his lover's stomach ripped open only feet from him in the living room.

'I was terrified.' Boydell wiped his running nose on his sleeve, his eyes red with tears. 'I was petrified.'

McCann looked at the young man. What could he possibly say?

'I knew I had to get out of there. They were sure to check the apartment before they left, and I knew they'd kill me if they discovered me. So I inched back and tried to open the window. But the fucking thing wouldn't move. I pushed and pushed, applying more pressure by small degrees. Then it suddenly gave, but just an inch. I think that's when they must have heard me. One of them called out to the other; I can't remember the words exactly. I fought with the frame, but I couldn't budge it open any further. I couldn't move it!' Boydell's voice had now reached a high-pitched intense whisper, his pupils dilated in terror at the memory. 'So I threw a chair through the glass, smashing the edges with a towel so I wouldn't be cut to ribbons as I pushed myself through. Then I was out and running.'

'Did you see them?'

'I looked back when I reached the end of the street. I saw one of them quite clearly. I was so surprised, I was frozen. Just couldn't move. Stupid. Like a fucking rabbit with a mongoose.'

'Why? Had you seen the man before?'

'Yes.' Boydell stared at a spot in space just above McCann's head. 'Yes. I'd seen him in London. He was Henry Trevor's man. *Sir* Henry Trevor, I should say.'

'Chris has never been found, has he?'

'Not as far as I know. I expect they preferred it that way.'

Boydell ran a hand through his tousled dirty hair. 'I need a drink. Give me the money and I'll buy you one.'

McCann held on to the envelope. 'What would you like? I'm buying.'

'Large Chinese beer and a whisky chaser.'

McCann walked inside. The elderly woman hadn't moved from the spot she'd occupied behind the bar the last time he'd ordered. She looked at him, raising her plucked eyebrows.

'Two beers and a large whisky, please.'

She waved him away with a smile. 'Is okay. I bring.'

'You have sandwiches?'

'Noodles. No bread, please,' she answered popping the two bottles. She poured the whisky into a tumbler, placing the drinks on a cheap beaten metal tray.

'Two times noodles then,' McCann said, adding 'I'll take the drinks with me.'

Outside Boydell was staring down the laneway, tapping the fingers of both hands on the table like a concert pianist. He didn't look up as McCann placed the tray on the table.

'We were fools to think they would keep their word. Why would they? Of course at the time we thought, *my God we're only asking for two million and we're delivering one hundred and eighty five. I mean, Christ Almighty! What did they want?*'

'Your silence.'

Boydell shot McCann a glance. That much was obvious. Boydell drank the Scotch in one, then took a long pull at the beer.

'Trevor was so damned smooth. So charming. He made it all sound so simple and between chums. I remember him saying quite clearly, *Look, we'll never see you again. You'll be in Costa Rica. We trust you, you have to trust us. We both have everything to gain. Division is disaster.* Well, we believed him.'

'It was Trevor's plan?'

'No. Trevor was just the fixer. He pulled the strings; did the organizational work and the hands-on stuff. It was Trevor who persuaded Chris to go along with the scheme. Chris wasn't a natural born criminal, but Trevor was like Iago in Othello's ear. *Easy money, no risk, one shot at easy street.* You see, Chris had met Trevor in London years back, and they'd been kind of pals for a while. Then suddenly he shows up. Before we knew where we were, we were committed, and Trevor made it quite plain there was no turning back.'

'Who did Trevor report to?'

'He and that swine Greville were the two line producers of the organization. Trevor operated out of Jersey, Greville was the boss here in Hong Kong.'

McCann recalled the conversation Rosalind had had with Whitey the day before she'd died. Sir Henry Trevor. Greville. Horan's threats to expose Greville's questionable dealings in the audit.

'Who was the executive producer?'

'We never knew his name. He used to come and go.'

'How often did you see him?'

'Three times. Once in London at Trevor's house, once in St Helier in Jersey, and once in Sydney at a private house. I never spoke to him, neither did Chris. Each time he was there, drifting around at the back of the room watching like a hyena while Trevor and Chris talked out the details.'

'When were you in Sydney?'

'Just over a year ago. No, a little longer. Maybe fifteen, sixteen months?'

McCann reached into his pocket, pulling out his mugshot photos. He took out the snap of Horan, and placed it on the table. It was worth a shot. 'Have you ever seen this man?'

Boydell studied the photo closely, then put it down by the others. 'No. Never.' He absent-mindedly picked up the other photos, shooting a sideways glance at McCann. 'Mind if I look? Who are they?'

'People who died in an explosion in Sydney recently. I'm working for the daughter of this man,' McCann said as Boydell looked at the head shot of Buchanan.

Boydell flipped the photo over then froze. 'That's him!' he said, staring at the photo of the dead Asian. 'That's him, for Christ's sake!' Quite suddenly he was again full of fear.

'Who?' McCann asked, placing a hand on Boydell's arm.

'The Harbinger of Death,' Boydell said quietly, regaining his composure. 'The man who used to watch us. Chris and I called him, the Harbinger of Death. There was something about his smile that scared both of us. The smug bastard just smiled as he wove his web of death.'

'This man is dead.'

'He's not. You're wrong. I saw him ten days ago.'

'Where?'

'In Wan Chai. I was watching the entrance to Wheelock House in Pedder Street. That's where Aust-Pac Finance is. I saw him arrive clear as day. I'd thought up till then perhaps they'd let me go; that if I lay low long enough, they'd lose interest. Seeing him persuaded me otherwise. It was then I decided to get lost permanently. Problem was, I had no money. Then along came the ad in the paper. Saved me.'

'Why Lamma?'

'It was just somewhere to regroup, think things out.'

McCann took back the photo of the Asian. 'Well you're misremembering the face. This man's body is in the Glebe morgue in Sydney. Your man must still be alive. You're sure you saw him ten days ago?'

'Absolutely. It's not a face you forget.'

At that point the elderly woman pushed her way through the plastic curtain carrying two steaming bowls of white noodles. She placed them on the table.

'Two more beers and another very large whisky,' Boydell called after her as she disappeared.

'Has someone actually tried to kill you, or are you just afraid they might.'

'My hotel room was broken into. All my papers were taken. So I moved from hotel to hotel, changing every other day. I hired a car and the brakes were tampered with. I was lucky to survive the accident. A week ago I felt I was being followed. I ran. I could hear his footsteps for three blocks, then I lost him in the subway. They're going to kill me because I know far too much - I saw the man who murdered Chris.'

McCann watched as Boydell drained his beer, then helped himself to the other bottle. 'Maybe you should eat something,' he advised. The man looked wasted.

Boydell pushed his plate away with a look of revulsion. 'Hate this shit.'

'Who arranged the forgeries?'

'The alterations to the letters of credit? One of Trevor's people. He was brilliant.'

'The banks never thought the drawdowns a bit odd?'

'The Harbinger of Death had a tame government minister in Kuala Lumpur. It was his job to soothe the ruffled feathers of the Malaysian bankers when the drawdowns took place.'

'He was paid by Greville or Trevor?'

'Neither. He belonged to the Asian. Deep in his pocket, all the way down to the knees. Look, it's all very complicated. The upshot was that Chris wired the money to a shell company in Hong Kong set up specifically for the purpose via Greville's DTC, Aust-Pac Finance. It was then immediately smurfed to about fifty accounts in offshore banks round the world. Came together again in a bearer corporation in the Caymans, then it vanished, God knows where. Greville took a commission in Hong Kong, as did Trevor in the Channel Islands. Probably everyone along the line.'

'What do you mean smurfed?'

'Well, if you wire a sum as large as a hundred and eighty-five million US dollars, it's going to hit the US Government financial PIs right between the eyes, isn't it.

So you split it into multiples of say five to thirteen million, place it in different shell corporations or front companies that cannot easily be distinguished from legitimate enterprises, shuffle the cash twice round the world till it comes to roost just where you want it. That's the joy of wire transfers. Of course it's not real smurfing. Originally the point was to get round the US ten thousand dollar rule – under that sum the banks had to file currency transaction reports, or CTR's, for anything over ten grand – but that's another story.'

'And the plan for you and Chris was to head for Hong Kong?'

'From Kuala Lumpur to Hong Kong for just three hours transit. Tickets and bearer bonds to be delivered at the airport.'

'What happened?'

'Greville was waiting, but not with the bearer bonds. He said there'd been a glitch; that the bonds would be ready in time for us to fly out in the morning. That night they killed Chris, but missed me. I've been living on my travelers' checks ever since - here on Lamma for the past week in a derelict house I found the other side of the Island. Then I saw the ad in the paper. Liu just happened to be over here with friends a few days ago having dinner. I'd met him before in Stanley, so I asked him to make the call for me. Told him to ask his own fee. No one knows I'm here. Except Liu.'

'How were Trevor and Greville involved with this Asian? Did he pay them a retainer? Was it blackmail?'

'Greville had large overdraft facilities personally guaranteed by the Asian. That was one of the holds he had over the man – that Greville owed him millions. You see the Asian owns his own DTC in Hong Kong called Simtra Finance. My guess is that you can dig for a week but you'll never see his name appear officially on any piece of paper. Greville also received a kick-back in the form of a cheque for two million dollars from the Asian for 'consultation services'. This was received a week before Greville authorized a sixty-five million dollar loan to another of the Asian's companies, Pac Seng Property Asia Ltd. It was around then that the parent bank in

Australia began to feel something wasn't quite right. It's all very complicated, but basically it means that the Asian bastard was controlling these guys so that he could shuffle his money around Southeast Asia passing it through several financial transactions via wire transfers thereby separating the money from its criminal origins. Sophisticated money laundering on a very large scale.'

'How did you come across all this dirt on Greville?'

'Sir Henry bloody Trevor told Chris. He hated Greville. Thought he was a common upstart. You see, Trevor was the snob to end all English snobs. A couple of glasses of bubbly, and he just couldn't help himself.'

'And the man you saw stab Chris Palmer was Trevor's man?'

'Yes. He was always with him in London. A Russian called Brokov. Of course I wasn't aware of his violent side then. He certainly didn't look it. Graceful bastard for a man of his height; six-two if he was an inch. I thought for a while he was Trevor's lover.'

'What made you think that?'

'Oh I don't know. The way he moved. He was incredibly handsome, almost beautiful. Perhaps too much so for a straight guy. Curly thick raven hair, aquiline nose, brooding eyes, thick full lips. Trevor told Chris that Brokov had once danced with the Kirov. He may have been joshing, I don't know. I'd like to break his fucking legs.' Boydell's eyes narrowed as he stared into the darkness.

'But he wasn't gay?'

'No. I only thought so the first time I met the man; the evening he was on his own with Trevor. Every time afterwards he was with the same woman. Slim, dark. By that time I knew Trevor had tastes similar to the Asian. He liked to screw young – and often.'

McCann sipped his drink. Brokov. Tall, graceful bastard. The slim dark female. Was this the pair that Kerry Whitehead had seen 'dancing' in the kitchen of his Wharf Road house? Had Trevor sent Brokov to Sydney?

Boydell picked up the photos again, glancing through them absent-mindedly.

'Is this who I think it is?' Boydell asked, staring with casual interest at the photocopy of Venice Messon that Torrance had given him.

'You know this girl?' McCann was incredulous.

'Well, I remember the face. But I don't *know* her. Never even spoke to her. She was with the Asian at the house in Sydney?'

'Whose house?'

Boydell thought for a while, then smiled wryly. 'This is where you get your money's worth, I suppose. That is, if you're after dirt.' He nodded towards the tape recorder on the table, as if making a point. 'Not that it's got anything to do with Chris and the Malaysian deal.'

'Whose house?' McCann was more insistent. He suddenly wanted to know badly.

'Senator Russell Croaker's house.' Boydell stared at McCann waiting for the obvious reaction to the mention of the legendary Australian political 'kingmaker'. McCann didn't rise to Boydell's sensationalist anticipation.

Russell Croaker was the power broker who had engineered the elevation of two Labor leaders to the party leadership, and subsequently the successful federal campaigns. Both had become Prime Ministers in their day. His political acumen and judgement of the mood of the rank and file of the Australian Labor Party was legendary. Croaker had accumulated a great many enemies over the years, but no one had ever successfully thrown any dirt that stuck. He was bulletproof.

McCann digested this bombshell. 'What was Croaker's connection with Palmer?'

'None, as far as I know. None at all.'

'Why were you all there?'

'Greville set it up. We had to meet and finalize arrangements for Telok Anson, the petrochemical plant. So when we flew in, he told us to meet him at a Vaucluse address. We didn't know it was Croaker's place, or that he was one of Trevor's cronies. I'd imagine Croaker had no idea we'd show up. I know he wasn't too happy about it. Seemed to Chris and me that he was embarrassed we'd seen him and the Asian together. He was livid with

Greville for inviting us along. Greville tried to laugh it off, but we could see he realized he'd compromised the Australian in a major way.'

'Compromised? In what way? He hadn't done anything.'

'Well, it was obvious to anyone with half a brain that the Asian had Croaker in his pocket. You know he's a Cabinet Minister?'

'Overseas Development, or something?'

'Minister for Development Cooperation and Pacific Island Affairs. Not a bad man to have by the balls when it comes to passing out aid to Vietnam, eh? The aid has amounted to many hundreds of millions of dollars over the last five years. And you can bet your life that the Asian takes his cut before it's passed out, as well as investing a tidy sum offshore for Croaker.'

'What evidence do you have that Croaker's corrupt?'

'Nothing that'd hold up in a court of law, I grant you. But what the hell was a government minister doing in the same company as corrupt bastards like Greville, Trevor and the Asian? Answer me that.'

McCann couldn't help smiling. Boydell had presumably forgotten his part in the two hundred and fifty million dollar carve up at Telok Anson.

Boydell held up the snap of Venice. 'The Asian and Croaker were quite obviously old mates. Add that to the fact that the girl in the photograph was quite clearly under age – '

McCann held up a hand. 'She wasn't.'

Boydell looked surprised. 'Well, if she wasn't, the others were. The Asian usually had a child on his arm. Blonde kid in London one time. Chinese twins the second time. The man was disgusting.'

'Did you ever see Venice Messon again?'

'This girl?' he said, tapping Venice's photo. 'No.'

'And Croaker?'

'No.'

'You never talked to Venice Messon that night in Sydney?'

'No, I didn't. She was the Asian's girl. No question.'

'Did it seem to you that she was doing it for the money?'

'No. She wasn't bought and paid for. She was all over him.'

A dog began barking way down the street and Boydell abruptly stopped speaking. He held up a hand for silence, listening intently, then seemed to relax slightly. 'Got to go pee,' he said standing. 'I'll order us another beer.' He looked at his watch. 'You'll have to be quick, your ferry back leaves in twelve minutes. I shouldn't miss it. It's the last one, and I wouldn't rely on the hotels here.'

McCann sat in the shadows as he waited for Boydell to return. He lifted the tape recorder. It was still running, maybe halfway through.

The dog stopped barking. The air was still, filled with silence and the stale stench of noodle broth. Only the smallest echoes of laughter from way down the promenade broke the silence.

The plastic curtain swished behind him. McCann turned to see the elderly couple exit the café. They both smiled politely at him, then set off back towards the ferry.

He held his watch up to catch the light of the moon. Eight minutes to eleven. Where the hell was Boydell?

Tucking the envelope and the recorder in his inside pocket, McCann walked back into the café.

The room was empty; no sign of the woman. He tapped on the bar with a spoon, calling out, but there was no reply. The smoke trail of a cigarette lifted lazily towards the ceiling from the full saucer on the bar top.

McCann looked quickly around the bar, then walked to the back of the room where a door led out to a small yard. At the back were twin toilets; the men's to the right, the women's to the left. The smell of stale urine was overpowering.

He called out Boydell's name softly in the darkness. No reply. Then again. Still nothing.

Very cautiously he pushed open the door of the men's toilet. Inside it was black as pitch, but the impression he gained was that it was a large enough room to accommodate both a urinal and a toilet. There was no light switch.

As his eyes began to adjust to the blackness, he could make out the outline of a metal urinal halfway up the wall to his left. Facing him was the door to the toilet. He moved forward slowly, then pushed the door to the toilet with his shoe, but it appeared to be jammed. He pushed harder, and it reluctantly moved inwards until it was just possible for him to crane his head round the door. The eyes of Philip Boydell stared up at him blankly, the pupils fully dilated with frozen terror. His body was twisted awkwardly across the toilet bowl. His Adam's apple had been blown outwards. This was without doubt the exit wound. He'd been shot in the back of the neck as he pissed.

McCann fell instinctively to a crouch, throwing Boydell's legs over his shoulder in case of incoming fire. Whoever had shot Boydell would almost certainly be watching him. Possibly debating whether to kill again or leave. After all he'd achieved his purpose, why stick around? He hadn't been seen. McCann wasn't a witness. But it was also possible the man had decided to take them both out and was waiting for the perfect moment, the safest shot.

McCann remained crouched in the center of the cubicle. He knew that, generally speaking, amateurs directed their fire into corners, presuming their targets would press themselves against walls. He was breathing long and deep to keep his heart-rate down, concentrating hard for sounds from outside. There were none, except the distant three bursts of the ferry's horn, signaling its departure.

Training had taught him to remain as still as possible, for as long as it took. He was without a weapon, and he'd be dead as soon as he presented a target. Of course if the man chose to start firing randomly into the toilet, McCann would have no choice but to rush him.

Ten minutes passed. The air in the toilet was thick with humidity, the sickeningly sweet smell of Boydell's blood and the stench of faeces.

Another ten minutes. Then another. And another.

The time was nothing to McCann. In the Falkland Islands he'd lain up in a field of long grass for sixteen hours, waiting for movement from an Argie sniper. Sixteen hours and one minute later, the Argentinean soldier had slowly raised his head, and McCann had blown it from the soldier's shoulders with a couple of two-round bursts from his MP5. That was the SAS way. Burst, pause, burst. The first had done the trick, the second was for insurance.

So the past forty minutes had been nothing.

McCann edged his upper torso silently round the rear of the base of the toilet bowl, so that now only a part of his legs were a target, and those were reasonably protected by Boydell's. Then he braced himself for possible violent action, and slowly pushed out his right leg, hooking the toe of his foot round the door, pulling it gradually open.

As it reached about sixty degrees open, he caught the unmistakable sound of shots from a silenced gun - as if pressure was being released from a bicycle tire for a fraction of a second. PSST... PSST... PSST...

The first bullet hit the edge of the door, ricocheting off into the side wall. The second and third were aimed at the sides of the cubicle.

PSST...PSST... The fourth and fifth slammed into Boydell; the first into his lower abdomen, the second into his right calf, missing McCann's legs by a fraction of an inch.

There was a second's lull. McCann remained absolutely motionless, looking through Boydell's legs past the door. Two seconds later there was the slightest movement in the shadows. McCann took a shallow breath of relief. If his adversary had decided to outwait him, he would have stood little chance, trapped as he was with only one exit. This evened matters considerably.

The elation McCann felt wasn't translated into the smallest body motion, as he mentally adjusted himself for action.

McCann watched as the outline of a slim athletic man took careful steps from the left hand side of the rear door of the café to a spot two feet from the front of the toilet.

Twenty seconds passed – the man was still little more than an outline. He was braced on the balls of his feet, a machine pistol held in front of his body at waist height, the other arm held to his left, his feet pointed outwards for added balance. He appeared to be debating the action he should take.

McCann drew back his legs so that they were now underneath him, the balls of his feet taking the weight of his body. He then wrapped his strong arms round Boydell's chest.

The man outside was now directly in front of the door, his right arm outstretched. McCann assessed the weapon. It was a Mini-Uzi, no question.

Taking a deep breath, McCann braced himself physically, firing up every brain cell into a state of extreme violence. He then sprang forward, screaming like a madman, at the same time throwing Boydell's body violently forwards.

The dark figure was taken completely by surprise. He had barely a second to loose off a burst of fire, three bullets smashing into Boydell's sternum, before the dead man hit him in the chest with the force of a pile-driver.

Know when to leg it. That was one of the most basic premises of the SAS - when to stand and fight, and when to run. It had nothing to do with courage. And now was definitely the time to run. The man still had a firm grip on the Uzi, and would be up and firing within seconds.

McCann leapt over the bodies of Boydell and his assassin, plunging headlong towards the rear door of the café. As he cannoned off the side of the door, he caught a flash of the body of the Chinese owner, lying behind the bar in a lake of her own blood. A second later he was out the door, sprinting down the dark laneway, the footsteps of his pursuer sounding on the cobbles behind him.

Fifty feet down the narrow street, McCann threw his body left, rolling onto the top of the low seawall, falling down to the foreshore twelve feet below. For an ex-sergeant of Para One it was the most natural thing he'd done since he'd landed in Hong Kong.

He immediately rolled to his right, curling into a tight ball under the overhanging stonework of the wall. *Freeze, listen, know your enemy, take command.*

A few seconds later he could clearly hear the footfalls of his enemy. They soon faded into the distance.

McCann remained where he was for half an hour, listening intently, while he assessed his situation. Was this the man who'd killed Whitey? Could this be Brokov? He was certainly tall and athletic. He'd moved with the grace of a stalking cat at the restaurant. If he could take the killer captive, a great many questions could be answered – not least of which was who had paid him to kill Boydell. However, without a weapon, in darkness, this option was fraught with problems. Innocent lives could be at risk if he decided to stalk Brokov through the streets of Lamma.

The next question was whether he should call the Hong Kong Police at once, or wait till he was off the island. He could beat on any door and ask to use the phone. But if he spent a second longer on Lamma than was necessary, it gave his attacker the initiative; the opportunity to hunt him down and kill him, together with whoever had been kind enough to give him help. No, it made sense to get off the Island immediately, then telephone the police when he reached Hong Kong Island, where he could lose himself in the crowds in Wan Chai.

The major problem with this option was that the last ferry was long since gone.

The rain had begun to beat down hard again. Despite his position, huddled tightly against the wall, his clothes were soaked through.

He wiped the water from his eyes as he gazed round the foreshore. The executive toys - that was the obvious answer. He could take one of the powerboats moored to the jetty.

Peeling his wet jacket from his shoulders, he retrieved his wallet, the envelope with Boydell's money, and the tape recorder from the inside pocket. He shoved them all deep in the pocket of his trousers. Then he pulled off his tie, stepping out of his shoes as he moved slowly forward.

Keeping contact with the sea wall at his shoulder, McCann made his way slowly round the curve of the bay towards the ferry jetty.

Thirty feet along, he began passing under the decks of the seafood restaurants, built on pillars out into the bay. The tide was all the way out, but the soft sand made the going difficult. His feet sank almost a foot into the quagmire with each step.

Every few minutes McCann paused to listen. The restaurants were now closed, the only sounds in the still night air the jangling clatter of pots, pans and dishes as kitchen hands cleaned the woks above him.

Thirty minutes later, McCann was under the landward end of the long jetty, the soft mud now up to his knees. The speedboats and launches were moored fifty feet further down the wooden jetty.

Pulling the tape recorder from his pocket, he waded out into the water under the pier.

He was up to his chest in the black water when he saw the figure of a man running down the center of the road towards the jetty. It was Brokov, judging by his outline and the smooth rhythm of his easy loping stride.

Immediately ducking his head under the water, McCann kicked downwards and swam for a good half minute underwater, watching the hulls of the speed boats pass like ghosts above him. It was just too bad about the tape recorder. Maybe the tape would still be useable.

Twenty feet forward, he caught sight of a set of aluminum steps above him, hanging in the water from the stern of one of the boats.

Grasping the steps, he lifted his head slowly out of the water, listening for footfalls on the wooden pier.

Nothing – just the gentle creaking of wood on wood and rope straining against wood.

The slim Scarab motor launch was moored aft to the jetty. Inch by inch McCann pulled himself onto the stern, sliding left over the gunwale onto the plastic seating. There he paused again to listen for movement. Still there was none.

Crawling on his stomach, he eventually reached the control console and tried his luck. There was always the one in a thousand chance that the key had been left in by a careless owner. Not this time.

Again pause and listen. Still just the gentle lapping of the water, and the creaking of the boats.

The spare. So many people kept a spare key in a magnetized box. Who knew? Perhaps he'd get lucky – the thought of silently hot-wiring the Scarab while an assassin methodically searched each boat didn't much appeal.

His fingers traveled lightly under the beveled edges of the console, then down each side. A foot down to the right, his forefinger caught on a metal square.

McCann picked the box from the hull of the Scarab and opened it. Inside, was the spare key.

The mooring lines fore and aft were now the first priority. If the tall man was checking the boats one by one, McCann's time was running out.

Inch by inch he raised his head to the level of the console and quickly looked left and right. The jetty was deserted.

McCann snaked along the side of the boat, across the polished foredeck till he came to the forward line, which he untied and slipped into the water. Then he crawled to the stern and did the same. One last quick look along the jetty, then he was back on his stomach crawling towards the console. One thing worried him like hell. Where was Brokov?

At the instant McCann turned the key in the ignition and the in-board twin turbos roared into life, a black shape scythed up out of the dark waters, bursting through the surface beside the Scarab like a grotesque Leviathan; an explosion of white water spray erupting into the air.

McCann instinctively thrust the gear lever into *drive* and the boat shot forward. But the Russian was already in the boat, one arm round McCann's throat, the forearm pressed hard against his windpipe. At the same time he was trying desperately to position the barrel of his Uzi into the small of McCann's back.

McCann thrust the throttle full forward, then pivoted on the ball of his right foot, parrying the Uzi with his left hand as the machine pistol came up level with his waist. He then seized the man's wrist, pushing the weapon to the side.

The Scarab hurtled forwards, crashing at an oblique angle into the bow of a cruiser to the right, the glancing blow bouncing the Scarab back hard to port as it headed out to sea.

For a microsecond, a look of shocked surprise registered on Brokov's face, his jet black hair framing dark eyes as they bored into McCann's. Then he set himself, swinging his left knee up towards McCann's groin. McCann swayed easily back as the knee swung forward. Brokov lurched, for once taken completely off balance. McCann immediately swung the flat of his free hand in a lightning fast arc in under the man's nose, trying to drive the bone of the man's nose up into his brain. The anticipation of the killer blow registered immediately on Brokov's face, and he whipped his head to one side, the blow still catching him under his right cheekbone with the force of a mallet.

Brokov sank to his knees, his eyes wide in astonishment. Then he lay still.

McCann immediately swung forword, wrenching the wheel violently to the left, avoiding one of the massive rusting metal harbor lights that marked the shipping channel by inches. The Scarab charged forward, sending walls of white water up like shields on either side of the bow.

As his hand reached for the throttle to pull it back, McCann felt an explosion of pain in his head, and his body crashed forward into the console.

It was only instinct and training that saved his life.

As if they had a will of their own, his limbs continued to function in a series of reflex actions as if on automatic pilot. *Timing. Distance. Position.* His programmed subconscious survival instincts took over.

As his body fell forwards, McCann twisted to his right, rolling onto his hip and kicking out with both legs as he screamed.

The counter-attack caught Brokov unprepared. As the Russian had delivered the karate blow to the base of McCann's skull, he'd begun to bring the gun up into the firing position. It had all taken less than a second and a half. But he hadn't anticipated McCann's roll – no one had ever survived his signature killing blow before.

Both McCann's legs caught him just above the hip, cannoning him into the pilot's seat. Brokov threw up his arms automatically to protect himself. McCann lunged for the throttle, crashing the lever back, then pushing full speed ahead. Again the Scarab lurched violently forward as the speed increased from twenty to thirty knots. Brokov was thrown back over the seat, his legs struggling to maintain a footing. McCann laced his fingers, stood, and smashed both fists into the side of Brokov's head. The Russian roared out a terrible scream as his body was catapulted over the side of the boat, plunging into the black waters of Victoria Harbor. In an instant he was left far behind, lost in the blackness.

McCann reached for the controls, pulling back the throttle and disengaging the gears. Then he sank into the pilot's seat, taking several very deep breaths.

He was alive. Somehow he'd survived. His head felt as though it was being struck every three seconds by needle lightning bolts, and waves of nausea coursed through his body.

He flicked on the navigation lights, and looked back into the darkness. He then re-engaged the forward gear, easing the boat round in a semi-circle. If Brokov was still alive, what to do? He was in two minds. To leave him to drown was easy; but to bring the man back alive to tell his story was really tempting. However, if he dragged the Russian back into the boat, who would be in better shape?

There was only one way to find out.

He eased the speed right down to eight knots and began slow sweeps of the dark waters; one hand on the wheel, the other grasping a wrench he'd found in a side compartment.

Twenty-five minutes later, McCann made for home.

McCann drove the Scarab at half speed through the sloe-black night, weaving in among the freighters and channel markers towards where he imagined Kowloon lay. His knowledge of the topography of Victoria Harbor was practically nil.

Eventually he correctly guessed the location of Green Island, and shortly afterwards recognized the silhouette of the Ocean Terminal and the World Shipping Center at Kowloon. Then he veered right, making for the front of the Regent Hotel, just past the Kowloon public pier. There he cut the engines, shouting long and hard until hotel security arrived on the quayside.

McCann didn't realize his face was a mask of blood from a superficial cut above his right eye. The two hotel security men took one look at him, then reached for their cell phones.

As he waited for the authorities in the night manager's room at the Regent, McCann telephoned Richard Chen. The man was as sanguine as ever, as if he'd guessed the evening would turn nasty. He was polite enough to ask McCann if he was injured, chiding him for not having taken up his offer of the services of Huey as bodyguard, while at the same time recommending a good lawyer. Chen informed McCann that he would rather not volunteer any information personally that night to the police - he preferred to wait for a call from them. His nature was to keep as low a profile as possible. It was only as Chen rang off that McCann remembered the tape recorder in his trouser pocket.

The machine looked remarkably unscathed, though it had received a good soaking while he'd been swimming at Lamma. The actual tape, however, looked in relatively good shape.

Next on his list of priorities was a call to Rosalind in Sydney.

By contrast to Chen, Rosalind was extremely solicitous. McCann assured her he was fine. Before he could get into the fine detail, Detective Sergeant Hankow of the Hong Kong Police from Central entered, and he had to cut short the conversation, promising to call her back in the morning.

The preliminary interview was conducted at the Regent with Hankow. Then McCann was driven to the Yau Ma Tei police headquarters on the corner of Nathan and Austin, where an Inspector Tsui grilled him till five in the morning.

Tsui listened intently to McCann's version of events. The tape was passed for analysis to the lab people. McCann told Tsui of his association with Task Force Acorn in Sydney. McCann's working relationship with the New South Wales Police Force in Australia, coupled with the fact that he was quite clearly the victim rather than the aggressor, significantly colored Tsui's attitude towards him.

At 4.40 a.m. the tape was returned to Tsui from the lab. It had been thoroughly cleaned. They listened to McCann's conversation with Boydell twice; Tsui nodding his head like a clockwork toy each time Boydell mentioned a name Tsui was familiar with in Hong Kong.

Finally, McCann offered the tape to Tsui provided he was given a copy to take with him. Tsui agreed to the deal. McCann was then driven to the Peninsula Hotel.

At eight the next morning, Chen rang. The police had removed the bodies of Boydell from the toilet of the Wing Lok, together with the owner of the café. Both had been shot with 7.62 millimeter caliber bullets. There was no information concerning Brokov. The harbor police had sent out launches just before first light, but had found no bodies. Chen concluded that either Brokov was dead and would probably not surface for three days or so, or had somehow survived, swimming to shore.

McCann informed Chen that Inspector Tsui had accepted his version of events. There was little room to doubt that McCann had been acting in self-defense, given the evidence of the tape. If and when the body of the Russian was found, there would be no question of charges being laid, so there was no reason to require McCann to remain in Hong Kong should he wish to leave. Tsui had wished him well.

Chen rang again just as McCann was drifting off to sleep. He'd made a reservation on QF 28, scheduled to depart at ten-thirty that night. This would give him time to recover before the flight.

As he replaced the receiver, McCann couldn't help thinking how incredibly coincidental it had been that Boydell had been run to earth within two hours of the disclosure of the details of the rendezvous to Richard Chen.

16.

**Brighton Beach, South Brooklyn,
New York City.
(Sunday) 19th May.**

Faint chords of a balalaika resonated through the air-conditioning ducts from the dance floor of the Klub Kreml up to Shirayev's elegant private office on the first floor. The hard-faced Russian Mafia *capo* sat facing his Italian counterpart. The silver inlaid Brazilian rainforest timber table between them was littered with half empty Vodka bottles of every flavor imaginable – lemon Pshenichnaya, pepper Russkaya, blueberry Moskovskaya, straight overproof Rasputin, Smirnoff, Derzhavnayaand, and the highly prized Pyotr Veliki with its signature picture of Peter the Great on the bottle.

Osip Alexandrovych Shirayev tapped his throat lightly with his fat forefinger as he eyeballed Vittorio Spettini across the table. One of the Russian's wiseguys stepped forward to refill the glasses until the menisci vibrated gently to the chords of the Ukrainian peasant music that drifted up from the nightclub.

Shirayev raised his glass to toast the Lucchese family crime boss. To the Russians, vodka was tradition. Prior to any important *dusha-dushe*, or heart-to-heart, copious amounts of *voda* were a prerequisite.

He exhaled deeply, then gulped down the white fire, chasing the liquid with two fingers of marinated mushrooms and a finger of blood sausage from the dishes of *zakuski* spread out on the table. He noticed with satisfaction that Spettini had difficulty draining his glass.

Maybe two more, possibly one. Then he'd suggest they begin discussions.

How different things were now, Shirayev thought with satisfaction. Five years ago it would have been the Italians who called the shots. The Russians had been the newcomers, the fleas on the backs of the Colombos, the Bonannos, the Genoveses and the Luccheses. Now he and the other three Russian families labeled by the FBI as the Brighton Beach *Organizatsiya* , were respected equal partners of the Italians. There was Grinkov from the Ukraine, Zetchev with his origins in organized crime in Vilnius in Lithuania, and Forlov from Riga - the cruelest, toughest, but fortunately the most inept *capo* amongst them.

Osip's father, Alexander Shirayev, a child of Tashkent in Uzbekestan, had been one of the thousands of Jewish émigrés allowed an exit visa by Brezhnev as a humanitarian gesture. The KGB had seen this gesture merely as the perfect opportunity to empty their prisons of the hardcore criminal element. And where better to send them than America? At the time, Alexander had been serving a five-year term for aggravated assault and armed robbery in a gulag in Eastern Siberia. He welcomed the opportunity to participate in the American Dream.

From his father's humble beginnings, running extortion rings, drug operations, and brothels in South Brooklyn, Osip had moved into more upscale white-collar crime, structuring an empire based on the profits he and the other Russian families had made from bootlegging tax-free gasoline. Very early on they'd agreed to cut in the Italians as a gesture of neighborliness. It made more sense than to put the Cosa Nostra off-side. Shirayev had agreed to a two-cents-a-gallon levy by the Lucchese family, and ever since they'd existed side by side, albeit a touch uneasily at times.

Yes, they'd all come a long way since those early violent days. Shirayev had read with pride that an investigator with the New York State Department of Tax and Finance had proclaimed the New York Russians 'the best white collar criminals in the world.' Certainly, that had appealed greatly to his vanity, yet he knew it was due in no small measure to his legal advisor, his *consiglière* Dieter Fischer, the former East German Stasi officer who sat to his left. It was with Fischer's guidance that Shirayev had moved the thrust of his organization into commodity trading scams, arms deals, narcotics, and money laundering. Now the alliance of the Brighton Beach Russians was a force to be reckoned with, even by the New York Italians. And respected even by their counterparts in Moscow.

This thought brought Shirayev back to reality with a thump. Khamovnikakh. The *Vory*. The Moscow Godfather of the '*Vorovskoi Mir*', or thieves' world, as the loose federation of Russian mobsters had become known with the fall of the communist regime. Powerful as the Russians were in Brighton Beach, there was no question of going head to head with Constantin Khamovnikakh. And right now, the *capo de capo* of the Russians in Moscow was one angry man who needed answers. It was now Shirayev's task, as a matter of professional courtesy, to provide them.

It had been over a month, and still he had not been able to deliver information to Constantin. Someone would have to pay for his financial loss, the Muscovite had told him. The finger would have to be pointed at someone. And Khamovnikakh's retribution would be terrible - that was without question. Shirayev had heard of a Chechin who had been caught skimming money. Khamovnikakh had ordered the skin of the man's upper torso to be flayed from his body. Raw vodka was then poured on his bare flesh, and he was buried alive in the forest outside Moscow together with his wife, two children and both grandparents.

Shirayev dipped a silver spoon into a silver bowl of Sevruga, smacking his lips as a few large gray grains of caviar dribbled down his chin. It was true, Khamovnikakh could be cruel at times.

He caught Spettini's eye and smiled broadly. One more vodka and they could begin. Till then, Russian etiquette dictated the Italians should sit, eat, and drink in silence.

To Vittorio's right was Pino Samiento, the Italian *capo's* advisor – one of the shrewdest men Shirayev had ever met. To his left, Massimo, 'Pig-face' Pieri, an appropriately named Italian who weighed in at over two hundred and sixty pounds. He was lashing into the finger food with considerable gusto.

Shirayev ran his short fat fingers over his bald bullet head, shifting his buttocks to ease his compacted testicles. Then he again touched his throat, and the vodka was poured once more.

As the Russian *capo's* bodyguard stepped back, Shirayev downed the vodka, wiped his lips with the back of his hand, and placed his glass on its head before him, smiling affably at Spettini. It was time to talk.

'It's good of you to come, Vittorio. I think this problem impacts closely on all of us, and I felt it couldn't wait.' The bi-monthly meeting of all the Russian and Italian families wasn't scheduled till Sunday week. In the interim, Shirayev had thought it wise to approach Vittorio, to sound out the Italian on his personal sources of intelligence.

'It's always a pleasure to sample your vodka, Osip,' Vittorio answered thinly, trying to make light of his obvious distaste for the raw spirit, though he knew it would be unthinkable to refuse the invitation of the Russian to drink.

'That anyone should even have considered doing what they did is inconceivable,' Spettini opened. It was true. To steal two hundred and fifty million dollars of Russian mob money was plain madness. Either a very major syndicate from outside now threatened the stability of the alliance, or the theft had been engineered by the smartest single player in the history of modern crime – someone necessarily with balls of steel.

'There is no question that delivery of the currency was made to the Delta flight as usual,' said Shirayev. 'The seals were checked, and the bags signed for by security. It is at Sheremetyevo Airport that we lose sight of them. And that is the puzzle. Our associate Constantin Khamovnikakh has asked me personally to look into matters this side of the Atlantic, for it is a matter that affects us all.

'We have to act swiftly. This time it is Constantin's money, next time it could be yours or ours. Those behind the action must be found and punished. If left unchecked, it spells disaster for the 'concordat'.' Shirayev referred to the alliance forged in Yerevan, Armenia in 1993 by mob delegations from all over the world; the Sicilian Mafia, the Brighton Beach Russians in New York, the crime bosses in Germany and Italy, the Turks, and the drug cartel Colombians. Every year since, a summit of international gangsters had taken place - the object to ensure a state of order and mutual prosperity, rather than allow the conflict that had existed before to continue.

However, the theft of the currency from Delta Flight 30, barefacedly ripping off a concordat member's stash, was beyond belief. Yet someone had planned and executed it, and as yet there was no trace of the currency. The trail had gone cold.

Spettini turned his head towards 'Pig-face' Pieri, motioning him to speak.

'Inside job. Not too difficult to figure that. It was never any secret about the money, that's the major problem. The whole world knew it was there for the taking every week. We all figured no one would have the shit for brains to try.'

'Someone did,' Shirayev snapped. He had no time for the fat Italian. Goons such as Pieri were the stuff of old Hollywood movies.

'Our union man at JFK, Tony Best, says one of the loaders went missing same day as the money,' Pieri continued. 'Guy called Poliakov. Never been seen since. Word's been out over three weeks. Nothin'. And that's unusual. We find people when we want to. Even if he's dead and buried.'

Shirayev spooned some more Sevruga into his mouth as he listened. It looked as though the meeting would be a waste of time. They had nothing to tell him. If they had, they would have come out with it by now. They were here for appearances, to show good faith. Poliakov had simply vanished off the face of the earth; the other handler who'd gone missing that day had been found dead at his apartment building; and Grasby, an employee at the Union Constitution, had been traced finally to a morgue in Fiji.

It looked as though Grasby was the insider. And now Khamovnikakh was beginning to make worrying inferences that the answer lay somewhere within the alliance, that someone was betraying the concordat. Soon the Muscovite would be pointing fingers at random. Someone would take the fall - that was for sure. Retribution would take place. And the last thing they needed in Brooklyn at present was an internecine war.

Dieter Fischer pushed his thin wire spectacles back up onto the bridge of his nose, then spoke.

'When we find the person who took out the hired help, we will find the culprit, will we not?'

Spettini nodded in agreement. Shirayev merely gestured to one of his people to pour more vodka.

'It is never possible to erase all evidence,' Fischer continued. 'The bags were delivered to the plane. The plane flew to Moscow. The trucks collected the bags from the plane, but the money was no longer inside. Hence, the switch took place inside the plane.'

'Sure, we all know that, Dieter,' Shirayev snapped. His bad temper was getting worse by the minute.

'Please indulge me, Osip, my friend.' Fischer paused. The Russian nodded as he gulped his vodka. Fischer continued. 'To steal so much money is not so very hard. The logistics are relatively simple. You switch the money for paper - that is all. But to *keep* the money,' he paused again for effect, stressing the word very deliberately, ' to *keep* the money and spend it is another matter entirely.'

'Get to the point, Dieter,' Shirayev barked, pushing a hand down the front of his trousers, separating his clammy testicles.

'With pleasure,' Fischer replied equably. 'The point I am making is that whoever took the bags of freshly minted currency would have thought long and hard about what to do with it afterwards. It's not the kind of money you keep on hand for pocket money. It's only usefulness would be to generate interest and profit.

Hence it would need to be banked somewhere, so it could be introduced into the worldwide money supply. And with such a sum, secrecy would be paramount, yet practically impossible.'

Now Fischer had the full attention of all in the room.

'Two hundred and fifty million dollars is a great deal of paper. It is high profile to say the least. To wash such an amount takes time and cannot be done in a vacuum.'

'Give the man a drink, for Christ's sake,' Shirayev shouted at the help, while he smiled at Fischer. 'Keep talking Dieter.'

'Outside of the members of our alliance, it would be difficult, to say the least, to launder so great an amount of cash without ringing bells around the banking community. Too many people are searching for it. I've made sure the word has been out in all the usual places; the Caymans, Turks and Caicos Islands, Vanuatu, Panama, Hong Kong, Switzerland, Bahamas – you name it. In short, anywhere there's an offshore Eurodollar economy, or somewhere US dollars circulate freely. If it's introduced anywhere, word will get back to me.'

'So where does that leave us, Mr. Fischer,' Spettini asked with interest. He was intrigued - money laundering, white-collar crime in general, had never been a staple of the Lucchese family interests.

'The bottom line is that in over three weeks there has been not the slightest indication that the money has surfaced anywhere. This would suggest that it is either still in its bags untouched, or that the person who took it into his head to steal the money has the means to launder the cash himself. That in turn would necessarily suggest that responsibility lies either with one of us within the concordat, a foreign sovereign government, or a substantial private bank.'

Fischer paused to let the import of his last sentence sink in. It was the last thing that either Spettini or Shirayev wished to hear. If Fischer's guess were correct, and one of the families had broken ranks, it spelt the end of the smooth running of an alliance that suited them all.

Pieri broke the subdued silence. 'If the guy Poliakov in the plane switched the cash, how the hell did they manage to make it disappear? Answer me that?' He was plain curious.

'The journey to the Ermitazh Bank took fifty minutes,' Fischer replied. 'There, the switch was discovered within fifteen minutes.'

'Why didn't they spot the broken seals when they pulled the bags out of the hold?' Samiento asked.

'They just plain didn't, okay?' Shirayev interrupted rudely, unable to control a brief burst of bad temper. Obviously, if they had, the money would never have gone missing. The guards had been doing the job, week in week out, for three years. They just got careless. Shirayev was staggered that Vittorio's consiglière had come out with such a remark.

Spettini's eyes narrowed as he stared at the big Russian. To insult his right-hand man was an affront to himself.

'Maybe those guys aren't paid enough, who knows?' Shirayev offered in a more conciliatory tone.

'Maybe they did a hell of a good job on the seals,' Fischer continued. 'Remember, Grasby at the Union Constitution was involved. Maybe his part of the deal was to supply new seals.'

'He's dead, right?' Spettini asked.

'Right,' replied Fischer, keen to finish his speech without further interruption. 'Anyway, an hour after the bags were hauled out of Delta 30, the airport was sealed by the authorities tighter than a cat's ass. Believe me when I say that Khamovnikakh made sure every inch of the perimeter was searched; every suitcase, every airport building, every vehicle.'

'What Dieter's saying is that it had to have been flown out during the time it took the armored trucks to drive into Moscow. That's plain as daylight,' Shirayev interjected matter-of-factly. This was old news to him. He and Fischer had come to that obvious conclusion a long time ago. He wanted to wrap up the meeting. He had better things to do than swap gossip with the Lucchese family. They plainly knew zip about the matter. It was all proving a massive waste of time.

'No shit. Flown out?' Pig-face raised his eyebrows in wonderment. Fischer eyed him with a tired expression.

'Khamovnikakh has compiled a list of aircraft on the apron at Sheremetyevo from 10.55 a.m. to 1.00 p.m. It's a matter of time. He will recover the money. I can promise that,' Fischer concluded.

'But in the meantime, we all have to watch our backs in case one of the alliance is a loose cannon. Is that what you're saying?' Spettini asked calmly, looking across at his Russian counterpart.

'Maybe,' said Shirayev. 'I've been giving that one hell of a lot of thought, Vittorio. But I wouldn't care to point a finger, would you?'

Spettini merely smiled evasively. 'The matter's hypothetical. Who would risk so much for one hit? Two hundred and fifty million can be made up in a matter of months. Why take such a risk?' He ran his tongue over his lips, shifting in his seat as he debated whether to share with the Russian the thoughts that were now running through his head.

Shirayev picked up on Spettini's hesitation. 'You got something to say, it stays in this room Vittorio. You have my word on that of course.'

Spettini smiled. 'Of course.' He arched his back, lacing his fingers. He then turned to Amiento at his left. The consiglière took his cue.

'If there's any weight to the theory that it's one of us, I would suggest that those whose spheres of operations were far from these shores would have the least to lose. And the most to gain, if we went for each others throats.'

'The Colombians?' Shirayev interjected.

'Possibly,' Amiento agreed.

'What about the Turks? Hell, it could be anyone not based here in the States.'

'That's true. I merely make the point that we should not be looking for treachery among ourselves here in New York. We have too much to lose. We should learn to trust each other.'

That much made sense, thought Shirayev. Also, the more he thought about it, the more he was inclined to agree with Amiento's logic. The fly in the ointment could well be many thousand miles away, possibly playing a game of divide and conquer.

Shirayev waved a hand. 'Hey, Vittorio, what am I thinkin' about? You'd prefer a glass of wine, maybe?' He raised his eyebrows as if the thought had just occurred to him. Spettini smiled his assent.

'Yeah. Maybe. Thanks.'

17.

The Peak. Hong Kong.
May 19th.

Qantas flight 28 wasn't scheduled to leave till ten-thirty that evening, so McCann decided to stir the pot a little.

Since it was possible that a telephone call might be traced to his room at the Peninsula, McCann walked down to the foyer to a booth next to the dining room. He flipped through the phone book till he reached Aust-Pac Finance, then dialed.

'May I speak to Mr. Greville?' McCann asked.

'I'm afraid he's in a meeting. May I take a message, and ask Mr. Greville to return your call?'

McCann had anticipated this reply. 'Yes, please tell him that a Mr. Brokov called. It's urgent.'

'Where can you be reached, Mr. Brokov?'

'I shall be out all day. Please tell him I shall be at the Peak Café at midday. Please impress upon him that the matter is urgent.'

Before the secretary had time to speak, McCann had replaced the receiver. He then walked through into the dining room, sitting at a table by the window.

The question was, would Greville bite? McCann knew that in the same situation he wouldn't. If Brokov had survived, it'd be a simple matter for Greville to call Trevor and establish where the assassin was. Either way, his call just now would be a shock to Greville. Unless Boydell's story was a tissue of lies, Trevor had ordered Brokov to murder Palmer, and logic dictated that the same man had also killed Whitey.

But why had it been Trevor's man who had murdered Palmer? Why hadn't Greville organized the matter himself. After all, Hong Kong was Greville's territory and the United Kingdom Trevor's. Why had Trevor taken on the responsibility? Perhaps Greville didn't have the stomach for the wet work himself? That was always a possibility. If they worked together, it would hardly be necessary to have more than one hit man on the payroll.

He scanned the dining room, searching for a waiter to take his order. Then his mind returned to Brokov. How long had he been in Hong Kong, searching for Boydell? Presumably for some time; with the exception of his short excursion to Birchgrove to murder Whitey, of course. Boydell had been hiding for a long long time, and the one person who'd known his whereabouts was Mr. Liu, the shopkeeper.

McCann began to follow the logical chain. Liu had told him at Stanley Market that Boydell could be found at Lamma. Subsequently, he himself had told Chen. No one but Chen. Yet within two hours Brokov was on the island, and Boydell was dead. Of course this didn't necessarily prove Chen was an informer, but it didn't leave much room for other suspects.

As he waited for his breakfast, McCann made contingency plans for the day. If Greville showed up at the Peak Café, it would provide the perfect opportunity to put the cat among the pigeons. Neither Greville nor Trevor was in a position to know how much Boydell had told him. Nor would they know if Palmer or his lover had committed anything incriminating to paper before they died. They'd have to be curious. Then there was the audio tape Boydell had made, minutes before his death.

But time and time again, McCann kept coming back to the dead Asian. Who was he? Boydell had identified the dead Asian in the photograph without question as the one they called *The Harbinger of Death*, the executive producer of the Telok Anson scam. But he'd clearly been mistaken. He'd said he'd seen the same man in Pedder Street, Hong Kong, only ten days ago. So who *was* the man at Wheelock House. Neither Palmer nor Boydell had known his name, nor had they ever spoken to him; he'd always been a man in the shadows. By sheer chance, Boydell had identified Venice Messon from McCann's photograph as the girl who had been *with The Harbinger of Death* at Croaker's house in Sydney. And from what Boydell had said, it was clear that man was still alive – at least he had been only ten days ago. So why had she chosen to blow up his double at the Savoy on March 26th? A simple case of mistaken identity?

Then McCann remembered the words of Mory, the bell captain at the Savoy. *Don't see how someone could have gotten to the fifteenth floor in that time.* Yet Mory had been as adamant in his identification as Boydell; he'd been certain the dead Asian had been the man he'd seen arrive at the hotel only seconds before the blast. So had Mory just been mistaken about the time? Was it conceivable that the dead man's double had been in Sydney moments before the bombing?

Another thought struck McCann. Brancusi had been pretty certain that Venice had never flicked the firing switch. It was still in the *off* position. Brancusi believed the explosion had been an accident; that the aerial had somehow or other made contact with the triggering switch. Whether or not Venice would have flicked the switch given time was another matter. If she'd decided not to throw the switch, then why not? Had she, like Macbeth, been infirm of purpose at the moment of truth? If Brancusi had been correct in his hypothesis that it was an accidental firing, then someone must have called Venice on her cellular phone while she *was screwing her courage to the sticking place.* Without a call, it was unlikely the bomb would have gone up, there would have been no electrical field. So who the hell had called her? Who knew her cellular number for starters – let alone knew the exact moment to make the call?

Hendrik Ohlson. The more McCann thought the matter over, the more the answer screamed out at him. His instinct had been right a long time ago. What the hell was Hendrik Ohlson doing at the Savoy that morning anyway? Coincidence? It stretched the bounds of credibility. So why had a man as astute as Torrance bought his story about a coincidental meeting in the street outside the Savoy? Why had Blackwood concurred? Merely because Ohlson had volunteered the fact that he'd been at the Savoy? And what had Blackwood said at Task Force HQ? *If you think you can do better than us, go and see him yourself.* Maybe the truth of it was that they had smelt a rat themselves, but, unable to break the boy's story, they were goading him to use a slightly firmer hand.

McCann signaled to a waitress, who hurried over.

'Will my breakfast be very long,' McCann asked, 'I'm in rather a hurry.'

Less than two minutes later, McCann's sausages were on the table.

As he poured the coffee, his thoughts leap-frogged to Brokov. With Palmer dead, presumably Trevor and Greville had been tying up loose ends when they sent Brokov after Boydell. Palmer's lover clearly knew too much. Whether or not the order came from Boydell's *Harbinger of Death* was another matter. Yet this was more than likely.

But would they think it necessary to send someone else after him now that Boydell, and possibly Brokov, were dead? McCann assumed this would hinge on his own course of action from now on. And what he had in mind would present himself as a dangerous adversary.

That was what he was counting on.

McCann sat at the corner table on the verandah of the Peak Café looking briefly away from the entrance to the restaurant towards Victoria Gap to his right. The blue waters of the South China Sea were an azure haze in the distance. It was ten past twelve, and as yet there'd been no sign of anyone who could have been Greville. Three times, middle aged business men had entered. But they had all joined tables of friends.

At twelve-thirty an elegant looking man of around fifty, with a shock of thick dark wavy hair entered. He was over six feet tall, with the kind of five o'clock shadow that suggested he was used to shaving at least twice a day. His suit was perfectly tailored, and his tie was stuck with a diamond pin the size of a small olive.

On his arm was a fragile yet fine looking woman of about the same age. They chose the table facing McCann.

As if by magic, the maître d'hôtel appeared and was suddenly all over the dark-haired man, smiling and posturing. McCann overheard the elegant man order a bottle of Dom Perignon. His attitude towards the wine waiter was a patronizing disdain that a Maharaja might have had for a houseboy.

Within thirty seconds, the wine waiter was back with the champagne. McCann watched the couple absent-mindedly. The woman looked tired and bored, as if she were a high class tart contracted for the day. Her partner didn't give her a second glance; instead he drummed his long fingers on the table, the black hair on the back of his hands giving him a certain lupine quality.

A few moments later, he turned his head slightly in McCann's direction, and their eyes met. McCann then looked away, debating whether he would order one of the Singaporean curries for which the restaurant was famous, or leave immediately. It now didn't seem likely that Greville would appear. It'd be necessary to confront the man at the bank after all.

McCann lifted the large menu from the table, and glanced down the list. As he put it down, by chance he again caught the eye of the dark wavy-haired man who this time held his eyes. His fragile female companion was no longer in evidence. Presumably she'd gone to the bathroom.

McCann looked around the verandah, signaling to a waiter who was brushing some crumbs from a recently vacated table. The young Chinese failed to notice him, so McCann stood and walked inside, threading his way between the tables, brushing past the dark-haired man who was still watching him.

Standing by the cash register was the diminutive figure of the maitre d', checking a bill. Sitting at the bar, two seats down from the register was the fragile looking woman. She shot McCann a glance as he entered. McCann tapped the maitre d' lightly on the shoulder.

'Excuse me. I wonder, do you have a reservation for a Francis Greville?'

The small man looked up, with an expression of annoyance. The servile demeanor that had been so much in evidence on the verandah less than a minute ago was gone, replaced by a haughty glare. 'Yes? I didn't catch your words,' he replied grudgingly.

'Can you tell me if a Mr. Greville has a reservation for lunch?' McCann asked.

'Mr. Greville is outside on the verandah, sir. Are you lunching together?' His tone hadn't changed.

'Could you please point him out to me? We haven't met before,' McCann asked affably, disregarding the small man's arrogant attitude.

'With pleasure, sir,' he replied, indicating the dark wavy-haired man, who was now staring directly at them from the verandah, a supercilious smile playing on his lips. He was shielding his eyes with one hand from the sun.

McCann walked back outside, stopping at Greville's table.

'You decided to come?' McCann said coldly. The man's smug smile of superiority annoyed him.

Greville said nothing.

'I can't see the point of just sitting there like the Cheshire cat, staring at me,' McCann continued.

Greville was unfazed. He merely shrugged his shoulders slightly as he reached for his flute of champagne, curling his long hairy fingers round the stem. 'You'll have to excuse me, old chap,' he said politely, 'but I'm afraid I haven't the first idea who the hell you are.'

The intention of his words was clearly to offend, yet they were counterpointed so cleverly by the soft tone and his calm easy smile.

'You know quite well who I am,' McCann replied crisply.

''Fraid not, old chum. I've just in come for a spot of lunch. Look, you're very welcome to join me, very briefly, in a glass of bubbly; I'm a friendly sort. However, if you're going to be aggressive, I suggest you get lost before I ask Hamish to see you out.'

McCann pulled back one of the chairs, adopting Greville's relaxed tone. 'You know, I haven't shared a glass of wine with a murderer in more than ten years. Needless to say, I had no idea that he *was* one at the time.' As he sat he added, 'He's dead now. Lethal injection.'

Rather than showing anger, Greville's expression remained relaxed. 'Anyone I know?' he replied archly, raising his full black eyebrows at McCann, and grinning. He then signaled to the waiter, holding up two fingers as he pointed to his glass.

'You have me at a disadvantage, old boy. You seem to know my name, but I'm afraid I don't know yours,' Greville said, studying McCann closely.

A waiter placed a champagne flute in front of McCann, then filled it.

'My name is Leo McCann. I work for Rosalind Buchanan.'

'Do you *really*. How *nice* for you,' he replied condescendingly. 'I knew her father. Not well, mind you. Such a shame – the bombing in Sydney, that is.'

'Mr. Greville, you are here because of the message I left with your secretary. Your curiosity got the better of you.'

Greville leant back in his chair and sipped his champagne. 'Is that so, Mr. McCann? Tell me more.'

'Last night I met with Phillip Boydell on Lamma Island. I have the entire conversation on tape. He also gave me copies of affidavits that he'd signed prior to the meeting.'

Greville's expression lost a touch of its former smugness. He was listening hard now.

'Boydell told me of the Malaysian conspiracy at Telok Anson to defraud Buchanan Industries of more than two hundred and fifty million dollars. He also told me of the involvement of Sir Henry Trevor, you and Senator Russell Croaker.'

It was McCann's turn to switch on the easy smile, Greville's face was all frost.

'You can tell Sir Henry Trevor that in the affidavit Boydell identifies Brokov as one of the two men that murdered Christopher Palmer. Boydell was an eyewitness. He states that Brokov was an employee of Trevor's. He talks of the meetings in London, Sydney, and the final meeting with you here in Hong Kong, where you, Trevor, and the Asian failed to live up to your end of the bargain.'

'Bargain? Asian? I've no idea what you're talking about, McCann.'

'The man you both work for,' McCann said, reaching into his pocket and pulling out the photographs, flipping through them while keeping them close to his chest. He then held up the photo of the Asian for an instant in front of Greville's eyes, before placing it face down with the others.

'Really? And who might that be? My one association is with the Australian Pacific Bank. With that one exception I work for no one but myself. Please surprise me with a name?'

Greville sat forward in his chair, challenging McCann to do so. A few seconds passed in silence, then he leant back again and resumed sipping his champagne. The arrogant self-satisfied look was back. He'd smelt the bluff.

'Last night you and Trevor discovered Boydell's whereabouts and sent in Brokov to kill him.'

'You have a very fertile imagination, Mr. McCann. Did this man Brokov also sign an affidavit to that effect? You could add it to the one Mr. Boydell gave you.'

Greville's relaxed look was evidence enough that he didn't buy a single word of McCann's bluff.

'You look to me like a hard man, Mr. McCann. *Are* you a hard man?' He reached for the champagne bottle, raising his wolfish eyebrows once more as he offered it to McCann.

'No thank you," McCann replied. "One glass with a man like you is enough. I wouldn't like to make it a habit.'

'You have a crisp turn of phrase, Mr. McCann,' Greville said, charging his own glass. 'However, I would be very wary indeed of calling people murderers in public places. Should you ever do that again, I will crucify you financially.' He took a sip, then continued. 'In answer to some of the issues you raise, let me tell you one or two things. Yes, I know Sir Henry Trevor well. We have been friends, and have done business together on occasion for well over ten years. As far as I'm aware, Sir Henry knew Christopher Palmer socially a very long time back. I myself met with the man in London shortly before his death. I vaguely remember the man you mention, Phillip Boydell, being at the same party. However, to draw the conclusion that I played any part in a conspiracy, instigated, so you state, by Sir Henry Trevor to defraud Buchanan Construction of their funds, is quite fanciful. I did no such thing. And I think I can state with the utmost confidence, neither did Sir Henry.'

'The money was laundered by yourself, passed through Aust-Pac Finance, then wired to a network of anonymous accounts in offshore havens,' McCann cut in. 'It's all detailed in the affidavit.'

Greville merely chuckled. 'Oh yes, the affidavit. I suggest you attempt to prove the money was wired to me, and that it was subsequently laundered by me personally. I assure you, it's harder than you think. It is what I do for a living, Mr. McCann; overseeing large sums of money passing from one party to another through the medium of the wire service. Have you any idea how many wire transfers pass through my bank every day? I can see by your face you haven't. Well, let me tell you it's many thousand.

"Mr. Boydell can swear till he's blue in the face that the money was wired to me initially. Maybe it was. I would suggest otherwise. It's beside the point really, because even if this were the case, I would naturally contend it was achieved without my connivance. If the proceeds of a fraudulent scheme were passed through my bank, and I was aware of it, I would certainly have no alternative but to inform the authorities.'

He paused to flick his middle finger and thumb at a passing waiter. It sounded like a pistol shot. The wine waiter was at his side in seconds.

'Another bottle, please,' he said without taking his eyes off McCann. As the waiter disappeared, Greville continued speaking.

'To suggest that I have something to hide is one thing. To suggest that I am personally involved in criminal conspiracies is something far more serious.' Greville leant both elbows on the table, interlocking his white curiously effeminate yet hairy fingers. They looked as though their one purpose over the past fifty years had been to count large denomination bank notes. His eyes narrowed to slits. 'To call a man a murderer to his face in a public place is going one step too far.'

His voice fell to the barest whisper. 'You would do well to heed my advice, Mr. McCann. You have two choices. One is to go home to wherever you've come from, and mind your own business. That would be the course of a judicious man. The alternative is to pursue this matter to a conclusion. If you choose the latter course, I would advise you to step carefully. Very carefully indeed. You see, I don't think you have any idea with whom you are dealing.'

McCann met the dark-haired man's eyes, untroubled by Greville's threats, merely thinking of another tack to take. The man obviously hadn't bought his story of Boydell's affidavit, and without them Greville was right – pointing the finger was one thing, proving the charges another entirely. Whether or not Boydell's hearsay evidence on the tape would be admissible in a court of law was debatable. Greville obviously felt secure.

McCann slouched back in his chair; perhaps he'd try one last shot with the affidavit. 'Suppose I was to decide to take your advice. How much would you be prepared to offer for Boydell's affidavit? I would naturally throw in the tape recording.'

Greville's contemptuous expression said it all. 'If you're suggesting for a second that I'd be blackmailed by a man such as yourself, you're sadly mistaken. I wouldn't wipe my arse with your ilk, let alone let them blackmail me. To do so would be to admit guilt, no?'

McCann had felt like breaking the man's arms several times during the last ten minutes. He tried hard to control himself.

Greville seemed to sense the promise of violence that lurked in McCann's eyes, so he eased up on his invective.

'Why don't you take the affidavit and hand it to the authorities,' he said, as the wine waiter arrived with the second bottle of champagne. Then he smiled, adding in a stage aside, 'Either that, or stick it up your arse.'

McCann stood, and walked to Greville's side, looming over the man. 'Just listen to this, you asshole,' he began quietly. 'I'm close enough to you right now to inflict so much damage to your face that it'd take a team of plastic surgeons a full year to fix it. Bearing this in mind, you'd better answer my next question damned quick. Okay?' McCann stared down at Greville, his balled fist inches from the banker's upturned startled face. Greville swallowed, but said nothing.

'Did you or Sir Henry Trevor have anything to do with the bombing at the Savoy Hotel in Sydney?'

'Absolutely not,' Greville croaked.

'I don't know if I believe you, asshole. I just had to ask for my employer's sake. Now let me tell you something else. I'm going to make it my business to make you one very unhappy man. You'd just better believe that.'

McCann lifted his right hand so quickly that Greville didn't have a chance to move a muscle before McCann pressed very hard with his thumb and forefinger on a pressure point just below and behind Greville's right ear, immobilizing him entirely. A shaft of excruciating pain shot down the right-hand side of Greville's face and body. Then McCann casually lifted the bottle of vintage champagne from the ice bucket and began pouring it slowly into Greville's lap as he continued speaking.

'Point one. Andrew Horan's investigations show quite clearly that you are a criminal. And though Andrew Horan is now dead, I have a copy of the computer tape that someone, presumably acting on orders from yourself or Trevor, attempted to steal from the bomb scene shortly after the blast. I know the same person removed three other computer disks. Please inform him he missed the important one.

'Point two. Imogen Whitehead, Horan's private secretary, was murdered by Sir Henry Trevor's man Brokov, as was Palmer. Last night Phillip Boydell was murdered, and an attempt was made on my life. All of this has made me really quite angry.'

In his peripheral vision, McCann could see the maitre d' approaching. Everyone on the verandah was staring at their table. McCann was still holding the empty inverted bottle over Greville's lap. The floor was awash with champagne.

'You're shortly going to be in the deepest possible shit, so keep looking over your shoulder, Greville. Tell that to Trevor, next time you see him.'

The maitre d' was now at McCann's side, tugging at his sleeve. McCann released Greville from his grip, the banker slumping back in his chair. McCann then turned to the head waiter.

'I'm told the Singaporean curries here are the best in Hong Kong. Problem is, I just couldn't force it down with a piece of shit such as this man here sitting in the same restaurant.'

The head waiter stared at the scene in disbelief. Greville was now holding a hand to the spot on his neck where McCann had placed his fingers, attempting to massage some blood back into his neck. He opened his mouth to speak, but no words escaped.

'Just one more thing,' he whispered to Greville.' Christopher Palmer is still officially missing. You seemed very ready to agree with me that he was dead. You know something the rest of us don't?'

McCann dropped the empty bottle in the general direction of Greville's testicles, then made for the door.

18.

Nikolskaya Ulitsa. Moscow.
20th May.

Nikolskaya Ulitsa stretches from Krasnaya Ploshchad, Red Square, at its lower western end, to Lubyanka Square at its top. During the Soviet era it was known as 25 October Street to commemorate the Revolution. Since *glasnost* the street was regaining its pre-eminence as a center of independent commerce. The most celebrated buildings in the street were the beautiful Zaikonospasskiy Monastery, and the Slavyanskiy Bazaar Restaurant, one of Anton Chekhov's favorite haunts.

The Ermitazh Bank was a comparatively dull building compared to the richly ornate nineteenth century wedding cake conceit that was the duck egg blue and white edifice of the Synodal Printing House, situated next door. Directly opposite was the Lubyanka metro station, and slightly to the right a building since 1918 the headquarters of the KGB in St Petersberg.

Khamovnikakh looked down from a bay window on the top floor of the bank building. His dark good looks and soft kind eyes belied the cruelty that lay at the heart of his character. Below him, a large group of children were walking hand in hand towards the Detskiy Mir, the world-renowned children's toy store. He smiled. He'd bought the building two months ago.

Life had been good for six years now. At times a struggle, certainly, but good nevertheless.

Once a high echelon KGB man, Khamovnikakh had welcomed Mikhail Gorbachev's *glasnost* with open arms, relishing the prospect of a free economy that would soon be his to rape. He'd made the right connections early in his career and amassed a fortune from the black market. It was a natural progression to take advantage of what was to prove a positive gold mine – the new Russian banking system.

Since the fall of the Soviet Union in 1991, government banks had been replaced by private institutions. Khamovnikakh had been first in the queue. A two hundred thousand dollar bribe had secured the charter for the Ermitazh Bank. Though in theory regulated by the Russian Central Bank, the private banks were predominantly left to their own devices. Now, the new Muscovite banks were quickly replacing Panama as the favored laundering venue for the Colombian drug barons and the Sicilian Mafia. The Ermitazh Bank was presently one of the ten leading banking fronts for the new order of organized crime in Russia. Yet though the world financial community was very aware of the new banking *Mafiya*, it was very much in their interests to turn a blind eye to their activities. As far as the US Treasury was concerned, a massive profit was being made on every freshly minted dollar shipped to Russia – ninety-nine point nine six cents in the dollar to be precise, provided the cash stayed out of the United States, which the great majority of it did.

Each year the US Treasury made approximately fifteen billion from sales of freshly minted currency abroad; their overheads no more than the printing costs. As far as Treasury officials were concerned, it was up to the American Banks who ordered the freshly minted hundred dollar bills to vet their customers. And, of course, the individual banks' compliance officers assiduously maintained that they would never dream of selling currency to any bank with known organized crime connections.

Khamovnikakh smiled at the naivete of the system. H.E Palfreyman, the compliance officer at the Union Constitution, was a stickler for the letter of the law. He'd publicly stated at a Senate enquiry that if the Chairman could prove to him that the Ermitazh was a 'mobbed up front' for the Russian Mafiya in Moscow, he'd have no more to do with the bank. After all, he was a man of principle. And a very rich one, thanks to Khamovnikakh amongst others.

A small girl in a red coat looked up at him from the street below, screwing up her eyes against the sun. She reminded Khamovnikakh of the wooden dolls his father used to buy him at Easter in Odessa.

Life had not been easy as a child. His father had struggled to provide the family with the few necessities of life, until the day he died of metal poisoning – the product of a day to day life in a metal smelter outside Odessa. Khamovnikakh had been twelve when he'd become the new head of the family, charged with bringing the bread to the table. He saw his father's relentless toil as a complete waste of life. It appeared far simpler to steal.

He laughed aloud at the recollections of his youth, a time when the black market had consisted of little else but luxury goods; electrical equipment, computers, cigarettes, and alcohol. Now it was oil. Now, with the connivance of corrupt plant managers in Siberia, he stole millions of barrels of crude oil. The oil was traded on the Dutch spot market each month, the proceeds wired through a daisy chain of front companies, until the money came to rest in a London Eurodollar account. It was then wired to the Union Constitution Bank in New York, which in turn sent bags of crisp uncirculated hundred dollar bills to Moscow. To the Ermitazh Bank. It was all so easy. American dollars arrived in truckloads each week from New York, supporting Khamovnikakh's entire organized crime network.

So easy, that was, until the 27th of March.

His eyes narrowed in anger. As if sensing an aura of evil somewhere above her, the girl in the red dress clasped the leg of her mother, burying her head in her full skirt.

For seven years the Russian economy had been falling into a pit, while the one growth industry had been organized crime. Crime bosses such as Khamovnikakh had gained control of the black market trade in the basic resources of the country via corrupt officials who traded in stolen petroleum and armaments, as well as diverting vast sums of international aid from those who desperately needed it to the likes of Khamovnikakh.

Khamovnikakh channeled his vast profits through a string of American and European companies with legitimate banking records, incorporated in Switzerland, London, Berlin, the Bahamas and New York. This way his dirty money, gained through narcotics operations in the Baltic States and Indochina, was fed through the Ermitazh Bank, back into the international banking system. The hot money was now freshly laundered, pressed, and clean as a whistle.

But law enforcement agencies in the United States were becoming increasingly uneasy. Where, in the past, the newly minted dollars had simply been printed and exported, seldom to return, now an ever-increasing proportion of the currency was finding its way back to the United States, invested in pseudo-legitimate businesses by the Moscow *Mafiya* through their connections in New York and Chicago. The threat of a highly structured organization of white-collar Russian criminals taking root in the United States - a possibility dismissed with derision only a few years before - had become a reality. The Russians were now viewed as a force that could well prove as dangerous to the wellbeing of American society as the Italian Mafia. And though it was initially those Russians living in America who were targeted by the FBI and the US financial crimes enforcement authorities, Khamovnikakh in Moscow did not escape their attention. He was now one of their top targets.

A telephone rang on the boardroom desk behind him. Khamovnikakh turned away from the window, lifting the receiver.

'Mr. Serov has arrived, sir. He is early.'

'Send him in, Sergei,' Khamovnikakh replied, then walked back to the window. The stolen money itself was not significant. Lloyds of London covered the currency. It was the principle, the fact that someone had had the audacity to steal *his* property. For that insolence, his retribution would be terrible.

Khamovnikakh heard the boardroom door open and close. He could just make out the reflection of the small figure of Serov in the windowpane before him.

'You have found my money?' Khamovnikakh began, still facing the window.

'We have narrowed the parameters of our search, *Vory*. Very significantly,' Valeriy Serov replied confidently, though his bowels had the consistency of thin gruel. 'We now believe we know how the currency left Sheremetyevo.'

Khamovnikakh turned theatrically, his kind eyes shining with good humor. Serov's heart rate reduced marginally, though he knew he wasn't out of the woods yet.

'We believe the currency was placed in unaccompanied cases labeled 'Optical Equipment' while it was in the hold of the Delta flight. These cases had been tagged through to Prague from New York. However, the consignee company in Czechoslovakia, Zorak Films, the one identified on the manifest, does not exist. The consignor, the New World Hotel Group, is also fictitious.'

'There can be no doubt that the money was placed in the cases marked 'Optical Equipment?'

'Every article that was in the hold of Delta 30, with the exception of the optical equipment, has been traced. No single group of more than five pieces of luggage belonged to any single passenger. It would be a logistical nightmare to have arranged to split the money between ten or more couriers, all with separate destinations. The majority of the Delta 30 baggage was still at Sheremetyevo when the airport was closed down. Some had been transshipped. These were intercepted and searched when they reached their final destination.'

'And my money?' Khamovnikakh prompted in a more threatening tone.

Serov blinked nervously. 'The so-called 'Optical Equipment' was never moved off the perimeter to the inside of the airport buildings. It was designated for transshipment. To a private aircraft.'

'Which private aircraft?' Khamovnikakh prodded.

'If you will permit me to explain further, *Vory*?'

Khamovnikakh waved a hand, his irritation showing.

'There were no flights to Prague until several hours after the airport had been closed,' Serov continued. 'Nor were the bags loaded on any flights that might have connected with Prague.'

Serov faltered momentarily; Khamovnikakh's fixed stare and stillness were unbelievably disconcerting.

'Tell me, Valeriy. Who flew the cases out of Sheremetyevo? Which carrier?'

'It had to have been one of three private jets.'

Khamovnikakh pounded the table with his bunched fist. Serov's feet all but left the ground, the shock was so severe. 'Three! Do the handers not recall loading the equipment on to a specific plane? This is all quite unbelievable!' Khamovnikakh snapped.

'I have spoken to all the men involved, *Vory*. They transported the cases to a Bay 23. A Lear Jet.'

'Then that should have been an end to the matter, surely.'

'I am afraid not. They were instructed by a man they took to be a member of the flight crew that the aircraft was not yet ready to load. The man asked them to return in an hour. Apparently there was some technical problem with the aircraft.'

Serov couldn't help noticing that Khamovnikakh was now grinding his teeth. He knew from experience that this was the premonitory sign of an outburst of violent anger.

'What happened to the cases, Valeriy?'

'They were not seen again by any of the members of the baggage handling team. The Lear Jet never took to the air. We must presume that this was a ruse, as was the consignee's address in Prague. The cases were in fact loaded into a different aircraft.'

Khamovnikakh continued to stare.

'Three private aircraft took off before we were able to shut the airport down,' Serov continued, his heart in his mouth.

'Why has this taken so long to establish?' Khamovnikakh asked with quiet menace.

'Tracing more than four hundred and eighty-six pieces of luggage took time, sir. I apologize.'

'I suggest it was the thought process that took the time. The three planes have been identified and traced?'

'All three identified. A German-owned Gulfstream – Hankerschmitt Worldwide. A 767 belonging to a Greek shipping company – Hellas/Apsos Marine. And a 727 owned by Buchanan Construction of Australia. The international authorities are dealing with the matter, as are we.'

The muscles of Khamovnikakh's face relaxed. 'Please let me know at once which of the parties is responsible.' He returned to the window. 'I would like to meet with whoever took my property. Here in Moscow. Do you fully understand me, Valeriy?'

Serov understood very well.

19.

**Pittwater. Sydney.
20th May.**

McCann was through customs by 7.45 a.m., and turning off the Mona Vale Road into McCarr's Creek by 8.50 am.

As the car rounded the final bend before the uphill stretch to the house, McCann could see L'Echapper Belle bathed in the early sunshine as she lay at anchor in the creek thirty feet below.

He wished, more than he cared to admit, that he'd never taken up Rosalind's quest. The job was turning decidedly nasty, and it didn't seem to be running in the direction Rosalind would have wished; one that provided clear, simple answers as to why Venice Messon had decided to kill herself in the Savoy. Instead, each upturned stone uncovered new details of some fresh malfeasance, seemingly quite unconnected to Maynard's death. It was beyond the realms of logic to believe that either Greville, Trevor, or the mystery Asian puppeteer of whom Boydell had spoken, could have put the girl up to killing herself as a favor to them.

However, what weighed most on McCann's mind was that it was just possible Whitey and Boydell might still be alive had Rosalind not asked him to start digging for answers.

Perhaps the most significant piece of information that Boydell had revealed was that Venice Messon was having an affair with an Asian who could easily have doubled for the man who'd died at the Savoy. And Boydell had seen this man in Hong Kong ten days *after* the Savoy bombing, though Mory, the bell captain at the Savoy, had been certain the Asian in the taxi was the dead Asian in the photograph.

McCann began to run possibilities though his head. Here he was theorizing about two men who were practically identical, and yet he hadn't considered the most logical explanation - that they were related. Twins. Not only did it explain the confusion of identities, it explained why both were at the Savoy. Both were there on the same business, except one arrived fractionally later than the other. The CIA had initially identified the photo of the dead man as a Vietnamese named Tran. Yet, as soon as they had established that Tran was alive, they'd dismissed him from their thoughts. If it had been his twin brother who had died in the explosion, naturally everything began to fit into place.

Mory had recognized the Asian in the photo, but had said he didn't think it was possible for the man to have had sufficient time to make it up to the fifteenth floor between the time of his arrival by taxi, and the explosion a short time thereafter. Brancusi's theory was that Venice Messon hadn't pressed the triggering switch on the bomb belt. Why hadn't she?

McCann considered the possibilities. Suppose when she entered the Stutton Conference Room she'd been confronted, not by the man she wished to kill, but by his twin brother - of whom she had no prior knowledge.

She was standing in the conference room with her finger on the switch when her cellular phone rang. She reached for the phone, and the aerial accidentally made contact with one of the wires as she pressed the 'Send' button. The rest was history.

McCann drew up outside his house, switched off the ignition but remained in the car as the thoughts sped through his brain. He could hear the phone begin to ring in the house.

So who the hell rang Venice in the Stutton Conference Room? Who knew her digital number? Her father didn't. She had few friends. Possibly Ritz or one of the Guardian Militia? That was possible.

Hendrik Ohlson. Who else? Suppose the young man was actually directly involved. Spotting the target for Venice? He sees the first man go in, and gives Venice the go-ahead. Then a minute or so later the twin brother arrives. This throws Hendrik for a loop - it's the last thing he's expecting. He immediately calls Venice, who is upstairs in the conference room unaware that her real target is in the lift on his way up. But before the second Asian can make it to the fifteenth, the bomb explodes.

The phone in the house rang again, and was picked up by the answering machine.

McCann was excited. If he was right about the twin, everything worked nicely. Even the footprint – the size nine European.

It was time to call Torrance.

He pressed the 'listen' switch on the answer machine, turning up the volume to full as he walked to the bedroom with his case. The accusing face of Cyclops, the lorikeet, stared at him through the window.

McCann stripped and searched for his toilet bag among his clothes as he listened to the messages. The first was from Matt. He told him to call any time day or night. He had information. McCann would be pleased. The second was from Rita at the Priory. A client called Roberts was insisting on personal attention. Could he call as soon as possible? The third was from Alan Messon. He sounded as if he'd pulled himself together. Would McCann call him urgently? The fourth was from Rosalind. Short and to the point. Call her. The fifth was from Torrance. A polite and formal message. Could he please call the task force office as soon as was convenient? The sixth, seventh, eighth and ninth were from Rosalind. All, with the exception of the last, were the same, asking him to return her call as soon as he got in. The last was different. She'd received a call from the Australian Federal Police. There was a meeting scheduled at the Buchanan building at midday. She wanted him there. And please call back as soon as he got in.

McCann was curious. What the hell did the Federal Police want? Perhaps Matt had pulled some strings, and the Feds had come up with some information for him. But if they'd been kind enough to spare the time to arrange a meeting, why hadn't they called him direct?

Ten minutes later, McCann was showered and dressed, Cyclops was tucking into an over-ripe plum, and McCann was dialing Matt. It would be almost half past eleven at night in London. After three rings the phone was answered.

'Matt? It's Leo.'

'Good to hear you, old buddy. Got some information you might be interested in. It's about your woman. Hugh Latimer was as thorough as ever. There's some interesting reading. Was going to fax it through, but I couldn't resist telling you personally. I know how satisfying it is to get just the answers you're looking for.'

'Fire ahead.'

'Latimer did a real number for me. Blue-coded the request through Interpol as well as getting his own boys on to it.'

'Yes, yes, yes,' McCann muttered. He was becoming impatient.

'Here goes. The girl. London to Charles de Gaulle, January 18th. Paris to Hong Kong, January 26th. Hong Kong to Ho Chi Minh City, January 27th.'

Shit, McCann swore softly to himself, the fact that she'd flown to Vietnam was good, it fitted nicely with his reasoning; but the interposition of Hong Kong was the curved ball. It was the last place on earth he'd have liked to hear Matt mention, since it brought Greville, Trevor and Brokov back into the picture.

Matt Hutton stopped speaking mid sentence – he'd picked up on McCann's expletive. 'What's that? Something not so good?

'Sorry, Matt. It was the mention of Hong Kong. The mention of the stopover there just complicates matters.'

'Paris to Ho Chi Minh goes via Hong Kong. There's no direct flight.'

'What about her visa?'

'The visa was applied for and picked up in Paris. Big Vietnamese community there. I presume that's why she was there for eleven days.'

'She used her own name for the tickets and visa?'

'Yes. Did you expect otherwise? Hell, I thought this was a straight-up enquiry.' Hutton sounded suddenly piqued. 'We've not been researching someone 'iffy' without your telling me, have we old boy? I hope not. Hugh will *definitely* not be pleased. I already owe the Thames boys a big favor.'

'Absolutely not, Matt, not in the least 'suss'. Where did she go from there?'

'Next time she shows up anywhere is November 16th. Hanoi to Bangkok. Then back to London same day.'

'Jesus Christ! She stayed in Vietnam for ten months? What was on the visa?'

'Student visa, valid one year. She flew back to Sydney two days later, 16th November.

'I don't suppose you can tell me where she stayed?'

'Sure. I'll fax the list through to you right now. I'll include the details of each meal she ate since she left Australia.'

McCann cut in quickly. 'Sorry, Matt.'

'Not to worry, just sending you up. As it happens we have an address in Paris, and one in Hong Kong. Both YWCA establishments. Nothing for Vietnam, I'm afraid. God knows why, they're usually pretty co-operative. If there's one country in the world I'd fancy my chances of getting lost, it wouldn't be Vietnam. Their immigration police are pretty spectacular.'

'Why do you think they didn't come to the party?'

'No idea. Latimer just said they were uncooperative.'

'Well, many thanks for the work, Matt. I appreciate it.'

'Not at all. How's Rosie?'

'She's well. Got to call her right now actually.'

'Well, give her my love, will you? Call if there's anything else.'

'There is something quite important you could do for me. May involve Langley.' He held the phone away from his ear – he knew Matt wouldn't take kindly to having to asking the CIA a favor.

'Hell's bells, Leo, can't you think of anything I can do myself!' Matt exploded. 'By the time I'm through doing you favors I'll owe a whole bunch myself.'

'I know, and I apologize.'

'Okay,' Matt said reluctantly. 'What is it?'

'A pal of mine who's heading up a police task force mentioned a Vietnamese national by the name of Tran.'

'That's his Christian name or surname?' Hutton interrupted.

'Don't know. Wasn't relevant at the time, so I didn't ask. I presume a family name. Anyway, his contact at Langley was someone called Harry Fine. He said this guy

Tran was on their hot list for a long time, then taken off around the mid eighties.'

'Why don't you ask your task force pal to ask Mr. Fine, or whatever his name is, rather than me?'

'I'd rather owe you one than him?'

'Oh great! That's fine,' Matt laughed good-naturedly. 'But who's Tran to you? What am I looking for?'

'I want to know if he has a brother. And while you're about it, can you ask them if they have an up-to-date photo, and any place of residence listed.'

'Anything else? Perhaps does he have any pimples on the bum?' Matt suggested dryly.

'Well, anything else from their files they wouldn't mind sharing, I suppose. Don't want to be a nuisance, do I?'

'I'd hope not. When do you need it?'

'Right now,' they both said at the same time.

'Speak to you soon, old friend,' Hutton said, then rang off.

McCann would have preferred to call Torrance, but the anxious edge to Rosalind's last message made him call her first.

'Leo! Thank God you called. You must have taken forever to get through customs.'

'Not really, it's only just after nine thirty, you know.'

'Seems later,' she replied defensively. 'Look, you've got to get over here by twelve. The Federal Police telephoned Ian this morning.'

'What's about?'

'I've no idea. I thought you might know.'

'Really?'

'Yes. I thought it might be part of the task force investigation.'

'Not as far as I know. And I'm sure Torrance would have mentioned it to me if it had been.'

'Well, I'd like you to be there.'

'Sure,' McCann replied, then a thought occurred to him. 'Is Bradley Radcliffe still with you in Sydney?'

'He's not with me right now. He's doing some business from home. International calls and so on. He's due here in twenty minutes. Why?'

'Just wondered.'

'He'll be here for the meeting, if that's what you're hinting at.'

This rang an odd bell. 'He's coming to the meeting? Why?'

'Because I asked him. He offered, actually. Do you have a problem with that?'

'No. Why should I?'

McCann was surprised by her sudden defensiveness.

'As it happens,' she continued, 'Brad's been associated with the company on and off for years. The Radcliffe family law firm has handled a few matters for us over the years.'

There was an awkward moment.

'How are you feeling anyway. Any bruises?' she said, to change the subject.

'Nothing much,' McCann replied fingering the surgical tape over his eye. He'd have to remember to change it.

'Got to go. I have a meeting with Torrance. See you midday.'

'Yes. Bye,' she replied, then rang off.

As McCann locked the front door, the phone rang inside, immediately reminding him that he'd forgotten to call Messon. As he walked through into the living room, he heard Messon begin to speak on the answering machine.

'This is Alan Messon for Leo McCann. Please call me urgently when you get in. I have some important news for you.'

McCann lifted the receiver.

'Just about to call you, Alan,' McCann lied. 'What's new?'

'Well, let's get something straight first. I'll tell you *my* news if you tell me how *your* inquiries are progressing. How about a trade?'

'I work for Rosalind Buchanan. She pays the bills,' McCann replied as diplomatically as possible. He didn't want to hurt the old man's feelings, but he could hardly spare the time to call Messon each day keeping him up to date.

'What happened to all your easy talk of compassion the last time we met. Remember? *Show some compassion for Miss Buchanan, I know she does for you.* I think that's how it went.'

'You've a good memory, Alan.'

'I'm not completely senile yet.'

'So what have you got for me, Alan,' McCann asked, hoping Messon would let his 'deal' slip.

'Something pretty interesting. I think Miss Buchanan is going to want to hear it. Concerns the man who procured the plastic explosive for my daughter.' There was a teasing edge to his voice. He was obviously not going to say anything more.

'Okay, Alan. Deal. I'll share my stuff. Now what have you got?'

'Have you heard of a man called Ritz?'

'Yes. Torrance at Task Force told me about him already. Have you found him? Torrance will be your friend for life.'

'To hell with Torrance. No, I haven't found Ritz. However, last night I came across a man called Kevin Jacks. On the street he goes by the name of 'Road Runner' or 'Roadie'. Said he knew plenty about Ritz, but it would cost me. I tried to persuade him to talk to me for nothing but he refused point blank.'

'So what? You want Rosalind to pay?'

'Please don't insult me, Leo. I'm meeting with the man tonight. You see, I didn't have the money last night. The man wanted five hundred dollars. And he won't talk to the police. Any sign of them, he's off.'

'What time tonight?'

'Ten o'clock, the Zero Dance Machine. It's a club halfway down Broadway towards Central Station.'

'Okay. I'm in. I'll see you then.'

'You're in when we shake hands on the deal. We share – right?'

There didn't seem any other way. He needed to talk to Messon's man, no question, and Torrance would be very grateful for the lead. But if he agreed to Messon's deal, he'd have to tell the man everything. McCann didn't believe in half measures. If he gave his word, that was that.

'Okay, Alan. Deal. Goodbye.' Quite how he was going to break the news to old man Messon that his pride and joy was screwing a criminal twice her age in the residence of a Cabinet Minister was a problem he'd have to address later.

Torrance unscrewed the cap of the bottled water, and took a long draw as he fingered the tape McCann had given him.

'We've taken three separate statements from residents of Wharf Road. All have given approximately the same description.'

'Six-two, curly thick black hair, aquiline nose, brooding eyes, thick full lips. The girl was small, slim and dark. How's that?' McCann prompted.

Torrance looked like a man who'd just told his wife he'd won the lottery only to find the Lotto people had telephoned ahead with the news. 'Go on, then. Tell me how you know so exactly.'

'A man called Boydell told me yesterday in Hong Kong.'

'Really. And he saw them in Birchgrove? My, he gets around, your friend.'

'He did. He's dead now. Murdered by the same man that killed Imogen Whitehead.'

Briefly McCann shared the details of the Hong Kong trip with Torrance. The Chief Super listened intently as McCann recounted his conversation with Boydell. McCann wasn't about to waste time; Torrance could listen to the tape as often as he liked when his secretary returned with a recorder.

'Your instinct tells you the man who killed Boydell was the same man Boydell says killed Palmer – Brokov?'

'Very definitely. Mind you I only have Boydell's description to go on. But given that it's accurate, I'd say it has to be the same man. How close was I to the description in the Birchgrove statements?'

'Pretty well spot on. Tall dark and extremely handsome was the way one middle-aged female described him. She didn't have much interest in the woman, just said she was thin. Both the others are similar.'

'What time did they notice them?'

'Around seventy-twenty. Two of them were on the way to catch the seven-thirty ferry to Circular Quay. The other man was just being nosey, bless him. I'll get straight on to Interpol and see if your man Brokov's got a record anywhere. Chances are he has. If so, I'll get them to fax a photo. I'll also put an alert on all points of entry in case he decides to come back here.'

'What do you think of my "twin" theory?'

'Very interesting.'

'You see, the brother's in the elevator on his way up as the bomb explodes. The doors open and the man's confronted by heavy smoke and debris. He's got two choices, either get the hell out fast or see what's happened.'

'You're assuming he had some criminal purpose.'

Torrance was on his hobbyhorse again. Assumptions; he'd never liked them. But what the hell was wrong with one or two? Where was his clinical approach based on fact getting the investigation?

'Yes, I think it's safe to assume that,' McCann replied with all the restraint he could muster. 'If he didn't have a criminal purpose he would have stayed to offer some kind of help. He doesn't. He knows his brother's in the conference room, and he can clearly see that no one inside could have survived. Nevertheless, he runs into room. Why? Because he wants to see if he can snatch whatever evidence Horan brought with him to the meeting.'

'How can he see anything at all? What about the smoke?'

'It's beginning to dissipate fast. The windows are out. As is the door. Brancusi said the smoke wasn't that bad when he entered.'

Torrance thought for a moment, then slowly shook his head. 'Nah, too *many* assumptions, McCann,' Torrance said quietly shaking his head.

'I don't think so. We know from Imogen Whitehead that Horan was on to Greville in Hong Kong and Trevor in the Channel Islands, and now we know from Boydell that the double of the dead Asian in the photo was the power behind them. It's Tran. Come on, even the CIA were initially fooled by the photo.'

'Hold on. Back a bit. You have a *theory* that the dead Asian had a twin bother, and it was this man, Tran, who had dealings with Greville and Trevor.'

McCann abruptly held up his arm. 'Mory!' he shouted. He'd quite forgotten the bell captain. 'Did anyone ask the Maori bell captain at the Savoy if he'd seen the Asian arrive?'

Torrance thought for a moment. 'We asked his partner, the concierge,' he began uncertainly after a few seconds, 'he told us he clearly remembered seeing the Asian arrive in a black Mercedes.'

'But did anyone ask Mory the same question?' McCann sensed he had Torrance flat-footed. The Chief Super was replying defensively, as though he felt he'd missed something.

'Not that I remember, no. Why would we ask the bell captain? His partner had positively identified the Asian arriving. End of story. We spent three days trying to nail the Merc!'

'Well, I showed the photo to Mory and he swears he saw the dead man arrive in a taxi only moments before the bomb went up. How does the "twin theory" stack up now?'

Torrance merely stared at McCann. He knew he'd made a major error.

'And don't forget we have the size nine European shoeprint partials. They are proof that someone entered the room before Brancusi got there. Why not Tran? He knows his brother is dead, and he knows Horan's in there too. Someone took the disks. That's an indisputable fact. Yet you've no idea who the hell that someone could have been.'

'We don't know for a fact the disks were there,' Torrance countered.

'We know Horan used the same computer disks as the one found in the shell of the bombed computer. We can safely assume, and I use that word with the greatest care, that it was Horan's computer. At his home I discovered that there were four disks missing from the box in his desk. That's three that Tran could have stolen from the plastic case at the bomb scene, and one, the blue one, the most recent, which was still in the laptop, because he couldn't dislodge it. I'd say all that points strongly to my theory that it was Tran who stole them.'

'And then he just skipped off home to Vietnam?'

'I'd say so. Somewhere out of Australia, anyway. There was no point in hanging around. His brother was dead. Horan was dead. And he had the computer disks, which were Horan's audit evidence.'

'All but the blue one; he couldn't get it out of the computer. He probably hoped it was too badly damaged to be able to recall data from it,' Torrance mused. 'Which brings us back to the shoeprint. The lab boys have done a great job on them. There were five partials in all. By the time they'd added them to the print you identified initially, they managed to patch all of them together with the computer, like a jigsaw. We called in a New Zealand podiatrist called Coyle. Seems the man who wore that shoe had a partial clubfoot, or something similar. Coyle was able to work that out by assessing weight and tread patterns. This man walked with pressure on the outside of the foot. That's what I'm told, anyway. The shoe would have had to be custom made by a specialist in orthopedic footwear.'

'Can we check the immigration computer records for the possible entry and exit of Tran either side of the bombing?' McCann asked.

'Absolutely. If you're right, and Tran was here in Sydney, he wouldn't have shown up on the immigration listings I asked for. You see, I made the request two days after the bombing. I couldn't do so before that because the forensic boys and the *detailer*, as I like to call Roy at the morgue, hadn't finished with the body. Of course at that stage I was only searching for the ID of the dead Asian, I wasn't looking out for anyone else. And by that time, Tran would have exited the country, and have cleared the computer system. If the dead body is Tran's brother, tracing his entry visa now should be a piece of cake. I'll make a request via ASIO to trace whether or not Tran did in fact have a brother.'

McCann cut him short. 'I've already called Matt Hutton. He said he'd fast track it.' He was about to continue, when a thought struck him out of left field. 'Damn,' he muttered to himself.

'What's wrong?' Torrance asked.

'I should have asked Matt to ask whether Tran's a Cham.'

'He is.' It was Torrance's turn to have the answers. 'It was in the file they sent from Langley, when we initially thought we'd ID'd the dead Asian.'

They sat in silence for a full minute. McCann felt a certain sympathy for Torrance. The police chief clearly felt foolish. He'd made some pretty fundamental mistakes during this investigation; errors that were quite out of character.

'What happens if Brokov shows up back in Australia?' McCann asked eventually.

'That would be someone else's responsibility, I'm afraid. You see, one thing I have to bear in mind is my terms of reference. Though the task force parameters are not set in stone, my focus is on the bombing and its social and political significance. I shouldn't be going off on tangents that don't concern the task force investigation; matters such as international fraud, money-laundering and murders unconnected with the bombing.'

McCann opened his mouth to protest, but Torrance held up a hand and sped on. 'The plain fact is that a young girl called Venice Messon managed to get hold of explosives from some source or other, and killed herself, three other people, and injured thirty or so passers-by at the Savoy. The State is concerned with the ramifications of the bombing. That's it, pure and simple. That was why Task Force Acorn was established. The Police Minister and the State Commander wanted to make damned sure it never happened again. Boydell told you Venice Messon was having an affair with an as yet unidentified Asian. If that was the case, it would seem to me more likely that Venice Messon had a purely personal motive for the bombing, a grudge against one or both of the Asians.'

'No. Just Tran,' McCann interrupted. 'Otherwise she would have triggered the firing mechanism herself when she saw that it was his brother in the conference room.'

Torrance rubbed his eyes with the base of his thumbs in a world-weary gesture. 'Whatever. Yes, all right, Tran for the sake of argument. However, the death of Imogen Whitehead is in the hands of the detectives at South Region. It's not our concern here at Task Force Acorn.'

'Why?' McCann could hardly believe his ears. That Torrance didn't consider Whitey's death came within Torrance's terms of reference was scarcely credible. 'I would have thought it was vital to your investigations.'

'McCann. I have to repeat that here at Task Force Acorn we are involved in the investigation into the bombing; who was responsible - whether it could happen again. I have determined that the murder of Imogen Whitehead is unconnected with the actual bombing. Unless of course you can tell me otherwise.'

'It *must* be within your terms of reference, surely.' McCann was astounded.

'Within the terms of reference, absolutely. But someone else's direct responsibility. As are Horan, Tran - if it's proved he was there - Brokov, Boydell – ' He smiled at McCann, adding, 'And yourself - as a victim of course.'

'Glad I rate a mention.'

'When I'm satisfied that I know why Venice Messon did what she did, where she gained possession of the explosives, and who else should be held responsible, that's the time I will inform the State Commander. He set up the task force in the first place. I shall recommend that, given the initial task force criteria, we should call a halt to our inquiries, wind up the task force, and leave investigations to the relevant authorities.'

They sat facing each other in silence for a couple of minutes. Then Torrance spoke.

'How's your coffee, by the way.'

McCann looked down at it. A skin had formed on the surface. It looked marginally more disgusting now than when Maggie had handed it to him twenty minutes ago. He put it down on Torrance's desk.

'I think I'll pass this time.'

'As for the involvement of Russell Croaker, I'd keep that snippet of gossip to myself at present if I were you. Meantime, I'll make it my business to make sure it reaches the ears of ICAC.' To Torrance's mind the Independent Commission Against Corruption was the ideal committee to hear of such unsubstantiated information. It would either go no further, or be acted upon. Either way, it would be investigated further, quite independently, and without political bias.

'Incidentally, Alan Messon called me this morning,' said McCann after a few moments.

'Did he? You know he still calls *me* every day. He says he won't rest till he finds the person who gave the explosives to his daughter. I presume he thinks that in some way that absolves her from any personal responsibility. He's like a dog with a bone. Spent most of his life ignoring his daughter; then, once she's blown herself to bits, killing three others in the process, he chooses that time to cast himself in the role of grieving father bent on personal vengeance.'

'That's being a bit uncharitable,' McCann observed. He had a soft spot for the old man. Sure, Messon had made some major mistakes in his personal life, but so had millions of others. Messon had guts and determination. He was also a genuine eccentric, and they were a dying breed well worth looking after.

'Messon says he's come up with someone who has the goods on Ritz. We're going to meet him tonight,' McCann said.

Torrance's sudden change in expression was startling. 'Who's he come up with? What's his name?' he asked.

'First of all, I'd better say that Messon cautioned me that this guy won't talk to the police. Says if there's any police presence this evening, he's off.'

'What's his name?'

'Look, I'll tell you exactly what he said tomorrow, word for word. Okay?'

The tone of Torrance's voice was doggedly insistent. 'Did Messon ask you not to reveal the man's identity?'

McCann tried to recall. 'No. Actually he didn't,' he conceded after a few moments.

'What's the man's name then?' Torrance demanded strongly.

'Kevin Jacks.'

Torrance thought for second, quickly flipped through a file on his desk, then looked up. 'Don't know him. Maybe a DEA informer.'

'Look, I've told you his name. Please hold off on Jacks till I've had a chance to talk to him.'

Torrance stared down at the desk, in two minds as to whether he should allow McCann to do work that was the particular responsibility of his own team. He then looked up at McCann. 'I'd like you to wear a wire this evening. Just in case you forget anything.'

'Sure,' McCann replied. 'I'll drop the tape in to you tomorrow.'

'Tonight, if that's at all possible,' Torrance said without any particular interest in the reply. He then shifted in his seat, reaching round behind him and opening the small fridge. He pulled out another bottle of mineral water.

'Gone on a diet?' McCann asked.

Torrance looked puzzled. 'Diet? Why do you ask?'

'The absence of toffees.'

'Run out. Simple as that. Sure I can't temp you to a nourishing bottled water?'

'A short black, maybe,' McCann muttered.

To McCann's great surprise Torrance put a couple of fingers in his mouth and whistled. A couple of seconds later his assistant, detective Lou, was at the door.

'Sorry to trouble you, Lou. Could you do something for me. Our friend here, Mr. McCann, is going to be helping us out this evening, and he really needs a short black right now. Could you send out for one. Giorgio's on the corner should be able to oblige. And can you ask Maggie to arrange a wire for Mr. McCann to take with him when he leaves?'

'Yes, sir,' Lou replied crisply, and was gone.

'One good turn deserves another, McCann. Here's one for you. In return for wearing the wire for me, I'll tell you where young Venice Messon spent her time during the time her father thought she was in England.'

McCann couldn't resist sending up Torrance's, despite the Chief Super's prior embarrassment at having failed to have Mory properly interviewed at the Savoy. 'In Vietnam by way of Paris, I'd imagine. January 27th? Left November? My guess would be... let me see. Back in Australia 27th?

McCann smiled affably at Torrance, whose face was a mask of granite.

'You can be a very annoying man, McCann,' he said eventually in the thickest Yorkshire accent. 'Who told you?'

'Matt Hutton.'

Torrance took a deep breath. 'Yes, I should have realized.'

'I'd say she was with Tran in Vietnam,' he said, looking at Torrance for confirmation. 'Just an assumption, of course,' he added, twisting the knife.

Torrance returned McCann's smile – he took the ribbing well. 'Spent a few months with the man, then came back here and made preparations to blow him to pieces next time he set foot in Australia? Can't have been too much of a good host, eh?'

McCann laughed. 'Tell me something. How would I get hold of a photograph of Sir Henry Trevor in a hurry? I like to be able to recognize my enemies.'

Torrance smiled wryly. 'You mean, short of having a buddy at the ABC, Newsdesk, or Reuters? I suppose you'd have to ask me a favor. Then I in turn would ask someone in London to fax me one.'

'Thanks.'

'Glad to help.'

'How did you find out about Venice Messon and Vietnam?' McCann asked.

'Interpol. Took a lot of bloody hard arm-twisting and graft I tell you. Next time I'll ask you,' Torrance answered mischievously.

At that moment Lou arrived and placed a small brown cup of coffee on the desk in front of McCann. In one side of the saucer was a sachet of sugar, in the other a small piece of lemon rind.

'It's a double,' she said, eyes on the cup.

'Looks delicious. Many thanks,' McCann said, draining the cold coffee in a single gulp. 'Wonderful.'

As Lou returned to her desk outside, McCann stood.

'Just one more thing. I'd like to have a word with Hendrik Ohlson. Can you give me an address or a telephone number for him?'

'If you hadn't asked about him, I would have pushed you in his direction again before you left. Glad you didn't disappoint me,' Torrance said, smiling.

'You never bought his story, did you.'

'Never. One of the few occasions when I had one of your "feelings".'

'Did he give any reason for being there?'

'Said he'd been in the arcade. A book shop. But he didn't buy anything. Maggie interviewed him again later, but couldn't find a chink in his story – stuck to exactly the same facts as he told me.'

'Why didn't you come right out and tell me how you felt? You could have quite simply asked me to "unofficially" lean on the lad a bit.'

Torrance winced at McCann's choice of words. 'Yes, that's about it. That's what I couldn't bring myself to ask. It's not in my nature. I've spent all my life in the force avoiding the easy options. You see, the moment you begin on that slippery path, you're lost. Next stop is planting evidence, fit-ups, coercing confessions. I'm sure you understand me, eh?'

McCann nodded. He knew exactly what Torrance meant.

Torrance opened a drawer, pulling out a file. He flipped through it, wrote an address on a notepad, then handed the top sheet to McCann, together with a passport-sized photograph. 'The snap's from the university registry. See what you come up with.'

'I'll see what I can do,' McCann replied. Then he remembered his conversation with Rosalind. 'By the way, do you know why the Federal boys would have asked for a meeting with the Board at Buchanan Construction?'

Torrance's face was a blank. 'No idea. Nothing to do with us.'

'Just have to see, won't we.'

'Don't forget to ask Maggie for the tape-recorder and the wire,' Torrance called out.

As McCann reached the door, he pulled a small box from his briefcase and tossed it across to Torrance.

'What's this?'

'A gift,' McCann replied, smiling. 'Toffees. Bought them in Hong Kong at the airport. They're Callard & Bowser. English of course. Supposedly the best.'

When he opened the door to Rosalind's office she was wrapped around Bradley Radcliffe. McCann stood by the door for a couple of seconds, feeling like a complete fool, mentally cursing Leila, Rosalind's secretary. Why hadn't she buzzed Rosalind as usual? Possibly she had, but they'd been too absorbed. Either way, he could hardly back out the door now.

'Good morning,' McCann said cheerily.

Rosalind's body reacted as though touched by an electric cattle prod. She was quite clearly a very private girl. She smiled and pushed her hair back behind her ears.

'Leo. Come and meet Bradley,' she said.

McCann joined them by the window.

Radcliffe smiled broadly, extending a hand. 'Hi. Bradley Radcliffe,' the tall man replied.

'Leo McCann,' he replied taking Radcliffe's firm grip.

McCann wasn't usually one to notice such things, but the media hadn't been exaggerating. This man was Hollywood material.

The men shook hands. McCann felt unaccountably awkward. For a moment he couldn't think of a thing to say. Bradley just stood there in total command of the moment, smiling relaxedly. All Leo could think of was how stunning Rosalind looked.

'How's your father's campaign progressing, Mr. Radcliffe?'

'Really well, I'm happy to tell you. Really well. I wish I could have come to Australia sooner, but it just wasn't possible. So many loose ends to tie up after the California primary. That was some convention.' He laughed easily. His teeth were perfect.

'So next stop the party convention, and the nomination?'

'I guess,' Bradley replied with a smile. It seemed to McCann a dumb reply for something the man knew for a certainty.

'How's your head?' Rosalind asked, looking at the inch-long scar over McCann's right eye, running her forefinger over the scar tissue.

'It's fine,' McCann replied, aware that Bradley was studying him closely. For some reason there was an atmosphere of tension in the room. Perhaps they'd had a fight, and he'd arrived just as they were making up. It didn't matter. He just wished they could get on with the meeting, and skip the small talk.

'I hear Bill Johnson may still run as an independent,' McCann said. Rosalind appeared to have lost her tongue, and Bradley was still looking expectantly at him.

'Looks that way. It'd be just great if he did. Split the democratic share clean in two. Well, he'd certainly steal a large wedge of voters from them. Wouldn't touch *us*.'

The Reverend Bill Johnson was the African American congressman from Illinois. He'd run four years ago, and hadn't done too badly. Now it was rumored an unrevealed backer from Utah had funded Johnson for a second tilt at the title.

'How long will you be in Sydney, Mr. Radcliffe?' McCann asked.

'Brad's got to get back tomorrow. I'm going with him for a couple of days.'

'Got to gear up for the convention,' Bradley said.

'When's the election proper?'

'November five,' Bradley replied.

'By the way - Whitey's cremation. It's tomorrow?' McCann asked Rosalind. Anything to end the stilted conversation with Radcliffe.

'Eleven a.m. Do you want to come?' Rosalind replied.

'I hardly knew her, but yes, I'd like to.'

Leila then mercifully buzzed through with the news that the Federal Police were in the boardroom.

'Thank you, Leila. Could you tell Ian and Bob we're on our way. Ask them to join us there.'

'Of course, Ms Buchanan.'

Mackintosh and Zeltis were sitting round the boardroom table, either side of an Australian Federal policeman. They rose as Rosalind entered.

The introductions took a few moments, then Rosalind sat. This time she chose the head of the table. Bradley sat farthest from her. McCann drew up a chair halfway down the table opposite the policeman, who'd introduced himself as Detective Inspector Richard Eade. He looked around thirty. He was slim, with intelligent eyes and bad skin.

'First of all I'd like to thank you for your co-operation Miss Buchanan. I appreciate you must be extremely busy,' Eade opened politely. His voice was confident, and rich with authority.

'Not at all, Mr. Eade. I asked Ian Mackintosh and Bob Zeltis, our Group Managing Directors to be here in case there were any areas that I'm personally unfamiliar with. Mr. McCann is here merely as an observer; he's not with the company. Mr. Radcliffe is a friend and sometime legal advisor.' She cleared her throat. 'So what exactly can we do for you, Mr. Eade?'

'The Buchanan Construction company jet is a Boeing 727. Is that correct?'

'That's right,' Rosalind replied.

McCann looked from Eade to Rosalind, who looked a trifle confused. It was clear from her expression that this line of questioning was the last thing she'd expected.

Eade unzipped his attaché case. In the silence of the boardroom it sounded like a whipcrack. He withdrew a sheet of closely typed A4 paper.

'The morning of March 27th at approximately eleven, the Buchanan Construction jetliner, a 727 registration number Victor Hotel nine seven seven nine, was standing on the apron at Sheremetyevo Airport Moscow. I'm sure you don't keep these facts in your head, but I'd be grateful if you could ask someone to confirm this for me.' Eade looked at Rosalind, who shifted her glance to Mackintosh who immediately rose from his chair.

'I'll just step outside and get the details,' he said with an easy smile. 'Won't be a moment.'

The door closed behind him, and they all sat in an awkward silence for half a minute or so.

McCann noticed Zeltis cast a look at Rosalind, as if he wanted to forewarn her of something, but she in turn was trying to catch the eye of Bradley, who was rubbing his forehead with his hand, looking down at the table. March 27th. The day after her father had been killed. Small wonder Eade's remark had thrown her for a loop.

'I don't suppose,' Eade said, breaking the silence, 'without the benefit of advice, that you'd be in a position to tell me whether the jet was on company business?'

'I would assume so,' Rosalind replied. 'It belongs to the company. It's not used for private business. My father broke that rule very rarely.'

McCann watched Eade open his mouth to speak, hesitate, then continue. 'Miss Buchanan. Please excuse me if I refer to matters which will still be very fresh and painful, but I believe your father Maynard Buchanan was in Sydney around that time.'

'My father was killed in the Savoy explosion the day before. The 26th.'

'Yes. I'm so sorry.'

'Thank you, Mr. Eade.'

The detective nodded. 'Were you using the jet at the time, Miss Buchanan?'

'I was in Los Angeles, attending a political convention. It was the day of the California primary.'

McCann shot a glance at Rosalind. She was coping well, not in the least emotional, just stating the facts in a controlled manner.

A studied look of puzzlement crossed Eade's face, one he obviously hoped wasn't lost on the faces round the table.

'Is the company jet often used to transport goods, Miss Buchanan? Or is its purpose mostly for the convenience of your father, yourself and board members?'

'It is also for the convenience of our clients,' Rosalind remarked. 'I can't remember the plane being used for transport, not for some time at least.'

At that moment the boardroom door opened, and Ian Mackintosh entered, carrying a manila folder. He held it up briefly, then tossed it on the table in front of his chair as he sat down, a cheerful expression on his face.

'This should answer any questions you may have, Mr. Eade,' Mackintosh said, riffling through the pages. 'March 27th?'

All eyes were on Mackintosh. Even Bradley Radcliffe looked up.

'Here we are.' Mackintosh's confident smile faded slightly, it was evident that the words on the page were not those he'd expected. 'It would appear that the 727 was leased out from the 25th to the 28th. I have to say I'm surprised. It appears from the records that – ' He was about to continue when Bradley cut in.

'Excuse my interrupting, Ian. Of course. I remember now. It should have rung a bell. I guess I was dreaming. Maynard rang me,' he took a deep breath as he struggled with his memory. 'It was around the 20th as I recall. We talked about one thing and another, and during the course of the conversation I mentioned a client of mine had been looking to lease a plane. Maynard seemed keen to lease his 727, so I said I'd get back to him. We worked out a leasing contract, and that was that. No big deal. Simple four-day lease agreement.'

'Was your client an individual or a company, Mr. Radcliffe?'

'I would have to make a call to my office to verify matters, but as I recall the company was The New World Hotel Group. I had no personal knowledge of the company at the time, merely their merchant bankers.'

Eade was taking notes on a pad. He looked up as the flow of Bradley's words came to a halt. 'Could you tell me who the bankers were, sir?'

'Rowe, Radley Associates. The Turks and Caicos Islands. I've dealt with them before. I assure you they're quite reputable,'

'Can I ask what this is all about, Mr. Eade,' Rosalind enquired.

'Of course. I apologize. Perhaps I should have filled you in with the background before I started with the questions. We have been asked, as a matter of courtesy, to make inquires on behalf of our counterparts in New York and Moscow concerning the disappearance of a shipment of banknotes. Fifty bags of US hundred dollar bills were stolen from the cargo hold of Delta flight 30 at Sheremetyevo Airport on the 27th of March.'

'How does this concern our company jet, Mr. Eade?' It was Ian Mackintosh's turn to be haughty.

'The Federal Bureau of Investigation, together with the Russian authorities, have determined that the cargo could only have left the airport perimeter in one of three planes that took off before the airport was closed. One of the aircraft was your company jet.'

'Have you been in touch with the other two?' Zeltis inquired. He patently was a devotee of the *what about the other guy?* school of thought.

'We haven't, ourselves. However, authorities in Greece and Germany have done so,' Eade replied. 'Anyway, I would be very grateful if you could confirm the names of your client and the merchant bank for me, Mr. Radcliffe. And I presume you have a copy of the lease agreement, Mr. Mackintosh. If it wouldn't be too much to ask, perhaps I could take a copy of it with me.'

Eade placed his notepad inside his attaché case, zipping up the side.

'I'll have my secretary fix you up with a copy of the agreement right now,' Mackintosh said as he rose.

'If there's anything else we can do for you, please don't hesitate to ask. I can't believe that our airplane was involved in any way,' Rosalind added

Bradley laughed lightly. 'Nor can I. I've been dealing with Rowe, Radley for many years. I can't believe they have international currency thieves among their clients.'

'I'm sure you're right, sir. But we have been asked to look into the matter.'

Mackintosh waved a hand. 'Quite understand. If you'll just come with me, I'll arrange the photostat.'

Rosalind stood. The meeting was at an end.

McCann headed for Bob Zeltis' office.

An elegantly dressed, bespectacled secretary in her mid-twenties sat behind a desk in an annex outside the Group M.D's door. McCann introduced himself, and she lifted the phone on her desk. A few moments later he was inside.

Zeltis' office was directly beneath what had once been Maynard's, and was now Rosalind's. In contrast to hers, his was high-tech. Every horizontal surface was crammed with computer equipment, accessories and gadgets.

'Welcome,' Zeltis said simply with the hesitant smile of a host who rarely entertains. 'What can I do for you, Leo?'

'Look, it may be nothing, and it may be a personal matter that is none of my business, but just now upstairs I got the impression that when Detective Eade mentioned the 727, you were trying to forewarn Rosalind about something with a facial expression.'

A look of incomprehension clouded Zeltis's face. 'Just now? You mean during the meeting?'

'When Eade referred to the company jet, and Ian left the room for the file, it seemed to me you were trying to tell Ms Buchanan something with your eyes, because you weren't in a position to say anything.'

Zeltis gestured to a chair. 'Why don't you take the weight off, Leo.'

'Thanks, but I can't stay,' McCann replied.

Zeltis sucked his teeth and looked out the picture window. 'It was nothing really. I mean, in the best of all possible worlds I would have preferred Rosalind to have known that Bradley had arranged the lease, rather than the fact coming out of left field. It's never ideal when the CEO is asked a question that everyone in the room knows the answer to but the boss. I would have liked to spare her the embarrassment - that's all. Particularly because it was her boyfriend who had done the legal work.'

'You knew of the arrangement?'

'Not at the time, no. Maynard handled the matter personally. He mentioned it, though, the following day.' He chuckled.

'Why do you laugh, Bob?'

'Oh, it's probably just semantics, but my recollection was that it was Bradley who was keen to lease the jet, not Maynard. He'd never done that before, leasing the plane that is. I remember him giving me the analogy of renting his home, and having strangers running through it. You wouldn't do that unless you were desperate for the cash. And he most certainly wasn't that short of a few thousand dollars.'

'So why did he agree?'

'He told me he agreed because he didn't have much of a choice. Bradley Radcliffe had asked a favor, and Maynard owed the family a few.'

'But upstairs, Bradley intimated he'd been doing Maynard Buchanan a favor.'

'That's my point.'

'By the way, Bob, where the hell are the Turks and Caicos Islands?'

'To the right of Cuba, above Haiti.'

'They have banks there? Banks that reputable law firms in New York do business with? Give me a break.'

'No, hold on, Leo. The Turks and Caicos are just one of a whole new breed of offshore banking havens. Used to be only a few; Jersey, the Bahamas, Panama, Switzerland, the Cayman Islands, Liechtenstein, among others. Now there's also Vanuatu, the Republic of Nauru, St Kitts, Niau, the list goes on. They're quite legit.' He screwed up his face, then smiled. 'Well, they have their legitimate *side*.'

'Why would Bradley Radcliffe be dealing with Rowe, Radley?'

'Why not? They're respectable merchant bankers; well, respectable enough, so I'm told. You've got to remember that when you're talking offshore banking, the Caymans represent the fifth largest banking economy in the world – that's judging by the wire transfer traffic of course, everything else is secret.'

Zeltis took note of McCann's expression of surprise, and chuckled.

'Not many people know that. Of course a lot of the attraction is the lack of regulation, and the high price put on secrecy by their clientèle – the protection offered of anonymous bearer corporations and so on. On the other hand, to be fair to the offshore banks, they've thrived partly because the world financial community is sick of the US regulatory requirements, and their onerous banking regulations. Same applies to the increased scrutiny of customers of US financial institutions by law enforcement agencies. Ultimately, you have to remember that the vast bulk of transactions in these havens are strictly legit.'

'For instance?' McCann asked.

'For instance, there's a Federal Reserve System requirement that a percentage of deposits held in the US be placed with the regional Federal Reserve Bank each night in a reserve account that bears no interest. So banks with a high volume of corporate accounts establish an account overseas. That way they sidestep the requirement, and don't have to forgo the interest even for one night. Offshore banking havens are also attractive because they often offer higher interest rates.'

'How can they compete in terms of interest rates with say, the Chase Manhattan?'

'They don't have to hold the reserve amount in a non-interest-bearing account with the district Federal Reserve Bank as the Chase does. It's a kind of insurance fund the government has always insisted on in the States. Doesn't exist offshore.'

Zeltis drew a Cuban cigar from the box on his desk and crinkled it with his thumb and finger, then drew it across his upper lip, inhaling the scent deeply.

'Never smoke them. Sometimes give them to valued clients. But I love the feel of them. Pure brilliant native craftsmanship. I love the smell.'

He replaced the cigar in the box without offering one to McCann. Clearly an investigator didn't qualify for a gift.

'Barings had an account in the Cayman's to cover margin calls for Nick Leeson's cavalier futures trading,' Zeltis continued, warming to the lecture. 'So you can see that the mere mention of places like Liberia, the Caymans and the Turks and Caicos don't necessarily conjure up the Colombian drug cartels. Mind you, my private belief is that they do everything they can to lure the legit corporations to their island paradises so they can traffic with the criminals. Can't deal exclusively with the crooks, can you? Might be a trifle obvious.'

Zeltis took a deep breath, suggesting by his body language that he'd prefer to move on. 'Drink?'

'Thanks, but no thanks, Bob. Got to go.'

Zeltis looked disappointed.

McCann stuck his head round the door. Rosalind and Bradley were deep in conversation on the sofa by the window. Neither looked exactly happy as a clam. They looked round as McCann spoke.

'Sorry to butt in, I've got a meeting across town. Thought you might want to see me before I left.'

'Of course! Come in, Leo,' Rosalind replied. 'By the way, I forgot to ask you. How was the meeting with Torrance? Are they any further forward?'

'Quite a lot, actually.'

'Going to share it with the boss?' she said, suddenly more cheerful.

McCann was silent. His eyes drifted imperceptibly from hers to Bradley's then back again, purely for her benefit. McCann noticed the slightest change of expression in her eyes as the muscles round them tightened in irritation. She knew he was attempting to exclude Bradley.

'I have a theory,' McCann replied reluctantly.

'What's that?' she probed.

'Look, I have to search out a friend of Venice Messon's, and then I have to meet with her father. I'd really rather talk to you either late tonight or early tomorrow when it's all come together.'

'Can't you give me an idea now?' She was all sweetness now.

'Yes, I could,' he said without further reluctance. 'Basically I now believe that your father was an innocent victim. Tragically he and Andrew Horan happened to be in the same room as the man that Venice Messon meant to kill.'

'And who was that?' It was Bradley who spoke.

'A Vietnamese called Tran.'

'Who is he? Do we know?' Bradley continued.

McCann shot Bradley a look. What did he mean, 'we'. Suddenly he'd included himself in the investigation, and McCann resented it.

'Yes *we* know,' McCann replied evenly.

'Well, who is he? Are you going to tell us, or keep us in suspense?' Bradley said good-naturedly, yet subliminally challenging McCann. Maybe his attitude reflected the fact that he could smell McCann's interest in his woman.

'I'm going to keep you in suspense,' McCann replied, as if in jest, yet shifting his glance to Rosalind, who seemed fully aware of the tension between the men.

'What was the Vietnamese's connection with the girl?' she asked, her face registering an intense concentration.

'Based on what Boydell told me, it appears that she was having an affair with him.'

'And what was this man Tran doing in the same room as dad and Horan?'

'That I don't know exactly, yet,' McCann replied, then held up a hand as Rosalind opened her mouth to ask another question. 'Rosalind, I would really prefer to speak to Messon's contact first.'

'Why?'

'I just have a feeling that he'll tell me what I want to know. If I'm right, then you'll have your answers and that'll be the end of the matter.'

'What do you mean, the end of the matter.'

Suddenly McCann knew this wasn't going to be easy. She was the kind of woman that liked getting her own way, and it didn't include his resignation. She clearly wanted him to pursue the matter to the end of the earth, but he had better things to do; not the least of which was to take a few days off and sail down the coast. It'd make a change from fighting for his life in a speedboat in Hong Kong Harbor.

'You wanted to know why your father died. Why Venice Messon did what she did. Now it's beginning to look as though her motive was strictly personal and quite unconnected to your father. You didn't ask me to investigate all the other matters that have come to light during my investigations - international corporate fraud, the murder of Imogen Whitehead, the murder of Phillip Boydell. That's the responsibility of the appropriate authorities, not me.'

'They weren't doing such a crash hot job until you started digging.'

'You mean Torrance?' he asked.

'Yes! I mean Torrance!' she replied. McCann could see she was getting angry. Bradley put an arm round her shoulders, which she shrugged off as she crossed to McCann.

'So you've had enough, have you, Leo?'

McCann pleaded with her with his eyes. He hoped to God she could read his thoughts. Now was not the time for an argument. To his great relief, she eventually cracked the faintest smile.

'What time tonight will you be through?' she asked.

'Maybe eleven. Could be later. Maybe tomorrow would be better.'

'No. Tonight. I want to know. Give me a call on my cell phone as soon as you get through.'

Bradley walked forward to join them.

'It was nice to meet you, Leo. Perhaps we'll see each other later tonight.'

Bradley put an arm round Rosalind's waist. This time she didn't shrink away.

'Either way, I hope I see you before you leave for the States, Mr. Radcliffe.'

'Please call me Bradley,' Radcliffe said with a warm smile. McCann couldn't help thinking it had taken the man the entire morning to come up with the offer.

'Sure. Bradley,' McCann said, shaking his hand at the door. Yet, as he smiled, a tiny part of his psyche swore. There it was again, that innate feeling of antipathy towards Radcliffe. Goddamn it, he thought, I'm jealous!

20.

20th May.

It was almost two o'clock, and the canteen was practically empty. McCann looked around. Ohlson was sitting at a table by himself, well away from the other few students who were still eating.

McCann had called Mrs. Ohlson at her home fifteen minutes earlier from the Buchanan building, explaining he was a Mr. Glover from the University Registrar's office. Was her son coming in today? A minor administrative matter. This time his mother had been quite helpful. Yes, he'd probably be in the library right now. Either there or in the canteen.

Several bulky textbooks stood on the table in front of Ohlson. He was making notes in a foolscap notebook. He looked troubled, glancing every few seconds at his watch.

McCann wove his way through the tables. As he came to a halt at Ohlson's, the young man stopped writing and looked up.

'Hendrik Ohlson?' McCann asked.

'Do I know you?' Ohlson replied without any warmth. He obviously wasn't in the mood for strangers.

'No, you don't,' McCann replied, as he drew up a chair and sat down.

'Look, I'm busy. I've got a seminar in about ten minutes, and I'm not adequately prepared. There are hundreds of tables here. Could you leave me in peace?'

'Ten minutes is all I ask. It's important to Rosalind Buchanan, important to Alan Messon, and could very well be of great importance to Venice Messon. You owe it to them.'

Ohlson looked up sharply for a second, then looked down at his books. 'She's dead. How the hell could it be of any importance to *her*,' he replied with hostility.

'Her memory. That's important. So let's get the facts straight, eh?'

Ohlson seemed unmoved, yet there was a hint in his expression that suggested the mere mention of Venice's name had tempered his abruptness.

'Well, as I said,' he replied uncertainly, 'I don't have your ten minutes.'

'I suggest you spare me the time I ask. You'll be doing yourself a favor - not me.' McCann's expression was hard and threatening. Ohlson met his eyes for a couple of seconds, then looked away nervously.

'Is that some kind of threat?' he replied, looking back to McCann, who said nothing.

'Look, I don't have the first idea who you are, but you seem to be threatening me. So leave me alone, will you?'

Still McCann said nothing, continuing to give the young man a confrontational stare.

Ohlson began to fiddle restlessly with a ballpoint pen, as he flipped through the pages of a book. Anything to avoid meeting McCann's stare. Half a minute later his nerve broke and he shot a furtive look across the table.

'Are you a policeman?'

'No, I'm not a policeman, Hendrik,' McCann said quietly. 'Interesting that you should think along those lines though. Make a difference, would it? Do policemen trouble you? Do they make you nervous?'

'I don't know what you mean,' Hendrik replied weakly. Then he seemed to find a semblance of courage. 'Who the hell are you anyway?'

'No need to be aggressive. Someone gets aggressive with me, I tend to get aggressive back. You wouldn't like that, Hendrik. Believe me.'

Ohlson ran the tip of his tongue over his upper lip. Possibly his mouth felt dry. Possibly he was getting the message. McCann hoped so.

'My name is McCann. I'm here on Rosalind Buchanan's behalf. She wants to know why Venice Messon killed her father. I think that's perfectly reasonable. Don't you, Hendrik?'

Ohlson was listening hard, tapping the ballpoint on the table. He looked distinctly jumpy.

'I'm sure if someone killed your father or mother you'd feel the same way she does,' McCann continued. 'Ten minutes is not so much to ask.'

'I keep telling you, Mr. McCann, I do not *have* ten minutes! I have to leave here right now.'

Ohlson began to gather up his books as he stood. McCann remained seated.

As Ohlson made the first turn to leave, McCann reached across the table, gripping the young man's wrist firmly.

'You may think you're home and free, but that's far from being the case. The police have serious reservations about the statement you gave them after the bombing. I've read the record of evidence, and I agree with them.'

'I couldn't give a toss if you agree with them or not,' Ohlson replied in a low voice, heavily laced with derision. He looked down at his wrist. 'Let go of my wrist. Right now!'

McCann continued speaking as if Ohlson hadn't said a word. 'You should agree to talk to me. Strictly off the record - just you and me. I may be able to help put an end to any further speculation on their part. Ten minutes is not so long, even if it means missing an important seminar. You see, you may not *have* a career in law if you decide not to talk to me. Do I make myself plain enough?' He then let go of Ohlson's wrist.

The young man stood motionless for several seconds, the books clutched under his arm, as he debated McCann's words. McCann's expression remained unyielding.

Ohlson took one step then halted. It was working, McCann thought. The boy did have something to hide. And it looked as if he had him on the run. Now was the time to strike.

'Before you say anything you might regret, Ohlson, let me say this. I know why you were there. I know about the Asian. So don't screw with me. Don't even think about it.'

Ohlson stared at McCann in shock as the words sank in. It was all in his eyes, to be read like a comic strip. *How can this man know? He's bluffing, no question. But I'm scared. Scared to death.*

'Neither Rosalind Buchanan nor I have any personal axe to grind with you,' McCann continued, varying his tone, now sounding warm and friendly. 'We don't give a damn why you lied. We know your part in this was innocent. It's the police who aren't sure. We don't believe you had the slightest idea what Venice was up to. But we do need to know exactly what happened that day. You just spell it out. You're the key.'

McCann paused briefly to let the words sink in. Before Ohlson had time to reply, McCann hurried on; he didn't want to give Ohlson the opportunity to make a rational decision, a negative one. Better to keep him rattled. 'Anything you tell me is off the record. Okay? Nothing you say to me now can, or will, be used against you in a court of law. I promise you that. But we *have* to know the detail. Rosalind has to know. You help me here and I'll tell the police I think they should back off.'

'Why would they back off just because you say so?' said Ohlson contemptuously.

'They will. Believe me.'

Ohlson stared back blankly, his mind racing. Then McCann stood.

'Look, Hendrik. You plain don't *have* a choice. You talk to me and walk away in ten minutes with a future in law, or walk away right now and I'll do everything in my power to make sure that one way or another the whole can of worms comes out into the open.' McCann leant across the table. 'You just tell me how the coin's going to fall, because you're beginning to piss me right off,' he concluded simply.

The young man stood motionless by the table for several seconds, his eyes riveted on McCann's. Then he sat, still clutching the books under his arm.

'Look, I already told the police everything about the day that Venice died,' he said.

Shit! McCann was losing patience with his lying.

'It's interesting you should choose that way to frame the events of that day. Not the day that four people were blown to pieces and countless others injured, but rather the day Venice died.'

'Semantics,' Ohlson replied defensively.

McCann abruptly stood, looming over the figure of the seated boy. 'Look, you little creep. Let's not go through all that shit again. I'm not stupid. I've *read* what you told them. Don't screw around with me, boy. Tell me the truth.'

Ohlson shrank back in his chair. 'Hey! Take it easy! She called me. Okay? We were going to have a drink. When she arrived she was in a strange mood. Told me to get lost. It's really as simple as that. You've got to believe me!'

McCann's expression took on a decided wintry quality. 'You really don't get it, do you. I wasn't joking when I gave you a straightforward choice a minute ago. Time's running out for you. You tell me everything, and it ends here. You carry on with this horseshit, and I nail you to the wall. No more seminars, no more law school, no more career.' McCann's expression hardened even further. He could look extremely menacing when he wanted to. He'd fronted the hardest men; Hendrik Ohlson stood no chance.

Ohlson expression took on an edge of real fear. McCann could see the panic growing in his eyes.

'Suppose I had anything to tell,' he stammered, 'you'd tell the police, and I'd be in serious trouble for withholding evidence and lying under oath.'

McCann spoke slowly and deliberately. 'Look, I'm going to tell you this just one more time. I will not repeat anything you tell me now in a court of law, that's a promise. You can't lose. Rosalind Buchanan just wants to know why her father died. She couldn't give a rat's ass about you. She wants to know what was going through Venice's mind that day. No one thinks you knew she was about to blow herself to pieces. Is that clear enough?'

'Are you recording this conversation?' Ohlson asked. He was in such a state now, his voice was scarcely audible.

'No. Search me, if you like.'

Ohlson watched as McCann took off his jacket, patting his chest and arms. Ohlson held up a hand. 'Okay, I believe you.'

'Good. Now tell me. Why were you there at the Savoy?'

'Look, I'll tell you in my own way. Okay? I'm buggered if I'll be interrogated again,' Hendrik replied. He was regaining a semblance of confidence, now that he'd finally made a decision to tell the truth.

'Okay,' McCann replied.

'We used to be close buddies, Ven and me. Nothing physical. Thought it might get that way once, but that's something else. Anyway, the long and short of it was she lost interest in me, then eventually dumped me. Disappeared. Not another word for the best part of a year. Then out of the blue she calls me and asks to meet, as if nothing had happened.'

'When was that?'

'About a couple of months before the bombing.'

'Her father said she'd changed.'

'To put it mildly. Last time I saw her she was a young happy kid. When I saw her again she was twenty, going on forty. Hard as nails. Looked as if she'd walked round the world.'

'Did she say what had happened to her in the intervening period?'

'Didn't want to talk about it. Said she'd just got back from London. You could see something bad had happened to her, but she wasn't saying.'

'You asked?'

'Sure.'

'What did she say?'

'Nothing. She clammed up.'

'So what did she want from you? Why did she contact you?'

'Said she wanted to be buddies again. But that was shit. She wanted me to do something for her. I could see that. It was obvious.'

'What did she want you to do?'

'Follow someone.'

Hendrik stopped speaking abruptly, and looked beseechingly at McCann, wringing his hands. 'Look, Mr. McCann. If I tell you the things you want to hear, please don't tell the police. I really didn't do anything wrong. I wouldn't. Ever. Not anything like that, anyway. Okay, I lied to the police, but I was just so scared! You would be too. When the bomb went up - I knew it was Ven. I just knew! Shit, I was so scared, I just ran. But I swear to God, I didn't know she had a bomb. That's the truth!'

'Calm down, Hendrik. Who was it she wanted you to follow?'

'She made it out to be a game. Said she was expecting a friend to arrive from abroad. When he arrived she wanted me to follow him from the airport, find out what hotel he was staying at, then call her. She said it was just a bit of fun, a 'lark' is how she put it. She even bought me a cell phone so I could call her when he'd arrived.'

'When did she buy you the phone?'

'About three weeks before he arrived.'

'Who was it?' McCann's tone was sharp. 'Who were you to follow?'

'I never knew his name. She gave me a photograph. Told me to carry it in my wallet until she called me that he was on his way.'

'Vietnamese?'

Ohlson shrugged. 'He could have been.'

McCann cut in sharply. He was so close he could taste it. 'Could have been? What do you mean, *could have been*? Did he *look* Vietnamese?'

'Yes! I mean just that. He *could* have been!' Hendrik snapped back. 'He could also have been Thai, Laotian, Cambodian. How would I know?

'How did she know he was arriving in Sydney?'

'I don't know. I wasn't interested in the bloody game. I only agreed to do it to shut her up, she was obsessed with the idea. After a few weeks I actually thought she'd forgotten the whole stupid thing.'

'Do you still have the photo?'

'No. She told me to destroy it. I did. Tore it apart and dumped the phone.'

McCann swore. The photo would have been solid gold.

'Let's get this straight. She called you the morning of the bombing, telling you to get to the airport with the photo and wait till the man came through?'

'Right.'

'What time?'

'Breakfast. Around eight. Said he'd be in around four.'

'You waited at the airport?'

'The Qantas Jet Base. It was a private jet. That's what she told me.'

'How did you get in there? What about security?'

'I parked the car opposite the exit to the base in Qantas Drive under the advertising hoardings. She'd told me approximately when he'd be through. So I just waited.'

'How long?'

'About an hour. Then a Mercedes came through the gates. I could see him quite clearly in the front passenger seat.'

'You identified him from the photo?'

'That's right.'

'Through the window from across the street.'

'Yes.'

McCann thought for a moment. The front passenger seat? It had to be the brother. Tran was the dominant partner by far. He'd sit in the back.

'Was anyone else in the car?'

'There was someone in the back.'

'One person?'

'Yes.'

'Another Vietnamese?'

'I couldn't see. It didn't matter at the time. My guy was up front. I didn't care about anyone else.'

So two men and a driver were in the car when it left the airport. Tran and his brother. Yet they arrived separately, Tran in a cab a few minutes after his brother.

'Did the Mercedes stop on the way to the hotel?

'Only at traffic lights.'

'And you were on its tail the entire trip?'

'Except for a couple of minutes when I lost the car on South Dowling Street.'

This had to be the moment they parted company. 'How come?' McCann asked.

'The guy in the back seat kept looking back through the window. I dropped back a bit in case he'd seen me following him.'

'Come on, Hendrik. If the guy was looking back at you all the time, why can't you describe him, for Christ's sake?'

'We were driving up South Dowling Street. Right into the sun. The guy was a silhouette! I could see his outline, that's all!'

'Okay. Take it easy.' It was important to calm Ohlson down. He was getting to the nitty-gritty now. 'So when did you lose sight of the car?'

'Along South Dowling, near Cleveland Street. The Merc was a couple of cars up ahead of me. Then it put on a bit of speed, wove in and out of the cars and just vanished in the traffic. Couldn't see it. I thought I'd screwed up.'

'What did you do?'

'Put my foot down. When I got to Taylor Square, I could see it wasn't up front, so I pulled in. I was going to go back. That's when I saw it in my rear view mirror. I let it pass, and was on track again.'

So it figured that somewhere in South Dowling Street the Mercedes had stopped and Tran had got out. But why had the car not waited? There could only be one reason. Tran had been sitting in the rear seat. A careful man, he'd kept a look out behind him for a tail. During the drive from the airport he'd spotted Ohlson. The amateur gumshoe. So Tran had taken the precaution of telling his driver to temporarily lose the car behind so he could get out, then allow the tail to pick them up again. His brother would run interference for him, should there be any problems at the hotel when they arrived in the Mercedes. He'd follow later in a cab. Evidently, Tran was travelling without a bodyguard. This surprised McCann.

'You followed the Mercedes to the Savoy, then called her to inform her that her quarry had arrived. Correct?'

'That's right.'

'How was she when you met outside the Savoy?'

'We didn't. Just told me on the cell phone to go home and forget I'd spoken to her. She was acid. But really.'

'Did you tell her he was in the Stutton conference room?'

'Yes. You see, I followed the man to reception. The girl told him to go right on up. She said it was the Stutton Conference Room.'

McCann thought hard for a moment. 'Did Venice know Buchanan? Or Horan?'

'Horan was the banker?'

'That's right.'

'You mean socially beforehand, or that they'd be in the room when she got there?'

'Both.'

'I've no idea. All I can say is that her focus was entirely on the Asian.'

'When the bomb went up you were leaving?'

Hendrik faltered. He looked down at the table and squared up his law books in an agitated manner. 'There's something else – ' Hendrik said in an undertone. It was clear from his demeanor that this was the part he felt least like divulging.

'I know. You fucked up, didn't you?' McCann knew the rest of the story.

Ohlson stared at McCann with disbelief. 'Do *they* know, or are you just guessing?'

'The police? No, they don't know. And yes, I am guessing. But I know I'm right.'

Ohlson stared at his hands. 'Yes, I made a mistake. Maybe I identified the wrong person.'

McCann said nothing.

'Shit, he looked almost identical,' Hendrik continued vehemently, as though justifying his error. 'For God's sake, I had the photo in my hand and it was him! Then Ven walks past me and into the hotel, I begin to leave, and there the bastard is! Getting out of the cab! I think to myself, Holy shit! What have I done? She looked mad as hell when she went on up. Well, I think to myself *shit, she's about to bust in on someone who wouldn't know her from Adam.*'

'So what did you do?'

'I could see the Asian, the second one that is, walk to the reception, say something, then continue on to the elevators. Last time I saw him, he got in and the doors closed. I was really confused. You see, I didn't know which one was which. Maybe the first one was the right one, maybe the second! I didn't know what I should do. Mind my own business or what. Should I follow the second Asian, or should I tell Ven that I'd cocked up. Then I made a decision. I called her on the cell phone. It beeped for a couple of seconds, then the whole place went up.'

'What did you do then?'

'I ran. Didn't stop for four blocks.'

McCann looked at him coldly. 'I see.' He paused for effect. 'You ran without looking back? You didn't think to stop to see if Venice, your childhood sweetheart, your friend, was safe?'

'I thought she was dead,' Hendrik replied lamely, staring at the floor.

'You watch Venice enter a five star hotel. Two minutes later there's a violent explosion, which you instantly put down to her. Yet here you are, telling me you had no idea she was carrying explosives?' McCann let the question hang in the air like an accusation.

'Mr. McCann, I'm telling you the truth! I've done everything you asked me. Don't ask me how I knew, or thought I did. There was something about her manner when she walked past me that was weird. Her eyes had a kind of dead quality. Yet at the same time, they seemed to be on fire! I really had no idea what was going on, it all happened so fast. Then when I called her on the cell phone and it went dead the split second the bomb blew – ' His voice trailed off for a second. 'I knew she was dead. I knew! So I ran. Can you blame me? Can you even imagine what it was like? It was mayhem everywhere!'

McCann remained silent. A sudden uninvited image of the body fragments of a young soldier flying towards him in a back alley in Ballymena, Northern Ireland, filled his mind like a mental explosion of its own.

'Why didn't you tell the police all this when they asked you?' McCann asked, trying to clear his mind of the nightmare pictures.

'Would you, Mr. McCann?'

'Would I what?'

'Try explaining it was you that had tracked the Asian to the hotel. That it was you who'd shown the assassin where he was? Would they have believed me? Do you believe me now?'

'As a matter of fact I do. Maybe they would have too.'

'Maybe,' Hendrik said sullenly. 'Maybe not. Either way Venice was dead. It wasn't as if the authorities were searching for a killer. It was over! You must understand that. It was over! They were dead. There was nothing I could do, for God's sake. I had to think of myself. It wasn't my fault! Why should I put myself in the spotlight? Shoot myself in the foot? What good would that have served?'

McCann thought for a few moments. The boy was right in some respects. It was over. He wasn't to blame. Yet he had seen the face of the man who had arrived late – the man that Venice had wanted dead. If anyone could place Tran at the hotel it was Ohlson.

'When the bomb went up, did you see the second man again at any time, either leaving the building or in the street?'

'No.'

'Can you think of anyone Venice was close to?'

'No,' Hendrik replied easily.

McCann was suddenly angry. 'You replied before you even thought about it, you little shit.' He could see a renewed look of panic flood through Hendrik's face. 'So let's get this straight. You bloody well think hard before you answer my questions, *then* maybe you say no. Is that clear?'

McCann studied Hendrik, as the young man closed his eyes, searching the depths of his memory.

'Did you meet any of her friends? Did she mention anyone, any names? Did she have any particular hangouts? Places where she could have got hold of the explosives?'

Hendrik's eyes snapped open. 'I didn't *know* she had explosives! You told me you believed me. Now you're asking me where she got hold of the plastic. Jesus Christ, Mr. McCann, I'm telling the truth!'

It had been worth a try, just in case Ohlson had been lying about the explosives. It looked like he really didn't know.

'So who were her friends? Where did she go? Where was she living?'

'She told me she was hanging out with a friend in the Cross.'

'Where?'

'The Cross! Shit, I never went there. I didn't want to know! We always met at some coffee place or other. Sometimes a bar. A couple of times she came round to my place.'

'Which bar?'

'The Bourbon.'

'How many times in all did you see her between the time she came back into your life and when she died?'

Ohlson didn't answer. He wasn't listening. 'Ritz,' he said suddenly in an undertone as if he'd just remembered he'd left the gas on at home.

'What *about* Ritz?'

'You asked me if she mentioned any of her friends. Ritz. That was the guy she was hanging out with. I'd forgotten.' He looked up at McCann as if willing McCann to believe him.

Time to lean on Ohlson again.

'Ritz? Not the sort of name you'd forget easily, Hendrik.'

'No shit, I really had forgotten. She only mentioned him a couple of times – for instance, like she had to get back before Ritz got home.'

'She was doing drugs. You knew that?'

'Kind of,' Hendrik replied defensively. 'I didn't want to know, so I never asked.'

'You're a swell guy when it comes to friendship, aren't you?'

Hendrik looked away. 'I've never been into drugs. But she looked as though she did - you know, the look, the skin, the eyes.'

'I know.'

'It did cross my mind that this guy Ritz was fixing her up.'

'But you've no idea where she was living?'

'No. And I mean that.' Suddenly his eyes pleaded with McCann. 'Please, Mr. McCann. I beg you, can I go? Look, if you give me your number, I'll give you a call if I come up with anything. I'll think really hard, I promise. All right? I've got to go!'

McCann reached behind him for his jacket, taking out a pen, writing his telephone number on the back of a scrap of paper. 'This is my number. Think hard.'

'I will. That's a promise. Can I leave, Mr. McCann?' The young man looked drained.

'Yes. You can go.'

'This conversation...' Hendrik began weakly, as he stood by the table, the books once more clutched under his arm.

'I gave you my word,' McCann cut in. 'I won't repeat it in court. I see no purpose in taking it further. As you say, Venice is dead.'

Ohlson took a step towards the door. Then he hesitated, turned and looked at McCann. 'Please tell Miss Buchanan that I am truly sorry if I caused her any pain by my lies. You see, I've never known such fear, and it still haunts me every day. I loved Venice and I let her down.'

McCann stood. 'Yes. You did. You let her down in a big way. Get out of here, Hendrik. It's over. Get on with your life.'

'Who the hell did that to your face?' McCann asked.

Messon's left eye was closed, and the skin beneath it a bluish purple.

'I took exception to someone's attitude the night before last. We came to blows,' Messon replied, unfazed.

It was just after 10 p.m., and the club was only just beginning to fill. Their table was the furthest from the dance floor, where conversation was still just possible. A halogen spotlight cut a narrow swathe through the smoke haze that hung in the still, fetid air. There was as yet no sign of Kevin Jacks.

'So, Leo. Our deal. What do you know that I don't?'

This was the hard one. McCann knew he'd have to face it sooner or later, but he'd hoped to put it off a while.

How would the old man react? That was the question. Would he lose control? He was obviously still emotionally unbalanced, as was evidenced by the fight he'd involved himself in two nights previously. He hadn't disputed that he was as much to blame as the other guy was.

'Apparently Venice was in Vietnam, not England, for the greater part of last year.'

Messon looked curious, rather than surprised. 'Vietnam? How do you know?'

'Immigration records. A friend of mine checked.'

'Why Vietnam?'

McCann braced himself. 'Did you know she had a boyfriend?'

'Hendrik?' he asked incredulously.

'No, not Hendrik. An older man.'

Messon's jaw set. Not a good sign. McCann continued. There was no choice, he'd given his word.

'A Vietnamese. A Cham actually,' McCann said, attempting to make the idea of an older man slightly more palatable by appealing to Messon's interest in Indo-Chinese history and ethnology.

'When you say an older man, how old exactly? Five years? Ten? Old enough to be her father?' Messon's words were measured, his eyes fixed on McCann's for any hint of duplicity.

'Older than myself; your junior by a few years,' McCann replied simply.

Messon's eyes didn't even flicker. The muscles in his jaw twitched slightly. 'You know she was sleeping with this man, or you assume she was.'

'I assume she was. At present we don't know where she was exactly in Vietnam, just that she was in the country.'

'I see,' Messon said in an admirably controlled voice. 'And was this man by any chance the man who was killed in the explosion? Is that what this is leading up to?'

'No. It's a long shot, but I personally believe that the dead man was the brother of your daughter's boyfriend.'

'And this man is still alive?'

'As far as we know, yes.'

'Why would she have killed the brother? Any ideas there?' Messon's face and body were still, but the fingers of the hand that lay on the table were beginning to tremble.

'Again, it's just a completely unsubstantiated theory on my part, but I believe her aim was to kill her boyfriend. However, there was a tragic case of mistaken identity.'

'Explain.'

'She thought she had her boyfriend cornered in the Stutton Conference Room, but discovered instead that it was his twin brother. Then, I think the bomb exploded accidentally.'

'Are you telling me the police now believe it to have been an accident?' Messon's expression changed to one of amazement.

'I believe it was an accident. At present the police are unconvinced. This may change.'

Messon blinked for the first time in almost two minutes, tears welling up in his eyes. A full minute passed as he looked up at the ceiling, trying to control his emotions. Then he again locked eyes with McCann. His stare was cold as an ice flow.

'What could this man have done to my girl that would have driven her to pack explosives round her waist?'

'I can't answer that question. I have no idea, Alan,' McCann replied.

'What is this man's name?'

'I'll tell you that when I'm sure of my facts,' McCann answered. He could hear Messon's labored breathing. There was no point in adding to the man's misery by providing him with a target that was out of reach.

Messon suddenly banged his fist on the table. 'What is the man's name, blast you! I insist you tell me!'

McCann quickly grabbed Messon's hand, pressing the top joint of the old man's thumb towards the palm. Messon winced. 'Please, Alan. You must be quiet or we'll be thrown out. I'll tell you the man's name when I've checked it out. Fair enough?'

Messon looked angry as hell, but he nodded.

As McCann let go of the old man's thumb, he smelt the distinct body odor of a man behind him. He turned as a finger prodded his shoulder.

'Hey, man. You mind takin' five. I got some business with your friend there. It's personal,' the voice behind him jived.

The thin Fijian looked in his late twenties. Without the obvious legacy of drugs, the gray skin, the sunken eyes, he could easily still have been in his teens. He smelt bad, a mixture of sweat, beer, clove cigarettes, and recent sex. He was dressed in a filthy two-piece sixties-style suit and wore an open-necked gray shirt. His trouser cuffs ended mid ankle to draw attention to his outsized black boots, the polished steel toecaps of which occasionally reflected the colored lights of the bar. His hair looked as though he'd just withdrawn it from a wind tunnel. The pupils of his eyes were dilated, and his speech was pseudo African-American hip. He'd watched too many movies.

His eyes flicked back and forth from McCann to Messon. Finally they settled on Messon. 'You going to talk to me, man, or am I wasting valuable time here?' The Fijian grinned. It wasn't a good look. Two teeth were missing on the left-hand side, and the rest were beiged by tobacco. His upper lip had an open sore that had puffed up the flesh, giving him a constant expression of contempt.

'Why don't you sit down,' Messon said.

'Who's your friend, man?' Jacks said, rocking his weight from one foot to the other as he eyeballed McCann.

'Just a friend. He's not police.'

Jacks' attitude sweetened marginally.

'You bring my money, man?'

'Yes, I brought the money. Sit down.'

Reluctantly, the gangling Fijian did so.

'You're Ritz's pal? You're Kevin Jacks?' McCann asked unhurriedly, moving his right hand to where the tape recorder was clipped to a belt under his jacket. He switched it on.

'Maybe.'

Jacks ran his tongue over his dry lips. McCann could see he was as high as a B-52 and gaining altitude. Each limb was in a state of perpetual motion, as if dancing to a slow interior rumba in his head.

'My name's McCann. Do you know where I can find Ritz?'

'Maybe,' he replied, then stood, shooting an angry look to Messon. 'Hey, man. Who the fuck's askin' the questions? This guy ain't payin'. You are! No?' He began to samba barely perceptibly from foot to foot, softly bringing his hands together in a silent clap as he eyed McCann.

'I pay. He's asking the questions. Please sit if you want any money,' Messon replied coldly.

Jacks sat.

'So Ritz is gone, right?' McCann began.

'You got it.'

'Can I buy you a drink?'

'Don't need no drink. Doing fine the way I am.'

'You were a friend of Ritz's?'

Abruptly the Fijian stopped his personal rumba, and he leant back in his chair. The pretence of good humor had evaporated. He spoke in a fast whisper now, his eyes doing the dancing.

'Look, I said so just now. An' I said so to your friend last night. I'm not here to waste my time with small talk. I'm here to make a living. Now, you want to tell me what you want to know, and I'll tell you what it's worth. Then we'll be through.'

McCann leant across the table and grabbed Jacks by the collar before the slim Fijian's eyes even registered movement. 'You listen up, 'Roadie' or whatever your name is. You might just be able to help me. But right now you're beginning to annoy me in a major way.' The gangling Fijian stared at the angry face before him. Any physicality would plainly be one major mismatch. He just held up his hands in a placatory manner.

'Easy, big guy. I'm listening. You're paying, right?'

'Maybe,' McCann replied. 'Why don't you relax and start answering my questions.'

McCann reached into his trouser pocket, pulling out a clip of bank notes, and showing it to the Fijian. 'How rich you get depends how much you know about Ritz.'

Jacks eased the chair back on two legs, one foot on the floor, the other tap dancing on the footrest. 'That's cool. Ask away. But I ain't got long.'

'When did you last see Ritz?'

'Five weeks ago, thereabouts. Now he's history. Did me a big favor. The man had a heap of clients. Now they're mine.'

'What can you tell me about Ritz?'

'Early fifties, maybe more. Ex-army. Hard man. But real hard. Crazy guy. You didn't want to fuck with that guy. No way. Been dealing round here on and off for about three years. Don't know what he did before. But if he took a shine to you, he was a good friend. Know what I mean - put a shotgun to your head and blow it clean off your shoulders if he took a dislike to you, but nice to his ma? Well, Ritz took a shine to me. Don't rightly know why. Shit, that was a couple of years ago. Called me his *black boy*. Hell, we were all niggers in his book, but he said I made him laugh. I used to run the errands, deliver the blow to customers. Meant *he* didn't ever have to take a fall. Made sense, didn't it? Mind you, I did all the time. But that was why I got paid. And I was a kid, so there wasn't much they could do to me. I was always out within a few hours.'

'Ever seen this girl?' McCann asked peeling off two fifties, slipping them to the eager fingers of the Fijian. They were in his pocket in under a second.

'Sure. It's the girl who trashed the hotel.' He looked up triumphantly. 'I'm right ain't I? It's her. The crazy gal.'

'You got it, Jacks.'

McCann glanced across at Messon, uncertain as to how he would react to Jacks turn of phrase. He obviously hadn't told the Fijian that he was the girl's father. Messon seemed to be coping well, more intent on the Fijian's answers, than on any gratuitous insults.

'Yeah, I seen her,' Jacks continued. 'That was Ritz's lady. Ritz fell for her in a big way. And she knew it. Anything she wanted she got. Never seen a man change the way Ritz did the moment he clapped eyes on her. He was putty in her hands, and for a man with that guy's violent background that's saying something. He'd had more than his fair share of skirt; beat on most of them - had no respect for women. She was different. She had him by the balls from day one. Don't ask me why. Maybe he was just getting too old; needed some young pussy. Maybe he thought he was in love for the first time.' He giggled.

McCann shot another quick glance at Messon. He was still okay.

'Special Squad have him on a list,' McCann said.

'Oh yeah? What list's that.'

'He was a member of a paramilitary group, the Australian Guardian Militia. That right?'

Jacks smiled dismissively. 'Shit, he just used to play around with them. Didn't have the first idea what their major game was though. Put it this way, Ritz was never what you'd call a thinker. I think his tour in the 'Nam cooked what passed for his brains. He just wanted to keep on pretending he was back in the thick of it. He really got his rocks off playing games with the Militia out Kempsey way. That was the closest he was ever going to get to killing people for fun back home.'

'You been up there?' McCann asked, peeling off another two fifties and passing them to Jacks' ready fingers under the table.

'The property at Kempsey? No way. Even Ritz was cagey about those people. Said they were mean as shit; and when you got a guy with as much compassion as you can balance on the head of a pin telling you that, you know these are people you do *not* fuck with.'

'Did he ever tell you about their agenda?' McCann asked.

Jacks looked back blankly.

'You know, their politics. What they had in mind. Their affiliations with other groups.'

'You mean overseas?'

'Yes.'

'Ritz told me the head honcho - name was Langren or something similar - had a thing about that Somalian warlord whacko. Know the one I mean?' McCann nodded. 'That was Langren's kind of lifestyle. That's how he saw himself. He believed in a new Australia, a white Australia naturally; no niggers, no immigrants, no gays. A regular Nazi. You wouldn't believe the amount of support he had from groups in Europe and America. Shit, Langren saw David Koresh as a *hero*! Wrote to a heap of people after Waco. See, there were lists of organizations all over the place in the papers after the Texas thing. Well, Langren wrote to 'em all.

'Did Ritz find the plastic for Venice Messon?'

Jacks said nothing, then glanced down at McCann's billfold. Another two fifties.

'Sure he did. He told me.'

'Details,' McCann said peeling a further two fifties and passing them under the table.

'Well, one night about three months ago he's drunk as a skunk. We'd had a real good night, made plenty, so he's real satisfied with life, and I'm his tame nigger boy, right? Well, he starts rapping on about what his lady had in mind. He's whispering, but laughing all to hell. Thinks it's the best fuckin' thing. Said she surprised the shit out of him. Said she'd watched the Oklahoma Federal Building thing on the TV. Said it would be a piece of cake to do the same thing here. Well, Ritz just sits there laughing as he tells me this shit. Says she's one ballsy lady, but hell, she could go right on and do it if she wanted to, far as he was concerned. Said they all deserved it. Like I said, he hated them all. Anyone that stopped him doing exactly what he wanted, right?'

'Who did she have in mind as a target? Did he say?'

'Ritz said she didn't rightly care.'

'How did he react?'

'He thought the idea was real funny. Said he was in two minds as to whether to fit her out - let her have a crack at it.'

'Did he have access to explosives?'

'Shit yes! He and his toy soldiers blow the shit out of the country most weekends. Man, he always had plenty.'

'So you think he gave her the explosives?'

'Makes sense, huh? I mean where's a girl like her going to lay her hands on enough shit to blow a hole through a building like the Savoy?'

'Let's get this straight. He told you this three months ago or thereabouts?'

'That's right.'

'Did he ever mention it again?'

'Sure thing. Next day I hear from a friend of mine that the mad bastard's looking all over for me. I'm in bad shape and in bed. He wants me to run a deal for him. I'm always supposed to be ready, see? Then suddenly he's at the door looking serious as hell. I get real scared thinking he's going to give me a serve. Sometimes he just laid into people for the hell of it, you know? Well, he grabs me, and looks at me as if I had done something real bad. Then he whispers into my ear that if I ever breathe a word of what he told me about the girl he's going to bite both my ears off and feed them to his pig out on the property. I say to him I can't remember what the fuck he said that was so important 'cos I was real drunk. That seemed to satisfy him. But he repeated his threat before he sent me on the deal.'

'When was the last time you saw Ritz?'

'Three days after the Savoy thing. He was scared to death. Came by to pick up a few things he'd left behind. Also some cash I owed him from a deal I'd made the night before. Said he was getting the hell out – off down to Hobart for a couple of weeks. I asked him why, but he wouldn't say. That's when I began to wonder if the scrawny girl had done the Savoy thing. Then I just plain asked him. Had to. Had to know.

'He was halfway down the stairs. Stopped dead in his tracks, then came right on up back to me and broke my nose. I mean - fuck - just like that! His eyes were real wild. Wild! Then he was gone. I was in the bathroom looking for a towel for my face when I happened to look out the small window, down into the street. Ritz was standing next to a dark green Falcon, shrugging his shoulders and waving his arms, like he was arguing. There were three guys round him. Then they pushed him into the car. Never heard from him since. Word on the street is they topped Ritzy that night.'

'Word from who?'

'Oh, you know - the word. It's seldom far from the truth. People know these things. It just slips out somewhere and before you know, everyone just knows. Except the police. They know nothing.'

'Langren?'

'I'd bet my life on it. I see it this way. The dumb fuck girl says she wants to blow the shit out of someone or other, and asks if Ritz can get her the goods. Ritz wants to impress the skirt, right? So he says, sure thing. Goes on up Kempsey way and steals some of Langren's plastic – the stuff the boss man's got other things in mind for. Then boom, the Savoy goes up and Langren finds he's short of his precious plastic. Puts the word about, and finds that Ritzy's been up sniffing around. So, boom boom, it's Ritzy's turn. I mean that's all Langren needs. The cops had been giving him a tough enough time for months, now he's got the whole fucking special services after his ass. That was some dumb thing of Ritz to do. Last thing he did do, if the word's right.'

The Fijian's feet were now tapping faster than Astaire. McCann had certainly got him going. He was definitely buzzing. He looked down for more money - he could almost taste it.

McCann peeled off the last four notes, and handed the money to Jacks.

'Anything you want to ask him,' McCann said, turning to Messon. It was only then he noticed Messon's expression – it was as dark as liquorice.

'As a matter of fact there is,' Messon said deliberately, staring at the Fijian. 'If you ever refer to my daughter as a *dumb fuck girl* again, I'll break every bone in your body.'

Jacks looked momentarily taken aback. Then he grinned. 'Sure, Pops. I'm scared to death.'

Just as Messon began to stand, McCann put a hand on the back of Jacks' neck, applying just the right amount of pressure with his fingers to wipe the grin from the Fijian's face.

'And when my friend's through, I'll be next. You won't be grinning then. You can bet your sweet life on that.'

To McCann's great relief, this appeared to satisfy Messon. The last thing he needed was an all up fistfight between an emotionally charged pensioner and a bombed out, drug-crazed pusher.

McCann withdrew his hand from Jacks neck. The Fijian's eyes flitted from McCann to Messon and back. Then he stood.

'Just one thing. Grandpa and me, we had a deal. I tell this little story once. Ask me to repeat it, put my gonads in a clamp, squeeze the eyeballs right out of my head, I'm not talking. You hear me Mr. Man?'

'I hear you,' McCann replied.

'I'm outta here,' Jacks said as he backed away through the tables.

'Can I buy you a drink before we leave?' Messon asked McCann, watching Jacks leave.

'No thanks. It'd be like having a drink at the scene of a hit and run. I don't know about you, but this place has all the charisma of the transit lounge at Jakarta Airport. I'm going home.'

'Keep in touch, Leo. I know you're a man of your word – you'll give me the name when you're ready.'

McCann rose, laying a hand on Messon's shoulders. The man had guts and determination. Not too much, he hoped. He was wading into dangerous still waters without a lifejacket. He was too old for it.

McCann looked at the coin scrape that ran the full length of the car. He didn't much care. Cars were for transport from A to B. If someone was trying to annoy him, he'd failed.

He unlocked the VW and opened the door. A quick glance at his watch. It was twenty to eleven. He extracted the tape from the recorder, slipping it into his top pocket, then punched Rosalind's number into the cell phone.

'Not too late for you, I hope,' he asked.

'Absolutely not. What have you got for me?'

'You want to meet?'

'Sure, where? My place?'

An image of Bradley sprang to mind. It was late, he was tired, and the thought of Bradley the gooseberry sitting at his elbow was the last thing he had in mind.

'Hey, what about I drive over to your place? What do you say?' Perhaps his silence had told her the story.

'Sure you don't mind? It'll only take half an hour this time of night.'

'Twenty minutes tops,' she replied with a chuckle.

'Thanks. But really. I'm beat.'

McCann turned on the radio. His mind was buzzing with random visions; Whitey struggling with the 'dancers', her eyes wide with terror; the upturned face of Boydell staring vacantly into space; Duncan McKintyre, his former SAS group commander, shot through the throat in the Mullins Road, Belfast. Perhaps it was time to retire – the violence was overwhelming. In the past he'd been able to deal with it, filing it away in his mind with various categories and degrees of justification. Now it sickened him. He'd probably had enough. Bringing Whitey's murderers to justice was not his responsibility. Nor was dealing with Boydell's killer, Brokov. Let others do the work.

McCarr's Creek looked quite beautiful. The moon was just two days from full, shining down with a fierce intensity through the fifty-foot gum trees that lined the road. The effect was mesmeric.

Suddenly the dark outline of a sports car loomed out of the blackness, sweeping round the bend towards him. McCann wrenched the steering wheel violently to the left onto the verge. His impression was of a two-seater - bluish. The car must have been doing over eighty as it flashed past him without any lights, taking up two-thirds of the road. In a second it was gone.

McCann swore, taking his foot off the accelerator, just tapping the brakes to keep them from locking up. It was only as he corrected the skid and made it back onto the road that he became aware of the pink tinge to the skyline ahead. Many times he'd driven home around seven and had marveled at the rich colors of an Australian sunset. But it was now ten after eleven at night. A sudden foreboding consumed his mind. Could it be a bush fire? He pressed hard again on the gas.

As he swept round the final bend he saw her. She was ablaze from stem to stern, the orange licks rising twenty feet in the air. Someone had cast L'Echapper Belle into the creek. She looked like a Viking funeral barge as she gently drifted towards the main river.

McCann sat on the grass by the pontoon and watched her die. There was nothing he could do. The Water Police launch stood off about twenty feet, training hoses on her, but it would only be a matter of time. The fire was through her like a raging cancer. The wheelhouse and upper decking had fallen into the hull, and she was listing badly to port.

'I thought she must have been a pal of yours, Leo.' It was Ken Davis at his elbow, the neighbor from next door. 'Otherwise I'd have come down and asked her what she thought she was doing on the boat.'

McCann held out a hand in a forgiving gesture, his eyes still fixed on his boat as she began to dip forwards into the black water. 'Thanks, Ken. You weren't to know.'

'I'd let Kissy out for a pee, you see. Christ, it was such a wonderful night.' Kissy was Ken's adorable pooch.

'I know,' McCann replied. But he wanted to grieve alone. He knew that it had been a warning to back off. The woman Ken had seen would probably turn out to be Brokov's woman. However, despite their warnings he was now utterly determined to be in for the duration.

'I'll leave you to it, then. Give us a call if there's anything I can do,' Davis continued, awkwardly.

McCann turned. Davis was a good man, he meant well. He lived alone, and always kept a look out for strangers when McCann was away. 'Thanks, Ken. I will,' McCann replied.

As Davis reached his gate, McCann saw headlights on the road. It had to be Rosalind.

As he walked back up the grass slope, he saw his boat slip forwards and disappear under the water, the moonlight highlighting the smoke that hung everywhere.

'It's the crudest possible message, telling me to back off. They're showing me the red light.'

Rosalind and McCann were sitting on the floor in the living room. The house was a mess, the study in particular. Whoever had broken in had made a thorough search of his papers.

'Maybe Greville thought I actually had something on them.'

'Maybe. What do you want to do?' Rosalind asked. 'It's up to you. You want to call a halt, so be it. Because you're right, I asked you to find out why she killed dad. You've done that. Judging by what Hendrik Ohlson said, I'd agree it was a personal thing between Venice and the Vietnamese. Her motive was quite unconnected to Telok Anson, Palmer, Boydell, and the rest. Perhaps it's best to let go, let the police handle things from now on.'

But McCann wasn't listening. 'They thought they were showing me the red light,' he said. 'But all I'm seeing is green.'

'What do you mean, Leo?'

His eyes were suddenly filled with fury. 'I want to go after those bastards. I want to see them pay, not read in the papers somewhere down the line that they've been taken down. I want to see it myself.'

Rosalind's expression changed from a sympathetic understanding to one of exuberance. 'You beauty!' she said, clapping her hands together. 'Deep down I hoped you'd react like that. Fact is, I knew it. You feel the same as I do.'

McCann smiled. Her attitude was infectious, and it made him laugh despite his loss. 'Oh yeah? You knew?'

'Of course I did. I knew you wouldn't quit. You wouldn't walk away now that someone has burned down the thing you love more than anything in the world, right in front of you. No way. I'm the same.'

'Oh yeah? You're the same, huh?' McCann replied mirroring her inflection.

'Sure! I owe it to Whitey to bring them to book. I also owe it to dad to make them pay for embezzling his money.'

'I'm glad we agree on things,' McCann replied, still smiling. She looked irresistible when she was pumped up. Her eyes were alive with passion and vitality. It was true, they probably were kindred spirits. He'd walk a long way for this woman - no question about it.

Rosalind looked curiously at him. 'You're staring at me, Leo,' she said after a beat.

'Can't I stare if I want to?' McCann replied with a grin.

She nodded her head from side to side, as if she were debating the matter. 'I suppose so. Sure. Why not?'

McCann stood. 'Another drink?'

'Better not. I'm driving.'

'A coffee?'

She nodded.

They walked in silence to the kitchen. Thin smoke slowly drifted by the window.

'I'm going to Vietnam. Want to stake me?' McCann said, as he filled the espresso machine with coffee.

'As far as I can see, you're still on the payroll. I know you threatened to resign a few hours ago, and I got decidedly snitty. But as of right now, I'd say you're still working for me. That means I stake you. What do you have in mind?'

'I want to find out what the hell Venice Messon got up to during all the months she was in Vietnam.'

Rosalind raised her eyebrows. 'Oh yeah?' She knew what he actually had in mind.

'I want to meet the sonofabitch who sent her over the edge.'

'What about Brokov and the woman?'

'Tran's the heart of the matter. I'd get nowhere chasing my tail trying to track down Brokov and the bitch that set fire to my boat.'

'And when they see you're not backing off?'

'I can look after myself,' McCann replied simply, placing two short black cups under the spout, and pulling down the handle. The smell of Kenya mocha was magnificent.

'And what do I do? Shall I come with you?' she said smiling.

McCann looked at her, her palms upturned in an inquiring gesture that gave her the air of a Javanese dancer. He couldn't think of anything he'd like more.

For one brief second he was tempted to agree, then his mind was filled with the reality of the trip. He'd be dealing with a very dangerous man, a man that didn't hesitate to send an assassin to kill an old woman just in case she knew something that might incriminate him. No, to bring Rosalind along for the ride was not the smartest idea. Then there was the question of Bradley. He'd quite forgotten her boyfriend's position in the equation.

'I think you should go to the States with Bradley,' McCann said, sipping his coffee.

'You don't want me to come with you?' she said, with just the barest hint of devilment.

'I'm thinking about your safety - pure and simple.'

'You're such a gentleman, Leo McCann,' she said with a captivating twinkle. 'You know, I'd like it if you called me Rosie. Could you do that for me?'

McCann was taken by surprise. Somehow she always managed to come up with the most offbeat remarks, just when he least expected them. 'Sure,' he replied. 'Rosie.' Then he tried to remember what he'd been about to say.

Rosalind watched him with a playful grin. McCann knew damned well she was sending him up.

'One thing you should do tomorrow, Rosie. Go see Gerson. Ask him what he's done, if anything, about Horan's findings. What was the name of the man that took over Horan's brief?'

'Duncan McKinley.'

'That's him. I'd wager a pile of money that he and Greville are working in concert, and that McKinley's covered all Greville's tracks by now. I'd be interested to see where Gerson figures in all of this, nonetheless.'

'Do you think they'll come after you if you continue digging?'

'Maybe. The only patch of blue I can see is that the bastards are obviously running scared. They're not sure how much I know, and it's bugging the hell out of them. They probably realize that Palmer and Boydell's affidavits don't exist - they're not stupid. But they can't be too sure about Horan's blue disk. Also, they'd be really concerned that I wasn't lying to Greville when I told him I'd taped the interview with Boydell on Lamma. That's why they went through my papers today. They've found nothing, so they still don't know if it exists. If I'd been in their position I'd have gone to ground, and done nothing. It's always best to see what ammunition the opposition has. It may be nothing. If someone's sniffing around, let them. One thing you don't do is add to the evidence.'

'You'll need a visa for Vietnam,' she said.

'Hell, I'd forgotten. That'll take days.'

'Maybe not. I'll tell Ian to put a rush on for you, say you're a technical expert vital to the proposed Hai Phong project. Last time we asked, we got one in twenty-four hours. Business is business, I suppose. Courier two passport photos to St James Travel first thing tomorrow. Where can I reach you in Vietnam?'

'I haven't even thought about my plans. Better if I call you. Can you give me a contact number?'

She pulled a small leather organizer from her bag, scribbled some numbers on a sheet of paper, then handed it to him.

'When do you leave?' he asked.

'Sometime tomorrow afternoon.'

'Taking the corporate jet?'

'Yes,' she replied, then narrowed her eyes as she caught McCann's expression. 'Why not, for God's sake? That's what it's there for.'

He didn't answer her question; he merely raised his eyebrows. If she wanted to kid around, so could he.

'Look, if I had my way, I'd sell up and give half of the proceeds to people who really needed it. But too many people's lives depend on the company.'

He believed her; he'd never seen her flaunt her wealth. 'Talking of the jet, did you ask Bradley about the lease of the Boeing?' This was the question that had been bugging him for some time.

'Sure. It was no big deal, as he said at the time. He was just doing dad a favor.'

'That's not how Zeltis sees it. Bob maintains it was the other way round,' McCann replied.

'Really,' she said with a sudden look of impatience. 'Look, what if it was? It's not really important. A reputable company brokered the deal.'

'Is that right,' McCann muttered under his breath.

'Are you suggesting otherwise? If so, tell me now,' she retorted.

He'd certainly got her back up. She was suddenly defensive as hell of Radcliffe.

McCann shrugged. 'If Bradley says Rowe, Radley are fair dinkum, I'll buy that. But they obviously made a fundamental error of judgment when they agreed to deal with whoever was behind the facade of the New World Hotel Group without checking their credentials first.'

'No one has intimated New World has done anything reprehensible yet,' Rosalind replied sharply.

'Not yet,' McCann replied with a tone that suggested they soon would be. 'The Federal boys obviously think there's a good chance there's a big smell about to escape. They just don't know exactly where. But it's as well to remember that they're not fools. I'd ask Bradley to check really carefully on his 'reputable' company. Then I'd check on it myself, if I were you.'

'Thanks for the advice, Leo.' She'd abruptly moved into corporate mode.

McCann put a hand on her shoulder. 'Look, Rosie. You hired me to give advice. That's what I'm doing. I call things the way I see them. I'm not a diplomat.'

'I'll say you're not. You're intimating my boyfriend's hand in glove with international criminals!'

'Steady. I have said no such thing. I just think it'd be prudent to cover all bases.'

They stood in silence beside the coffee machine for a few seconds.

'Can I have another coffee,' Rosalind eventually asked, in a manner suggesting she regretted her acerbity.

'Sure,' McCann replied, pouring more water into the top, and adding the ground beans to the cup beneath.

'You don't like Bradley much, do you?' she said simply.

McCann's head swung round to her. She was just so damned direct!

'I hardly know the guy. How can you say I don't like him?'

'He's a fine man, Leo. So is his father. You just don't know him yet. Smart, loving, generous. Kind.'

'Well, I'd say we're diametric opposites in everything but the smarts and kindness stakes. He's everything I'm not. Fancy bloodline, megabucks, youth, good looks.'

Rosalind snorted. 'You're not exactly the Elephant Man, Leo.'

'How long have you known him?' McCann said, ignoring the backhanded compliment.

'Since I was ten,' she replied, then laughed lightly. 'Ridiculous isn't it?'

'No. As long as you weren't sleeping with him then,' McCann replied straightfacedly.

'I could go right off you, Leo McCann,' she replied with a grin. 'Seriously, our family has known the Radcliffes for years and years. Brad and I were kids together. Sometimes they'd spend holidays over here, sometimes us with them. The Radcliffe's had a wondrous beach house near Martha's Vineyard. We used to joke that the whole town belonged to Brad's grandmother.'

McCann pulled the lever down, and the coffee bubbled into the espresso cup. He then passed her the coffee, crossing to the verandah window, staring into the night. The air was still outside allowing patches of gray smoke to hang in the air like phantoms, reminding him of his loss.

'We need new financial terms?' said Rosalind.

'The mast and refit? I suppose we do. Maybe we could talk about that later. It's too early now.'

'Whatever. Give it some thought.'

She finished her coffee, then picked up her jacket and purse, and walked to the door.

'It's late. I'd better go. See you tomorrow at the funeral. Ten forty-five?'

'See you then,' he replied.

'Do you need money for the trip?'

'I'll use Amex.'

'If there's anything you need, just let Leila know at the office.'

The headlight of a car on McCarr's Creek road shone through the kitchen window and was reflected in her eyes. There was no doubt in McCann's mind any more. She was without doubt the most captivating woman he'd ever met.

21.

21st May.

McCann woke at 8.30 a.m. He'd eventually fallen asleep approximately an hour earlier, still sitting where Rosalind had left him the night before, in the kitchen by the window looking down to the empty space where L'Echapper Belle had stood at anchor.

Was it plain crazy to hop a plane to Ho Chi Minh City? What exactly did he hope to achieve? Was it purely in the heat of the moment last night, while he was filled with pain at the loss of L'Echapper Belle, that the thoughts of revenge had burned so strongly? Was it because of Whitey? Could it have been to impress Rosie?

And though some of the pieces were beginning to fit together, the center of the jigsaw was still a gaping void. Why had Horan and Buchanan met with Tran and his brother at the Savoy in the first place? All he had to work with were Whitey's conjectures based on Horan's investigations. And what exactly had Horan meant when he'd said *the wheel is come full circle*. What exactly *had* he uncovered?

Now there was also the curious question of the plane. Was it conceivable that Buchanan had been in on the hijacking of the money at JFK? It seemed scarcely credible.

Of course it was by no means certain that the Buchanan jet had been the aircraft used. The authorities were still checking at this stage. It was still possible that it was one of the other two at Sheremetyevo.

But if it turned out to be the Buchanan jet, where did this put Bradley? An innocent who'd merely put Rowe,

Radley together with Maynard Buchanan? If so, then who had been the guilty party? Had Rowe, Radley been duped by criminals? Or were they involved in the conspiracy?

McCann was re-filling the coffee machine when the first call of the day came through. He let it ring till the machine picked it up.

'Good morning, Mr. McCann. Meg Poole of St James Travel speaking. Ms. Buchanan has asked me to inform you that we will be handling all the details of your Vietnam trip. Whenever you're ready, just give me a call. I'd be grateful if you could courier two passport photos ASAP. Thank you.'

McCann smiled. There was no way that Rosalind was going to let him off the hook. He was going to Vietnam.

He was on the verandah drinking his coffee, looking down at the creek, when the phone rang for the second time. Again he let it ring; the doors were open, he'd listen to the message. There was always the option of picking up.

'Morning Leo. Matt here. I have the info about your man. Give us a call.'

McCann was inside in a flash.

'Matt? Leo. What've you got for me?'

There was a beat, then Matt replied in measured tones. 'I'm seriously beginning to regret doing young Rosie all these favors. I seem to be doing nothing but your legwork.'

McCann laughed. Matt was a good friend, there was no disputing it. 'Cut the crap, Matt. What have you got?'

'Your man Tran. Full name Tran Van Luc. Luc means 'force' in Vietnamese. Pretty appropriate moniker. War hero of sorts. Full Colonel in the North Vietnamese Army. Fought for the duration. But word has it he was seldom near the sharp end. Lost half his foot in an argument with a Claymore very early on.'

McCann smiled. The shoeprints. It all added up. 'What made him a hero then?'

'Made sure he was around when they were handing out medals, I suppose. He was in the supply arm, you see. So he was a good friend to have, if you needed anything.'

'Did he have a brother?'

'Steady junior, I'll get to that. Haven't finished the bio,' Hutton continued with a chuckle. 'Moved from Hanoi to Saigon when it fell in '75. Well, then he was like a sow in a truffle patch, as you can imagine. All that hardware left behind, and he was the supply chief!'

'Black market?'

'Too right. Made a damned fortune. Then did the right thing and spread the cash around a bit in the right circles. He made a lot of powerful friends, and they let him get on with it. They weren't stupid.'

McCann could hear the rustle of paper over the line as Hutton turned the page.

'The CIA was after his ass till '84. They were pretty burned up he was selling off the US hardware they'd had to leave behind. Around the same time he turned legitimate. Banking. Now runs the biggest merchant bank in Vietnam. Bigger even than the Foreign Trade Bank there. Called the Viet People's Commercial Investment Bank. That's the translation, anyway. His twin brother's full name is Tran Tuan Hung. Hung means 'strong'. He runs a DTC in Hong Kong, The Fortress Hill Investment Bank. It's big. Word at Langley is that it's Tran's twin Luc who calls the shots. By the way, Tran Tuan Hung has lived in Hong Kong for seven years. He now goes by the name of Fook Lam Chau. Maybe it's smarter to do business with a Chinese name, as opposed to a Vietnamese one.'

'You've got an address for Tran Luc?'

'Nothing more specific than Hoy Tay Lake, Hanoi.'

'What about the twin, Hung?'

'Nothing on him. They were never interested in him, you see, just big brother.'

'Do you have any contacts in Vietnam?'

'Our people? Or cousins?' Hutton was aware that the line was not secure. 'Cousins' were the CIA.

'Both. I'm visiting either tomorrow or the day after.'

'Better make it two days. I'll have to send whatever I come up with to Vera.' Vera was a post office box in central Sydney. Anyone monitoring their conversation would have no way of knowing what Hutton was referring to.

'Which carrier are you using?'

'May as well fly Vietnam Airlines to Ho Chi Minh. They could do with some support I'd imagine.'

'I'll organize a reception.'

'Thanks Matt.'

'Not at all,' Hutton replied in a voice rich with sarcasm. 'Any time.'

McCann dialed again. Next in line was Torrance's direct line. As usual he was at his desk.

'Morning, McCann.'

'Good morning. Just heard from my friend in England. Thought you'd like to know the news.'

'I suppose you've rung to crow,' said Torrance without a hint of resentment.

'Tran Van Luc had a twin brother, Tran Tuan Hung. Lived in Hong Kong for years. He adopted the name Fook Lam Chau. One more thing - want to know something about Tran Van Luc's feet?'

'You *have* rung up to crow,' said Torrance resignedly.

'Lost some toes to an anti-personnel mine during the war.'

There was no reaction from Torrance.

'The size nine orthopedic European?' McCann prompted.

'Okay, I follow you. No need to beat me over the head with it.'

'They came in together on a private jet the morning of March 26th.'

'That I do know, McCann.'

'You know? How?'

'Based on your *assumptions*,' he said stressing the word with distaste, 'I asked immigration to check on our Tran Van Luc. He arrived 26th 4.10 p.m. Private jet. Qantas Executive Services handled the flight. Left that evening, 9.45 p.m. Remember, I told you, we were only checking for aliens still in the country, because we were trying to identify the dead Tran not his living brother.'

'Why didn't Tran Tuan Hung show up on the records?'

'He was travelling on a Panamanian passport under his Vietnamese name. He had a multiple entry, one month, visa. Expired today. We'd been targeting Asians.'

'Why not the name?'

'When Langley came up with Tran Van Luc as a possible, it was so quickly knocked on the head we didn't bother to run with the name. They assured us he was alive and kicking in Hanoi, so he couldn't be our man, remember?'

'So you now agree with my theory that Tran Van Luc took the computer disks?'

'If they existed. The plastic container could well have been empty.'

There was no point in pursuing the computer disks angle further, he could see Torrance had dug his heels in on that point. 'Okay, forget it. I'd have to be able to present you with a Polaroid of the man stealing them to convince you. But you can see now that the reason it was so bloody hard to identify Tran Tuan Hung was because his brother took his wallet and any other identifying material from his dead body. That's why there was a partial shoeprint next to Hung's body.'

'That again is hypothesis, McCann.'

'Look, for a man that assumes a lot I've had my fair share of success to date – grant me that won't you, you difficult bastard?'

Torrance chuckled good-naturedly. 'All right, all right. But why make the identification so hard. What's in it for him?'

'Tran Van Luc was making the most of a bad situation. On the down side, his brother was dead, but on the up side, so was Horan. And it was Horan who had the goods on him, at least so Imogen Whitehead maintained. So Tran looks around to see if Horan brought the evidence with him. He sees the disks and takes them. But he doesn't want anyone to know he's been there helping himself to the evidence, so he takes the brother's ID to slow the authorities down till he's back in the air and off home. The bad news is that he's got to wait until his brother's visa expires, and he's officially notified of

Hung's death, before he can arrange for the body to be flown home.'

'What's he going to say when we ask him why he left his brother behind?'

'He'd just say he had no idea his brother had been at the Savoy, that they hadn't planned on returning together, and that he presumed his brother was off on business somewhere.'

'Was your friend Matt Hutton able to tell you what Tran Tuan Hung did for a living?'

'He ran a merchant bank in Hong Kong. Worked for his brother, I'd presume. Must have had a Hong Kong passport as well.'

'That's right. He must have had three. The Panamanian one you buy. The Hong Kong one comes with time and the right amount of money, and the Vietnamese one's a gimme - he was born there. Tell me, though, how come Tran Van Luc arrived at the Savoy after his brother?'

'I haven't told you the best bit yet. I had my chat with young Hendrik Ohlson. I gave him a touch of the Leo McCann slow burn, and he changed his story radically.'

'Tell me.' Torrance sounded excited. McCann detailed the entire conversation as accurately and concisely as possible to the eager ears of Torrance.

'My guess is that Tran spotted Hendrik Ohlson following him,' McCann continued a couple of minutes later. 'He didn't know who was in the car. It could have been anyone. So he jumped the limo somewhere in South Dowling Street. He left his brother to run interference.'

'He did that in a big way.'

'Sure did.'

'By the way, you've got the interview with Ohlson on tape?'

'No,' McCann replied hesitantly. He knew what Torrance's reaction would be.

'What! You've got to be kidding me. You didn't tape the boy. Jesus H. Christ!'

'I gave him my word.'

'Shit, McCann. What the hell did you think the recorder was for?'

'Knock it off. I got a tape-full of goodies from Messon's man. It's so good, you'll forgive me right away. I'll send it over by courier.'

'Can't wait.'

'By the way, all Ohlson's stuff is off the record,' McCann added.

'What the hell do you mean? I'm going to roast the little toad!'

'Look, if I hadn't given my word, he'd never have told me. I'm sure of that.'

'Heard you the first time. You gave your word,' Torrance replied through clenched teeth.

'Hey, at least we now know the truth. By the way, was there anyone else on Tran's plane from Vietnam?' McCann asked.

'You mean Brokov? No. But we do have his entry/exit details. Arrived from London exactly one week ago. Left for Kuala Lumpur three days ago.'

'That figures. Killed Imogen Whitehead, then heads off to kill Boydell. Any record?'

'None. He's clean under that name. I've checked him with Interpol and the FBI. Nothing. As for the photos, I've one of Sir Henry Trevor, but none of Brokov. Want me to fax it? What's your number?'

McCann gave the Priory fax.

'By the way, Brokov's woman torched my boat last night.'

Torrance was silent for a moment.

'You know that for a fact? That it was her?'

'I know it, yes. For a fact, no. I just know it. The man who lives next to me saw a young woman on the boat just before she went up. I must have passed her on the road, she was going fast as bat shit. Almost took me out.'

'I'm sorry to hear about the boat. I mean that. By the way, what did the Federal Police want with Rosalind Buchanan?'

'They asked a lot of questions about the Buchanan executive jet. Apparently it's one of three jets that could be linked to the theft of a major amount of currency at JFK.'

'Never rains, eh? Rosalind Buchanan's got a heap on her plate right now, I'd say.'

McCann had to agree. He just hoped for her sake that Bradley Radcliffe wasn't about to add to her woes.

To his immeasurable embarrassment and shame, the cell phone in his pocket began bleating during Rosalind's eulogy. He'd quite forgotten it was there. To her great credit she continued speaking, as if selectively deaf to this most intrusive of twentieth-century conveniences.

McCann was seated at the back of the chapel, which was sadly somewhat empty. Kerry sat in the front row. He looked happy as a clam; clearly without the first idea what was going on. On his left was an empty space where Rosalind had been sitting. To his right sat a female nurse of around forty, her arm threaded through his. Zeltis and Mackintosh were in a pew three rows behind, next to Rupert Gerson, who presumably was representing the Australia Pacific Bank. Everyone held the white roses handed to them as they'd entered. Whitey's rosewood coffin stood on a low catafalque.

The moment he heard the phone start up, McCann put his rose aside, thrusting his hand in his pocket. In the confined space it had the sonority of a foghorn. He rose and walked quickly from the chapel.

'Leo? It's Alan Messon. I just heard about your boat. I'm so very sorry.'

'Thank you, Alan. Look, I'm afraid I can't talk right now. I'm actually attending a funeral.'

'Oh, I see. I'm sorry.'

'I'll call you later, right?'

But before McCann could hit the 'end' button, Messon began again. 'You promised you'd tell me his name. The Vietnamese. When you were sure of the facts, you said. Remember?'

'I do, Alan. And I will tell you. But not now. I really have to go.' Messon was still speaking when McCann cut him off and slipped the phone back into his pocket.

As he walked back up the steps of the crematorium, he noticed two men in raincoats standing by the gate that led to the street. They stood apart from the funeral cortège drivers. One was considerably taller than the other. It seemed to McCann that they were watching him.

Inside the hall everyone was kneeling in prayer. The Reverend Sebastian Green, the family cleric Rosalind had chosen for the service, was reciting the twenty-third psalm. The congregation was then invited to pay their respects by laying the roses on the coffin. The committal followed. Then Green pressed a switch on the dais, and Whitey's coffin moved backwards. Purple curtains closing discreetly behind it.

It was at this precise moment that Kerry chose to escape from the mental prison of his insanity. Quite suddenly he looked wildly round the room, then at the purple curtains that confronted him.

'Oh dear Lord, she's dead,' he called out, his cries echoing round the building. 'What's happening? Oh sweet Jesus, please don't take her yet,' he cried, placing his head in his hands and beginning to sob uncontrollably.

The service continued for a few minutes, despite Kerry's weeping. Then came the blessing, at the end of which Kerry was led from the chapel, Rosalind on one side, the nurse on the other.

Outside were perhaps less than a dozen wreaths. McCann was saddened that such a wonderful woman should have so few friends present to mourn her passing.

As a distant rumble of thunder sounded in the sky, McCann looked down towards the gate. The two raincoats were still standing there, looking in his direction.

Without waiting to speak to Rosalind, McCann walked purposefully over to the two men, who held their ground, continuing to eyeball him.

'Are you waiting for a member of the Whitehead party?' McCann asked, in none to friendly a fashion.

'Actually, we were waiting for you, Mr. McCann,' the taller of the two said pleasantly. 'My name's John Cate, I'm with AUSTRAC, the Australian Transaction Reports and Analysis Center. It's a federal agency.'

He held out a hand. McCann had no alternative but to shake it. The man seemed friendly enough.

'And this is my colleague Scott Boesel,' he said, shooting a sidelong glance at the other raincoat. Boesel was a stocky five foot eight, with a small black goatee and a tonsure. 'Scott's with FinCEN, the Financial Crimes Enforcement Network; a somewhat similar organization to ours in the States. We're working together as part of a FATF initiative.'

'And what exactly is that?' McCann inquired.

Cate smiled embarrassedly. 'I'm sorry. It's the Financial Action Task Force. It's an international organization set up in 1989 at the International Economic Summit to foster cooperation between law enforcement agencies all over the world, and document and compile national programs targeting money laundering.'

So what did they want with him? And how did they know who the hell he was?

'We appreciate this is a somewhat inappropriate moment. However, we'd be grateful if we could arrange a time to meet.'

'With regard to what exactly?' McCann asked.

'We think we have a common purpose, Mr. McCann. We worked closely with Andrew Horan prior to his death.'

That was enough. It said plenty. They had McCann's full attention. Nevertheless, he still took issue with their sense of timing. 'Could you excuse me a moment while I say goodbye to some people?' he replied crisply. 'This is, after all, a funeral of sorts, not a convention center.'

Cate and his friend looked suitably chastened as McCann made his way back towards the chapel. After a couple of paces he stopped, looking back at Cate and Boesel.

'Aren't the raincoats a bit of a cliché?'

Cate smiled, Boesel didn't respond.

Kerry was still sobbing at the chapel doors – a child who didn't want to return to school. He'd wrapped both arms round Rosalind. Bradley Radcliffe stood to one side with the solemn air of a very stylish funeral director. He was dressed in an elegant knee length black cashmere coat.

McCann caught Rosalind's eye, and they communicated very briefly and discreetly in sign language - he'd be in touch before she left for the States. Then it was time to return to the raincoats, to see what they were after.

As he reached them, the rain suddenly started to beat down. Boesel turned up the collar of his coat with a smug look of satisfaction.

'I see you don't have a raincoat, Mr. McCann. Why don't we sit in the car? Beats the hell out of getting wet,' Cate suggested, indicating a Ford Falcon just across the street.

'Why me?' McCann asked, as he settled into the back seat of the car. Boesel sat beside him, Cate leant over from the front passenger seat.

'As I said, we were working with Andrew Horan before he died. He came to us at AUSTRAC for help,' Cate replied. 'We had common interests. He was compiling an audit.'

'Yes, I know.'

'It so happened that we found ourselves investigating the same companies; the same merchant banks. Their names kept cropping up, so we agreed to share material. Then he was killed, and we lost access to a great deal of the data he'd promised us. We've been continuing our investigations along lines indicated to us by Horan since then. His wife told us yesterday that you'd been in touch with her; that you were inquiring into his death. She mentioned you'd shown some interest in Andrew Horan's computer records. Is that right?'

'I'm actually investigating Maynard Buchanan's death, rather than Andrew's, but I suppose it amounts to the same thing.'

'I suppose it does, yes,' said Cate.

'How did you get on to me?'

'Well, we were talking with Detective Inspector Gattenby of South Region Major Crime Squad who is investigating Imogen Whitehead's death. He told us you'd been really helpful, liaising via Task Force Acorn. He also mentioned you'd been to Hong Kong recently.'

'That's right,' McCann replied. Word seemed to travel very fast between the various police departments. Quite what interest his trip to Hong Kong would have been to Gattenby he couldn't fathom.

'I'll tell you what drew our attention,' said Boesel. They seemed to be taking it in turns to ask the questions. 'It was the names that cropped up during the course of our conversation with Gattenby. They appeared to be the same names we'd encountered in our dealings with Mr. Horan. Apparently you'd brought up the names of three men in your discussions with Chief Superintendent Torrance of Task Force Acorn; Francis Greville, Sir Henry Trevor, and most recently a Vietnamese named Tran Van Luc. Is that accurate?'

'That's correct,' McCann replied. Presumably Torrance had passed on his entire conversation to Gattenby. 'When did you speak to Torrance?' he asked Cate.

'Less than an hour ago. We then called Buchanan Construction for a contact number, and they said you'd be here.'

'Do you remember meeting a federal policeman called Eade?' Boesel asked.

'Of course. He asked all the questions about the Buchanan jet.'

'Correct. It's been a strange few months, but it appears to us that the theft of the millions in Moscow and the bombing in Sydney could be interrelated.'

They now had McCann's attention in a big way.

'How's that?'

Boesel glanced at Cate for confirmation, then looked back to McCann.

'Do you have time to come down to our offices right now?'

'Wouldn't miss it for the world. What's the address?'

'We can drive you, then drop you back here.'

'No thanks. I have to drop off a tape at Task Force Acorn for Chief Superintendent Torrance. He'll be champing at the bit. Where's your office?'

Cate reached into his wallet and pulled out a card.

'Shall we say an hour?'

'An hour.'

McCann stepped out of the car and closed the door. Then a thought struck him and he tapped on the driver's window. It slid down.

'By the way, Scott. How did you know it was going to rain?' McCann asked.

Boesel shrugged. 'You've got to be a Fed to be able to pick the weather, Mr. McCann.'

22.

21st May.

'This is our office – has been for over a year,' Boesel said as he pushed open the door to the third level.

It was a computer jungle. All four walls, with the exception of one small window, were covered with hardware. A Tandem Mainframe had pride of place in the center of the room. Three Mackintosh workstations stood to the left, a Hewlett-Packard workstation to the right. Ropes of color-coded wires, secured together with tape in groups of four or more, ran across the floor between the furniture. It reminded McCann of the scanning room at GCHQ, the British Intelligence Communications Headquarters in Gloucestershire, England.

Boesel stood just inside the door, hands behind his back. 'The Financial Action Task Force is an international forum for promoting anti-money laundering legislation. It's got members in twenty-six countries, one of whom is Australia. It has established secretariats in various locations round the world. Though strictly speaking it doesn't have an investigative role, it encourages countries to form their own task forces. Its initial purpose was to fight narcotics-related money laundering worldwide. But the parameters are no longer quite that narrow. We're no longer restricted to drug money; any dirt will do. Take a seat. I'll give you a bit of background, then show you around. Okay?'

Boesel indicated a beat-up fifties three-piece suite that stood in a corner near a coined coffee vending machine. It looked like a yard sale.

'Actually, in the last few years it's achieved a lot internationally,' Boesel continued, searching in his trouser pocket for some change for the machine. 'Pressure has been brought politically on all member countries to make laundering a criminal offence, to beef up rules regarding the reporting of suspicious banking transactions. A whole heap of things.'

As he began loading coins into the vending machine, Cate stepped forward and tapped Boesel on the feed arm, indicating McCann with a swivel of the eyeball.

'Can I get you a coffee? Tea,' Cate asked, turning to his guest.

The second coin had already slipped down the shute before Boesel had time to react. 'Oh, I'm sorry, Mr. McCann,' he said, 'I wasn't thinking. What'll you have?'

'Nothing right now, thanks,' McCann said, sitting in one of the vinyl armchairs. 'So FinCEN are the computer cops that fight money laundering in America?'

'Pretty close. Actually there are a heap of organizations in the States that focus directly on money laundering. Most have a narcotics angle, because in the past most of the money being laundered was the proceeds of drug-related crime. Top of the list of organizations is the Office of National Drug Control Policy in the President's Executive Office. That's not hands-on, it merely controls policy. The main coordinating body is the Multi Agency Financial Investigations Center, or MAFIC. They try to coordinate the FBI, DEA, IRS, US Customs, and the Post Office. I tell you, if it wasn't for the MAFIC, none of us would get anywhere. There's too much of the *hey, asshole, that's my patch* attitude in the States.'

'The MAFIC's an internal organization?'

'That's right. But quite obviously the great majority of international money laundering crosses international borders, and that's why the FATF's role's so vital,' Boesel continued.

'Are you with FinCEN or the FATF?'

'I am a FinCEN man, working with a regional task force set up very loosely under an FATF umbrella.'

'What's the name of this one?'

'Task Force Lotus,' Boesel said, as he clicked the knob marked *coffee granules* and the machine spat a miserly portion of brown dust into the waxed paper cup. 'It's a multinational task force based here in Sydney. We've got quite a few agencies represented. John Cate, as you know, is from AUSTRAC, as is Kyle Rosen over there,' he said indicating a young man surrounded by hardware, staring at a computer screen in a corner. 'Avery Suschor is our FBI rep – he's been working on financial crime for twenty odd years. I'm the rep from FinCEN, as is Noah Jennings, who's not here at the moment. Then there's Gordon Mascon – ' Boesel hesitated for a moment. McCann knew at once that he was the CIA man. 'He's with the US State Department. He's out.'

Boiling water began to dribble into Boesel's cup.

'Plus we've got a terrific support team of technicians, care of the Australian Government.'

'You're investigating specific people, or money-laundering in general in Australia?' McCann asked.

'We're working right alongside four other international task forces; Red Ruble, Blue Quays, Old World, and Homeboy. Ruble is concerned primarily with Russia - Moscow in particular; Homeboy's zone is New York; Blue Quay's is the Caribbean; Old World's Europe. Our zone's Southeast Asia.'

'You get half a continent, and some of them get a city? Doesn't seem too fair to me.'

Boesel laughed. 'In financial terms it amounts to about the same thing. The world still more or less revolves round the dollar, so New York is still *it* when it comes to international wire service transactions. That's Homeboy's zone.

'Outside of the States it's the Eurodollar Market that's paramount. Eurodollars are US dollars circulating in the financial community anywhere outside the US. This market is based in the thirty or so offshore banks – for instance the Caymans, which boasts 546 banks at the last count. That's Task Force Blue Quay's' zone of operation.'

Boesel joined McCann. It was now Cate's turn to pop coins in the machine, clicking the coffee knob four or five times. He obviously liked a stronger brew than Boesel.

'There was an estimate made back in '94 that around two-thirds of all the US currency in circulation was either overseas, or in what we call "the underground economy," Boesel continued. 'That was around 260 billion dollars! Imagine that. All that cash, and we have no idea where it is. Quite a proportion of it is rushing round the world via the wire services every day. Do you know, two-thirds of all newly minted US currency flies straight off to Russia and Eastern Europe.'

'Like the money stolen in Moscow recently?'

'Exactly, Mr. McCann. I'm glad you drew attention to the stolen money, because it ties in with what I'll tell you in a minute.'

Cate pulled his coffee cup from the vending machine, and began stirring the liquid with a wooden paddle. 'In the opinion of most western governments today, money laundering is the most critical problem facing law enforcement,' said Cate. 'Federal agencies in the States estimate this to be around 300 billion dollars of dirty money a year. This isn't just drug money, Mr. McCann, it's savings and loan fraud, organized crime, white-collar fraud, real estate fraud – you name it.

'But not all money laundering's illegal, is it? Wiring flight capital from one country to another for instance. It could be that I merely wanted to disguise the ownership of my funds,' argued McCann.

'You're quite right. But we have to look at the big picture, and the big picture is this. Take away the profits of narcotics trafficking, and there's no incentive to peddle it on the streets. Same principle applies to all major organized crime. This is where FinCEN in the States, AUSTRAC here in Australia, and Trac-Fin in France, among others, come in.'

He sat back and looked at McCann as would a teacher in class. 'What would you say is the quickest and most risk-free pipeline for moving and hiding money?'

'The international wire services,' McCann replied.

'Exactly. But when you consider there are approximately half a million wire transfers daily, valued at more than two trillion dollars, of which less that one half of one per cent represents money laundering, you can see our problem.'

That much was clear. McCann was glad it wasn't his problem.

'What you're looking at over there, Mr. McCann,' Cate said, indicating the techno-jungle facing them, 'is a kind of marriage between all the artificial intelligence and intelligence amplification systems of the various international partners of FATF. We keep each country's data bases separate, since the systems vary operationally, but we can crosscheck on the motherboard using every byte. FinCEN's AI system's acronym is FAIS. It includes knowledge-based systems, which automatically make inferences about wire transfers and other data; and link analysis, which helps identify relationships among individual accounts, people, and organizations. The Australian system is called ScreenIT. Any unusual transactions? They show up like fleas on a white dog. Beautiful, no?'

McCann had to agree. George Orwell would have been out of his depth – Big Brother had nothing on this techno-amalgam of databases.

'Where do I fit in?' McCann asked.

'Your trip to Hong Kong,' Cate began. 'You were following up leads that Andrew Horan had given you?'

'No. I went to meet a friend of the man who defrauded Buchanan Construction in Malaysia of a hundred and eighty million.'

'Palmer? Telok Anson?' Boesel chipped in.

'You're familiar with the facts?' McCann asked.

'We are. But first, may I give you some background as to our overall purpose. This will answer your question as to why we asked to speak with you.'

'Sure, go right ahead,' McCann replied.

'Well, the five FATF task forces I mentioned earlier, of which we are one, are all part of an umbrella task force called Mainstream. Each of the task forces has a target list of names. These are those people we believe to be top of the hill so to speak, the godfathers of financial crime in the various areas. They're the ones we're after.'

'You've identified exactly who they are?' McCann asked. He already had a shrewd idea who one of them was.

'Hold on a minute. Don't jump the gun. Before I go into that, let me tell you something else, because it goes to the very heart of a theory we have concerning the connection between Maynard Buchanan, and the man whose name surfaced in your discussion with Chief Superintendent Torrance - Tran Van Luc.'

'Okay. I'm listening.'

'With the break-up of the Soviet Union in '91, there was a slow disintegration of the structure of government. One of the most significant areas to change radically was the Russian banking system. Before '91 it had been government controlled, now it was replaced by chartered private institutions. Given that corruption was at that time endemic in Russia at every conceivable level, it was a safe bet to assume that many of these chartered banks would fall into the wrong hands. And that's exactly what happened. The banks were unregulated and many undercapitalized.

'On July 2 1993 the first of the so-called international gangster summits took place in Yerevan, Armenia. You see, it was becoming plain to the worldwide criminal fraternity that the international banking opportunities available to the Russian Banks for processing dirty money were unlimited. The new criminal aristocracy, the Russian *Mafyia* in Moscow, wanted to process the dirty money of criminal syndicates around of the world. So they issued invitations to criminal delegations from the US, South America, Italy, Turkey and Germany to come to Armenia.'

'No Asian delegation?'

'No. That was what intrigued us initially. The man who called this first summit was called Rafik Svo. His premise was to bring an end to division amongst the international criminal community, by drawing the Colombians, the New York Italians, the Brighton Beach Russians, the Italian Mafia and the Moscow Russians into a loose alliance. The Russian banking system would be used to launder the world's dirty money for them all.

The Moscow banks would supersede Swiss banks, Panama, Liberia, offshore banks and the like. After all, why do business with a bank when you can own one?'

'I wouldn't have thought they would have trusted each other to deal through the one system, owned and controlled by a single arm of the alliance,' said McCann.

'Good point. That was a major sticking point at the summit, and though subsequently a major percentage of mob money from all of the world was processed through Moscow, the families continued to spread their cash around the Caribbean, and continued to bank to a limited extent in Switzerland and South America.

'Then in '93 there was another summit in Prague, Czechoslovakia. The biggest thing to come out of that was a mutual cooperation agreement between the Russian and the Sicilian Mafia. The Russians agreed to launder drug money for the Sicilians in return for a franchise on some drug-smuggling routes through central Asia. But it was here that they began to tread on the toes of people outside the Alliance - the very people who had been excluded from the party in the first place. The Asians.

'They were doubly pissed. To their mind, Asia was their turf. Not only did they feel they were being moved in on, but they quickly realized that they'd be badly affected if they were excluded from this very powerful club.'

'Rather like the European Economic Community?' McCann interjected.

'Exactly. They knew they'd be better off being on the inside looking out. The alliance was becoming too strong.'

'It was Tran Van Luc who wanted in?'

Boesel smiled. 'He very much wanted in.'

'All very interesting, but how is this relevant to my trip to Hong Kong?'

'The money that was stolen at Sheremetyevo airport on March 26 this year was Russian mob money to be processed through a Russian mob bank.'

'I don't see your point exactly,' said McCann.

'It seemed too much of a coincidence that you were investigating Tran Van Luc's possible involvement in the theft of the money at Telok Anson, while at the same time there was a strong possibility that the Buchanan Construction 727 was used to transport the US currency from Sheremetyevo airport. And at the center of it all was a meeting at which Tran Van Luc, his brother, Andrew Horan and Maynard Buchanan were participants – a meeting from which, either by chance or design, only one man walked away alive.' He paused momentarily to gauge McCann's reaction. 'You have to admit, the coincidences are strong.'

McCann held up a hand. It had only just struck him. When had Boesel and Cate placed Tran at the Savoy? Where was all their information stemming from? 'Hold on just a second, will you,' he said. 'How long have you been aware that Tran Van Luc had a twin brother?'

Boesel smiled, Cate looked sheepish.

'Chief Superintendent Torrance has been good enough to share the fruits of his investigations with our office, together with your theories.'

'I see,' McCann replied with a wry smile.

'Regardless of the coincidences, you not suggesting Maynard Buchanan was a confederate of Tran's; that they were partners in crime?'

'I don't personally believe so, though we have to consider the possibility. Certainly Andrew Horan did.'

'Did what? Think his oldest friend was a criminal?'

'No, he merely considered the possibility. You see, during his audit the specter of Tran kept appearing in the spreadsheets. The man is clever; he works through daisy chains of shell companies and bearer corporations. You won't find his name on the registers of suspect corporations – others manage and front them. But to a man of Horan's capabilities, the smell was overwhelming.

'One of the last things he confided to us was a theory that Tran Van Luc had stage-managed the Telok Anson affair, a theory that has since been confirmed by Phillip Boydell to you in Hong Kong. Or so Detective Superintendent Torrance has informed us.

'Then another thing occurred to Horan. If Tran had persuaded Palmer to steal the money, he'd know only too well that Buchanan would require refinancing double quick.'

'The rationale behind the theft?'

'Quite possibly. For who would be in a better position to offer his services than Tran himself, through his merchant bank. Buchanan would naturally be very relieved to secure refinancing so quickly, without the smallest inkling that Tran had stolen the money in the first place.'

'*The wheel is come full circle,*' McCann murmured to himself.

'I'm sorry?' Cate said, leaning forward.

'Hold it. You're saying that Tran Van Luc financed the loan?'

'Effectively, yes. Not through his own bank in Hanoi, but via banks he controlled. Horan had done his homework, and with our help traced the financing. The Union Constitution was the lead Bank. The syndicate participants were the St John's Commercial in Jersey, where Sir Henry Trevor is a director; the Fortress Hill Investment Bank in Hong Kong, the chairman of which we now know, thanks to you, was Tran's brother; and the Weddle Commercial in London, which has cropped up time and time again on our computers, and more than likely has links with Tran.'

'Tran in all three cases.'

'We think so.'

'Answer this. Did Buchanan know he was dealing with Tran when the loan was negotiated?'

'Possibly, though it's by no means certain. I doubt that he'd be familiar with the power behind Fortress and Weddle anyway, and he'd have no reason to think that Sir Henry Trevor was a crook. Remember it's only specialists like us who know the full extent of their darker side. Otherwise, they would cease to function.'

'But he would have known by the time the meeting was arranged?'

'I would say quite definitely. Horan would have told him of his suspicions,' Boesel replied.

'If Andrew Horan believed Tran to be the intelligence behind Telok Anson, why would he consider meeting with Tran at the Savoy? A dubious reputation's one thing, but a belief that he was dealing with a criminal is totally another. For that matter, why would Maynard Buchanan have been present at all?'

'As I say, I presume Horan shared his theory with the man who, as you rightly point out, was his oldest and closest friend. I'd say the plan was for the two of them to confront Tran.'

'If Tran realized they knew of his involvement in Telok Anson, surely he would never have shown up?'

'From what Horan indicated to us, Maynard Buchanan had been at the point of entering into further negotiations with the same bank syndicate when Horan brought his findings to Buchanan's attention. If that was the case, I'd presume Tran thought the meeting was arranged to discuss future business. He would have been happy to show up.

'I'd say the strategy was to give Tran an ultimatum – if he agreed to repay the stolen Telok Anson money, they'd agree not to take the matter further. It'd be in the interests of both parties – Tran could well afford the repayment, and would thereby avoid criminal prosecution, and Maynard Buchanan would avoid the financial press painting him as a man of poor judgment and questionable ethics. And you have to remember that as soon as the authorities were alerted, the judicial system would have tied up the money for years. Plus there'd be no question of the Australian director of public prosecutions being in a position to bring Tran to trial; Tran would make sure his pals back home saw to his interests.'

'Can I just go back a bit. If the money at Sheremetyevo airport was mob money, how was it allowed to leave the United States?'

'Although we may *know* it is mob money, it's up to us to *prove* that it is. And most of the time that's damned hard. That, my friend, was the whole point of setting up the Russian Banks. Often we know money's dirty, but we can't prove it. For instance, the Union Constitution Bank in New York is happy to do business with mobbed up Russian Banks. It's great business, so they turn a blind eye to the obvious fact that the money has passed through the giant world washing machine and they are a part of the laundromat sending around twenty billion in squeaky-clean bills out of the country. And where does it finish up? In banks like the Ermitazh in Moscow, owned and run by the Godfather of crime in Moscow, the *Vory*, a man named Khamovnikakh.'

'And he's Task Force Ruble's target man?'

'Now you're getting the picture,' Boesel said smiling.

'Let's get this straight. You're saying Tran Van Luc stole the money at Sheremetyevo, and either blackmailed Maynard Buchanan into granting the lease of the jet to transfer the money, or that Buchanan was unaware of the proposed theft.'

'We'll get to that in a minute. First I'll let John give you one last piece of background. Can't have all the fun myself, eh?'

'Well, as Scott mentioned a few moments ago, the summits never invited the Asians. Why, we can only guess at. There were no reps from Southeast Asia; and let's face it, the bulk of the raw material of narcotics comes from that theatre of the world.'

'They invited the Italians, though, and they were running the stuff into Europe,' said McCann.

'True, but they were ignoring the market itself – a vast one named Asia. So it was in the early part of '96 that Tran Van Luc made contact. How much do you know of Tran?'

'That he made his fortune out of the black market and became a merchant banker and money launderer.'

'All that's true. As far as the banking side went, his big break came in '87. That was when the State Bank of Vietnam relaxed their banking regulations, and the first wholly commercial bank was capitalized. Naturally, the first was state controlled. However, Tran greased the palms of the right ministers, officials of the Council of State and high ranking bureaucrats, and ended up in control of the second commercial bank.'

'Is private ownership of a bank allowed by law in Vietnam?'

'Strictly speaking no – not that there's any Statute Law in Vietnam anyway, it just doesn't exist. But to all intents and purposes it's Tran Van Luc's private bank. At present it's one of the top fifty in the whole of Southeast Asia.'

'How was it capitalized?'

'With his black market profits, and through governmental stock issues organized by Tran's corrupt buddies in the Council of Ministers.

'Within six months Tran was operating a giant Indochinese money laundering operation with arms in Hong Kong, Shanghai and Kuala Lumpur. To appease his pals in the government, he provided an avenue out of Vietnam for the various ministers flight capital to banks in Hong Kong, the Caymans, and so on. But the big picture was laundering funds from other South East Asian and Indochinese sources; drug money, Hong Kong Triad money, hot money from Australia – in fact criminal money from all over his area of influence.

'One of his most important clients was a Triad gang, the Sun Yee On, the largest in Hong Kong, with a membership of more than forty thousand. To give you some idea of the scale of Tran's operations, listen to this. In Communist China five billion movie tickets are sold every year. The famous Cheung brothers who own and run Golden Cheung Asia, a film production distribution company set up to do cross-border business in 1997, are effectively owned by the Sun Yee On. Guess who are their bankers?'

'Tran.'

'Spot on, Mr. McCann. The Vietnamese People's Commercial Investment Bank. So, by operating through Tran Van Luc's bank in Vietnam, and his DTC in Hong Kong, the Sun Yee On can launder all their drug money and other criminal profits through films. With the mainland takeover of Hong Kong in 1997, the Triads tapped into a gigantic market, and it's safe to lay odds that a communist official is *marginally* easier to bribe than a Hong Kong one.'

'So Tran made contact with the Alliance because he didn't want to be shut out as a world money center, along the lines of Moscow?'

'Partly right. But it was the bigger picture that interested him most, and one he thought would appeal to the Alliance.'

'And that was?'

'An interlinked banking cooperative structure that would circle the globe. Up till then, thanks to arrangements the Russian banks had with banks like the Union Constitution in New York, and the Weddle Commercial Bank in London, the Alliance operations extended from the west coast of the States right across Europe as far as the Chinese border in the East. But that stopped short of Hong Kong, Indochina, China, and Japan.

'Tran was certain that the prospect of the financial possibilities of a China on the verge of opening itself to western trade would make the members of the Alliance's mouths water.'

'Then why the hell would Tran want to upset the apple cart by stealing the Russian *Mafyia*'s money,' McCann interjected.

'We have two theories here. First, we think Tran was squeezed for liquid assets. Remember, thanks to Horan's audit his operations in Hong Kong had to be very speedily put on hold, and all funds returned in cash to where they should have been prior to a possible full-scale investigation by Gerson and the Hong Kong banking authorities.'

'And the second theory?'

'Maybe he felt he wasn't getting fair recognition from the Alliance. Tran has a massive ego, bordering on megalomania, and it's well known that he loathes Khamovnikakh. He wanted to set the various partners at each other's throats so that he could emerge more powerful in the aftermath of a feud – one from which he could easily distance himself.'

'Tran's your particular target?'

'Lotus' target. Khamovnikakh's Ruble's. Osip Shirayev and the Brighton Beach Russians belong to Homeboy.'

Cate leant back in the chair and crossed his arms in satisfaction. 'As far as Tran's concerned, I'm here to tell you we're getting pretty close. The major problem lies in the fact that we won't be able to touch him if he stays put in Vietnam, even when we get the goods on him.'

'Aren't we forgetting that the man is responsible for the murders of Imogen Whitehead, Palmer and Boydell?'

'Not to mention three others in New York connected to the cash hijack,' Boesel added.

'Surely there would be ways and means of bringing him to book internationally,' McCann argued. Boesel and Cate merely smiled as though McCann was being a trifle naive.

'You mean,' McCann continued, 'that providing he stays in Vietnam, or keeps clear of any country that has an extradition treaty with the States or Australia, you can't lay a finger on him?'

'Right,' said Cate.

'Wait a minute, what about Noriega? He wasn't even a US citizen when he was picked up in Panama and prosecuted in Miami for trafficking.'

'We've thought of that, and it's a possibility. Believe me it's the major fall back position at Mainstream headquarters. Of course the attendant political problems are huge. Pulling Noriega out of Panama was a cakewalk. No one was in a position to argue with us. How the hell could we do the same with Tran Van Luc in Hanoi? Send in a team of kidnappers?'

McCann smiled inwardly. It wouldn't be out of the question logistically. It would be bread and butter work if Matt asked him to set it up. But the political fall-out would be the problem.

'No way are the Vietnamese Communists going to give up their man to the US authorities. Task Force Ruble might have slightly better luck with Khamovnikakh; but either way, we couldn't snatch him the way we did Noriega. He'd have to be handed over. Panama's a very different kettle of fish to the People's Republic of Vietnam. As far as Khamovnikakh's concerned, the Russians might do us that favor in return for all the favors we're doing them in foreign aid. But with the Vietnamese, it would be a very different matter.'

'So what is it you think I know? Why did you search me out?'

'Two reasons. The first concerns Andrew Horan.'

'He'd contacted AUSTRAC for assistance with regard to the audit he was undertaking. When he returned to Sydney from Hong Kong we asked him for a copy of his findings to add to our database at Lotus. But he told us it was his fiduciary duty to first show it to his chairman at the Aust Pacific - Gerson. He would at that time tell Gerson that he felt bound to pass on his findings of criminal activities to the requisite authorities.'

'But he was killed before he could do so?'

'Correct. We believe he had all his findings on computer disk rather than on paper.'

'Did he hand the disk over to Gerson?'

'He planned to. Whether or not he had time to do so before he died we don't know. However, he did confide in us that he had a back-up if Gerson's reaction was not as he anticipated.'

'You mean he feared for his life even at that stage?'

'He didn't think he was in danger, no. He was just covering his bases. For instance, if Gerson refused to act on his findings.'

'Horan thought Gerson might be a player?'

'There was always that possibility, though Horan didn't think it likely.'

'So there's a back-up disk somewhere, and you think I might know where it is?'

'We hoped you might have some ideas,' Boesel said.

So they thought he knew the whereabouts of a back-up disk? But did one exist, or had Horan taken it to the meeting? If he'd taken the original to his office at the bank, Horan would hardly have taken the sole back-up evidence to a meeting with his enemy. So where would he have left it? In a safety deposit box, or elsewhere? In Horan's shoes, he wouldn't have taken it to the bank in case there was criminal involvement there. No, it was much more likely that he'd leave the disk, or disks, elsewhere. It was a longshot that it was still at Horan's home; the police, and the Lotus people, would have searched the place thoroughly. So were they just covering all bases in asking him for his thoughts? Presumably.

'*The wheel is come full circle*'. The line from *King Lear* ran yet again through his mind. That was what Horan had muttered to his wife the night he'd returned from Hong Kong. It must have suddenly become crystal clear that by refinancing Buchanan Construction in Malaysia, Tran was merely re-cycling the money he'd stolen from Buchanan at Telok Anson.

His eyes re-focused on Boesel and Cate. They were still staring at him in silent anticipation. He abruptly stood. 'Do you mind if I take a quick break for a second? Where's the washroom?'

Cate gave him directions.

McCann locked the door of the small toilet, pulling out his cellular phone.

A few seconds later Torrance was on the line.

'McCann. I'm at task Force Lotus with Boesel and Cate. Tell me what they look like, could you?' It was always best to be double sure who you were dealing with. He'd been caught out once in Nigeria; taken to a government building by two high ranking security officers to meet a government minister. Except the whole thing had been a set-up. The men were revolutionaries with forged papers, and the building a very convincing sham. He'd had to fight his way out of the place.

'Boesel's the short priest in mufti, Cate's the long drink of water. The furniture's a nightmare.'

'Enough said. Thanks. Just thought it wise to check the credentials.'

'You don't take many chances, Mr. McCann.'

'Try not to, Mr. Torrance.'

'Thanks for the audio tape.'

'My pleasure.'

'Hope you don't mind my passing on all your stuff to Gattenby and Lotus, Leo.'

'Not at all.'

'By the way. We matched the size nine European. Italian Orthopedic shoe company in Rome, Armando Vergnano. So you see, despite the methodical, rather than inspirational, nature of my work, I sometimes get results.'

'Shoes made for Tran Van Luc?'

'The very same,' Torrance stated. He sounded well pleased.

There was a slight beat. 'Every now and then the ball lands in double zero, Mr. McCann. Got to go. Good luck.'

Boesel and Cate were sitting exactly as before, like ventriloquist dummies abandoned in a burlesque club dressing room. Even their expressions were the same – one of concentrated expectancy.

'I take it you've been through Horan's house?' said McCann as he sat.

Cate nodded. 'Mrs. Horan was very cooperative. We've been through every inch.'

'It's just an idea I have. Take another look. See if the Horans have a copy of Shakespeare's *King Lear* in the study. I have a feeling he might have hidden the disk inside it.'

'Why?' Boesel asked.

'Just a feeling,' McCann replied – he didn't feel like long explanations. 'Tell me one thing that's been really bugging me.'

'Ask away,' said Boesel.

'When you heard that Horan and Buchanan had been killed in an explosion at the Savoy, why the hell didn't you come forward and give Torrance a hand with the identification of the Asian.'

Cate held up a placatory hand. 'Look, I know it may seem odd to you, but see it from our point of view. First of all, Horan didn't tell us he was meeting with Tran that day. Secondly, the first we hear is that a young girl had strapped explosives to her waist and blown away Buchanan and Horan in a hotel. Sure, the first thing Gordon Mascon did for us was check with Langley on Tran. Torrance at Acorn did the same through Harry Fine. But word came back that he was in Hanoi. We had no knowledge that Tran had a twin, so why would we think the dead Asian was in any way linked to Tran? Also, we couldn't see any possible link between a twenty-year-old terrorist suicide bomber and what we were investigating.'

McCann shook his head. There'd certainly been a major shortage of lateral thinking in the aftermath of the bombing. Torrance had been responsible for some pretty fundamental errors during his investigation, and these boys had only seen the picket fence of their own particular financial patch.

'Why do you think Horan didn't tell you he was meeting with Tran?'

'Well, we can only guess at that. I'd say he hoped he could persuade Tran to deal with Buchanan. Maybe Horan was going to offer to bury the evidence against Tran, provided he returned the Telok Anson money immediately.'

'You think Horan was that kind of man? That he would compound a felony?'

'That's a tough one, McCann. Maybe he saw it as helping out his oldest friend, and it was the most expedient way of doing so. He didn't want his pal exposed to the financial press as an incompetent. It wouldn't have been the truth.'

Cate rose abruptly. 'Why not show Mr. McCann our baby while I check on his theory,' he said to Boesel.

Boesel stood and they wandered over to stand in front of the hardware. Boesel was about to speak when McCann forestalled him.

'A question. For the sake of argument, if I wanted to run someone through your Intelligence system, how would I start?'

'This is someone you suspect of financial criminal activity, such as money laundering?'

'For the sake of argument, yes. Possibly.'

'Well, before we go into how we sniff out the bad guys, I'll just explain the three basic steps in laundering. They're placement. That's getting the cash into the legitimate system. Layering. That's separating the cash from its criminal origins. And integration - losing the cash among legitimate funds. How would your hypothetical target fit into the scheme of things?'

McCann thought for a moment. If the Buchanan jet had been used for the cash hijack, and Bradley had known of the criminal identity behind Rowe, Radley Associates, then he was part of a conspiracy. That was it, pure and simple. He'd had no hand in the actual laundering himself.

'Possibly a kind of very tenuous integration, maybe,' he replied.

'Integration. Well, that's a start. What we do at FinCEN, and AUSTRAC, is use sophisticated artificial intelligence systems to search for the bad guys. Wire transfer screening determines where to target further investigations.'

'How does it accomplish that?'

'By cross-referencing vast databases. It comes up with anything it finds unusual,' Boesel replied quickly. 'If your hypothetical kept cropping up in suspicious circumstances, the system would take note of it.'

'He'd develop a file?'

'In a way, yes. The computer would be on the lookout, so to speak, for him in other areas.'

'I see.'

'Then there's what we refer to as knowledge acquisition. This constructs new profiles for use during screening. The computer is programmed to process data as close to the way a human would, but using vast amounts of data and doing the job in microseconds. It has hundreds of thousands of rules that direct the computer towards its final conclusions. The collection of rules is in essence what's referred to as its *knowledge base.*'

'A computer that thinks laterally? Thank God for that,' McCann quipped. If the humans were incapable of it, it was just as well that machines weren't.

'That's about the size of it, yes. That was the idea, anyway. The computer actually explains its thinking process once it's delivered its findings. AUSTRAC's ScreenIT system was set up to automatically detect information on all unusual transactions. Its database is huge.'

McCann was impressed. It certainly beat the hell out of his word processor, which so often simply told him in the middle of some task that what he was doing was not possible.

'So if I asked the computer why it thought my man was financially dubious, it would be able to tell me why?'

'Absolutely. You'd be able to track back, step by step to see the reasoning behind the computer's findings. That's where link analysis scores. It explores any associations that exist between large numbers of objects of different types, like people, banks, accounts, corporations, wire transfers. Investigations of such links help tell us where to investigate further. Link analysis works on databases called Fields, which are information points of varying kinds. Fields can be addresses, account numbers, phone numbers, names of people or corporations. The object is for the system to spot matching Fields. Put very simplistically, if a bank is consistently linked to a company that has a director with prior convictions for money laundering, we look into it closely.'

'If every currency transaction report has to be lodged with you, then how can anyone hide their identity from you?' asked McCann.

'Shouldn't be easy, but I'm afraid it is. You see, there are around 500,000 wire transactions a day. Add to that the fact that some foreign banks, bound by their secrecy laws, simply refuse to name their originator. There's also the question of privacy. And while it's perfectly possible for us to subpoena transfer records held by US banks, foreign banks may have left the originator details blank. That's what gives the offshore tax havens like the Caymans, Bahamas and the Turks and Caicos their appeal.'

'Hold it right there. Why would a reputable company set up shop in the Turks and Caicos?'

'A great many do. There's a great deal of legitimate business brokered there. Just because it suits criminals to deal there as well doesn't make every bank in the Turks and Caicos a front for the mob. The appeal is that for as little as ten grand you can buy a fully anonymous shell corporation there, and then launder fifty million dollars through it. Makes it pretty cost effective, eh?'

'But there must be records of who owns the company?'

'Not if it's a bearer corporation. It's owned by whoever holds the shares, and there are no public records of the holder of the shares.'

'Have you heard of a company called Rowe, Radley Associates?'

'The merchant bankers whose clients leased the Buchanan jet,' Boesel replied with a sly grin.

'You know them?'

'We do. They're *very* well known to Blue Quays.'

'Are you saying they're corrupt?'

'I'll put it this way, they have a great many very questionable clients. That's where the link analysis comes into its own. Rowe, Radley crop up time and time again when the criteria for money laundering fed in by our knowledge-based experts are met. The real identity of more than two-thirds of their clients is a mystery!'

'But simply to do business with Rowe, Radley Associates doesn't necessarily mean you're a crook?' McCann felt had to go through the motions of being fair.

'Is Bradley Radcliffe a felon?' Boesel replied without batting an eyelid. 'Is that what you want to ask me?'

Boesel smiled at McCann's reaction. 'He's your hypothetical isn't he.'

McCann said nothing.

'Not as far as we are aware. I knew you had him in mind the moment you mentioned "a hypothetical". I know we wear trenchcoats, but we're really not that dumb.'

'It was Bradley Radcliffe who allegedly referred Maynard Buchanan to a firm in Hong Kong called the Jensen, Rollason Partnership. Bob Zeltis told me that they brokered the loan to re-finance Telok Anson.'

'Yes, we're aware of that. As you can imagine, we've done a great deal of follow-up work on the facts that Horan made available to us.'

'What's the reputation of the Jensen, Rollason Partnership?'

'Clean, as far as we know. They're a very large and reputable firm. But it only needs one man on the inside, paid off by one of Tran's people, to make contact with the three banks which when formed constitute a syndicate. Once contact was made, the banks would have jumped in.'

'Where does that leave Bradley Radcliffe?' McCann asked.

'Still in the clear. All he did was point Buchanan towards Jensen, Rollason. I have to presume he knows of them, and thinks highly of them. I'm sure the Radcliffe law firm and Jensen, Rollason have done business countless times,' Boesel replied carefully.

'You don't view his hand in both the re-financing of the Buchanan Telok Anson loan, and brokering the lease of the Buchanan jet with suspicion?'

Boesel gave McCann a very old-fashioned look indeed. 'Let's put it this way. We have to be very careful. You're entitled to your thoughts. No one's proved that the Buchanan jet was involved. Nor is there any proof whatsoever that Radcliffe knew of any wrongdoings on the part of Jensen, Rollason. To make inferences to the contrary would be unethical on my part. Even if I thought he was up to his neck in it all.' He looked up briefly at the ceiling and closed his eyes. Then he opened them and smiled at McCann. 'You have to remember that his father's looking good as the next Republican President of the US of A.'

'You mean you're going to tread carefully?'

'Like in a snake pit with bare feet,' Boesel replied, drawing his lips back, and running his tongue over his teeth.

The door flew open and Cate entered, holding out a floppy disk in triumph. 'Eureka, Mr. McCann,' he said, 'In his study. In the *Complete Shakespeare* edition.

'Lucky guess. What's on it, anything useful?'

Cate looked at Boesel, then back at McCann. 'I'm afraid I won't be able to share it with you for a while. Not till we've had a chance to look at it.'.

'That's great. Thanks, my friend. I give it to you, and you won't even let me have a look-see.' Actually he'd expected it.

'There are secrecy laws that govern our operation here at AUSTRAC,' Cate said. 'You can't look at the disk, but I can tell you about it. Pretty stupid, huh?'

McCann nodded. Pretty standard bureaucracy.

23.

21st May.

Rupert Gerson sat back in his chair. 'My dear Rosalind, if you're merely going to repeat your fanciful theories concerning hypothetical conspiracies, I'm afraid I'm going to have to pass. I'm happy to *make* time to help you, but not *waste* it.'

Rosalind was close to losing her temper. Gerson was both arrogant and a chauvinist of the worst kind. He was also making a very big business mistake. Antagonizing the major shareholder of one of the fifty largest companies in Australia was not too smart.

'Please don't patronize me, Rupert. I am not *your dear Rosalind*. I'm asking a very simple question, and if you are indeed happy to help me, you'll answer it. Has any action been taken concerning Andrew Horan's findings?'

Gerson looked at her as though she'd withdrawn an Armalite rifle from her handbag.

'Andrew Horan's internal audit was exactly that – internal. It is private and is absolutely none of your business, young lady. Whatever path I choose to take is my decision. I will not be held to account by you or anyone else.'

'Perhaps the Australian Securities Commission?

Gerson gaped.

'I spoke to Imogen Whitehead shortly before she was murdered, and she confided to me then that both she and Andrew had serious reservations as to the position of the Australian Pacific Bank in Hong Kong. To put it as succinctly as possible, she said the bank's exposure in Hong Kong through your DTC was huge. She talked of corruption and kickbacks to a senior bank employee who I won't name right now in view of the laws of defamation.

'She also spoke of continuing dangerously speculative loans to a company called Pac Seng Investment. She maintained that Andrew Horan had proof that Pac Seng was siphoning off funds from monies it had been loaned by Aust-Pac Finance, and redirecting them to an offshore company, Meridian-Zenith - a company controlled, but not owned, by Sir Henry Trevor - while maintaining fraudulent profit statements on its books. And at the heart of it all is the real power behind Pac Seng – a Vietnamese called Tran Van Luc. I have to take it as read you are familiar with this man and his track record.'

She paused briefly. All that was audible was Gerson's labored breathing.

'I could continue, but I know you will be familiar with all these facts, thanks to Andrew's report.'

Gerson's face was now bathed in sweat. His thick neck was livid with rage.

'How dare you speak to me in this fashion, Miss Buchanan,' he began.

That at least was a step in the right direction. He was now treating her as an adult - though still as a woman, rather than his equal.

'Perhaps you'd prefer me to have a word with the shareholders? They deserve an answer, they have the most to lose,' she shot back. She wasn't about to be cowed by Gerson.

Gerson lifted his phone. 'Margaret, please send Duncan in at once.'

As he replaced the receiver, his eyes narrowed. 'As a mark of respect to your father, I will say this much. Duncan McKinley and I have gone to great lengths to reassure ourselves of the bank's financial position in Hong Kong. As it turns out, it has become abundantly clear that the chairman of our deposit trading company there, Francis Greville, has at all times acted with the utmost probity. The loans that Andrew found questionable, in that they presented too great a risk, were never proceeded with. I must point out that this was Francis Greville's decision, not mine.'

The door opened and a tall, good-looking man of about thirty, dressed in a fine pin stripe, entered the room.

Gerson introduced Rosalind to the Englishman. Then McKinley drew up a chair and sat next to Rosalind. Gerson took a succession of deep breaths in order to regain some semblance of composure, then spoke.

'Rosalind has, in her own particular way, voiced concern that we have not adequately safeguarded the shareholders' interests regarding Andrew Horan's audit. Perhaps you could put her mind at rest, Duncan.'

'With pleasure, Rupert,' McKinley began. His voice was pure Devonshire cream. 'Mr. Gerson and I have looked at every possible angle. I flew to Hong Kong myself and talked to Mr. Greville, informing him of our concerns. However, as it turned out, none of the proposed transactions that Mr. Horan found questionable had been proceeded with. Mr. Greville apparently was also of the opinion they were too high risk. So I'm happy to be able to tell you that our position in Hong Kong is now quite stable.'

As she'd thought, Greville had quite obviously gone into fast damage control. But it would have to have been with the co-operation and connivance of McKinley, that much was clear.

Rosalind studied McKinley. He stared back, a supercilious expression on his smooth patrician face. She then turned to Gerson, who was taking turns cleaning his bifocals, and mopping his fat red neck with the same spotted handkerchief.

'I can't imagine why you didn't tell me this when I asked, Rupert,' she said with a sugary smile. 'When you think about it, simply telling someone to mind their own business is never the most diplomatic approach.'

She stood and both men rose, Gerson holding out a hand. 'I'm sorry that there should have been any unpleasantness, Rosalind,' Gerson said. Perhaps a little voice in his head had reminded him of the capital value of Buchanan Construction.

'So am I, Rupert,' Rosalind replied. The hell she was going to apologize, though she could tell by his expression that he fully expected her to do so.

'Goodbye Mr. McKinley,' she said, turning to the Englishman.

'I'm sure we'll meet again,' he said.

'I hope so,' she replied politely. She meant it. She had every intention of making sure it was in a criminal court of law.

Thirty minutes after his meeting with Cate and Boesel, McCann was opening a medium-sized post office box at the Central Post Office, in the heart of Sydney's central business district.

Inside was a DHL plastic-coated envelope addressed to Vera McCann marked "no signature required" across the top.

He re-locked the metal box and walked back down Pitt Street in the rain, among a sea of fast-moving umbrellas. He debated whether to drop in at the Priory to see if all was well. Probably there was no need - Rita always coped. He decided to do so anyway, if only as a gesture of goodwill to his secretary. He'd use the opportunity to call the travel agent, and make arrangements for the flight to Vietnam.

He was fifty feet from his office building when his cell phone began to bleep in his trouser pocket.

'McCann? It's me. Just met with Toad of Toad Hall.' It was Rosalind.

'You spoke with Gerson?'

'The same. I tell you they're in *major* damage control. He had a shot at trying to flannel me, you know, the *smile and smile and be a villain* bit. Then I let him have it between the eyes – allegations of major fraud, the involvement of Trevor, Greville and Tran. That had him buzzing McKinley on the intercom within seconds.'

'What did McKinley say?'

'More of the same. They've covered their tracks all right. All the cash is back in place. Just as you said.'

'You think Gerson's involved?'

'Not personally, he hasn't the balls. But McKinley? Certainly. Proving it, though, is another thing. I'll have a friend of mine do a complete background on the man.'

'Who?'

'Headhunting firm we use in Chicago. They miss nothing.'

'When do you leave for the States?'

'I'm in the car right now,' she replied.

McCann breathed deeply. Thank God he'd asked, he was about to raise the subject of Bradley.

'Sorry we didn't have a chance to catch up before you left, Bradley,' McCann said, hoping Rosalind would reply that she wasn't using the speaker and that Bradley couldn't hear the conversation. If Bradley was driving, there was an outside chance she'd be in the passenger seat with the phone to her ear. If that were the case he'd chance a remark to her concerning her boyfriend.

He was out of luck.

'Next time you're Stateside, give us a call,' Bradley replied, a definite smile in his voice. 'Who knows you might have to call the White House.'

That was that, then. Bradley was listening. Too bad.

'Good luck with the campaign,' he replied, then altered his tone as he directed his conversation back to Rosalind. 'When are you due back, Rosie?' The more intimate form was deliberate. He hoped it put smug Bradley's nose ever so slightly out of joint.

'Day after tomorrow. Got heavy business meetings in Sydney. Don't want Ian and Bob to think they're running the show.'

'Take it easy and enjoy yourself for a few days,' said McCann. 'By the way, happy birthday.'

'You remembered!' she cried out, laughing with all the sophistication of a five-year-old at a surprise party.

McCann smiled. She really was quite delightful.

As he reached the VW, a meter man was lifting the windscreen wiper, placing a parking ticket underneath. He looked up furtively as McCann approached, snapped the wiper back into place, then hurried away down the street – it was never pleasant to be caught red-handed handing out bills; better to be far away from the possibility of violence from irate drivers.

As he stuffed the ticket in his pocket, McCann looked down Pitt Street. A few short weeks ago, only a couple of hundred yards down the same street, a young girl who had lost the will to live had strapped plastic explosive to her body and irrevocably altered the lives of so many people around the globe. The fall-out was still settling. He had to know why she'd done it, what had driven her.

It wasn't until eight-fifteen that he was back in the car driving north across the Sydney Harbor Bridge. It had been a major mistake poking his nose in at the Priory. Rita had virtually locked him in his office with a mountain of "most urgent". The first hour had flown by, the second had passed more slowly, and the third had ground to a halt around six-thirty, when Rita popped her head round the door and wished him goodnight. She handed him a single page fax. It was a photograph of a very ordinary looking man. Underneath Torrance had written: *This is latest Reuters snap of Trevor. Keep in touch. Torrance.* Trevor had more the look of a suburban bank manager than an international player.

The travel agent had arranged a Vietnam Airlines flight leaving 9.55 a.m. The visa had been expedited and would be couriered to the airport, together with his ticket.

Once more doubts began to intrude into his mind. Did it really matter a damn if all he ultimately determined were the reasons for the girl's mental state? There was little he could do to bring Tran Van Luc to judgment. The world's best law enforcement agencies were finding this a hard enough ask. And in the meantime, how would Greville, Sir Henry Trevor, not to mention Tran Van Luc himself, react? Would they make the sensible decision to leave him alone, thereby avoid risking any further negative profile? Or would they consider he was proving too dangerous? He was fast putting too many pieces of their international power game together, and they might well believe their interests best served by silencing him for good?

McCann leant forward, rubbing the palm of his hand over the inside of the windscreen, which was so fogged he could hardly see through. The rain had picked up again, and was beating down with almost the force of hail.

Greville would certainly have reported back to Tran. It would have been more than his life was worth not to inform the Asian of the events in Hong Kong. But Greville probably felt more secure now because his personal affairs were in order. The same went for Trevor. It was probably Tran who had the most to lose. Did he know of the existence of Task Force Lotus; that he was their public enemy number one? Did he realize they were closing in - that Boydell had identified Brokov as a direct link in the killings? Though Boydell was now dead, McCann had witnessed his killing, and could identify Brokov. The link was there.

Most importantly, was Tran aware that Lotus was close as two whoops and a holler of pinning his tail to the Moscow currency hijack? And even if they couldn't prove his involvement, he would surely realize that they could let the rumor drift.

McCann smiled. How would Khamovnikakh react when he found out it was his concordat associate who'd ripped him off? He wouldn't be too pleased.

McCann turned left off Mona Vale Road into McCarr's Creek Road. The rain was still bucketing down, and the wind had swung round, the nor' easterly now replaced by a strong southerly buster.

A mile from the house McCann cut the lights of the car, pulling in to the side of the road and killing the engine. He looked through the condensation on the windscreen towards the next bend along the road. Better to leave the car, and do the rest on foot. Just to be safe. They'd been there before, maybe they were there right now, waiting. He'd get as wet as a shag on a rock, but it hardly mattered.

He sat in the car for fifteen minutes with his eyes closed, to give him night vision. The heavy low cloud base effectively obscured the moon completely; outside it was as dark as a wolf's mouth.

McCann loped along in a half-crouched position, hugging the cover of the bush and shrubs at the side of the road, the water driving into his face. *Twenty feet, stop, freeze, look, listen. Move forward twenty feet.* Always the same routine. The closer he came to the house, the shorter the distance he covered between stops.

At the bend in the road where he'd encountered the sports car the night of the fire, he squatted by the edge of the road. From his position the ground dropped away steeply through the dense bush and trees to the creek below. Through the profusion of ferns, rhapis palms, black boys and grass trees, he could clearly see his house two hundred feet or so round the curve of the road. He'd turned on the bathroom light when he'd left in the morning. It was still burning in an upstairs window. There was no sign of movement.

He looked left to Ken Davis' cottage, the only other house in the immediate vicinity. A light shone in an upstairs room.

He checked his shoelaces, untying then re-tying them tightly. It was essential to have balance and security underfoot when running over uneven ground in the dark. He then undid his leather belt and pulled it from the loops of his trousers, coiling it round the fist of his left hand. Then he slipped carefully over the edge of the roadway, climbing down into the deep gully that lay between his present position and his house, which stood on the crest of the slope opposite.

Half an hour later he was couched in the pouring rain thirty feet below the verandah of his cottage, the boathouse ten feet below to his left through the trees. His waterlogged clothes felt heavy as lead and were torn in several places by the blackberry bushes and the jagged edges of fan palms. His hair clung to his forehead like seaweed to a submerged rock. Rain water streamed down the contours of his face.

Deciding to scout the right-hand side of the house first, he began the slow climb up through the mud and trees. He was vaguely aware of an insect that had found its way inside his shirt and was moving down his left side, but his concentration remained absolutely focused on the house and its environs as he searched through the trees that surrounded the area for the slightest sign of movement.

It was as he reached the apex of the arc round the house that he saw a small movement by the front door. The rain had eased slightly, making vision marginally better. He stayed absolutely motionless, looking to a spot five degrees to the right of where he'd seen the movement. It was an old army trick – which was where to focus in limited light conditions.

A slow minute passed. McCann remained frozen in the same position, but there were no further signs. Though his present position was hardly the ideal LUP, an attitude the SAS referred to as a "lying up position", it would have to do until he knew more about what was going on at the side of the door, whether there was more than one person. He knew he hadn't been mistaken. Someone was waiting for him. Now he'd wait for them.

Ten minutes later he saw movement again. Someone was standing in the shadows by the door. Judging by the height and contours of the body, it was a man. Not a professional, the movement was too erratic. There had been no sign of any motion elsewhere, so the chances were the man was not part of a team.

McCann was faced with a choice. Call the police on the cell phone in his pocket, or take the stranger himself, and have a quiet word with whoever it was - one on one. The latter alternative seemed overwhelmingly superior.

McCann moved forward until he could see the shadowy figure by the door moving forwards and backwards, rocking restlessly.

Soundlessly, he moved through the discontinuous bush, one minute up to his ears in thick grevilleas, the thorns of the pyracantha tearing at his face and clothes; the next minute, brought almost to a standstill as he reached a clearing that provided no cover.

He paused five feet behind the dark figure, winding his plaited belt round both fists, pulling the leather tight as he rose from his crouching position. He took a deep breath, then leapt forward.

The sheer impact of McCann's body threw the man forward away from the door, crushing his body face first into a flowerbed. The leather belt was drawn tight round the man's upper torso, binding his arms to his chest.

McCann leapt immediately to his feet, then straddled the prone man, pushing his head down face first hard into the soft earth with one hand as he wrenched the man's right arm round behind his back with the other. It was only then he saw the side of the man's face. It was Alan Messon.

'I suppose you were just trying to get your own back,' Messon quipped good-naturedly. 'After all, I did my best to kill you in the warbird a few days ago. It's only natural you'd have your revenge.' He was lying on a sofa in McCann's living room, holding a towel to a graze on his forehead. Mercifully, the full extent of Messon's injuries was a few bruises. McCann had given the old man a blanket to keep himself warm, while he'd quickly changed, then fetched the first-aid box from the bedroom.

'I hope you can see it from my point of view, Alan,' McCann replied, walking over from the dining room with two glasses; a gin and tonic for Messon, a beer for himself. 'I thought you were the enemy.'

'I've been ringing you all bloody day. I don't suppose you check your messages when you've got that damned mobile thing,' Messon said as he took the glass from McCann.

McCann looked across at the blinking light on the answering machine. It was true. He rarely checked messages till late, sometimes not till the next day. 'Well, here I am. What can I do for you, Alan?'

'We had a deal, Leo. And I firmly believe you to be a man of your word. Am I mistaken?'

McCann knew damned well what Messon was hinting at. Damn! Why wouldn't the old fool leave the issue alone. It was a road with a dead end. Ultimately, there would only be a brick wall for Venice's father to beat his head against. Why did he persist? To be fair, McCann knew the reason. It was because the man had to *know*, the same way Rosalind had to know. After all, why the hell was he going to Vietnam himself, for heaven's sake? It was as simple as that – for knowledge. And Messon had been correct, he had given his word.

'You know the name of the man who hurt my child,' Messon said quietly.

'I don't know why she should have wanted to kill him. That's the truth, Alan.'

'She had her reasons. He drove her to it. What is his name?'

'What do you want, Alan. Vengeance? It's just not possible. He's too powerful. I've just finished talking to an international law enforcement agency. They're after the same person, and they don't think they'll ever get near him. So what possible use is it going to be to you knowing the man's name?'

Messon abruptly stood. 'Tell me his name, damn you! You promised! Does no one have a sense of honor any longer?'

There seemed little point in trying to convince the old man to the contrary. 'His name is Tran Van Luc,' McCann answered deliberately. 'He lives in Hanoi somewhere on Ho Tay Lake. He is an extremely well connected merchant banker with high-placed friends in government circles, both in Vietnam and the West. There is no way on earth that you will ever be able to touch him.'

Messon stared at McCann in the silence that ensued. 'We will let time be the judge of that, Leo,' Messon said eventually, as he pulled the blanket from his shoulders and laid it down on the sofa. He looked tired, but relieved, as though a great weight had been lifted from his shoulders. 'So your investigations are at an end?'

The last thing he was going to do was tell Messon he was off to unravel the mystery ten months of Venice's life in Vietnam.

'Life has to go on, Alan,' he said evasively.

'Providing one has a purpose,' Messon replied with a thin smile.

There was an abrupt crash upstairs and the smoke alarm in the bedroom began screaming. A second later, with a shattering sound of breaking glass a ball of flame exploded through the living room window.

McCann threw himself at Messon, pushing him down on to the sofa, then pulling him to the floor. As he looked back up, he saw the bullets rip into the wall opposite at around chest height. The flames had taken an immediate and firm hold on the coffee table and Jarrah floorboards. To attempt to douse the flames would make him a target – which was out of the question.

He pressed his hand to his trouser pocket then swore – the cell phone was upstairs beside his bed where he'd left it when he'd changed. And the smoke alarm, which continued it's high-pitched scream, attested to another fire up there.

Ten feet or so away was the phone, upturned beside the blazing coffee table. Was there time to make a call? It had been less than twenty seconds, but already the living room ceiling was completely obscured by billowing black smoke. Messon was looking wildly at the front door.

'Stay where you are!' McCann screamed. 'They'll cut you down the moment you open the door!' Then he kitten-crawled towards the phone, snatching it away from the flames, desperately punching in triple zero.

As a voice responded to the emergency call, he shouted as loudly as possible into the receiver. 'Someone's shooting! It's a massacre! The house is on fire. 1204 McCarr's Creek Road!' McCann knew the word "massacre" would get them moving fastest. The police had a horror of multiple deaths, it had been their continuing nightmare since the Hobart killings. They'd be there within minutes. The question was how to stay alive till then.

Messon was beginning to choke. If they stayed where they were they were dead. By the same token, if they made for the doors they'd be dead too. Shot down.

The sound of the fire upstairs had become a roar. The flames had now taken hold of the far wall and the entire ceiling of the living room.

McCann had to make a decision right now or they were both history. Somehow he'd have to draw the fire of those outside, while Messon made a break in another direction.

Rising to squatting position, he grabbed Messon's arm, dragging him behind him through into the kitchen. Throwing two tea towels into the sink, he turned the water on full, then handed a cloth to Messon who placed it over his nose and mouth. McCann tied the tea towel round his face, then pulled open the bottom drawer in the kitchen, grasping the handle of a heavy hammer.

Messon's eyes darted in panic from the living room, which was now a fireball, to McCann, who was on his hands and knees in the middle of the kitchen smashing the floorboards in the center at their weakest point, then ripping them up, exposing the ground underneath. There was around three feet of space beneath the floor.

'Get down there fast. Head in the towel. Lie flat.'

Messon looked at him blankly. 'I'll be burnt to death,' he shouted back.

'DO AS I SAY! Stay put under the house till you hear me shout your name, then get out of there fast before you fry!' McCann screamed. He then pulled the old man over to the roughly hewn hole in the kitchen floor. Messon gave one last look, squared his jaw, then scrambled through.

McCann watched as Messon dropped to the ground beneath and lay flat in the dry earth under the house. Then McCann stood, lining himself up with the kitchen window, mentally calculating a trajectory that would see him clear the edge of the verandah outside and land him on the sloping lawn that fed down to the water thirty feet below the house.

A burst of automatic fire slamming into the wall three feet to his left made up his mind.

Pushing off from the wall opposite the window, he ran forwards, leaping upwards, curling his body into a ball, his arms shielding his head as the glass exploded around him.

He cleared the verandah by inches, barely making the lawn, landing with a mind-numbing impact far worse than any para jump he'd ever experienced in his life. As he rolled for the first time, he roared Messon's name through the night, then abruptly bounced for the second time on the grass.

The air was crushed from his lungs as he executed a succession of para rolls at speed, the momentum of his body taking him like a living projectile down the sloping grass to the creek below.

The following minute was a blur. McCann was vaguely aware of the jarring impact of the water, the pain in his left shoulder and leg, and a burning sensation in his eyes and lungs as he flailed upwards towards the surface. Then his head broke through, and he took the first desperate gasp of air. The night sky shone bright as day, a livid yellow/orange from the inferno that had been his house only minutes before.

As his brain began to function clearly again, he plunged headlong towards the bank of the creek, holding himself close to the edge, his body hidden by the lip. His heart was running faster than a train. Where was Messon? Had he survived? Had the would-be assassins left, or were they fanning out along the bank searching for him?

Then he heard the unmistakable throp of a police chopper as it suddenly appeared through the trees, out of nowhere, playing a powerful searchlight on the lawns round the back of the house. Great waves of relief flooded through his veins as he heard the fire trucks. It was quite overwhelming. Seconds later he could see two red Scania trucks racing down McCarr's Creek Road towards the house. They were followed by three police cars.

Pulling his body out of the water, McCann followed the searchlight's pool of light as it swept round the grounds. It was then that he saw Messon. He was caught in the beam, waving his hands over his head, his hair standing on end like a scarecrow, his clothes as black as a coal seam.

24.

21st May.

Ken Davis had also called the emergency number the second he'd heard the breaking glass and seen the flames. He'd heard no gunfire, they'd used silenced weapons.

Considering his age, and what he'd been through that night, Alan Messon remained surprisingly calm as he was stretchered to the ambulance and taken to hospital. The burns to his neck and back were relatively minor, probably first degree.

The medics tried to persuade McCann to go with Messon, but he refused, preferring to join the police in a thorough search of the garden.

McCann found shell casings at the back and front of the burnt-out house. From their locations it seemed there had been two of them. They'd staked out both exits to the house, intending to firebomb the house, then shoot McCann as he tried to escape the flames.

The casings were found in two clusters. The first was fifteen feet from the back door. There were nine casings at this location, all 9mm. The second cluster was ten feet to the right of the front door. Here were twelve casings, again all 9mm. The location of the second gunman suggested that they must have arrived after he'd surprised Messon – they'd have had no compunction in killing them both, had they arrived earlier.

McCann turned one of the casings over in his fingers, examining the indentation of the firing pin. The weapon was almost certainly fully automatic. That much he felt sure of, judging by the pattern of the spray in the kitchen – he remembered the burst of five or so rounds, hitting almost simultaneously. Possibly one of the Heckler & Koch MP5 series; the MP5K, the silenced model. This was the shortest in length and thus the easiest to conceal, with an overall length of 12.8 inches. Then again, it could just as easily have been the Mini-Uzi, which was the same caliber, but had a fractionally better firepower at 950 rounds a minute.

McCann handed the casing to one of the detectives. The Mini-Uzi. Brokov's preferred weapon. Only a close examination of the spent rounds dug from the debris, together with an examination of the shell casings, would tell for certain. But it was a logical step to think along the lines of Brokov and the woman. If so, how had he been able to re-enter the country with such ease? Either way, these were professional killers. They didn't give a damn about leaving the casings, so they obviously felt secure their weapons were untraceable. He and Messon had been mighty lucky to escape with their lives - that was certain.

The police interview was conducted at Dee Why Police station. It lasted close to two hours. When they were through, the detective inspector was kind enough to loan

McCann an old raincoat. Anything was better than arriving at a Sydney hotel in torn muddy rags.

McCann signed his statement, then took a cab to the Medusa, where he booked in, ran a bath, stripped, and examined his naked body.

The pain had been bad enough, but as he stood before the full length mirror in the bathroom, he was shocked by the extent of the bruising down the full length of his right side – from shoulder to knee was a blue/black blur of flesh. His face, hands, arms, legs, and feet looked as though he'd been whipped by a crown of thorns. He raised his eyebrows and smiled at his reflection in the mirror. He was alive. A man without his training and background wouldn't have stood a chance.

He emptied the contents of a box of bath salts into the bath, then stepped in. Any pain he'd experienced before that evening paled into insignificance as he lowered his body into the slightly less than hot water.

After a chicken and spinach salad, and a bottle of Hill of Grace, McCann eased his bruised limbs between the sheets, and almost instantly fell into a deep sleep.

He awoke just before sunrise. For a few seconds he was disorientated, then the events of the previous night washed through him with frightening clarity, and a feeling of intense anger overwhelmed him. It was an anger directed at himself. Because of his dogged persistence Alan Messon had narrowly escaped death. First it had been Whitey. Then Boydell. Had they become victims simply because Rosalind had refused to let go? Yet he was as much to blame as she was. He'd guessed wrong about the intentions of Tran and his people. He'd thought they'd back off, after the warning. He'd guessed wrong.

But Tran certainly wasn't as smart as he'd given the man credit for. He'd risen to the bait – unless the orders had come from someone down the chain of command, without the Vietnamese's knowledge.

He reached for the phone and ordered breakfast from room service. His bones felt as though he'd participated in an endurance rodeo ride.

Someone had obviously upped the ante from a warning to a contract hit. Having failed, would they try again? Probably not - at least not for a while. But he didn't want to count on it; his hunches hadn't been too accurate recently.

He threw on a toweling robe and walked to the desk. He'd need to buy some clothes and a suitcase. Then he'd have to drop by the Priory to pick up his passport. It was just as well that he'd always kept his most important documents in the fireproof wall safe at the office. Perhaps Rita could send it.

At 7 a.m. the phone rang. It was Rosalind.

'Ian called me last night. It was on the news. I've been ringing around for an hour. I was so worried. I didn't know where you were. Are you all right?'

McCann walked back to the bed and sat. 'A bit stiff, but okay. I called Mona Vale Hospital twenty minutes ago. Messon's recovering too. He's one tough nut. Where are you?'

'Somewhere over the wheat belt. Kansas? I really don't know. Thirty-four thousand feet up, anyway. I called because I was worried.'

'Thanks.'

Several seconds passed, neither seemed to know what to say.

'Do you still plan to go to Vietnam?'

Though he'd been debating the issue all morning, he knew he'd made the decision the night before. 'Yes,' he replied. 'Why not? I don't feel ready to throw in the towel quite yet.'

She didn't say anything, which surprised him.

'You want me to?' he asked.

'Quit? Hell, no. I worry for you - that's all,' she replied quietly. Then her voice quite suddenly changed gears. It lost its intimacy, and was more businesslike. 'Almost forgot. I've heard back from London, they faxed me. Guess where McKinley's parents live?'

'No idea. Out with it, Rosie, I've got a plane to catch.'

'Petit Port, Jersey.'

'Trevor's territory?'

'And guess who gave him his first job, when he was a nipper?'

'Sir Henry?'

'The very same. He worked at Meridien, Trevor's company.'

'Great stuff. Look, I've really got to go.'

'Sure,' she replied. 'One last thing. Do you carry sufficient insurance for the house?'

'It's a rental,' he replied.

'What about your stuff?'

'Doesn't matter - there's not much I can't replace. I just hope to God Cyclops isn't scared to death when he comes visiting this morning at sun-up.'

'Who?'

'Forget it,' McCann said gently, reminding himself to ask someone to put out some food for the bird.

'Keep in touch, Leo. Ring me when you get to Vietnam, okay?'

'Sure.'

'Promise?'

'Promise,' he replied. Then he swore. He'd made a decision to distance Rosalind from any violence in the future. Now he'd have to give her a blow by blow account each day.

The next fifteen minutes were all spent on the phone. He spoke to Messon at the hospital. The old guy seemed quite chirpy. He told McCann that since he'd carried top medical insurance cover for more than forty years and had yet to see the inside of a private hospital - he'd decided to move to the St Vincent's Clinic for a few days R & R. The service and the food were reputed to be five star. It seemed like a good idea.

Next call was to Rita at home. She told him she'd just heard about the fire on the early morning 'Today' show. She'd been shocked to hear the news, but greatly relieved when they'd reported McCann was fine. Yes, she'd be happy to send his passport by courier to the airport.

McCann knew the next call would be harder, but it was essential. It was something that had nagged at him since he'd left Hong Kong. He looked at his watch. It was too early, he'd have to call Inspector Tsui in Hong Kong from the airport.

By eight he'd finished a light breakfast, showered and was pulling on the jogging suit he'd had sent up from the shop in the foyer. It looked absurd matched with his brown brogues, but it couldn't be helped. He could hardly go shopping in the torn clothes he'd arrived in last night.

He made the international terminal at Mascot at 9.45 a.m. after stopping briefly at David Jones department store for some new clothes. It was one of those times he was glad to be carrying a first-class ticket. You were never too late to check in first class.

It was 8.40 a.m. Hong Kong time when McCann was put through to Tsui.

'Good morning, Mr. McCann,' Tsui said in his perfectly unaccented English. 'This is a surprise.'

'Look, I'm sorry to take your time. I was hoping you could answer a question for me, based on your police experience.' McCann's experience told him it was generally a good move to appeal to a policeman's vanity.

'I'll see what I can do,' Tsui replied. 'As long as it's not classified.'

'I don't know if you remember, but I had an associate in Hong Kong while I was there. His name is Richard Chen?'

'Of course I do. He's been around as long as I have. He's somewhat of an institution amongst gumshoes here in Hong Kong.'

'That's really what I'm calling about. How would you assess his reputation? Straight up, or unethical? Strictly off the record, of course.'

'Nothing's ever off the record, Mr. McCann. That's my view. Anything you say or do can return to haunt you. The only solution is a commitment to the truth. So to answer your question, I'll tell you. Chen is more than a halfway decent man; Machiavellian to a degree, but no criminal. There's never been even the slightest rumor in the force that he's drug or underworld connected, and I tell you that's a rare thing here. I'd say his organization is the best PI firm on the Island, and he generally gets results.'

He'd somehow expected this answer, though it was not the most welcome news. This vindication of Richard Chen made matters much more complicated. If Chen hadn't passed on the whereabouts of Boydell to the other side, that left only Liu, and he had absolutely nothing to gain, unless he was selling his services to both sides. And even if McCann believed that, how did Liu know whom to contact with his information?

'May I ask why you're making inquiries about Richard Chen?'

'I was considering the possibility that Chen sold out to the people who killed Boydell. You see, no one other than Liu and myself knew where we were to meet on Lamma.'

'It's a puzzle certainly, but I would not be pointing the finger at Chen. That's just a personal view. I can't vouch for Mr. Liu, but I've interviewed him, and he appears a very simple man to me, quite artless.'

'Has the body of the Russian been recovered from the harbor yet?'

'Not yet, no. Sadly we pick bodies out of the harbor every day, but none of the Caucasian cadavers have remained unidentified.'

'You're no closer to a resolution of the Boydell case?'

'I'm dancing as fast as I can, Mr. McCann, believe me,' Tsui replied, his voice smiling down the line.

A steward walked to McCann, indicating his watch. Presumably his flight was ready to board.

25.

New York
22nd May.

The Radcliffe apartment was a large yet unostentatious duplex on Fifth Avenue between 71st and 72nd. For years it had also been home to Bradley and his elder brother Conrad; now the parents, Theo and Blanche, had it to themselves.

Theo sat at the head of the long candelabra'd Georgian dining table. Martha sat to his right, Rosalind to his left. At the far end sat Blanche, flanked by Conrad and Bradley. Between them, seated on either side, were the key members of Theo's staff. To his right, Sheila Pasca, his chief-of-staff, and Charles Scheer, his speech writer and media strategist. To his left, Mariel Proby, his foreign policy strategist, and Dreek Brookbank, whose responsibility was domestic issues.

It had been an easy-going dinner to welcome Rosalind back to the States, with little talk of politics and the intricacies of the campaign ahead. No mention was made of recent events concerning Buchanan Construction in Australia and Hong Kong, though quite clearly all round the table would have been appraised of them by Bradley as a matter of course. The last thing anyone inside campaign headquarters needed at this point was even the most tenuous link to any 'unpleasantness'.

Martha Radcliffe, Theo's mother, was as ever dominating the conversation - Rose Kennedy's alter ago. Rosalind studied the faces round the table as the family and political staffers lapped up Martha's pearls of wisdom. Theo looked tired but serene, a gentle smile playing on his lips as he gave his complete attention to his mother.

Over the past few months Rosalind had come to see a very different side to the man the general public saw at rallies and on television. She had witnessed the obvious rush Theo experienced on the campaign trail from his celebrity status as the front-running presidential candidate. It was the lifeblood that gave him the energy to put in consistent eighteen-hour working days. But though he fed off the roar of the crowd in public, she'd come to know his private nature – that of a modest, sincere and caring man, dedicated to doing his best to ameliorate the basic living conditions of the disadvantaged in society.

His mother, however, was a win at all costs woman. She had her agenda, and was determined to see it fulfilled regardless of ethical niceties. If a certain sector of society had to be appeased to secure a block of votes, then she'd do all in her power to convince her son to do so. Often she failed; Theo had the moral backbone of his father, rather than the vaunting ambition of his mother, and she knew it.

Martha said something Rosalind didn't quite catch and everyone laughed, Bradley more so than the others. By contrast to his father, Bradley came to life as the sun set. He was a night bird. Not that he wasn't a tireless worker in his father and grandfather's mould. As campaign fund manager, Bradley had accomplished miracles. Though they'd all known from the word go that Theo would need every red cent of the thirty-seven million dollar legal limit for the primaries, Bradley had come up with every last dime, despite the fact that the Radcliffe family fortune was around thirty million short of that total. The coffers had been full from the first day of the Louisiana caucus campaign.

But financial genius that he was during the day, he became the classic society animal as the sun set. It was a deeply ingrained part of his nature to want to sparkle at a dinner party. The only exception was in the presence of his family. There, he loved to watch his father and grandmother take the spotlight.

For no reason that she could fathom, Rosalind suddenly felt weary. Perhaps the past week had taken more of a toll than she'd imagined. There'd been the emotional pain of losing an old friend in Whitey, then the shock of the events in Hong Kong. Finally there had been the firebombing of Leo's boat, his house and the attempt on his life. She'd been looking forward to a long-deserved break from the pace of work in Sydney. It had been a hard struggle fighting to keep her head above water, attempting to prove to herself as well as Ian McKintosh and Bob Zeltis that she was up to the task of running one of the largest industrial companies in Australia. Yet now, as she was looking at two straight days with the man she loved, her thoughts nevertheless were drifting from Bradley to concerns for Leo McCann's safety.

'I hope you're going to be able to find time to be with us all on August seventeenth?'

Rosalind's mind refocused from Sydney to the smiling faces round the table. She could tell by Sheila Pasca's expression that the question had come from her – though 'fired' would have been a more accurate description. Her eyes shone with the expectancy of an affirmation.

'Wouldn't miss it for the world, Sheila.'

The national convention was to be in Atlanta this year. Though Dick Stockton, Theo's closest contender, was still in the race, and Larry Harms still resolutely refused to throw in the towel, every political commentator agreed that Radcliffe's nomination was a certainty. Small wonder then that the faces round the table were so relaxed, cheerful and assured.

'The way the figures are panning out, it kind of makes my job a mite easier, when your brief's an acceptance speech, rather than one to snare the floating voter!' Scheer quipped, and again everyone laughed dutifully. Though capable of crafting humor on paper, extempore wit wasn't Scheer's long suit.

Theo cut through the laughter. 'Be a whole different ballgame come November five. Don't need to remind us all about that one.' But his easy smile mirrored his confidence.

Aware that possibly they'd picked up on her lack of concentration throughout the latter part of the dinner, Rosalind lifted her glass. 'If you'll allow me, I'd like to propose a toast to the next President of the United States, Theodore Radcliffe!'

Scheer, Proby and Brookbank pounded the table with their hands as they voiced their approval. Blanche fidgeted with the stem of her wineglass, but looked happy enough. Conrad placed a hand on his mother's arm. Martha beamed at her son, who smiled modestly. Bradley looked Rosalind dead in the eye and winked as they all raised their glasses.

'To dad!' Bradley said, and they all drank.

They sat in the rear of the chauffeur-driven Cadillac in silence. Bradley looked preoccupied. Whether by the upcoming Republican convention, or the state of his golf swing was debatable – Rosalind had never been able to second-guess his thoughts.

He held her hand in his, but his body language suggested something less than intimacy as he stared out through the tinted glass at the crowds on the sidewalk.

'Why don't we drive up to Augusta tomorrow, Brad? I'd like to see Avery before I leave, he's such a sweet man,' Rosalind said, shifting her body closer to Bradley's.

Bradley smiled, yet continued to look out the window. 'You know, he cultivates that 'sweet old man' image. Works every time on pretty girls. They just want to cuddle the old boy to death, and he's not complaining.'

'I'm one of the pretty girls, am I?'

At last Bradley turned to her. 'That came out all wrong, Rosie. But you know what I mean. Pretty girls are drawn to sweet old guys. My granddad's cuter than most, is all.'

'Shall we go visit him? I'd like you to myself for a day or so, away from the city. The drive would be heaven.'

'Can't. Too much to do. Simple as that. Dad relies on me.'

The limousine made a left on 86th and entered Central Park, dipping under East Drive.

'I could organize a dinner party tomorrow night. Invite Avery. He'd come, for sure.'

'Let's eat out. The TriBeCa Grill?'

'Hell, no. Avery'd hate it. Too showbiz. Café des Artistes is more his bag. Old fashioned, with all those frolicking nudes on the wall.'

Bradley again looked out the window. For some reason the limousine had braked heavily, as if it had encountered some obstruction. Abruptly it halted, and the glass partition that separated the passengers from the driver slid down.

'Mr. Radcliffe, we may have a big problem,' the young driver said, pointing forwards, his eyes full of fear.

Bradley looked past him through the front windscreen, then immediately back through the rear window. The limousine was boxed in tight – a black Mercedes in front, a Chevy four door to the rear.

'What's going on, Brad,' Rosalind asked. The driver's frightened tone was infectious.

A dozen disparate thoughts flashed through Bradley's head. He had to think quickly. 'Are the doors locked?' he asked the driver with as much sang-froid as he could muster.

At that moment the phone on the console beside Bradley's seat began to ring.

'Sure are, sir,' the driver answered. 'No use trying to break out of here, though. We're jammed in.'

The phone continued to ring insistently.

'Stay calm. Do and say nothing, we're going to be just fine,' Bradley said, pulling Rosalind close to his body. He then grabbed at the phone. 'Whoever you are, get off the line. I need to call 911 right now!' he shouted. To his surprise and dismay he heard a mocking laughter.

He slammed the phone down, then picked it up again, but there was no dial tone. Just silence.

'Do you have communication with your base, up front?' he asked the driver.

'Yes, sir.'

Through the windscreen, Bradley could now see a well-muscled man in a leather jacket step from the driver's side of the Mercedes, and open the rear door. Another man wearing a full-length black coat exited the Mercedes and began to walk slowly towards the limousine.

'Well, make the call! Tell them we're being carjacked for Christ's sake!' he screamed at the driver, who was sliding down to the pedals, his hands over his head.

Now the man in the black coat was at the door, tapping at the glass. Rosalind watched with horror. Bradley held her hand tightly. Then the man stepped back momentarily, and his leather-jacketed offsider stepped forward, the butt of an automatic in his hand. Almost at once the window glass shattered, and a hand reached inside to unlock the door. It was pulled slowly open and a well-dressed man in his late forties stepped into the car, pulling down a jump seat, and seating himself opposite Rosalind and Bradley. He left the door open.

'I'm sorry for any inconvenience,' the man said with all the apologia of someone who had butted in on a cocktail party conversation. 'But unfortunately your driver saw fit to lock me out. I did call to introduce myself, but you sounded so hysterical, I'm afraid I couldn't help being amused.'

Rosalind looked quickly through the windscreen, then behind her, then through the open door. There were three men in dark overcoats in the road, as well as the leather-jacket by the door. One was standing by the raised hood of the car in front, as if attending to a mechanical problem. One was standing in the road to the rear and the third was standing by the open door, making no attempt to conceal the automatic in his right hand. She glanced at Bradley. He'd seen the weapon, and his face was set, the muscles in his jaw tensing. It was evident that this was not about a simple robbery. But if they planned to kidnap either or both of them, why was the man taking his time?

'What is this about?' Bradley asked.

'My name is Dieter Fischer. With a 'c'. I have a question for you, and I require your full attention. I believe I now have it.'

'What's the question?' Bradley asked quietly.

'The New World Hotel Group,' he said very deliberately. 'Do these words mean anything to you?'

Rosalind studied Bradley's reaction closely. Bradley's expression didn't change. The eyes narrowed a touch if anything.

'I have knowledge of the company, yes.'

'Do you indeed, Mr. Radcliffe?' Fischer asked rhetorically. 'Do you indeed. Now that's a conundrum, since no such company exists.'

'If it doesn't now, I assure you it did once, Mr. Fischer.'

'Mr. Radcliffe. We tend to get to the bottom of things very quickly in our own particular way. You see, we have friends in the most exotic corners of the globe. For example, just yesterday an associate of mine had a short conversation with a Mr. Jonathon Rowe. He is a business associates of yours, I believe.'

Rosalind felt a sudden pressure on the hand that Bradley held. She shot a glance at him, but he wasn't sending messages. It was apparent the name had touched a nerve. Rowe, Radley Associates. She remembered the name from the interview with Eade. They were the people who had brokered the jet lease.

'You see, we are searching for some missing property. After some considerable time and trouble, we came to the conclusion that the New World Hotel Group might be able to help us locate our valuables. However, it turned out that the company in question was merely a shell company. It was created for a particular purpose – to relieve us of our property. You see, the company had no substance. Are you with me this far, Mr. Radcliffe? I do hope so.' Fischer's voice was as sweet as syrup. The eyes, however, told a very different story.

'Whether or not New World was a legitimate company at one time is a matter for Rowe, Radley. I merely put them together with Buchanan Construction, who was anxious to lease out their property.'

'That's not the way Jonathon Rowe remembers it. Not at all.' The soft voice was gone, replaced by a very hard edge. 'Mr. Rowe maintains it was you that introduced New World to him.'

'I beg to disagree,' Bradley started, but was immediately cut short.

'Don't smart-talk me, Radcliffe,' Fischer snapped. 'Don't you *ever* underestimate me. I know who you are and what your game is. Fuck with me and your father's future's in the toilet. I guarantee that.'

Rosalind winced. Bradley was now holding her hand so tightly she felt pain. He looked frozen with fear.

'I know you are aware of who I am,' Fischer continued with more control, 'so I will give it to you straight. You tell me who took our goods, and you walk away. So does she,' he added indicating Rosalind, 'And so does your father. That's the deal.'

'I have no idea what you are talking about,' Bradley replied slowly after a few seconds.

'That a fact?' Fischer said. He then leant forward so that his face was less than two inches from Bradley's. His eyes had the opaque glaze of a fish on the slab. 'Listen up kid. I click my fingers, you're dead. Same goes for the lady. I've seen your kind come and go. And believe me they always go. So this is the deal. You think things over, and get back to me tomorrow latest. You tell me all I want to know. Don't even think about an alternative. You know whom I represent. *Just do it*, as they say.'

They stared at each other for a few seconds, then Fischer relaxed his body language, sitting back in the jump seat and adjusting his cuffs. He looked at Rosalind.

'Sorry to have put a damper on your evening, Miss Buchanan. Looks like your wellbeing is in this asshole's hands.'

He stepped from the Cadillac, then ducked his head back briefly in the door.

'Think smart, eh?' he said. Then the leather jacket beside him closed the door.

Rosalind watched the man climb back into the car in front. The Mercedes moved off, followed shortly by the Chevy.

Rosalind sat in stunned silence for fifteen or so seconds, certain she could hear her own heartbeat, it was pounding so violently. Bradley looked turned to stone. Then he leant forward, looking over the partition down at the terrified driver who was still curled up on the floor by the pedals.

'Driver? Get moving.'

'Where to, Mr. Radcliffe?' the young man said, lifting his head to face Bradley.

'Where do you think? My home!'

The driver gaped. 'You want me to call the cops? I can call the company?'

'No. Take us to Riverside. Now!'

Ten minutes later Rosalind was standing in the foyer of the Crichton Building on Riverside, watching Bradley through the plate glass speaking to the driver. She had been too shaken to say a word since the incident. Bradley had offered nothing, content to hug her close to him in silence.

She watched as he peeled off some notes from his money clip, placing an arm round the young driver's shoulder.

'How do you plan to handle this, Bradley?' Rosalind asked as they entered the apartment, 'Speak to Theo first, or call the police right now?'

'Let me handle this, Rosie. Please,' Bradley replied with more than a hint of irritation.

'Hey! Don't snap at me,' Rosalind said. 'I just went through the same ordeal you did. I simply want to know how you plan to handle this, because if you're planning to sit back and do nothing, I'm not!'

'Look, Rosie. We have to be damned careful here,' Bradley said in a placatory tone. 'That hood was right about one thing. The moment we involve the NYPD, my father's campaign is dead in the water. You think they'd keep wraps on all of this? The story'd be worth a fortune. Stockton would go to town throwing innuendoes at dad.'

'You have nothing to hide, for heaven's sake!' It was a statement, but no sooner were the words out of her mouth than she wished she'd couched them as a question. 'That's right, isn't it?'

'Of course I have nothing to hide!' Bradley snapped, making for the liquor cabinet. 'My God, what do you think of me? Christ alone knows what that man Fischer's got on his mind. I have to talk to Sheila. Work out a course of action.'

'I'd say your father has a right to know, wouldn't you?'

'You want a drink?' he asked from across the room, ignoring her question.

'No thank you. Are you going to tell Theo?' Rosalind persisted.

'Yes, of course I'll tell dad. Just give me a moment to think, will you. I don't tell you how to run Buchanan, do I?'

Rosalind had never seen Bradley like this. He looked shaken to the core. Sure, the incident had been frightening, but they'd both been there, and the long and short of it now was that they'd both survived, and should now be looking to making sure the madman Fischer couldn't harm them in the future.

She watched him pour a whisky into a shot glass. His hand was shaking.

'Who was he? Do you know?' she said quietly. There was no point in shouting at him.

'I haven't the first idea. I know as much as you do. He said his name was Fischer. Some damned caricature of a gangster. How could I know who he was?'

'He said you did.'

'Well, I don't! End of story. The missing property he referred to is quite obviously the currency stolen in Moscow. He must think I had some hand in a conspiracy with New World. How you can even think to ask me whether I know the man is staggering. I had no reason to believe New World was anything but a reputable company. As I'm sure did Jonathon Rowe. If the people behind New World stole this man's money, it had nothing to do with me. I can promise you that!' He put his drink down on the mantelpiece, then hugged Rosalind. 'The question now is how to handle the matter. I'm not going to provide even the most tenuous link between my father and organized crime, just for the benefit of dad's political opponents. Not for any money. If that means having to convince this madman that I had no part in any conspiracy to steal his money, so be it.'

Rosalind stared at him in total disbelief. 'That man threatened to kill me. Can you remember that far back? He said he could happily snap his fingers and you would be dead, *and so would the lady*. Yet here you are, concerned about the damned campaign, considering how best you can put that madman's mind at ease. Are you crazy?'

Rosalind looked deep into Bradley's eyes. They were filled with anxiety and irresolution. Whatever decision he came to, the result could easily spell the end of Theo's career, that much was clear. But it was now equally clear where Bradley's priorities lay, and the shock of it was a lance through her brain. She hoped for Theo's sake that Bradley would have the sense to tell his father what had happened. She knew he'd be horrified by his son's reaction.

'I need to make some calls,' Bradley replied at length. 'Why don't you go to bed, I'll be up soon,' He made a move to kiss her, but she pulled back.

'You have to tell Theo right now. It's his decision - not yours, not Sheila's. Theo's!'

'All right! You don't need to hit me over the head with a baseball bat. I will tell my father! Now can you let go?'

Rosalind walked across to him, taking his hands in hers. 'Brad, I think it's best if I fly home tomorrow.'

'Because I shouted at you? Come on. I'm sorry. I apologize,' Bradley replied truculently.

'No. It's because of us.'

'Because of Fischer, you mean?' Bradley continued without listening. 'You'll be safe, I can guarantee it. Please stay. I need you with me.'

How often since the day her father had died had she needed Bradley, she thought. But he'd never come to her, he'd always been too busy on the campaign trail. His priorities had been clear enough then, but she'd been blind to them.

'You don't need me by your side. This is a political thing, and you've got to sort it out with your father and the police. To my mind it's simple. Fischer is a criminal, and deserves to be treated as such. You tell Theo what happened, then you tell the police. I fail to see how it could hurt Theo's bid for the presidency. There's not the smallest whiff of wrongdoing on your father's part, and you are merely tainted by association. You've done nothing wrong. So please, for God's sake, don't think you can deal with the man. He's obviously too dangerous.'

'Trust me to do the right thing, Rosie. Trust me,' he pleaded.

'You do whatever you feel best. It's none of my business any more,' she said, 'Just don't ever suggest I'm quitting just when you need me. I'm not scared, believe me. I'm emotionally drained and I can't take even the scent of violence.'

There wasn't anything else to say, and they both knew it.

'I'm going to take a bath. Why don't you make the calls,' she said.

As Bradley reached for the phone, it began to ring. Rosalind walked to the bedroom.

A stewardess placed a glass of champagne and a small china plate of hor's d'oeuvres beside him. McCann smiled up at her, then slit open the envelope addressed to *Vera*, pulling out the contents. He then reclined his chair. There were two photographs, and a letter from Matt. One was a head shot of Tran Van Luc. It was practically identical to the photograph of the dead Asian Torrance had given him eight days before. The other was a photograph of a middle-aged man he'd never seen before, with wavy fair hair, crisp starched shirt collar, and an Irish Guards tie. McCann flipped open the short letter.

My dear Vera,

Here's a snap of Tran Van Luc. Took an awful amount of finding. I'm told they had to chop it and blow it up from a group shot taken with the Chairman of the Council of State and several members of the National Assembly no less. So it looks as though he's still well connected.

The American Embassy in Hanoi is at 7 Lang Ha Road. A good contact there is Larry Wykoff. He's expecting a call. One of us. Nice fellow, been around a long time. Thirteen years in various parts of Indochina. Quite a specialist in things Viet. Lots of good stories, I'll be bound. I've sent him a note.

As for Ho Chi Minh City, our cousins suggest you go see a man with the unlikely name of Milo Ganzini. tel: 291 516. War veteran. A trifle touched by the sun, but what he doesn't know... you get my drift?

I also asked Toby Croft to meet you at Ho Chi Minh. A company man all his life. Burma, Middle East, North Africa, Thailand. Twenty years in Vietnam. Retired five years ago and married the former Arts Minister in the Thieu Government. They run a restaurant in a converted shoe factory. Don't think he's spent more than ten days in England his entire life. You'll like the old codger a whole lot, he's a company icon, very Graham Greene.

Don't call me, I'll call you. I enclose an early snap.

Uncle Matthew.

McCann folded the letter and slid it, together with the photographs, back into the envelope. Matt had, as usual, come up with the goods, even though his contacts sounded like founder members of Eccentrics Anonymous.

26.

Ho Chi Minh City.
22nd May.

The final twenty minutes approach to Tan Son Nhat International Airport was through dense gray-black cloud, which accounted for the turbulence. Then quite suddenly the 747 broke through into clear air, and the variegated green mosaic of the trees and rice fields that was the countryside of Vietnam was revealed beneath.

The airport buildings flashed past McCann's rain spattered window as the engines were thrown into reverse thrust, and the jumbo began to slow.

By the time McCann had made the bus journey to the terminal building and was in the immigration hall, he was soaked through. It was 5.30 p.m.

At 5.55 p.m. he was still four back from the passport control desk. A uniformed Vietnamese immigration official of around forty was taking his time examining the documents. A pace behind him stood two much younger men, dressed in checked short-sleeved shirts. They were undoubtedly members of the *Tinh Bao*, the Vietnamese security police.

As the queue shuffled slowly forwards, McCann watched them without appearing to do so, by focussing on a spot several feet to one or other side of them. They were sharing a joke, not taking much interest in the new arrivals.

As McCann stepped forward, their attitude changed radically. The young man in the broader check looked up and began to stare fixedly at him, whispering something to his colleague. Their smiles evaporated, replaced by professional concentration.

The uniformed official flipped through McCann's passport, extracting the paper visa. He studied McCann closely for several seconds, as he'd done every arrival before him, then punched the details into a computer that stood on the desk. He then stamped the paper and waved him through.

On his way through to the baggage collection, McCann glanced quickly back over his shoulder – the broad check shirtsleeve was reaching for a phone behind the desk.

In the main concourse of the arrivals building, a rolling sea of humanity confronted McCann.

To the swarming animated cab drivers around him, McCann was a day's wages, and they weren't about to give him up to a rival easily. They pushed and crushed towards him, each beckoning and shouting their 'special price'. The vociferous bargaining began at around thirty dollars. By the time the melée had reached the road outside, the price had dropped to around twelve.

A voice rang out behind him. 'I say, is that you McCann? Hold on, for pity's sake, I can't keep up.'

McCann turned, still holding on to his bag which a young Vietnamese boy of about twelve was trying to ease from his grasp while his even younger companion held open the boot of an old Fiat taxi.

A tall man in a crumpled beige linen suit, the trousers secured by an Old Etonian tie, was hurrying along the concourse towards him. He was waving a Panama hat that had surely witnessed the establishment of the Democratic Republic of Vietnam in 1945. A mane of snow-white hair danced in the stiff breeze.

'The name's Croft,' the old man wheezed, holding out a hand as he fought for breath. 'Hutton told me you were coming. Thought I'd welcome you, myself. Still got your luggage I hope? Didn't let the little devils take it off you, I trust?'

'No, I've still got it,' McCann replied pulling the bag sharply from the young boy's grasp.

'They'd never steal it,' said Croft, handing the boy a five thousand-dong note, the equivalent of around fifty cents. 'They're a good bunch – it's just business, you know. Once they've got the luggage, they've got *you*. Makes sense, doesn't it?' He laughed as he slapped McCann on the back, thrusting him forwards through the crowd. 'Car's just up ahead to the right. You'll have to push if you ever want to get out of here. You're a commodity, see?' He chuckled again.

The car was a maroon Peugeot, circa 1952. Beside it stood a very small and very old bald-headed Vietnamese with a wispy beard. As Croft and McCann approached, he opened the back door of the car, placing the palms of his hands together in a gesture of welcome.

'This is my associate Nguyen Dinh Minh,' Croft said returning the old man's suggestion of a polite bow. 'He is kind enough to drive me round this city of automotive madness. Minh, this is my friend Leo.'

McCann extended a hand, which Minh shook with a surprising ferocity, considering his age. 'Pleased to meet you. Is that Minh, as in Uncle Ho?'

The bald-headed driver laughed self-deprecating. 'No, sir. Ho was great big man – I am so very small.' Minh then took McCann's bag, tossing it in the front passenger seat.

As the old car chugged its way out of the airport car park, turning onto the main highway to the city, the last rays of sun were covered by cloud. Almost immediately the air felt a good ten degrees cooler.

Despite the fact that all the windows had been completely wound down, the interior was as oppressive as an orchid house. The air conditioning unit consisted of a six-inch metal fan that had been attached to the dash of the car with gaffer tape.

'So, welcome to my country,' Croft said, running a spotted handkerchief inside the collar of his shirt. 'How's Hutton?'

'In good form,' McCann shouted over the bedlam roar of truck engines, horns, scooters and cars.

'Glad to hear it. I believe you're searching for someone?'

'That's right. A girl.'

'Makes a change from MIA's,' Croft replied. American families still paid fortunes to local investigators to search for kinfolk who had never returned from the war.

'This girl was here for the best part of a year. Returned to Sydney a few months ago. I'm trying to find out what she was up to while she was here.'

McCann was finding it very hard to concentrate. Minh was driving the car to the limit of the manufacturer's stress specifications, and although fifty miles an hour was not in itself a dangerous speed, on this particular road it felt suicidal.

Only the central six feet of the highway looked in any way derivable, the five feet on either side a mass of mud and potholes. There was no central marker line; not that it would have made a difference since no one paid the slightest notice to the rules of the road. It was a case of *sauve qui peut*. Once in the flow of traffic there was no question of slowing down unless a traffic cop was insane enough to step into the road and hold up a hand. The Peugeot was carried along on a wave of Honda scooters, cars, trucks, and buses.

McCann studied the antics of the rush hour commuters with astonishment. The motorized bicycles were the worst. They ducked and wove in and out of the trucks and cars, risking life and limb as they jockeyed for an advantageous position to advance forward a mere car's length. They carried on average two to three adults plus a child or two. Many had twenty or so chickens or ducks hanging from the handlebars.

'This is the girl,' McCann said, passing the photo of Venice to Croft. He took the snap and stretched his arm forward, accidentally hitting the back of Minh's head. He then redirected his arm out of the window, screwing up his eyes to focus properly.

'Pretty,' he said.

'Yes, she was,' McCann replied, terrified that at any moment a truck would shear Croft's arm clean off at the elbow.

'Was? She's dead? I thought you said she returned to Australia?'

'She did. She then killed herself.'

'I see. I'm sorry,' said Croft. The sympathy was a point of form presumably. He had no way of knowing who she was. Besides, dealing with the fall-out of death was a part of his job. 'Nationality?'

'Australian.'

'Well, let me see. What would I do if I were you? I suppose I'd check the Embassy in Duc Ton Thang first. You're supposed to register there but no one does, so maybe that's useless. Nevertheless, she looks like a good girl so she may have done so.'

McCann doubted this very much. It was quite possible that by the time she arrived in Vietnam she was anything but the goody-two-shoes Croft was staring at.

'May I have the snap back, please?' The anticipation of serious injury was becoming too much. Croft brought his arm back inside the car as a truck roared past, the baby-faced sweating driver leaning on the horn.

'I'd also check with all the foreign correspondents if I was you. They don't miss much. There are a heap of them here, most with bugger all to do all day. *Agence France Presse, Associated Press, Time , Reuters*. Might even try the *Bangkok Post*.'

'Do they all have offices?'

'No need, dear boy. They're in and out of the Rex like bunnies in a warren. I presume that's where you're staying?'

'No. The Majestic.'

'Well change. Kill two birds with one stone. Besides, everyone stays at the Rex. It's gloriously fifties kitsch, and has the most unusual cocktail bar in Indochina. Served as a home away from home for American officers and journalists during the war.'

The Peugeot hit what felt more like a moon crater than a pothole, and both he and Croft were momentarily launched into the air.

'Road's a bastard, isn't it,' Croft shouted to McCann as he clung to the window strap.

The Peugeot flew along the tree-lined road, past fields where peasant farmers worked knee deep in the rice fields, ploughing behind water buffalo. The brand new Omni Saigon Hotel flashed past, shimmering in the late afternoon sun like a diamond lost on a gravel and dirt path. Every fifty feet or so along the road children squatted beside the road at small wooden tables, on which stood recycled green and brown bottles filled with petrol for sale to the scooter drivers.

'Everyone has to register with police, so there'd be a record of the hotel she stayed at when she arrived. How long was she here in Vietnam, all told?'

'Eight months or so.'

'That long? Then she'd probably have applied for a visa to study the language. Wouldn't get one otherwise. If she moved about the country she'd have to re-register again each time she changed hotels.'

'What if she stayed with a local?'

'Same thing. It would be their responsibility to register her locally. You see, internal security has never posed a real problem to the Viets. They've always had a good handle on that. The most effective instrument of social control in the '80s here in Vietnam was the 'revolutionary vigilance' surveillance system. Each village, school, district, even city blocks, had their own Revolutionary Vigilance Committee. It's not strictly speaking an arm of the state or the party – it merely assists the government in monitoring the behavior of the citizens.'

'They spy on each other?'

Croft gave McCann an old-fashioned look. 'Really, Leo, you make it sound vile. It's not so bad. Don't you have a 'neighborhood watch' system to control crime in the United Kingdom and Australia?'

'Yes,' McCann replied. That was certainly another way of looking at it.

'Well, here we have the *Ho Khau* registration system. Every individual is required to carry an identity card, and each family must have a family registration certificate or residence permit listing the names of all persons authorized to live at each address. So you can see that tracking the girl would be a piece of cake if you had the cooperation of the *Tinh Bao* - our equivalent of the CIA.'

McCann couldn't help noticing how each time Croft referred to Vietnam, he referred to the country as his own. McCann was impressed by the commitment of the man to his new country. He could see the warts, but still loved the body.

'How can I arrange that?' McCann pressed Croft.

'The cooperation of the *Tinh Bao*? You can't. But it's possible I can. It will cost money of course. They'll expect to be paid for their time and trouble. Even our local police expect a little gratitude if they attend a burglary, you know. Seems fair to me, it's our way of leaving a few beers for the garbage men at Christmas.' Croft could only see the silver lining.

'Could you possibly organize that for me?'

'Certainly. A couple of hundred dollars should do the trick. I'll make a call as soon as I get home. Should have a reply for you at dinner. You will be dining chez nous?'

'Love to,' McCann replied.

As McCann pulled out his wallet, peeling off four fifties, his attention was drawn to a motorized bicycle passing them on the right. Two fair sized pigs were strapped to the frame with hemp twine – one each side. The elderly driver was shaking the fist of his left hand at Minh, who was squeezing him out of the center of the road into the potholes while studiously ignoring him.

'I'd also check the Club Opera and the Indochine. Both restaurants are popular with rich Westerners.'

'She wasn't rich.'

Croft smiled, then winced as another pothole pitched him sideways, his head missing the doorframe by less than an inch. '*All* Westerners are rich as far as the indigenous population is concerned,' he said righting himself.

'Someone follow us, Mister Toby,' Minh shouted from the front.

Both McCann and Croft resisted the temptation to turn. Both knew better.

'How very boring,' Croft said. 'It can only be you. They know me too well, and I'm just a boring old tosspot.'

'I don't see what interest they could have in me. No one apart from you, Matt, and the woman I represent knew I was coming.'

'Would your name by itself be likely to trip the burglar alarm on immigration computers? Ever been associated with the firm?' he asked, referring to the Secret Intelligence Service.

'I've done some work overseas, yes, but never east of Kuwait.'

'Well, it's a matter of no consequence,' said Croft. 'Just tedious to have them hanging around.'

But to McCann it was of some very real consequence. If Minh was correct, and they were being tailed, it was more than likely someone associated with Tran Van Luc had arranged to put his name on a list, just in case he should choose to visit. And if Tran could command the aid of the *Tinh Bao*, then McCann's task was going to be doubly difficult.

'You want I lose the company behind, Mister Toby?' Minh shouted from the front.

'Absolutely not, Minh. Slow down if anything,' Croft shouted back. The SIS rules of combat stated very clearly that you never tried to shake a tail unless you were carrying the most incriminating material. It was always best to remain calm and abort only those rendezvous that could compromise either party.

'Anyone else I can help you with?' Croft asked as they bounced over a succession of small ridges that crossed the highway.

'The address of Tran Van Luc.'

Minh suddenly swerved, braking hard to avoid a buffalo which had stumbled into the road. Croft and McCann were thrown violently forward.

'Oh dear me, not the ubiquitous Tran,' replied Croft with equanimity as he sat back in the seat, brushing his white hair back into place. 'He's been a thorn in all our sides since the early seventies.'

'Yes, I know. I'd like to meet him.'

Croft raised his eyebrows, turning the edges of his mouth down in a pantomime look of horror.

'Wouldn't bother. He's not a very nice man. Not at all. You know anything about him?'

'Just how he made his money. That he likes young girls.'

'Well I wouldn't bandy that kind of chat around here too liberally. He's become a very major cheese indeed. Owns the largest merchant bank in Indochina.' Croft paused, then gave McCann a wry grin. 'Well, as far as anyone can own anything here. They could take it away from him in a matter or hours, but they never would. Same as China. Many a millionaire in that bastion of hard-line communism. But the Party turns a blind eye because it suits them.'

The car was by now well into the heart of downtown Ho Chi Minh City. Rush hour had given place to the time of day when the entire population of the city took to wandering the streets, gathering in doorways, snacking on chicken or beef noodle soup prepared by the *pho* ladies on almost every street corner.

It was family time. The wide boulevards were rivers of men in military dress or loose fitting shirts and trousers, and women in delicate silk *ao dai*, the Vietnamese national dress. Children ran in all directions. The girls were dressed in starched white Crimplene dresses, the boys in short-sleeved shirts and shorts. It was the time of the evening reserved for relaxing and socializing after a hard day's work.

'Our humble hostelry is down there on Don Dat Street,' Croft said, pointing to the right. 'It's called Le Sabot. It's a short cyclo ride from the Rex. Talking of which, we've arrived.'

The Peugeot drew up outside the Rex on Le Loi Boulevard. Minh struggled from the front seat, picking McCann's bag from the passenger seat and opening the rear door on McCann's side.

'Look, I'd love to join you for a snifter, but I think I'd better get off to the restaurant,' Croft said as McCann got out of the car. 'We're open till late. You must meet my beloved. We'll be very hurt if you don't come.'

'I'll be there,' McCann replied as he took his bag from Minh, at the same time peeling off a ten dollar bill and handing it to the aged driver. Minh smiled gratefully as he pocketed the money, whispering discreetly to McCann as he did so. 'The men who follow us are in white car parked directly opposite.' Minh then placed his hands together and nodded a farewell.

The receptionist was a little surprised that McCann had made no reservations. There were several conventions in the city, but fortunately one suite was still available. Unfortunately it was on a floor where there were some renovations taking place. So sorry. The suite was on the third floor facing the boulevard. A snap of the receptionist's fingers, and his bag was on its way to the elevators.

The young porter opened the door to McCann's suite and switched on the air-conditioning. The propeller blades of a Sopwith Camel would have made less racket. He handed McCann the key, nodding politely as he took possession of the two-dollar tip.

McCann dropped the bag on the bed farthest from the door. On the nightstand was a sheet of typewritten paper on which was written: *You are respectfully informed of a room maintenance work that is progressing, 8 to 11.30 a.m. and 2 to 5 p.m. There will be moments of unpleasant noise.* The time frame specified seemed to cover most of his waking hours, McCann thought idly - not that he planned to spend many of them in the room.

He crossed to the window and parted the white net curtains a fraction with his forefinger. The white Toyota was still parked across the boulevard from the entrance. Even though it was clearly obstructing the flow of traffic, the police weren't moving it on. The *Tinh Bao* clearly meant to tail him a little longer. It didn't much matter as long as they left him alone.

A quarter of an hour later he'd showered, changed into an open-necked shirt and loose cotton pants and was dialing the number Matt had given him for Ganzini.

The phone rang for some time, then a woman answered, speaking in very speedy Vietnamese.

'May I speak with Milo Ganzini please?' McCann asked quickly, as soon as there was a pause.

'Milo out for now. Please call later. Thank you so much,' a female voice stated in a polite and friendly fashion. Then the line went dead.

McCann looked at his watch. 7.40 p.m. Perhaps now was the time to check out the places Croft had suggested.

The second he emerged from the revolving doors of the Rex Hotel, the cyclo drivers were on him like locusts.

Short for the French *cyclo-pousse*, cyclos were the three-wheeled pedicabs that were the most convenient and popular transport for those without the means to buy a scooter. McCann handed five dollars to the man he thought looked the poorest and showed him the scribbled address the concierge had given him for Café Indochine.

As they turned into Ngyen Hue Boulevard, McCann turned his head sharply to the right, as if to look in a shop window. The white Toyota had just pulled out into the traffic.

Less than five minutes later they arrived at the Indochine. As Croft had suggested, the clientèle was predominantly well-heeled young Europeans. Perhaps too well-heeled. Venice wouldn't have had much cash. She'd most probably have mixed more with the backpacker set.

McCann sat at the bar and quizzed the young barman, showing him the picture of Venice, to no avail. An hour later, he was still no further towards finding anyone who recognized Venice. Next stop was the Club Opera.

The white Toyota continued to follow them on their journey from the Indochine to their next port of call. The old cyclo driver was spectacularly fit and agile considering McCann had not seen him once without a Marlboro hanging out of the corner of his mouth.

The Club Opera was another chic minimalist eatery cum nightclub. This time the patrons were more mixed ethnically, though the prices attested to the socio-economic standing of them all. Again McCann chatted to as many people as possible, showing the photo around. Again with no success. It was dispiriting. Still, he had to remind himself that the population of Ho Chi Minh City was just under five million.

Before he left the club he called Ganzini once again. The female voice repeated the request to call later, but this time McCann was able to leave his name and that of the Rex before she cut him off.

McCann looked at his watch as he left the Apocalypse Now Bar. It was close to ten-thirty. It was time to get over to Croft's restaurant or risk upsetting him. Together with his faithful yet now fatigued cyclo driver, he'd visited well over ten bars and clubs, and had struck out in all of them. The photo meant nothing to anyone. McCann glanced down the street – the white car was parked twenty feet behind his cyclo. He could just make out the faces of two young men in the glow of their cigarettes.

Le Sabot on Don Dat Street was much smaller than McCann had envisaged, considering that Matt had referred to it in his note as a converted factory. In reality it measured less than six hundred square feet, yet Croft had managed to squeeze in around thirty tables and a hundred and fifty people.

The restaurant was still packed with patrons when McCann arrived. All were Vietnamese or Chinese.

Croft was eating at a table by the bar, partnered by two elderly women. He waved cheerily at McCann, then beckoned him over. 'Couldn't wait any longer, I'm afraid. Hope you don't mind our beginning without you,' he said. 'Tuyet, this is a friend of mine Leo McCann,' he continued, presenting McCann to the fine looking woman on his right, 'And to my left, this is my sister-in-law, Nguyen Thi Hong.'

McCann made a small bow. 'How do you do.'

'I'll order for you, shall I? The specialty of the house is the fried chicken with lemon grass and chili. But we'll include a few of the more esoteric dishes, just for fun, eh?'

'Sounds good to me,' McCann replied.

'Oh, while I think of it, only the very aged die-hards still bow. Sadly, it's considered old-fashioned and a trifle reactionary. I know old Minh does it, but he's as old as the Southern Highlands.' He smiled as he tapped McCann affectionately on the shoulder - as though relieved to have completed an awkward man to man chat with a favorite son.

The food came with surprising speed; beef, lobster, curried goat, vinegared eel. All were quite delicious. Though the fish bladder in oyster sauce was a trifle more confronting, it tasted good nonetheless.

Tuyet talked of how radically the country had changed since the unification of North and South, and how it had impacted on her lifestyle – one day a minister in the Thieu administration, the next a working men's restaurant owner.

'The new order left me to my own devices. They obviously never saw me as a threat. Surprising really, when you bear in mind the power of intellectual dissent in North Vietnam over the decades, especially in the late fifties. They should have known better than to underestimate the literary classes. Intellectuals are always a nuisance, aren't they? I mean, in the eighties they called literary cabals such as The Hanoi Barefoot Literary Group in the north, and the Literary Flame here in Ho Chi Minh City, 'subversive', so quite why they imagined a former minister of the arts would be an innocent kitten is beyond me. Not that I complained at the time – I was extremely fortunate not to be sent to be 're-educated'.'

The conversation passed from the arts to the politics of Asia and the new role Hong Kong would play as part of China. It eventually drifted to questions from Croft of life back home. There was a part of his psyche that was essentially 'terribly English' regardless of the years abroad. He babbled on about the "good old days", every now and then reaching out under the tablecloth and taking Tuyet's hand. She would then turn to him and smile. You could see that they adored each other.

It was close to midnight when the women took their leave. Croft filled McCann's glass with rice wine.

'Now, I expect you'd like to know how I spent your money, eh Leo?'

'You have some details?'

'I've had a response,' Croft replied cryptically.

'There's a difference?'

'Indeed. I called on an old friend of mine and gave him the money to share around in the usual way. There's a well-worn pecking order you know. Anyway, he called round here personally around ten o'clock. He's never done that before. That in itself started me thinking. He asked me what my interest was in the girl. I said I was asking on behalf of a client, and he replied that perhaps I should not involve myself any further in this particular client's business. Naturally I asked him why, and then he really began to pick his words carefully.'

'So her name did mean something.'

'Quite clearly. What he told me surprised me for several reasons. Firstly, she's on the subversive list. They've been looking for her for eight months or so. My friend didn't know why, and he'd be the first to know. You see, categories are normally annotated at the top of the file under the name. Intellectual dissent is one, religious and socio-religious resistance element, political sedition and counter-revolution are some of the others. Her category slot's vacant, yet she's been among the top "must-finds" since February last year.'

'Everyone's been telling me the *Tinh Bao* knows what you had for dinner last night. Now you're saying they couldn't find a young girl in eight months.'

'Well naturally they had the initial records. Then they lost her, and pressure's been applied from high up to find her.'

'Who by?'

'He didn't say, but the intimation was the Minister himself.'

'Would this be in the way of doing Tran Van Luc a favor?'

'Hold on a moment. You didn't say so before, but I take it there's a connection between the two. A sexual one quite possibly?'

'Correct.'

'They were lovers?'

'The facts point that way.'

'Then why would he be searching for her? Had she left him?'

'That I don't know.'

'Was she a political activist? It could be you've got it all wrong. That it wasn't Tran that was looking for her, but the *Tinh Bao*. The Central Highlands for instance has had a history of counter-revolution. An armed guerrilla group called FULRO once controlled the area. Used to be active in the early eighties.'

'I doubt she was a rabid activist. It's conceivable, I suppose, but at this stage I'd say no.'

'One thing he did tell me was that you're probably in the wrong city. Last contact was in Hanoi. The My Guy Club.'

'Sounds like a brothel.'

'It is. At least that's what my source tells me.'

'Does he know who put the word out to find her?'

'Every time I asked, he gave me the look.'

'I know it. *Please don't ask, I can't tell you*?'

'Right. It's clearly way over his head.'

'I'll tell you one thing that will definitely interest you. *Your* name caused a *great* deal of interest. I think my friend may have told me more until he put two and two together and asked whether you were my client. Then it was a whole different ball game.'

'It sounds very much to me as though Tran Van Luc was expecting me, and asked someone to make life difficult.'

'That he could do with ease. I'd watch my back if I were you, Leo.'

McCann shrugged. 'It's just going to make my job a great deal harder, that's all.'

'You had no luck in the bars and clubs? You tried the Indochine? The Club Opera?'

'I did. No bites,' McCann replied.

'By the way, I'm afraid you don't get the money back. In their book you asked for their time, not necessarily a successful outcome. Sorry.

'You still got a tail?'

'All evening.'

'Well, don't worry about them. *Leave them alone and they will go home*, as the rhyme goes.' Croft refilled their glasses. 'What are your plans?'

'I have to see a man called Ganzini tomorrow.'

'Milo. Good choice. Keeps his ear to the ground.'

McCann was banking on it. He lifted his glass and toasted his host.

The air was oppressively humid outside. The shirt was sticking to his back within seconds of stepping out into the street. It was now well past midnight. The traffic had maybe halved. McCann looked around for his cyclo driver. On every other occasion during the evening, the Marlboro man had come running within seconds, pointing to where the bicycle was parked. Now there was no sign of him. Nor of any other cyclo, which was unusual. The drivers normally congregated outside busy bars and restaurants. It felt like the Taj Mahal with no tour guides.

As McCann debated whether to walk to a busier street or wait for a passing cyclo, the front of the restaurant was abruptly lit by the high beam of a car just down the street. The white Toyota. So that was it – they'd scared the drivers off to force him to walk back to the hotel. Well, that was just too bad. This wasn't the country to confront the police. Croft was right. Don't rise to it. See what they do next. He set off in the direction of the Rex.

The street lighting improved as he turned left into Le Thanh Street. The curbside bars were doing a busy trade, each no larger than ten feet square, lit by candles or a single hanging bare light bulb. The locals chatted and joked, some eating inside, sitting on small wooden benches, some squatting on their haunches outside on the pavement drinking beer, smoking local cigarettes and munching on nuts.

McCann walked slowly, relying on his good sense of direction. He knew the street he was on would lead him past the Hotel de Ville, where a right turn would take him directly past the Rex. The lights of the white car remained on high beam twenty feet behind, cruising at his walking pace. With any luck the engine would overheat. He smiled to himself. He didn't mind the walk, but the effect of the car on the locals was an education. The cyclo drivers would catch sight of him – a westerner walking the street – veer across the road and call out to him. Then the white car would flash its headlights. The cyclo drivers would take one look, then peddle away without another word.

Five minutes later he was in Le Loi Boulevard, pushing against the revolving doors of the Rex Hotel. In the glass he subliminally caught sight of the white Toyota reflected in the glass. It had parked directly in front of the Hotel, and the doors were opening.

'There is a small problem please, Mr. McCann,' the night manager said hesitantly as McCann asked for his room key.

'And what is that?'

'Your papers are not in order.' The sharp voice came from behind him. McCann turned. The two young men in the white car stood behind him. The one who hadn't spoken was trying hard not to smile, as though privy to some private joke. The other was quite serious.

'What papers are you referring to? I wasn't aware we had to carry papers,' McCann replied.

'You say in visa you stay at Majestic Hotel. Not Rex Hotel. Why you say this thing?' the more earnest of the two young men asked.

'I changed my mind. I filled in the visa form in Australia. When I arrived, a friend told me the Rex Hotel would be more convenient for me. Look, the hotel has my passport, what's the problem?'

'There is a fine for incorrectly filling in visa and immigration forms, Mr. McCann,' the night manager said helpfully.

'Please may I see passport and papers,' the hard-faced young man said, holding out a hand towards the night manager.

He looked through the passport for some time, every now and then looking up at McCann, then back to the passport. He then returned it to McCann. 'No fine this time. Please now carry at all times.'

'I would have done so, but I was told to leave my passport at the desk this evening.'

'I say please carry all times. Thank you,' was the curt reply. The two young men turned and walked back outside.

McCann held out his hand for the door key. The night manager apologized for any inconvenience, at the same time handing him two folded and sealed message forms. On his way up in the lift he opened the topmost. It was from Ganzini. The message was timed at 11.45 p.m. He left his address, suggesting a rendezvous at 10 a.m. The second was from Rosalind. *Please call when you can. R.* Just that. She left a number. McCann was curious.

Inside the room, McCann walked quickly to the bedroom, picked up the telephone and removed the baseplate, checking the input condenser. Then he unscrewed each end of the receiver. The tiny sophisticated listening device was in the top half, where most wouldn't think of checking. He replaced the receiver, then opened the room door and stepped back into the corridor. Maybe there was a way to turn the bug to his advantage.

The roof terrace restaurant and bar on the fifth floor was a treasure house of mellowed kitsch. Caged birds of every description hung everywhere – some happy with pals, some on their lonesome. A red marble semicircular bar stood under an awning. In every corner were elaborately topiaried trees in pots. At the apex of the terrace, sandwiched between a life-sized blue plaster elephant and a seven-foot grisly bear, stood a giant revolving crown richly decorated with tiny fairy lights, the letters R–E–X beneath it.

He ordered a beer at the bar and enquired whether there was a telephone in the restaurant – it would save him the trouble of returning to his suite. Would it be possible to charge his room, he asked fingering a ten-dollar bill? The barman directed McCann to a booth beside a large fountain, accepting the money with a smile. The billing would be no problem, he said, as he made a note of the number of McCann's suite.

It would be around 1 p.m. in New York. He hoped she wasn't in the middle of a power lunch.

Rosalind sounded surprisingly jolly when she came on the line after six rings.

'McCann? It had to be you. I felt it in my bones. Maybe I'm psychic! Just about to tuck into a Caesar. Where are you? Still in Ho Chi Minh City?'

'Yes. Listen, I've encountered a spot of local resistance here. The immigration boys are making life a bit boring.'

'How?'

'For some reason they've been on my tail since I arrived. Maybe Tran thought I might come after him, I don't know. It's almost as if he were definitely expecting me today. Couldn't call you from my room because it's bugged, so I thought I'd give you a call from the bar then call you in a few moments from the room and feed the listeners a load of bullshit. Okay?'

'Sure, but have you come up with anything positive yet about the girl's movements?'

'Looks like Venice headed straight for Hanoi. That's what Matt's man says anyway. I've a meeting planned with another of his contacts early tomorrow, then I'll head up to Hanoi.'

'Where can I reach you?'

'No idea, I'll have to let you know,' he replied. Then he caught sight of an advertisement on the inside of the booth listing hotels. 'The Pullman Metropole,' he said, reading the address and phone number of the most elegant. 'Look, I'll call you back in five from the room. Just remember who's listening.'

McCann drained the beer, handed a ten to the barman and walked back to the lift.

Back in his suite he again dialed New York.

'McCann? It had to be you,' she said as she picked up the line. 'I felt it in my bones. Maybe I'm psychic! Just about to tuck into a Caesar. Where are you? Still in Ho Chi Minh City?' McCann had to resist laughing – she had a nice sense of humor. 'How are you enjoying yourself?'

'Having a great time. Wish you could have come. Pity, but there you are. Got into a bit of trouble this evening with the police. You see, I wrote on the visa that I was staying at the Majestic, then I decided on the Rex. Thought they'd arrest me.'

'That's too bad, darling.'

Despite the fact that he knew she was pulling his leg, he knew he could learn to like the intimacy. 'How was New York?' he asked.

'Don't ask. Tell you when I see you,' she said.

She put down the phone before he had time to reply.

27.

Ho Chi Minh City
23rd May.

Ganzini looked as thin as a blade of grass. He moved like an insect in a disco, swinging his arms, bent at the elbows. The short stubble on his head was the same two days growth as on his face. His skin, crinkled like a discarded passionfruit, was baked dark ochre by the sun. As he spoke, his head bobbed from side to side like a fast action metronome. The 'boonie-rats' in his platoon back in the Nam of '71/'72 knew him as 'Grinna'. The left side of his face had been badly scarred during a firefight, and his lips were now forever turned upwards in a grimace. In front of him on his roof terrace was a wooden bowl of fruit and a canvas bag filled with San Mig beers.

Half a pace behind and a foot to the right of him, sat a strikingly handsome Vietnamese woman around forty, squatting on her heels in the Vietnamese way. Wrapped around her head was a richly embroidered green scarf, edged in crimson. Her cheekbones were sharply defined, her brown eyes wide and open. The full lips were slightly parted to reveal teeth as white as Indian Ocean sand. Her skin was unblemished and smooth as liquid chocolate.

Across the roof near the door, a fragile looking copper-skinned girl of around ten sat in the hot afternoon sun, her shining black hair falling past her shoulders to her tiny waist. She stared at McCann with an intense concentration. Her right hand clasped a leather thong that served as a lead for a small black bear cub which pawed the air with a bandaged arm.

Ganzini lived in District Five, the huge Chinese district of Saigon called Cholon. His apartment was the top floor of a three story French colonial building on Hung Vuong Boulevard, the street famous for its distinctive Cholon mixture of Chinese and French architectural styles. His pale blue shirt flapped gently in the breeze that funneled down the street past the curbside kitchen chefs as they stirred their various brews and soups.

McCann listened as the thin man spoke with the velocity of an M-16 on full automatic. Perhaps he was speeding, perhaps it was just a mixture of too much beer and weed. Whatever it was, Ganzini was high as the Empire State.

'Weapons! Look there were a million soldiers serving with the South Vietnamese Army alone. They were all issued with M-16's. So that's a million of those little suckers, and that's just for starters. There were machine guns, M-60's, Thumpers – that's the 40mm grenade launcher, Laws, Mini-guns... And when you get to the bigger stuff, there's heavy artillery, tanks, armored personnel carriers, the M-113's – I mean the list is endless! Just think of this. Uncle Sam supplied the South Viets with over seven hundred Iroquois choppers. When Saigon fell, I'd estimate no more than 20 made it to the fleet. Then you'd have to guess that another 250 or so were written off. So that leaves maybe 400 of them. That's before you even estimate the numbers of Chinooks, CH-47's, Hueys, and the odd Cobra AG-IH that were left behind in the rush to shift ass.'

'Tran cornered the market?' McCann asked.

'I shit you not! In '86 I heard that Tran was dealing in the export of all this stuff. He'd made all the right connections, and it was like he'd got the only license to trade. Must have been major kickbacks to the military. The Vietnamese had given quite a bit of hardware to the Cambodians when they pulled out of there, but there was still plenty, believe me! He was crating up the stuff and shipping it out in freighters. There are a hell of a lot of people out there who just love cheap hardware. Most of it went by sea to South America – Panama, San Salvador, Argentina, the drug barons in Bolivia, Colombia. Some to Africa, Angola, and later on places like Somalia.

'And you don't have to guess too hard how the South Americans paid for the stuff. Cocaine. Which Tran arranged to be shipped via Florida to the States and Europe. And wait till you hear this – the deal was *they* shipped it, they took all the risks, and Tran collected at the end of the line.

'So he stood no chance of being busted.'

'Ain't that a "numba one deal", man!' Ganzini exploded with delight.

Ganzini's woman bobbed up and down on her heels, a broad grin on her face. McCann could see the respect for Tran's ingenuity written all over her face. As she chuckled, Ganzini reached behind him, laying an affectionate bony hand on her shoulder. She nuzzled it with her cheek.

Ganzini's eyes flashed across to the little girl and her pet. 'Hey, Marcie! Take the bear inside, will you sweetheart. It's too damned hot for the little fella out here.'

The young girl pouted, then pulled the uncooperative black bear inside the attic doorway.

'Found the little critter a couple of weeks ago near the Ngoan Muc Pass on the way to Phan Rang in the Central Highlands. Looked like she'd taken a hit from a truck or something. Fixed her up. Now I'm stuck with a black bear. Shit, things you do for the family, huh?' He held out his arms to either side in a gesture of martyrdom.

'Anyway, as soon as the Communists thought they could get away with selling US hardware on the black market, they did. And who better to do it for them than Tran? He had all the contacts overseas, and he had the financial infrastructure to wash the dough and bring the hard currency back home. Well, that's what the Communists had in mind. Tran preferred to keep the bulk stashed in Miami, Panama and Nassau. Bet your sweet ass he made sure they never knew the true scale of his operations. Hell, he even crated Skyraiders and shipped them abroad.'

'Skyraiders?'

'Single engine bombers. Sturdy tough bastards. Of course a lot of the hardware was unserviceable – the choppers in particular. But at the price they were being sold, who cared? They could be whipped back into shape at the other end, no problem. That's where I came in. I knew what was still good and what to throw away; what to keep for spares, and what to sell to ignorant numbnuts that didn't know any better.'

His eyes flicked to McCann's can of San Miguel, and he reached inside the sack for a fresh one, gently tossing it over. 'Have some fruit. It's good. Never liked fruit much as a kid, but I tell you, after a couple of weeks on C's out in the boonies you'd kill for a tin of peaches, and that's something you *never* forget. Always have a big heap of fruit round now. Help yourself. That one there,' he said pointing, 'that's *thanh long*, dragon fruit, literally blue dragon. *Dee-licious*! The smaller one's sapodilla. Light brown inside, tastes vaguely of sweet coffee. Taste grows on you.'

McCann popped the San Mig, then picked a sapodilla, peeling back the thick skin. 'How did Tran reach you?'

'Shit, Tran never came near us. The man was some major big cat. He wasn't about to mess around with the mechanics! Word was he needed guys like us, guys who were back in the Nam and knew the hardware. The NVA were good, don't get me wrong, but that was our shit! I was a dream come true to Tran's people. I'd spent two tours of duty babying those mothers! I'm telling you, Charlie could knock down a Slick and I could get it back in the air in under a day – I mean I was *good*!' He beamed with pride, the scar tissue crinkling up to his eye. 'They brought 'em to me in trucks. Choppers of every size and description; snakes, shit-hooks, red birds. When I'd finished they *flew* those motherfuckers outta there, and that's a fact!'

'How many guys like you did he have?'

'Wouldn't rightly know exactly. Maybe twenty, all over the Nam. In the early days it was one dangerous game. As soon as the CIA caught wind of what Tran was up to, they set out to stuff up his business. They were mad as hell and just wanted to put a spoke in the wheel. I know for a fact that there were two freighters that left Haiphong in '89 that were never heard of again. Never showed up where they were supposed. Your guess is as good as mine as to why not. Sank in a storm? I don't think so.'

'How come the condition of the gear was so good after all those years?'

'It wasn't, man. A lot of it was garbage. But there was just so much to choose from, you get me?'

McCann nodded. 'Sure.'

'Over the years Tran realized the price he'd been charging was less than they'd been worth. But you have to remember that as the stuff rusted, it was worth less too, so the price remained pretty steady. As the quality went down, the markets changed. Now Somali warlords like Adeed could afford the odd choice item.'

'It's all gone now?'

'Yeah, there's not much good stuff left now. I mean there was always a finite amount of the stuff anyway. But that's how Tran made a fuck of a lot of the seed money for his later schemes.'

'What about ammunition?'

'There was precious little of that at the best of times. See, we wouldn't re-supply the South with ammo. Uncle Sam's priority was to wash his hands with the war and get out the last of the guys snappy. So the South had a dwindling supply of ammo, and Uncle Sam wasn't about to re-supply. What could the South Viets do? They had the guns, and nothing to put up the spout. So they got their ass well and truly kicked by the Communists. That's the real shame of the war, far as I'm concerned. The years that followed the treaty were by far the worst for the South in terms of suffering and bloodshed.'

'You don't hear too much about those years.'

'Right on! Truth is, the Western media lost interest when the Yanks went home. As far as they were concerned, the war was over and a peace treaty had been signed. Try telling that to the ARVN regulars in the middle of a nowhere jungle still fighting a war of attrition as the Communists took over the country. Charlie beat the shit out of these people, while their own artillery couldn't give them cover because they had no shells. They just had to watch their buddies die. So, to answer your question, no, there was no ammo on the sale list.'

McCann helped himself to a dragon fruit and began to peel it. If Ganzini was going to answer all his questions with this a similar attention to detail they'd be here till nightfall. Ganzini's eyes were wide with expectancy as he waited to field McCann's next one.

'The kick-backs must have bitten into Tran's profits.'

'True, Tran had to factor in a lot of kickbacks. The greater part went to the top. He had to buy it from the Communists after all. Couldn't just knock it off, could he? But there were people all the way down the line that wanted their share – the Cong An Nhan Dan, otherwise known as the People's Police; the Cong An Bien Phong, a.k.a. the border police; and most importantly, the Cong An Bao Ve Chinh Tri, the Special Protection Police, sometimes called the *Tinh Bao*, the Viet equivalent of the KGB.' His face suddenly lit up as a thought scythed in from left field. 'Ain't it interesting now that everything in the Nam is the People's this and the People's that, that there's one exception, and that's the Central Bank; that's the 'State' bank!' He laughed loudly, then shouted indoors. 'Hey, Marcie! Where are you, sweets? Come out here to poppa!'

'You have any other children?' McCann asked as Ganzini guzzled his fourth beer and popped a fifth.

'Just Marcie. We lost one a couple of years back.' Suzie leant her head on his shoulder.

'Yeah, provided everyone got what they thought was a reasonable slice of the action, everyone was happy,' Ganzini continued in a rush, quickly banishing all thoughts of the miscarriage from his mind. 'Tran walked away with three-quarters of the loot. And all the while the CIA were sick as hell. Payment was made in Panamanian Banks, Argentinean Banks, in Hong Kong. All in hard currency. This is all common knowledge, man,' he said holding up the palms of his hands to McCann. 'Some of it came back into Vietnam via Tran's companies. So he bought drugs and Western consumer goods and smuggled them into Vietnam via Colonial Route 9 and Khe Sanh. It was a circle that never let up. It's still the major smuggling route into Vietnam, Khe Sanh. Stuff comes in from Laos and Thailand, and to a lesser degree Cambodia. Cigarettes, liquor, videos, any electrical equipment, auto parts, tires, movies. Everything.'

Suzie grinned, 'Numba one. Heh?'

Ganzini took her small hand in his and squeezed it affectionately. 'You'd think she couldn't speak the language, wouldn't you? Not so. She understands it all. Just doesn't want to speak it. Says it's an ugly language. Way I speak American, I reckon she's got that right.'

'What is it about Vietnam that draws people back to it? With respect, you'd think the Vets wouldn't even think of coming back to a place most knew as a living hell.'

'Well, that was then. Now is now, as they say. Some can't see it that way, an' I respect that. For me, it's a glorious mixture of everything. Vietnam means so many different things to different people. The draw of Vietnam? Lotta people call it the 'Bite of the Lotus'. Bites you in the butt when you're not lookin', and then you're screwed. Gotta come back. The French call it 'Le Mal Jaune,' the yellow sickness. Not so romantic.'

Suzie prodded Ganzini in the gut with a long finger and smiled a gentle rebuke at him. He winked back at her.

'For me it's Suzie and the kid. And the philosophy of life - everyone doing their own particular thing. The color of the country, the smells, the tradition. God knows, a lot of the boonies come back for pure nostalgia. Some for the women, who are undoubtedly miraculous.'

Ganzini pulled a bag of weed from his pocket and rolled a thin greyhound, then offered it to McCann.

'Care for a spliff?'

'Not right now, thanks.'

Suzie flicked her Zippo and Ganzini inhaled deeply, passing the cigarette behind him, as he looked to the door. 'Marcie, where the hell are you? Come out here, honey. Bring the bear if you have to!'

'This is your home now?' McCann asked.

'Yeah. Took a while to adjust though. Wasn't always laid back like I am now. I was one angry motherfucker I can tell you. Wanted to kill anything that moved when I was shipped back home. Didn't matter if they were white, black or yellow. Spent a few years back in St Paul getting my mind right. Now I can only see today. I leave the yesterdays to those miserable mothers who can't move on.' His hand slid into the beer bag and a sixth was extracted and popped.

Now was the time to get to the point, while Ganzini had taken the time to draw breath. It was now or never. 'How do I get to meet Tran?'

'You?' Ganzini's thin shoulders shook as he laughed. Behind him, Suzie giggled as she drew on the spliff.

'Where does he live?'

'Up in Hanoi. Ho Tay Lake some place. Least, that's what the word is. He's organized himself a fortress there. Big major house on the dyke.' Ganzini smiled again as he took back possession of the cigarette. 'I wouldn't expect he'd be in the habit of entertaining visiting PIs.'

'Do you know exactly where?'

'No. Haven't been up Hanoi way for years. You'll have to have a look see yourself.'

'I will.'

Ganzini reached into his pocket, pulling out a battered leather wallet.

'Here's an address of a buddy in Hanoi,' he said scratching a name on an old cigarette paper. 'Vargas. Runs a drug club up there. Likes money. He'll do anything if the price is right. Mind you, you gotta be careful. Someone may come along five minutes later and offer him more than you did. Then you may just end up dead. Know what I mean? So just make sure you pay him. If he won't take your money, if he says it's a freebie, you're up shit street. He means to sell you out.'

As McCann stood, Ganzini held up a hand. 'I mean it, McCann. Watch yourself there. Tran's got the *Tinh Bao* in his pocket.'

'I know. They've been up my backside ever since I left the airport.'

'If they start twitching their tails, back off. Can't beat 'em. They can lose you in a minute and no one will ever know. Nothing those bastards don't know. They could tell you when I last had a crap.'

Suzie rocked back and forth on her heals as she peeled with laughter.

But maybe Ganzini was wrong. Maybe they weren't so damned clever. Venice Messon had led them a dance for months.

McCann pulled out the photo of Venice and passed it to Ganzini. Suzie rocked forward so she could also see.

'Did you ever come across this girl? It's a long shot, but I've been showing it to everyone.'

'Pretty thing. Looks just like that little girl in the movie Taxi Driver,' said Ganzini.

'Yes, she looks very young. She's actually seventeen in that shot.'

'That a fact?' he said, handing it back to McCann.

28.

Hanoi
23rd May.

McCann was aware of the tail from Cholon back to the Rex, and again on his way to the airport. But there seemed nothing to be gained by attempting to shake the *Tinh Bao* since he knew they'd pick him up again at the airport, so he didn't even bother to think about them. He'd picked the brains of the journos who had been propping up the bar at the Rex when he got back to the hotel, but none had shown any interest in his questions, and when pushed, knew nothing of Venice.

Though the flight to Hanoi was an internal one, his passport and visa were again demanded and thoroughly scrutinized as he checked in.

Three-and-a-half hours later, McCann fought his way through the seething mass of humanity packed into the arrivals building at Noi Bai Airport and strode purposefully towards the first cab he saw, waving a twenty at the driver. A minute later he was on his way into the city.

As the battered Ford sped down Highway 3 towards Hanoi, McCann glanced in the left wing mirror. A relatively new Nissan four-wheel drive followed at a discreet distance with two different, yet almost identically dressed, young shirtsleeved Vietnamese in the front.

It was now obvious he was going to be shadowed everywhere. But if Tran had organized the exercise, why had he stopped short of violence? Brokov had tried to kill him twice, once in Hong Kong and once in Sydney. Now that he was in Tran Van Luc's backyard, why was the Vietnamese content merely to observe? Was Tran waiting for him to come closer, waiting for the most convenient time and place to take him out?

The cab crossed the wide, burnt ochre, Red River at Chuong Duong Bridge and entered the old quarter of Hanoi. With its maze of narrow tree-shaded streets, it was known once to the French as the Cité Indigène. The ambience of the city was a stark contrast to Saigon. There were fewer cars and motorbikes - more bicycles and cyclos. Less noise and pollution - more trees and parks. Where Ho Chi Minh City was brash, Hanoi was dignified - the architecture pure thirties French provincial.

The Hotel Pullman Metropole was without doubt the newest and most impressive hotel in Hanoi, City of Lakes. The cost of a room for the night was many times the monthly working wage. Yet despite the expense, it was almost always full, the only room available to McCann a small single at the rear of the building. The last front double had been booked an hour previously.

His first call was to Larry Wykoff at the Embassy. The CIA man was friendly and helpful. Yes, he knew of the My Guy Club, and also of the Green Parasol Of the Universe, the contact address that Ganzini had given him. But he had never frequented either. He cautioned McCann against any thoughts of a run-in with his two shadows. It could only end in a swift deportation without an opportunity to ask questions. Presuming his telephone line to be bugged, McCann made no mention of the possible connection to Tran.

As he prepared to leave his room, the phone rang.

'McCann? It's Rosie. When did you get in?'

'About twenty minutes ago. I'm just about to leave to follow up on a lead. Are you at home or at the office?'

'Neither actually. I'm in the bar downstairs,' she replied. 'I'll order you a beer, shall I?'

McCann opened his mouth to reply, but no words came to mind.

'I'll take that as a yes,' she added, after a moment's silence, then hung up.

Though the bar was crowded with rich Western tourists, McCann spotted her almost at once. She was sitting at a corner table, dressed in a simple white silk shirt and jeans, staring off into the distance. She looked preoccupied, tired and unhappy.

'You're a surprise a minute, Rosie,' he said as he pulled back the chair next to hers, sitting down.

For a second he wondered why he hadn't kissed her on the cheek as he usually did women he knew socially. But for some reason it didn't feel right.

'Not that much of a surprise, surely. Hanoi's on the way home,' she replied. McCann just stared at her. It was hardly just down the street. 'Well, Cathay Pacific flies home via Hong Kong, and that's just round the corner isn't it?' she protested. Then she smiled.

'Whatever. It's good to see you. I can only presume it was you that took the last decent sized room. When did you check in?'

'About an hour-and-a-half ago.'

'That figures,' he said smiling. 'How was New York? Last time I asked you, you said *don't ask*. If it was purely personal, tell me to mind my own business.'

'It was, and it wasn't,' she replied, picking some nuts from a bowl on the table and arranging them abstractedly in a line on the table. 'The limousine we were travelling home in from Theo's dinner party was carjacked by some gangster in Central Park.'

McCann listened in stunned disbelief as Rosalind recounted the details of the episode with the man who'd called himself Fischer.

'I couldn't stay in New York. I had to get away. Perhaps it was weakness. Maybe I owed it to Brad to stay. I don't know.'

'Do you think he'll tell Theo?'

'That's his call, not mine. I hope so. If he's the man I fell in love with, I think he will.'

McCann could almost read her thoughts. She was willing Bradley to do so, but her secret fear was that he'd do nothing of the kind. 'Rosie. I hope you don't mind my asking you this question, but I think I have to.'

She looked up from the nuts on the table. 'Do I think Bradley has any criminal involvement? That's it, isn't it?'

'I'm afraid so, yes,' McCann replied quietly.

She looked off across the room. McCann felt she knew the answer, but found it hard to admit it to herself.

'Before you say anything, maybe it's best if I tell you how I see things. First of all we have the matter of the lease of the jet. Bradley brokered the lease through Rowe, Radley. Bob Zeltis recalls that it was at Bradley's instigation, while Bradley says he was doing your father a favor. Either way, the company that leased the jet was a fly by night shell company. No one's been able to trace them. Rowe, Radley, who arranged the lease, are well known to international financial enforcement authorities as the most questionable of merchant bankers in the Turks and Caicos.

'Secondly, we have the matter of the miracle loan that came out of nowhere just in time to save your father the embarrassment of having to go public with the Telok Anson debacle. Horan firmly believed that Tran engineered the fraud at Telok Anson so that he could provide the funds for a fresh loan to Buchanan Construction to finish the job. Again, it was Bradley who initially referred your father to the Jensen Rollason Partnership in Hong Kong. Through contacts at the Financial Crimes Enforcement Network, I've been able to identify the syndicate bank members of the loan deal. The Union Constitution was the lead bank. Their link to the Russian mob banks in Moscow is a matter of public record.'

Rosalind said nothing. She looked ashen as she listened.

'The syndicate banks were Sir Henry Trevor's, the Fortress Hill Investment Bank in Hong Kong, of which Tran's brother was chairman, and the Weddle

Commercial in London, which has cropped up time and time again on FinCEN's computers.'

'You're saying that Brad's directly linked to Tran? That he was part of the Telok Anson conspiracy. Not only that, but that he was part of the theft of the millions in Moscow. That's what you're saying, isn't it?'

'I'm afraid so.'

Rosalind took her hand away from McCann's, cupping her forehead in the palm as she closed her eyes for several seconds. 'Oh sweet Jesus,' she whispered barely audibly.

McCann knew he had to continue. There was no alternative; it had to be said. 'Rosie, I must ask you this. When I called you from Hong Kong telling you where I was meeting Boydell, was Bradley in the room with you?'

She leant back in the chair, her eyes still tight shut, taking deep breaths.

'I told Brad that you'd made contact with Boydell, yes. I told him you were meeting him at Lamma.' Then she opened her eyes, staring hard at McCann. 'I told *him*, he didn't ask. I think there's a difference.'

McCann softened his tone a fraction. It wasn't going to be easy to come to terms with the possibility that Bradley was so deeply implicated. 'Possibly,' he replied.

'You realize what you're intimating now?'

'I think so, yes.'

'It's one thing to suggest that Brad's involved in a criminal fraud, but now you're suggesting he was an accessory to the murder of Boydell in Hong Kong.'

'I'm afraid that it looks that way. He's the only person who could have betrayed the rendezvous.'

'Bullshit! What about Chen? What about Liu, for Christ's sake?'

'I've checked Chen out with the Hong Kong Police, they say he's clean as a hound's tooth. Liu was Boydell's choice as a go-between. He didn't know who Tran was.'

'Sure. Okay,' she began with a heavy sarcastic lilt, 'Well, if the police say Chen's a good fellow, then let's assume Brad's a murderer shall we?' Her fuse was burning dangerously short.

'Rosie. There are just too many coincidences. Why did I get the third degree at Ho Chi Minh Airport? They *knew* I was coming. You think Torrance sent them a fax? Who else knew, apart from you and Brad and the men from Task Force Lotus? Why did Fischer take it for granted that Bradley would know who he was? He was certain enough of Bradley's involvement.'

Rosalind's shoulders slumped, and her expression softened from anger to a weary despair. 'Dear God,' she breathed as she wrapped her arms round herself.

'Look, I'd like to believe that Brad had no reason to think they'd kill Boydell. It's still possible they found him by other means. But it just doesn't look too good for Bradley. It looks black as night to put it frankly, and I'm damn glad you're out of New York.'

But Rosalind wasn't listening. She was still hugging herself, rocking gently back and forth on the chair. 'What do I do now?' she said softly.

'What you do is up to you. I feel I have a responsibility to tell the authorities everything I know when I get back. As far as I'm concerned, Theo's race for the White House is beside the point – three people have been killed in the past ten days!'

'Jesus, what do I tell Theo? That his son's an accessory to murder? It'll kill him.'

'Maybe Bradley has had the courage to tell him. I hope so. Either way, someone has to tell him before Fischer makes good his threat.'

Rosalind picked the nuts from the table and placed them deliberately in the ashtray. 'I'd like to give Brad the opportunity to tell Theo himself. I'd like to give him a day to decide.'

McCann looked at her and his heart went out to her. Her expression was flat and impassive. The tears that rolled down her cheeks were the only sign of her desolation. She certainly had guts. And what she'd suggested seemed fair, to her anyway. It put off the moment she dreaded, and she'd suffered enough over the past months. Possibly it wasn't fair to Theo. He deserved to know at once. And no one deserved a son like Bradley.

'Do you want me to pack in my investigations?'

Rosalind looked up, taken by surprise. 'Why would you say that?'

'Venice Messon killed your father. Not Tran Van Luc, Greville, Trevor, nor Brokov. Venice is dead. There's nothing I can do to hurt Tran, short of assisting the police to build murder charges against him, and hoping that somehow he'll be extradited to face trial. There's more than a fair chance that the net Task Force Lotus has woven may be closing around him as we speak. But I really can't see any point in digging into Venice Messon's private life any further in a search for her private motives for killing Tran. Can you?'

'We've come this far, Leo. I have to know. I always did. It may seem ridiculously inconsequential to you, but to me it's vital to my being. Maybe I've become as obsessive as she was, I don't know. It's similar to the pain a mother feels when a child disappears. It's almost a relief when they find the body. Perhaps you're tired of it all. Perhaps you think it's time to back off and let the authorities back home get on with it.'

McCann put an arm round her shoulder, hugging her to his side. 'It seems to me I've only just got here, so I may as well continue for a while. So, if I'm still on the payroll, I'd better be on my way. I'd ask you to join me, but I've an appointment with a man who runs a cat-house up in the old quarter, and that's hardly your speed. The other contact runs what Milo Ganzini in Ho Chi Minh City referred to as 'a drug club'. After those two stops, who knows?'

'Sounds like a generous slice of life to me. I think I'll join you,' she said, taking a couple of deep breaths. 'Besides, I can't just sit in a hotel room while I give Brad the chance to do the right thing. I've got to keep busy.'

McCann was glad. He'd missed her, and though the next few hours was hardly going to be an evening at the theatre followed by dinner at Sardi's, he felt he could look after her. She had more than her share of courage. She deserved a little moral support. If she wanted to tag along, so be it. Provided the *Tinh Bao* continued to hang back and be content to watch as they'd done up to now, all would be well.

She looked at her watch. 'It's not even eight o'clock! Too early to go clubbing. Let's go eat. Any ideas?'

'None whatsoever. Hanoi is uncharted territory. As long as it's Vietnamese, I couldn't give a damn.

The air was still, hot and humid, scented with jasmine, cigarettes, soup and petrol. They rode in two cyclos, side by side. Rosalind sat back in her seat inhaling the night air, staring at the architectural legacy of French colonial rule; the second floor wrought iron balconies, the shuttered windows, the muted ochres and creams of the houses. A double cyclo followed behind at a discreet distance, the two young short-sleeved Vietnamese squeezed together in the wider seat.

The narrow streets were buzzing with motorized bicycles, pedal bikes, and the occasional Vespa scooter. The boulevards were crowded with happy Vietnamese. Women, young and old, squatted beside mounds of dried fish, baguettes, and sweetmeats. Old men played mah-jong in the narrow cafés. Children ran in and out of the shops, their eyes wide with excitement, every now and then catching sight of westerners and calling out a greeting, their smiles wide as the Red River.

The two cyclos threaded their way through the labyrinth of streets, past lottery vendors, women sitting beside rattan baskets of spinach and fresh tiger-lily buds, spice merchants and pavement kitchens.

'Leo! Over there!' Rosalind called out at him, pointing to a small restaurant that wouldn't have been out of place in the Boulevard St Michel in Paris. She turned to her driver, indicating the café.

The ambience of the place and the friendliness of the staff were a good deal better than the food. The chicken was stringy and covered with the ubiquitous overpoweringly pungent fish sauce.

Though Rosalind made a good fist of putting New York behind her for twenty-four hours, it was apparent to McCann that she was fighting a losing battle.

'Are those the security guys who've been following you?' she asked.

McCann followed her brief glance through the glass of the French doors. Outside, across the street, the two *Tinh Bao* youths were sitting on onion boxes at a low table under a flame tree, their faces highlighted by a hurricane lamp. They were eating bowls of rice and what at a distance looked like jumbo prawns. Either the Vietnamese Secret Service had deep pockets, or the local vendors were circumspect enough to provide them with free food.

'Yes, that's them. Sometimes I wonder if I'm being paranoid. It could be they've got nothing to do with Tran. Look at it this way, a few years ago in Moscow you might have been followed by the KGB, but that wouldn't have meant Beria or his modern equivalent had ordered it personally.'

'Has it ever occurred to you that they hope *you're* leading *them* somewhere?'

'You mean if it is actually Tran that asked them to tail me.'

'Yes.'

'Where could I be leading them? What could I know that Tran doesn't already?'

A smiling waitress approached the table and began to clear away the dishes. McCann ordered two green teas.

'How far is the My Guy Club?'

'We passed it on the way here. About a hundred yards back on the right.'

As they left the small restaurant, their two cyclo drivers appeared, as if by magic. McCann tried in vain to explain the proximity of their destination, but both Vietnamese affected incomprehension, smiling broadly and gesturing to the cyclos as they bowed and nodded.

Rosalind laughed. McCann was relieved. 'I wonder if there's any chance of us ever being able to just take a walk in this town?' he said, laughing with her.

'Forget it, McCann,' she replied stepping up into her cyclo.

'Maybe we could pay them to follow us. Pedal at a discreet distance?'

McCann held up the address of the My Guy and the driver nodded his head in recognition. Across the road, the two young Vietnamese put their rice bowls aside and stood.

If the My Guy Club in Bat Dan Street was a bordello, it certainly didn't look it. It seemed exactly like any of the other tourist bars in the busy street. A beaten copper bar stood to one side of the room; wooden tables, Bentwood chairs and a small dance floor occupied the rest of the space. There was no evidence of girls in short skirts and low-fronted tops. Instead, the clientèle was a mixture of men and women of all ages, both European and Asian.

A slim middle-aged woman in a turquoise sheath dress showed them to a table, pointing to the extensive list of exotic cocktails at the foot of the menu. Her movements were a mime signifying she spoke no foreign languages. She clearly assumed few westerners spoke hers. McCann ordered two beers. A look of disappointment clouded the waitress's face. Cheap beers – no expensive cocktails.

'Who do we know here?' said Rosalind.

'No one. Croft merely said this was the last place that Venice had been sighted before she vanished.'

'Probably worked here,' Rosalind replied, then gestured with her eyes over McCann's shoulder towards the door.

The *Tinh Bao* pair had just entered. One stared very deliberately at Rosalind, then smiled at her. The other stepped up to the bar, ordering drinks.

'One of your boys is getting a mite fresh,' she said.

'Ignore them. They're trying to pull your chain.'

'Is that so, Mr. McCann? I hadn't considered that possibility.'

As the middle-aged woman returned with the beers, McCann pulled the snapshot of Venice Messon from his inside pocket and held it up for her.

'Do you remember this girl?' he asked very slowly.

The woman screwed up her eyes, then shook her head. McCann was about to take the photo back when she pointed towards a tall thickset Vietnamese tending the bar. She then made a gesture, raised her plucked eyebrows, and seemed to be asking permission to take the photograph to her friend. McCann handed her the snapshot.

McCann could see the barman study the photo. He then whispered to the woman, at the same time glancing furtively towards the two young *Tinh Bao* boys. His hand was on the bar-flap, about to lift it, when one of the boys snapped his fingers at the man and barked something aggressively in Vietnamese. The barman stopped dead in his tracks and dropped the bar-flap as he met the young man's gaze. The one who'd snapped his fingers beckoned the barman in a gesture of arrogance. He then snatched the photo, studying it closely, questioning the barman in short aggressive sentences. McCann could see the older man was clearly intimidated by the two boys. He held his head low in a submissive fashion as he answered their questions. Finally, one of the two waved him away in a dismissive way as the other directed him towards McCann.

The two *Tinh Bao* boys watched with interest as the barman approached McCann and Rosalind. The aggressive youth had his chin tucked into his chest, his eyes wide and hostile. His partner leant casually on the bar-top, sipping a beer and smirking as he stared at Rosalind.

'We do not know this woman,' the barman said, as he dropped the photo of Venice Messon next to McCann's beer. He was sweating.

'She was here?' McCann replied holding the barman's stare.

'I know nothing,' the barman repeated, a look in his eyes that pleaded with McCann to drop the questions.

'Her name was Venice Messon. Where did she go?'

'I cannot help you. This is a bad thing. You make me big trouble. Please to go now. I ask you, please?'

'We'd better leave,' McCann said to Rosalind. 'There's nothing to be gained asking this man anything more.' He then stood, pulling a twenty-dollar bill from his wallet and placing it under his glass. It was three times the cost of the drinks, but would maybe make up for the incident. Rosalind pushed her beer into the center of the table, then rose. 'Can you give me a name?' McCann continued in a low tone to the barman, whilst looking at Rosalind, at the same time slipping his wallet into his back pocket. It wouldn't have been possible for the two at the bar to have heard the words, nor seen his lips move. As McCann passed the barman, he heard him whisper back, 'Sammi Chung. Please leave!'

The Green Parasol of the Universe was a small bohemian café halfway down Hang Ga Street. As he parted the heavy green brocade curtains, McCann was reminded of his favorite Montmartre haunt, Le Bouffon, on Rue Lepic just below the Sacre Coeur.

The air was so thick with smoke, the interior looked like an impressionist painting. Smudged human shapes sat at low tables; their shadows cast on the walls by candles stuck to wooden cups hanging from the ceiling just above head height.

As they stood inside the door, acclimatizing to the light, a door at the rear of the room opened and a small Chinese stepped through.

'How may I be of service?' the Chinese said softly, with the utmost grace. 'This house is not tourist house. I am so sorry.'

'Please, is Mr. Vargas here tonight? Milo Ganzini sent me.'

The name had a therapeutic effect on the man. 'Please wait one moment, thank you sir,' he replied, then turned and walked back through the rear door.

They took in their surroundings while they waited for the old man to return. There was no evidence of mainline drugs, just Vietnamese and Chinese men lounging on richly decorated Persian rugs by low tables. There were no women. Most of the men were simply chatting in low tones as they drank rice wine and played cards or mah-jongg. In the center of the closest table a Siamese cat was curled up in a large bowl, nestled among a selection of fruit. Tables set against the walls were laden with small esoteric Indochinese collectibles; vases of pale pink lotus blossoms, vine root carvings, and small stuffed birds. The framed artwork on the walls was of such a profusion that scarcely more than a few inches of the wallpaper were visible anywhere.

A minute had elapsed when the rear door opened once more and the Chinese beckoned McCann and Rosalind to follow him.

The narrow corridor led to a narrow flight of steps, at the top of which was a landing. The Chinese knocked lightly on some sandalwood doors, then opened them inwards, stepping politely to one side to allow Rosalind and McCann to pass through into the room.

As they entered, a robust man pushed himself out of a winged chair and stepped forward to greet them.

'Hi. I'm Tony Vargos. Mr. Kwok informs me you're a buddy of Milo's. That right?'

McCann shook his hand. 'That's right. This is Rosalind Buchanan. I'm Leo McCann. Thank you for sparing the time.'

In stark contrast to the downstairs room, this one was as comfy and cozy as a professor's study. All the furniture was thoroughly western, from the standard lamps to the sofas and chairs. To one side of the winged chair was a butler's table crammed with bottles of liquor.

'What can I get you?' Vargos asked affably. 'Make yourselves comfortable. How's Milo? Quite a character, eh?'

Rosalind and McCann stuck to beer while Vargos poured himself a Bourbon.

'He's well and happy. Needs to slow down though.'

Vargos chuckled. 'That's Grinna. Never could relax. Did he tell you we made two tours together?'

'He said you were close, yes,' McCann lied, it was probably a good move to soft soap the man until he could judge him better.

'I used to fly the old C-141's in and out of Saigon from Sydney, the Black Flights. Remember the Starlifter? It was one hell of a big mother. Grinna was the mechanic. You heard of the black flights?'

McCann shook his head.

'We carried body bags. Hundreds of 'em. There was this cold storage depot outside of Saigon someplace. All KIA's were transported down to Saigon for the trip back

Stateside. Policy was to send the bags back in a steady stream; not too many, not too few, just the right amount. That way it never looked as if we'd encountered a major set-back.'

'What about major casualties - there must have been times…?'

'They shipped the overage to Sydney. Kept the guys in cold storage, then eased them home from there, piecemeal. No one knew. Well, that's not strictly true, a few journos did; but it never was common knowledge. Brought back a mess of black market stuff each time; booze, electrical, hash, dew, clothes, soap – anything and everything. Someone was making a fortune and it sure wasn't Grinna and me.'

Vargos settled back into the wing chair evaluating McCann briefly, then resting his eyes on Rosalind. 'So – what can I do for you both?'

McCann pulled out the photo of Venice and passed it over to Vargos, who had to tear his eyes from Rosalind to concentrate on the snap. 'We were just in a place called the My Guy.'

Vargos smiled thinly, never taking his eyes off the photo. 'This girl work there?'

'Maybe once. She's dead.'

'I'm sorry to hear it,' Vargos replied casually, offering the photo back to McCann.

'Is the face familiar, Mr. Vargos?' Rosalind asked.

'Yes. But I never knew the girl personally.'

'You knew who she was?'

Vargos ignored her, switching his attention to McCann. 'You know you've got spooks in tow downstairs, don't you?'

'Yes,' McCann replied

'Don't worry. They'll stay outside. Their bosses are in the library on the second floor, and they don't like surprises.' His attention drifted back to Rosie. 'You smoke opium, Miss Rosie?'

'Never tried,' she replied diplomatically.

'Care to sample one of my hand-rolled O-J's? Marijuana soaked in opium solution. Very sweet and mellow. Only thing between me and madness in '72.' His right hand hovered over a carved wood box on the table beside him.

'Maybe another time,' she smiled back.

'Leo?'

'Thanks, but no thanks.'

Vargos shrugged, his hand reaching inside the box for a perfectly rolled joint. He struck a match and inhaled deeply.

'Did you know of her connection with Tran Van Luc?' McCann ventured after a few moments silence.

McCann could see Vargos debating whether to reply. The fat man closed his eyes for a brief moment, then stared at the ceiling as he drew on the slim cigarette. 'Sure, I knew. Everyone did.'

'The girl in the photograph was his girlfriend.' Rosalind interposed.

Vargas's eyes flicked down from the ceiling to stare at her in amusement. 'Not exactly,' he replied ambiguously.

'What do you mean by that, Mr. Vargos?' she probed.

'Tony. Please,' Vargos chided with a lascivious smirk. 'But before I continue this wonderful conversation, let me say just one thing. Mr. Tran Van Luc is a very influential man in this neck of the woods. I would walk a long way before I would put a man of his authority offside. It just wouldn't be the smartest thing in the world to do. Now, he may not care for me to discuss his personal affairs with strangers, bearing in mind we've only just met. No offence, Leo, but I have a business to run. Do you follow me?'

McCann nodded. 'Does the name Sammy Chung mean anything to you? You know him?'

'Her. She's a *her*, not a *him*,' he replied laughing. 'Used to work at the My Guy. Retired now. An angry young buck threw acid in her face a few months back. Maybe you'd be better off quizzing Sammi.'

'You have an address for her?'

'Sure do. But I wouldn't show up on her doorstep with the spooks on your heels. They have a thing about Sammi. Never saw eye to eye.' He chuckled again to himself as he sipped his bourbon. 'Yeah, why don't you go speak to Sammi. Tell her I sent you. You might like to give her a few dollars, she could use the help.'

'Any way you can help us lose the spooks?' McCann knew it was probably pushing Vargos a bit too far, but it was worth a shot. Vargos drew on the last of his O-J then stubbed it out.

'Hell, why not,' he replied with a grin.

Vargos and his offsider Mr. Kwok led the way down another long corridor and through a small door that connected the house they'd originally entered to an equally large house at the back of it. They then descended two flights of stairs.

'Mr. Kwok will take you to Sammi. You'd never find it yourself. I have to get back,' Vargas said, as he shook McCann's hand. He kissed Rosalind on the cheek with surprisingly propriety.

'I've told Kwok to take you directly home if the spooks attach themselves before you get there – it's only fair to Sammi, she's had enough problems to last her a lifetime.'

McCann held out a sealed envelope in which he'd placed five hundred dollars at the hotel for just such an eventuality. Vargas looked taken by surprise.

'What's this,' he asked, confused.

'A present. Just to thank you for your hospitality.'

Vargas waved the money away. 'Don't be ridiculous, I'm glad to help. Wouldn't dream of it,' he said pleasantly.

'Please,' McCann insisted. Ganzini's caution was at the forefront of his mind.

Vargas shrugged and took the envelope. 'Sure, if it makes you happy. Thanks. Come and see me again if there's anything I can do for you in town. I can usually fix most problems.'

'I'm sure you can, Tony,' Rosalind said with a winning smile.

'Rosie, *you* can come by *any* time,' Vargas replied theatrically.

They followed Kwok through a rabbit warren of corridors and passages until they passed through an archway into an ill-lit back alley. Two old men sat on the red earth playing Chinese checkers on a board scratched into the earth, cigarette butts substituted for the pieces.

At the top of Hang Ga Street they passed under a railway bridge, heading northeast for a few hundred yards. McCann kept a constant watch behind him, as did Kwok, but there was no sign of the *Tinh Bao*. It was now just before midnight, yet the small tree-shrouded streets were still busy. The pavement bars were still doing brisk business.

'Why do you think Vargas was so cagey about Venice Messon?'

'He's caught between trying to do his buddy Ganzini a favor, and pissing off Tran. So he's keeping schtumm personally, yet pointing us in the right direction. That'd be my guess.'

'How much did I give him?' Rosalind said archly.

'Five hundred. It was Ganzini's advice. Said if it was for free, Vargas'd sell us out.'

'Hey, five hundred seems fine with me,' she continued playfully. 'Just like to know what I'm spending. Makes it more fun.'

As they turned left into Hang Than Street, three small children ran up to them, two girls and a boy. They were laughing and giggling, trying to catch Rosalind's hand. When she realized the nature of the game, she held them both out to the little boy, and he caught hold, squeezing them tightly. Kwok winked at the children, handing out some barley sugar sweets that he pulled from the pocket of his baggy trousers. The eldest girl looked about eight. She was carrying a tiny baby in her arms.

'They ask if you are American,' Kwok said.

'Can you please tell them I'm Australian, Mr. Kwok?' she replied. She now had the boy by one hand and the youngest girl by the other. Both were skipping along beside her, laughing their heads off, their mouths full of sweets. The eight-year-old girl and her tiny charge skipped beside McCann, cradling the baby's head carefully with both hands.

They passed the Dong Xuan Market, which three hours ago had been crowded with shoppers, monkeys, mynah birds, potted plants, spices, medicines and snake spirits. Kwok abruptly halted, pointing to an upstairs window. The children stared upwards at the light.

'Please to remain here. I will see if Miss Sammi at home. I explain to her.'

Kwok disappeared down a narrow alleyway at the side of the wooden building, leaving Rosalind and McCann standing on the pavement hand in hand with the children. They all gazed upwards; open-mouthed and expectant, as if Michael Jackson might appear on the balcony.

Two minutes later Kwok returned, glancing up and down the street for unwanted company.

'You come now with me, see Miss Sammi? Then I leave. This okay?'

'This okay,' McCann replied, handing a few dollars to each of the children. Only the eldest seemed to appreciate the money. The little boy and girl had shown more enthusiasm for Kwok's sweets.

Rosalind looked briefly back over her shoulder as she walked down the alleyway to Sammi's house. The children were standing where they'd left them; the eldest was staring at the money McCann had given her, the other two looked somewhat forlorn, as though a good game had come to an end.

Kwok pointed to some exterior wooden steps that ran up to the first floor.

'Miss Sammi is second door. Please, I leave you here. Thank you.'

McCann shook the old man's hand warmly, surreptitiously slipping a twenty into his side pocket as he turned to leave, just in case the old man was too proud to accept the money face to face.

The upstairs verandah was crammed with potted palms of every description, most in urgent need of re-potting. The first door was painted black and nailed shut. The second showed a little light under the bottom edge. McCann knocked lightly.

The door opened, and a young woman stood in the doorway, silhouetted by a bare light bulb that hung from the center of the room. Her black hair fell straight to her wide shoulders. Though her features were indistinct, at first sight she looked Chinese, slim-waisted and around thirty.

'*Moi vao*,' she said motioning them inside with a graceful sweep of her arm.

The room was sparsely furnished. A low table stood in the center; two small cushions either side. In one corner was a dark wood futon bed frame with a mattress less than two inches in thickness. Beside it was a thick white candle in which several scented sticks had been stabbed. Under the small window was an altar. In the center stood a Buddha, a burning candle either side. A china bowl of cooked rice and fish had been placed in front as an offering. Beside the door was a pitcher of water standing in a wide bowl, a white cloth draped neatly over the side. Next to this was a mini propane burner on which was balanced a small enamelled kettle. There was no evidence of a kitchen.

'*Ten toi la Sammi. Ten ba la gi?*' she asked Rosalind, as she knelt down beside the low table.

'My name is Rosie, and this is Leo,' Rosalind replied. 'I'm afraid we don't speak Vietnamese.'

'I did not really expect that you would, but it is so insulting to assume these things, don't you think?' Sammi replied with a smile. 'You're friends of Tony Vargos?'

'We met him only this evening. He said you might be able to help us,' Rosalind replied.

'Tony has a good heart. He has his dark side, as do we all I think. But he's always been a good friend to me,' Sammi replied. 'May I offer you some green tea?'

'Thank you,' Rosalind replied.

As Sammi rose, the shadow that had cloaked her features fell from her face. The entire right hand side, including the side of her nose and lips was white scar tissue. The left-hand side was quite extraordinarily beautiful.

'What kind of help do you need, Rosie?' she said, as she filled the small kettle from the pitcher of water.

'Tony suggested you were a close friend of Venice Messon,' said Rosalind.

Sammi looked up sharply, then quickly composed herself and continued making tea. 'Yes, I knew her. Ven was my very good friend. She was a sister and a mother to me, though she was just a child.'

'Do you mind talking to us about Venice?' Rosalind asked.

Sammi poured the water into a metal teapot, stirred the contents once, then placed the spoon beside the kettle. 'No I don't mind,' she said with more than a hint of emotion that indicated she minded very much.

'Tony told me how she died' she continued. 'Can you tell me what interest you have in Venice?'

'I am a friend of Venice's father,' McCann said. 'Rosie's own father died in the explosion. We don't believe Venice meant to kill him. We think he just happened to be in the wrong place at the wrong time.'

'Karma,' she whispered to herself as she poured the tea into small cups and brought them across to the low table.

'Venice's father needs to know what drove her to end her life in that way,' Rosalind said. 'Also, I think it might in a strange way help me adjust to my father's death if I could begin to understand how she felt the day she died.'

Sammi picked up a cloth, reached up to the bare white globe and twisted it till the light was extinguished. She then sat, lighting the candle in the center of the table.

'I am sorry for your father.'

'You knew Venice from the My Guy Club? She worked there?' McCann asked.

'She was a prisoner there,' Sammi replied simply.

'Who kept her prisoner?'

Sammi looked up from the candle, leaning her head on her right shoulder as if to mask the scars. 'Perhaps I should tell you in my own way. You will have so many questions, and I will answer as many as I am able.'

She closed her eyes for a few moments and inhaled deeply, placing her hands, palm against palm before her.

'I was a bargirl at the My Guy. You may not have seen the rooms. It is a club for *our* people, not tourists. One day they brought her in. She had been drugged. He locked her in a room.'

'Who?'

'Kien Khanh. You do not know him. He was my boyfriend once. He is dead now.'

She looked into the flame of the candle. The images were clearly indelible.

'I asked him who she was, and why he had locked her in the room. He replied that he had orders to keep her safe. She was Tran Van Luc's woman.' She looked up at McCann. 'You know of this man?'

'I do, yes.'

'He is the most depraved man I have ever known. His cruelty is unmeasured. When I heard she had died, yet he still lived, I cried for two days.'

'You knew that she intended to kill him?' said Rosalind quietly.

Sammi hesitated, averting her eyes from Rosalind's. Then she continued. 'I could tell you no, but I would be lying. Yes, I knew she meant to kill him. I did not know how.'

'But you do know why?'

'She loved him very deeply. He rejected her.'

'That is no reason to kill,' Rosalind replied. McCann could see Sammi's easy answer had wounded her.

'They met in Australia. At a recital, she once told me. He must have seen her and wanted her. Few of his desires are left unfulfilled. He is undoubtedly a fine looking man. And so very charming when he wishes. But it is all a mask to hide his depravity. He has the heart of a wolf. He wanted her, so he seduced her and took her. She was an easy prey. An innocent.'

'She told no one of the affair – not her father, nor her friends. Can you think why?' McCann asked.

'I knew her a short time, but I came to know her as a very private woman. Her feelings were her own.'

She lit a joss stick, pressing it into the wax of the candle.

'She came to Vietnam and he rejected her? If that's what happened, why would he keep her a prisoner?' McCann asked. He could see by the look in Sammi's eyes that she was being less than frank. There was something she was holding back.

'He was angry. She had visited his house unannounced and shamed him before his people. He wished to punish her,' she replied, staring at McCann, willing him to believe her. 'I cannot tell you more,' she continued vehemently, 'I cannot step into his mind.'

'How long was she a prisoner?' Rosalind asked in a soothing voice.

'For four months.'

'And there was never an opportunity to escape? In all that time? She couldn't use a telephone?'

'She was locked in a room. Kien Khanh feared very much that she would escape, and he would have to answer to Tran Van Luc. So he fed her opium in her food. She spent her days and nights in a dream world. I would feed her and talk to her. I did not know of the drugs in her food. I thought merely that she was ill. Khanh began to spend more and more time with her. He no longer wished to touch me. I could see he wanted her too, but she was Tran Van Luc's woman.'

'Did Tran visit her?'

'Only once.'

'When was that?'

'Two days before she escaped. I had been in Bac Ninh visiting my brother. When I returned she was unconscious. Khanh was asleep. He had injected her with pure heroin to keep her quiet. It was his karma that Tran Van Luc chose that day to visit his woman. When he saw what Khanh had done, he cut his throat as he slept.'

'Did he take Venice with him?'

'No. He felt no compassion for Venice; she was merely his prisoner. He was angry with Khanh - the injection could have killed her. He had disobeyed – that was all. He was to have kept her safe. Tran Van Luc left her locked in the room and gave me the key. He said he would return to take her elsewhere. I knew I could not allow that. So when he had left, we planned her escape.'

'We?' Rosalind interjected. 'Did others help you?'

Sammi looked momentarily flustered. Then she rose from her cushion, walked towards the altar and stared up at the small bronze Buddha.

'Are you afraid of Tran, Sammi?' McCann said softly.

'I am afraid of nothing now. But before, yes, I was full of fear.' She turned to face them. 'When Tran Van Luc discovered that Venice had gone, he came here to my house. I had returned briefly for my possessions. I was to join Venice. He told me I had betrayed him by helping his woman to escape him. He said I had taken a special thing from him, so he would take from me the thing I valued most. He held me down and poured acid onto my cheek.'

In the soft light of the altar candles McCann could see her eyes ablaze with a primal hatred. She'd said she was afraid of nothing now, and he believed her.

'There's more, isn't there,' McCann said softly.

She turned and walked slowly back to the table, kneeling again. The anger had drained from her face, replaced by a weary resignation. 'Yes, there is more.'

'Can you tell us?'

'There are things I have kept from you, you are right. I swore an oath to Venice that I would never talk of her secret. I cannot break my word.'

They sat in silence for a long while.

'Do you know of the Dong Xuan Market?' Sammi asked.

'We passed it tonight.'

'There is a medicine shop at the far end. Come tomorrow at nine o'clock. Make sure you come alone. I cannot tell you what you wish to know, but I may perhaps show you.'

'Thank you, Sammi. I would be so grateful. You must excuse us for disturbing the peace and tranquility of your evening.'

'You are friends of Venice's family, that is enough for me to know.'

Rosalind held out a hand across the table to Sammi, who took it in both of hers and held it.

The streets were quiet as they walked back through the deserted old quarter in the general direction of the hotel. Unlike Ho Chi Minh City, Hanoi slept at night. A fine misty rain had begun to fall, giving Rosalind and McCann some relief from the oppressive heat. Even past midnight it was in the mid seventies – but it was the humidity that was the killer.

The meeting with Sammi Chung had been a revelation, yet little of her story made sense. Venice had traveled to Hanoi to see Tran. He'd clearly been severely embarrassed by the appearance of a teenage girl on his doorstep, professing undying love. It certainly painted a picture of a considerably more naïve Venice Messon than McCann had initially imagined. She was a bright young girl. Could she really have believed that a man of Tran Van Luc's age and position would have welcomed her with open arms?

But if Tran, angry and humiliated in the face of his friends, had simply rejected her out of hand, why had he arranged for her kidnapping and imprisonment? Why had he not simply arranged with his secret police friends to have her deported at once, never to return? That would have been a swift resolution to his problem. So what point was there in keeping her prisoner? A punishment? It seemed almost medieval. From what Sammi had said, Tran no longer had the slightest interest in her sexually.

Yes, there is more, Sammi had said. Throughout their conversation Rosalind and McCann had both felt her reticence. Rosalind was adamant the reason was simply as Sammi had stated - that she'd given her word to Venice to keep her secret, and she could not break her word. The fact that she was prepared to find other ways of pointing them towards the answer only demonstrated her wish to help.

Croft's source had confided that the *Tinh Bao* knew of Venice's presence at the My Guy Club. If that was so, it suggested a connivance between Tran and the *Tinh Bao* – they must have known she was a prisoner and sanctioned it. That gave the entire abduction an official rather than a personal flavor.

So what was Venice Messon's secret? Was it something that she knew, something so vital that Tran was prepared to keep her locked away for an unlimited period? Why not simply kill her?

At the intersection of Hang Chieu and Hang Duong, they spotted a cyclo driver draped over the seat. In his arms he cuddled a bantam chicken. Both were fast asleep. Rosalind stood by the pedal bike and clicked her tongue. The chicken's eyes blinked open. Startled, it began to struggle. Within seconds the driver was awake and negotiating the price of the trip to the Pullman Metropole. Glad of the fare, he sang a succession of Vietnamese peasant songs as he pedaled them through the drizzle back to the hotel.

Because it was a single cyclo, Rosalind was obliged to sit in McCann's lap, her arm round his neck. It was the best bicycle ride of McCann's life.

Two very sour-faced young Vietnamese sat on the low wall beside the entrance. The taller of the two *Tinh Bao* men stared aggressively at McCann as he and Rosalind walked up the steps. McCann looked straight ahead, the last thing he needed now was a confrontation.

They collected their keys from reception and walked to the elevators, arranging to meet at seven-thirty for breakfast before leaving for the Dong Xuan market. Sometime before then McCann would have to construct a way of losing the two shadows outside.

McCann barely had time to pour himself a Scotch before the phone in his room rang. It was Rosalind. She was sobbing and could not form words coherently at first. A terrible wave of foreboding ran through McCann's body.

'Oh God, Leo,' she said finally, her voice choked with emotion. 'They've shot Bradley.'

29.

24th May.

McCann looked at his watch. It was six-thirty and he could hear the traffic already beginning to build up in the street. The first light of dawn was visible through a small gap in the curtains. Rosalind was in the bathroom, packing her toiletries.

The night had been spent on the telephone in Rosalind's suite. It had been Ian McKintosh who had left the initial message to call, and he who had broken the news to Rosalind. Bradley had been shot twice in the chest outside his apartment on Riverside at 8.30 a.m. New York time, 8.30 p.m. Hanoi time. It had been Theo who had rung McKintosh, desperate to reach Rosalind.

The facts were that a gunman had opened fire from a car as Bradley walked out the doors of the Crichton building. Due to concern for his son's safety – there had been a recent death threat reported by Bradley to his father – Bradley had been assigned an armed FBI detail. The FBI men had returned the fire, wounding the gunman and killing the driver, a woman. Bradley was in a critical condition at Mount Sinai. The gunman was at the Metropolitan Hospital with wounds to his arm and stomach. His condition was not life threatening. Both were under armed guard.

Rosalind called Theo immediately at the number he'd given McKintosh. She reached him at the Mount Sinai at 2.25 p.m. New York time. Bradley was out of the theatre, but was still listed as critical. The media had arrived in a feeding frenzy at Mount Sinai within minutes of the Crichton doorman's call to NBC with his scoop. The news of the shooting had then hit the TV network stations as the lead story around the country.

Theo sounded calm and in control, though Rosalind knew he'd be an emotional mess. Martha, Blanche and Conrad remained at Bradley's bedside in case he regained consciousness. Rosalind told Theo she'd be flying back as soon as was logistically possible. Then she called the Buchanan pilot, Jack Cousins, in his room down the hall, explaining the situation, and informing him they'd be leaving for New York as soon as he could arrange it. Cousins estimated a take-off time of around nine was achievable. He always made a point of refuelling on arrival for just such eventualities. He'd arrange a car to pick her up at 7.15 a.m. to take her to Noi Bai.

McCann kept her company all night as she made her calls. By the time he'd initially raced round to her room from his, she'd ceased crying. During the hours that followed she had kept her emotions in check and was in damage control. He'd watched her with admiration as she'd talked calmly and succinctly to Radcliffe Snr, McKintosh, and Cousins. At five she'd taken a shower and changed. Then she'd packed.

There was a knock on the door. A young waiter entered with a tray of juice, coffee and toast, which he put down on the coffee table beside McCann. As he left, Rosalind walked through from the bathroom.

'What are you going to tell Theo?' McCann asked, as he poured the coffee.

'Everything I know, of course. That was always my plan. Now it's made easier, in that I no longer have a moral choice.'

'Did Bradley tell his father? Did he lay it on the line? You spoke to Theo – what's your guess?'

'He said Brad had told him of the death threat, but Theo didn't go into any detail. There's no way he would have, on an open line to Vietnam. Maybe Brad didn't give him the full story, I don't know.' From the tone of her voice McCann judged that she feared he hadn't. 'I'll have to see when I get there.'

McCann offered her toast, but she shook her head. He could see her hands were trembling.

'Would you like me to come with you?' he asked. Though she was showing amazing emotional strength, he wondered just how much more she could take.

'Thanks, Leo. You're a wonderful friend, but I have to do this alone.' She noticed with embarrassment that he was watching her unsteady hand. She instantly cupped her coffee with both to reduce the shakes.

'Do you think it could have been Fischer?' asked Rosalind

'That arranged for someone to gun down Bradley? I'd have to say I don't think so. Logic's against it.'

'Against it?'

'You told me the last thing Fischer said to Bradley in the car was that if Bradley didn't tell him all he wanted to know, he was a dead man. That's right?'

'Yes, that's what he said. Brad refuses, so Fischer sends in a hit man. That's logical, isn't it?'

'Not in my book. If Bradley hadn't yet told Fischer what he wanted to know, the last thing Fischer would do is kill him. He'd find another way to squeeze the truth out of him.'

'Maybe he was plain angry.'

'Wiseguys get angry, not the men at the top. Business first, vengeance second.'

'So who tried to kill him?'

'Someone who wanted to make sure he said nothing to Fischer.'

'Tran?'

'Tran. Look at it this way. Suppose over the last few days Tran's been getting pressured from all sides. Now he sees no alternative to putting his finger personally in the dyke before the water pours through. Greville would have been the first to get on his back. He'd have told Tran that I'd spoken to Boydell before he was killed. He'd have said that I knew of the Greville, Sir Henry Trevor, Tran connection, and that I knew who was behind the Telok Anson affair. He'd know I could at any time make public the truth behind the refinancing of the petro plant with laundered funds.'

'Something you'd find very hard to prove.'

'True. I grant you that. But the reason I did my best to stir up Greville in Hong Kong was to goad Tran into making some irrational moves. That's why I bluffed that I had Horan's computer disks and Boydell's affidavits. Greville didn't buy the affidavit angle because he knew damned well there hadn't been time to take them legally – Bradley told him of the rendezvous as soon as I told you. But Tran was unsure about the existence of Horan's back-up disk, and the audiotape of the conversation on Lamma Island, so they searched my home and torched my boat as a warning to back off. When they saw I wasn't intimidated, they sent someone to kill me.'

'But why? Everything you learnt from Boydell would amount to hearsay. And as for Horan's disk, wouldn't Greville and Tran have been able to cover their tracks financially before you made the facts public?' argued Rosalind.

'They did just that. Searching my house for the back-up disk was insurance, just to buy time. Judging by Gerson's attitude when you saw him, it looks as though McKinley had already managed to convince the bank of Greville's probity. Tran sent in Brokov and his wife to take me out because he felt I was capable of stirring up more trouble.

'Within forty-eight hours he's proven right. He's informed by the *Tinh Bao* that I'm right here on his doorstep, and he's wondering what the hell's happening now? He's afraid to send in a hit team until he knows exactly what's going on. And all the while Tran knows Dieter Fischer and the Brighton Beach Russians are getting closer and closer to the truth of who masterminded the theft of the Moscow *Mafyia*'s millions, and he's bitterly regretting the rush of blood to the head that made him do it. Because, if they ever get wind of who is behind the heist and inform the Moscow banks, that's the end of the alliance for Tran - the end of his dream of a worldwide banking network.

'And with Bradley running scared, Tran knows the whole house of cards is teetering on the brink of collapse. Once Bradley starts talking, the media fall-out's going to be world-wide, inevitably involving Telok Anson, his tame Malaysian government cronies, and eventually culminating in the exposure of his corrupt association with the son of the next President of the United States.'

Rosalind said nothing, neither did she drink her coffee. The logic was compelling.

'You see, if my way of thinking is at all close to the mark, Bradley was seriously scared. He was caught between Fischer and the mob in New York, and another hard place – Tran in Vietnam. So he got word to Tran. He asked him for guidance, help, protection, anything. Tran do doubt told him to calm down, saying he'd fix things. But he knew then that Bradley was a gigantic liability. Tran tightened the screws, and Bradley's nerve broke. So Bradley had got to go. Tran knew it would mean the end of his American connection to the Oval Office, but it was too dangerous to do otherwise. Tran then ordered the hit.'

'But, reading between the lines, it looks as though Brad came clean to Theo, before he was shot.'

'Maybe he did. I hope so. But maybe he told him some story that made him smell sweet as a rose.'

He was about to continue, then thought better of it. It wasn't the best time to debate what might happen if Bradley didn't pull through. But the fact remained that if Bradley *hadn't* come clean, and he didn't pull through, it was going to be very hard fingering Tran with any crime at all. There was little or no direct proof; no direct evidential links to the deaths of Palmer, Imogen Whitehead, or Boydell. Tran had the convenient buffer of Trevor. Rosalind was right. All McCann had was just hearsay; such as Boydell's account of events recounted over a bowl of white noodles on Lamma Island. As long as Trevor, Greville and Tran remained calm and stood firm, unshaken in their commitment to each other, it would be difficult to nail any of them.

Brokov was the closest thing to a weak link. More than likely it was Brokov the FBI had under guard in the Metropolitan Hospital. He and the woman operated as a team. The driver had been a woman, but she was now dead. The Russian had tried to kill him on Lamma Island – he'd take pleasure in identifying Brokov if he lived long enough. If Brokov broke and named names, Trevor and Greville would be in deep trouble. From there it was a short step to drag Tran down. The question was, would Brokov live long enough to name names?

'The sad fact, Rosie, is that Tran's made damned sure we have no hard evidence. We still have to pin the tail on Tran. So where do we find the evidence?'

'We don't need evidence,' Rosalind said calmly.

McCann looked into her eyes, and knew they were thinking along the same lines. 'We tell the Russians who took their money?'

'Right. We let them tear each other's throats out like rabid dogs. Beat's the hell out of a judge and jury.'

It was the first time in many hours that he saw her smile.

Cousins called from the airport at five to seven. The slot time for the jet was 9.15 a.m. The limousine came ten minutes later. McCann walked Rosalind down to the lobby and out to the car. As the driver held open the door, she turned and hugged McCann. Then she stepped into the car and it threaded into the rush-hour traffic.

There'd been a changing of the guard as far as the two *Tinh Bao* men were concerned. The new pair was unmistakably internal security. The trademark short sleeved shirts, the arrogant stare. McCann wondered what they'd be like working undercover – the idea was laughable. The problem now was how to lose them, never an easy task in a country where Caucasians were few and far between.

As he re-entered the hotel, he saw one of the two men disappear round the side of the building, presumably to watch the back.

Up in his room, McCann dialed Torrance in Sydney, hoping the policeman would be at his desk. Maggie Blackwood answered. They exchanged a few pleasantries, then Torrance came on the line.

'Morning, Leo. Where are you? Still in Vietnam?'

'Hanoi. Look, we heard of Bradley Radcliffe's shooting late last night. Rosalind Buchanan just left for the States. I gather the FBI shot the gunman and he's still alive.'

'Correct,' replied Torrance. McCann was about to speak again when Torrance pre-empted him. 'I'm one step ahead of you. I wired Brokov's sheet to New York soon as I heard.'

'And?'

'It's him.'

'Will he live?'

'If they guard him properly. He's not going to die of his injuries.'

'They realize he'll be a target?'

'I've impressed that on them in the clearest possible terms.'

'Anything else I've missed since I've been away?'

'Russell Croaker put a twelve-gauge shotgun in his mouth last night at his house in Bowral. Loose lips at the

Independent Commission Against Corruption maybe. Things are heating up.'

The international lines out of Hanoi were jammed. It took McCann twenty minutes to get a line through to Scott Boesel at Task Force Lotus HQ in Sydney. When he did get through, it was Gordon Mascon, the CIA rep, who came on the line. McCann introduced himself. Mascon knew who he was immediately, though he'd been out when McCann had visited the Lotus HQ. Mascon asked how he could help, sensitive to the fact the line was unsecured, and that practically all international calls to Vietnam were rumored to be monitored.

'I need to reach someone urgently. I thought either you or Scott might be able to help me with a fax number.' If the CIA couldn't help him, no one could.

'We'll do what we can. What's the name? I'll take a look.'

'Fischer. Christian name is Dieter. Lives and works down at the beach in Brighton.' With any luck the Viet Interior Ministry monitoring staff wouldn't have the first idea that he was referring to. If they checked, they'd most probably come up empty-handed. The name would only ring Tran's alarm bells.

'Hold on. I'll check.'

The connection was so good, McCann could hear Mascon breathing, together with the clicking of his computer keys.

'There's a note here that says he can be reached at the Club Kreml in New York. I've never used the number, so I can't vouch for it. But try it, if it's urgent.'

'It is,' replied McCann.

Mascon ran through the digits twice. McCann copied them down on the pad next to the phone.

'Can I tell John or Scott why you called?'

'Not right now. Wish I could.'

'I understand,' replied Mascon.

McCann wished him well then hung up. He then sat at the small desk in his bedroom and composed a detailed single page fax. He addressed it to Dieter Fischer.

Fifteen minutes later McCann had changed from the khaki shirt and trousers he'd been wearing in the lobby earlier, into white linen slacks and a cotton shirt. A Panama hat he'd had sent up from the lobby shop and a pair of Ray-Bans completed the new outfit. Slipping his street map of Hanoi into his pocket, he closed the door of his room behind him and stepped into the corridor.

The fire stairs at the side of the building snaked down to a well between the hotel and the ballroom. McCann looked down from the corridor window. There was no evidence of a third man below in the well of the building. But once at ground level he'd still have to walk from the building into the street behind the hotel, and the second *Tinh Bao* man was bound to be stationed there.

As he looked down, he saw a small white truck back up towards the service doors that stood to the right of the stairwell.

Once he'd persuaded the fire door to open with a short sharp blow of his shoulder, McCann was down the stairs in twenty seconds and at ground level.

Just then the rear doors of the old white truck were flung open. A young man wearing a threadbare Yankees baseball cap stepped down from the cab and walked towards some very primitive hydraulic lifting gear that stood next to the truck. As McCann approached, the young man called out to him.

'Hello, man! You have Marlboro maybe?'

'Sorry,' replied McCann, smiling. 'Don't smoke.' What wouldn't he have done for a pack, though - Marlboro were solid gold currency in Hanoi. It was a mistake not to have carried them. The young man shrugged, grinned, pulled a butt-end from the pocket of his shorts and lit up. As he did so they were joined by two hotel employees, pushing a heavy metal cart filled with bed linen. The cart was attached to the hydraulic lifting gear and the contents emptied into the back of the truck. The hotel employees then walked the cart back inside.

McCann pointed to the truck, then towards the street. 'You go to Ba Dinh District maybe?' he asked.

The young Vietnamese laughed lightly. 'I go Hai Ba Trung,' he replied, gesturing with his thumb into the back of the truck. 'You want come? Five dollar taxi, heh?'

McCann smiled broadly, nodding his head. 'Sure. Five dollar.' He peeled off a five from his billfold, handing it to the young man. 'My woman no see me go,' he said, pointing up at a window several floors above, winking conspiratorially. The Vietnamese laughed loudly as the hotel men returned with more linen.

Five minutes later the truck swung out into Ngo Quyen Street with McCann among the linen.

To reach his rendezvous with Sammi, McCann needed to retrace his steps from the laundry in Hai Ba Trung, which was south of the city center on the banks of the Song Hong River, and head two miles north. He picked up a cyclo within seconds near the Dong Mac Gate, directing the puzzled driver west towards Lenin Park. He then pointed north past the eleventh century Temple of Literature on Pho Nguyen Tri Phuong. The driver nodded. It was only then that he gave the driver his final destination - the Dong Xuan market.

By the time McCann could see it up ahead, they'd executed the most circuitous route north imaginable, giving the widest possible berth to the Pullman Metropole.

As the cyclo began to slow, McCann passed the driver two fives. He then jumped lightly down into the street, immediately weaving in among the crowds that thronged the entrance to the market. He walked with head bent, shoulders rounded and a slight limp, his Panama hat pulled down over his brow. To the casual observer, here was a man of over sixty.

He passed a small pharmacy just inside the entrance. The shelves were crammed with bottles of herbs, alcoholic syrups, and bunches of dried snakes hanging from a hook. He let the momentum of the crowd carry him along into the maze of narrow alleyways.

The hot air was thick with the scent of spices, animals, freshly butchered meat, and body odor. The dirt underfoot was slippery with vegetable matter, water and rubbish from the day before. Racks of brightly colored clothes and shoes hung above the shoppers. Scooters were parked between the stalls, draped with bolts of cloth and second hand silk *ao dai*. An orange clad bonze walked by, deep in meditation, carrying a bowl of uncooked rice. A young girl looked up at McCann, grinning as she turned some small cookies on a griddle over a small open brazier.

Glancing at his watch, McCann saw he had just ten minutes to spare – time enough to find the medicine shop Sammi had mentioned, while making sure he was not being followed.

He limped into a space between a vegetable stall and a butcher's shop, looking back down the alley – to all intents and purposes an infirm old man catching his breath.

Pig's trotters, snouts and entrails were laid out on trestle tables to his left. He'd been taught by the best how to spot a tail. After ten minutes he was satisfied that there was none. He then looked in the opposite direction towards the back of the market where Sammi had told him the medicine shop was situated.

As the crowd wove in and out in front of him, he suddenly caught a fleeting glimpse of Sammi in the crowd, looking towards him. She didn't appear to recognize him - her expression didn't change. She looked to her left and right, then stepped into a doorway.

Pulling his Panama hat down, McCann rejoined the moving sea of market-goers and shuffled forwards.

The door of the shop was open. A sign above it read *Thuoc*, Vietnamese for 'medicine'. The only other indication that it was indeed a medicine shop was the multitude of small blue bottles in a window above and to the side of the door.

As he stepped inside, he immediately sighted Sammi standing at the rear of the shop beside a primitive counter. She turned her head towards him as he entered, looking straight past him – she still didn't recognize him. She was expecting Rosalind and McCann, not one old man. McCann shuffled up to her, lightly tapping her on the shoulder as he spoke.

'Sammi,' he whispered. 'It's me, Leo McCann.'

Sammi jumped backwards, then focused her eyes on McCann.

'Rosalind had to fly back to America,' McCann continued in a low voice. 'She had bad news. I'm alone.'

Sammi lifted her right hand slightly, looking over McCann's shoulder into the alley with an expression that seemed to beg a question of someone outside. McCann caught the look, and followed her eyes. An elderly man stared back at her from the hardware shop opposite, nodding his head.

'It's all right, Sammi. I've checked. I've not been followed,' said McCann.

'I know,' she replied, grasping McCann's wrist and pulling him towards the rear door of the shop.

As they hurried through a small door that led into the street, a young boy snatched the Panama hat from McCann's head and replaced it with a *non*, the conical woven straw hat all the locals wore. At the same time he draped a length of faded orange cloth round McCann's shoulders.

Outside, a fifteen-year-old ten tonne Soviet built Ywat truck blocked the street. The engine was throbbing, devoid of any cowling, the noise deafening. Up in the back, a man and two boys were tossing sacks of cassava and sapodilla fruit down to barrows assembled by traders under the tailgate.

'Please get in, hide yourself,' Sammi shouted, thrusting McCann forward. The man on the back held out a hand, pulling McCann up and inside.

The smell inside the rear of the Ywat behind the driver's cab was overpowering, a mixture of rotting banana, over-ripe mango, and putrid vegetables left over from a previous delivery. But the all-pervading stench was of gasoline and exhaust gases. McCann pressed himself into a corner between mounds of green bananas, bags of poppy seed, and neat stacks of *go lat*, a highly prized hardwood from the northwest. He squatted Vietnamese-style, the cloth wrapped around his body.

A few minutes later a voice in the street shouted something in Vietnamese, and the two children McCann had seen unloading the fruit jumped up into the vehicle with him. Then he was plunged into darkness as the canvas flap was pulled down and secured at the back. With a tortured scream of protest the gears were engaged, and the aged truck rolled slowly down the street, the two boys giggling in the darkness at the far end.

McCann remained where he was for more than an hour, until he judged they were well past the city limits and thundering down the main highway. Then he shifted his position and stretched his legs, searching for and finding a tear in the canvas so he could peer out.

There was no possible way to judge in which direction they were heading. The route out of the city had been a Chinese monkey-puzzle. He'd have to wait until Sammi saw fit to ask the driver to stop the truck and invite him into the cab with her – if she had chosen to come along herself.

The chartreuse paddy fields sparkled in the burning sun, stretching away across wide viridian valleys to the distant mesas topped every few miles by pagodas. Trucks and buses sounded their horns as they fought for prime position in the center of the road. Scooter drivers wove in and out of the mainstream traffic, their shock absorbers straining under the weight of perhaps three or more people or as many as fifty live ducks. It was a constant dice with death; it never showed on their faces.

Every five miles or so they passed through a small village. The trucks always maintained their speed. To brake was considered wasteful of fuel. Chickens, dogs and ducks ran for cover. Only the buffalo remained calm, wandering suicidally across the paths of the speeding metal beasts, refusing to acknowledge the supremacy of the automobile.

An hour and twenty minutes into the journey, the truck suddenly lurched to the side of the road and stopped. McCann could hear muffled voices inside the cab. A few moments later the canvas flap at the tail was lifted and he saw the friendly face of Sammi standing in the road, peering in at him. She was wearing course blue pajama-style peasant clothes, her hair tied back behind her head in a queue.

'We think it's safe now to ride up front with us. No one follow. You want?' she said, smiling. The two boys sitting on bags of poppy-seed laughed aloud. They understood English – they knew how bad the truck smelled.

'Yes, that'd be good. Thank you,' McCann replied gratefully, jumping down into the road.

'We are almost at Hai Duong. That is southeast of Hanoi, halfway to Hai Phong.'

'Is that our destination?'

'No. We go further. From Hai Phong we drive east then down to the Gulf of Tonkin.'

'Is this the way you brought Venice?'

Sammi nodded. 'I had no means to know when Tran Van Luc would come for Venice. So I had no time to plan things properly. I relied on the kindness of the family who had taken me in when my parents were killed in the war.'

'Where is our destination?'

'You will see. I cannot tell you. I promised I would never.' She smiled at McCann. 'You think I cheat a little? Maybe. I choose to do so for Venice's father. He has a right to know the truth.'

The truck driver and the two children returned from the tall grass on the far side of the ditch where they'd been peeing. The two boys scrambled back into the rear of the truck, pulling two large plastic containers of gasoline and a funnel to the edge of the tailgate. The driver filled the tank, then walked round to the driver's door. McCann joined Sammi in the cab.

'This is my friend Diem,' said Sammi, introducing the driver to McCann. The good-looking man smiled through brown broken teeth, nodding cheerfully.

'*Ten toi la Leo McCann*,' said McCann returning the driver's nod.

Sammi laughed. 'That's very good, Mr. McCann. I'm impressed.'

They thundered on along National Highway 5 for another hour and twenty minutes. Sammi pointed out the famous Tay Phuong Pagoda, three parallel single-level structures dating from the eighth century, built to resemble a buffalo. Just before 1.40 p.m. they hit the city traffic in the outskirts of Hai Phong.

'We must stop to make just one delivery,' Sammi said apologetically as the truck turned left off the main highway, passing the Hotel de Commerce, before drawing to a halt close to a small street market.

McCann walked down the roadway to the Cam River to stretch his legs and find a toilet. Behind him Diem and his sons unloaded the vegetables and fruit.

Where the hell was Sammi taking him? And what was waiting at the end of the rainbow, to make all this subterfuge necessary?

The great clock atop the Hai Phong Post Office told him it was 1.55 p.m. It would now be just before 2.00 a.m. in New York. Rosalind wouldn't be touching down in Los Angeles for another ten hours or so, and wouldn't reach New York till 6 p.m. tomorrow. He prayed that Bradley would survive. Rosie deserved a break. If he lived, she'd have the chance to make a rational unemotional decision to leave him. If he died, she might develop a romantic image of the man that he didn't deserve.

As he walked back up Hoang Dieu Street, he saw Sammi, Diem and the kids squatting beside the truck tucking into bowls of what looked like rice gruel. When she caught sight of McCann, she held one up to him. Despite the heat of the day, steam rose into the air.

'It is *chao thit*. Rice porridge with pork. Very tasty. Please try,' said Sammi, holding out a set of chopsticks to McCann.

In turn, McCann held out a plastic bag of beers and soft drinks he'd bought in a bar on the way back from the river. Sammi took a coke, as did the children. Diem took a large beer. They ate in silence. The food was simple yet delicious.

A quarter of an hour later they were back on the road, racing full-bore east towards Hon Gai. They crossed the Cam River, then turned south towards the ferry that took them across the mighty Red River just outside the city. They then continued southeast.

The landscape was now dry and more barren. On each side of the road the rice harvest was spread and raked out to dry in the fierce sun. The terracotta villages they passed became fewer and far between, as were the rice fields. In their place were groves of sapodilla trees, laden with fruit.

It was 3.50 p.m. when McCann saw Ha Long Bay for the first time. He'd been aware of Sammi looking in his direction at frequent intervals for a reaction.

The image of the bay through the strong heat-haze brought to mind the landscape of some strange planet. Across miles of salt pans were the bright clear emerald waters of the South China Sea; three thousand limestone islets rising almost vertically from its depths.

Sammi smiled as she saw the look of wonder on McCann's face. It was always the same for those who saw the miracle that was Ha Long Bay for the first time.

'Is this where you're taking me?' he asked.

'We are not there yet. Bai Chay is still twenty miles from here. We must first take the ferry at Phan Rang.'

Another half an hour. The hot wind continued to scream in through the open windows. It didn't appear to affect Sammi or Diem. McCann's face felt as though it had been sandblasted.

Ten minutes later Sammi pulled two cloths from her pocket, handing one to McCann.

'It is to protect against the salt. It will eat your skin,' she said tying the handkerchief over her nose and face. Diem had already pulled his neck-scarf up over his face. McCann could see the workers in the salt pans, covered from head to foot as they raked the salt. He fastened the neckerchief round his face. The relief was instant.

They followed the road towards the sea until nothing but a low wall separated them from the Gulf of Tonkin.

At 5.00 p.m. they entered Bai Chay. Diem pulled the truck off the road and rubbed his eyes with the heels of his hands.

'We get out here,' said Sammi.

'We've arrived?' asked McCann.

'Not quite.' She pointed to the far side of the road. A string of more than fifty brightly colored tourist boats were moored bows facing the sea wall. Moored beside the largest of these boats was a weather-beaten fishing barque. A Chinese fisherman was waving from the stern. 'That is my uncle Wing. He will be our captain.'

'We're going to take a ride to China?' McCann asked with a wry grin.

'We take a ride, but not to China.'

30.

Brighton Beach. Brooklyn.
New York.
24th May.

To say that Osip Shirayev was pleased would have been an understatement. If he'd been a man with an inclination towards dancing he would have been hoofing a polka in his nightclub. Instead he ate. Large amounts of Beluga caviar, thick slices of sourdough bread, and unsalted butter.

Dieter Fischer sat opposite his boss, watching the fat Russian with fascination. When would he stop this time? Two five hundred gram tins? Three? Perhaps he would witness a record - four.

'So what do you reckon, Dieter? You'd better tell me now, 'cos once I send it on to Moscow we're committed. We'd better be sure we got our facts straight. This is some heavy shit.'

'It fits with everything I've discovered till now; like the last piece of a jigsaw.'

'Yeah, but is that enough? If it's all true, and you're right, Khamovnikakh owes us big-time. But if we got this thing wrong, he and the Asian together – ?' The rest of the sentence was implied by his expression. 'What keeps bugging me is the fax didn't come from Radcliffe. He's the one running scared. So who the hell is this guy McCann? And why would he sign his fuckin' name anyway? In his place I'd have kept my identity under the soap. What's his angle, tell me that?'

'He's trying to get Radcliffe off the hook. He says he's working for the Buchanan woman.'

'He knows we didn't whack Radcliffe!' Shirayev spat out, along with well over five grams of sturgeon roe. 'He's trying to cause trouble maybe – you thought of that one?'

'Sure I have. You know I'm careful. It was the first thing that came to mind. But I've checked everything he said in the fax. I've had Walter on the case all day.'

Walter Hill was their man on Wall Street. It would be hard to find a smarter man when it came to unraveling financial daisy chains. 'He says it all adds up. All the names are linked, as are the companies and banks. The one hard place is the New World Hotel Group. There is no way to prove absolutely that it was the Asian's shell company. He's too clever.'

'He'll deny it. You know that,' Shirayev observed, well into his third tin of Beluga.

'He can deny it all he likes, but it's a financial smoking gun when you add up all the facts, then put them together with Bradley Radcliffe's confession.'

'But he hasn't fucking confessed to *us*,' Shirayev snapped.

'McCann says in the fax that he came clean to him. I tend to believe him.'

Fischer took a deep breath. Five minutes ago his boss had been one happy barrel of fat. Now he was getting cold feet. What did he want, a signed confession from the Asian? 'Walter says it figures, and he's one very cautious man. Let's put it this way. Constantin Khamovnikakh wants answers. You can give them to him. It's that simple.'

Shirayev unwound the tape of the fourth tin, easing up the lid with his thumb. He ran his tongue over his lips. The black eggs gleamed in the glow of the halogen light. He briefly looked around for the bread, realized he'd eaten it all, then returned his attention to the fish roe.

'Don't get me wrong, Dieter. I just got to make sure we got this thing figured right. See all the angles. Don't want it coming back and biting us.'

'One way or another, things won't be the same. If it's Tran Van Luc who's dipping his fingers, then there's going to be some major fall out – but not in our patch of blue. Look at it another way, the Asian would find it difficult to reach out this far, but we don't want to make Khamovnikakh mad. We need him.'

Shirayev paused from eating, putting the desert spoon down on the table.

'What does this guy want, for Christ's sake,' said Shirayev waving the fax. 'And what's the guy doing in Vietnam anyway? That's the Asian's territory.'

'All he wants out of it is for us to ease off Radcliffe and make sure the Asian doesn't whack the guy. That's what he says. He's got nothing to gain out of making trouble.

'He's got it in for Tran. That's what he's got to gain. Revenge.'

Fischer sat back. There was no answer to that one. Sure, it looked like the man McCann had it in for the Asian. But when did information ever come without strings? It was always someone with a grudge, or someone who wanted money. And despite a possible motive of revenge, all the information detailed in the fax had panned out. So why not simply pass it on to Moscow? The alternative was to do nothing, to sit on it. But if Khamovnikakh ever discovered they'd done so, when he'd put so much pressure on them to come up with the information, they were dead in the water.

Shirayev picked up the spoon once more, and began to make headway into the fourth tin, his fat lips smacking a counterpoint to the dance music which had begun to drift through the air ducts from the dance floor below.

'Okay. I say go with it. Make Constantin happy,' said Shirayev, scraping the last of the roe from the fourth tin whilst eyeing the fifth.

Valeriy Serov re-read the fax for perhaps the eighth time as he sat in an anteroom at the Ermitazh Bank, in Moscow, waiting to be called in to see Khamovnikakh. It had been sent him by Dieter Fischer less than an hour ago.

Serov's feelings were decidedly mixed. He was relieved at last to be able to provide answers to his boss - yet fearful as to the ramifications of the information. The details confirmed all his private suspicions, based on his own investigations around the world. For two days he had vacillated, debating whether to share his thoughts with Khamovnikakh. And now came the fax from Fischer. These details could not have come at a better time, or from a better source. No longer would he be obliged to point the finger at Tran Van Luc. That privilege would belong to Osip Shirayev.

The door to the *Vory's* office opened and Sergie Probin, the Russian banker's private secretary, stepped into the room. 'Mr. Khamovnikakh will see you now, Mr. Serov.'

Serov stood, taking a deep breath. No way would he have wished to be in the shoes of Tran Van Luc.

31.

Vinh Ha Long.
24th May.

The old barque punched its way through the slight chop out into the bay. Only the foremast was set, square-rigged. Sammi stood at the prow looking out to sea, McCann a pace behind her. The weather had taken a turn for the worse, the upside being the refreshing breeze that blew in their faces, bringing welcome relief from the sultry heat they had endured all day.

They were sailing due south.

'The name Ha Long means "Where the Dragon Descends to the Sea," ' said Sammi. 'According to a Chinese myth a dragon once came to Luc Hai Bay, literally the Azure Sea, and trod so heavily on the earth that he gouged out deep valleys with his feet and tail, crevasses that quickly filled with water when the great dragon plunged back into the sea. The peaks of the mountains were the only remaining visible land, and formed the islands you see today.'

'Is this the final stage of our journey,' asked McCann.

'We are an hour from home,' Sammi replied.

'Home? Your home?'

'It is Wing's home. Be patient, Mr. McCann, all your questions will be answered.'

She pointed to an islet to the right. 'On that island is the Dau Go Cave. It is cut by the elements into the Isle des Merveilles - the Island of Wonders. We have names for all the islands – the Islands of Buzzards, Monkeys, Toads. They consist mostly of dolomite and limestone.'

Wing stood at the wheel, a man after McCann's heart – not given to idle chatter while at sea.

They sailed on past Hon Ti Top Island then took a starboard course into a narrow fiord, the sheer limestone walls of the islands on both sides rising hundreds of feet above them. Every twenty minutes or so, they caught sight of other fishing boats heading out to sea. All recognized Wing's boat and waved cheerily as they passed.

A half-hour into the journey, Wing broke open a bottle of sweet rice wine. Sammi poured it into three earthenware mugs and gave one to McCann. Wing lifted his and toasted McCann. Ten minutes later they rounded a point and McCann could see a small island dead ahead. Small houses clung to the cliff top.

'This is my home,' Sammi said. 'I call Wing my uncle, but he is not exactly so. My parents died in the war. Wing took me in, and I came to live here. It was a sanctuary for me, so I knew it would be the same for Venice. No one would find her.'

'But wouldn't she have had to register? What of the *Ho Khau*?'

'We are all family here. Wing and his family have lived here for ten generations; since his ancestors fled the pirates of Macau in the mid eighteenth century.'

Wing let down the last remaining sail, and they drifted the final few yards to a wooden pontoon where three smaller fishing boats were moored. A woman of about fifty was waiting to welcome them. Her eyes sparkled through a mass of happy brown wrinkles.

'This is my aunt Mei-Li,' said Sammi as McCann stepped onto the pontoon. The woman bowed politely. Sammi then directed McCann towards the small village.

A steep flight of steps cut into the cliff face led upwards to the hilltop where twelve or so small stone and wood houses stood in a semi-circle facing the sea.

Two small children chased after a lean and hungry dog, a few old men sat on porches mending nets and smoking pipes. A young girl was tending a pot of stew.

'Venice and I lived in the house at the far end. I will show you,' Sammi said setting off down the street, greeting everyone as she passed them.

'She stayed here until she returned home to Australia?'

'Yes,' Sammi replied, opening the front door of the house she had indicated earlier.

'No one lives here at present. It is out of respect for Venice. She was much loved by us all.'

McCann entered the low-ceilinged house, walking to the rear of the single room and looking out of the small window towards the garden.

'May I ask you a question, Sammi?'

She nodded.

'Why did you ever leave here to work at a place such as the My Guy Club?'

'As a child I would look out to sea and wonder what was beyond. I was a romantic, I suppose. I was always curious as to what lay beyond the fiord, on the mainland. On my sixteenth birthday I determined to see for myself.'

'You traveled to Hanoi?'

'I did. And there met Kien Khanh. I fell in love. I had no concept of evil before I met him. I soon learnt. He made me please other men. I could not refuse. If I did, he would beat me. He told me if I attempted to leave him he would find me and kill me. Besides I had nowhere to run because I had told him of my sanctuary at Ha Long.'

'But when Tran Van Luc killed Kien, you were able to escape?'

'That is right. I could live again. And give a life to Venice. Only Kien knew of my home. That is why I brought her here. Many friends helped me - good friends who would give up their lives for a friend.'

'Why did you return to Hanoi?'

'To fetch my Buddha and my books. It was foolish, I know. That was when Tran Van Luc found me.' She ran a finger self-consciously across her scarred face.'

'When Venice left, you again returned to Hanoi. Why?'

'Before I tell you, I would like you to walk with me,' Sammi replied.

She opened the back door of the small shanty, leading the way through the tall grass to a copse of tamarind trees. Then she gestured with her arm. A small hardwood cross stood between the two largest trees. In front of it were scattered some wild flowers.

McCann walked over to the grave and crouched before it. Sammi remained at a distance. The inscription read, 'Paris Messon. Died among friends.'

They sat under the tamarind trees watching the sun set behind the Isle des Merveilles.

'Paris was Tran's son?' McCann asked.

'He had told her many times he had no heir. It was a great sadness for him. So she determined to tell him face to face that now he did. But when she came to his house he would not see her. He was shamed by her appearance before his business associates. She was turned away from his house on the third day by force, taken to her hotel and left there. It was only then that she told him of the child in a letter. She was numbed with unhappiness and anger. She told him he would die of old age, never having set eyes on his child - his heir.

'But of course her anger had not been good sense. When Tran Van Luc received her letter, he at once sent his people to take her. He determined that she would remain his prisoner until her time came. He informed her she would then be sent home. The child however, was his and therefore would remain. It was she, not he, who would never set eyes on the child again.'

'Tran had no idea Kien was feeding her opium until the night he visited her?'

'Never. He would have been enraged had he known Kien was endangering the life of his child. That is why he killed Kien; because he might have harmed his offspring.'

'He searched for her?'

'He searched everywhere. Everyone looked for her. There was a price on her head of five thousand American dollars. But no one here would give her up. We nursed her here for five months.'

'The effects of the drugs?'

Sammi nodded. 'She was very ill when we brought her here, and for weeks afterwards. Slowly she improved. She fought hard to regain her strength for the sake of her child, but the damage had already been done.

'We would spend our days here on the island talking of our childhood, our hopes and dreams, our disillusionment, our happiness, and our fears. She was terrified that Tran would one day find the child and take him from her.' Sammi looked across at McCann. 'She knew it would be a boy.'

'She meant to return to Australia with the child?'

'We planned to drive them in the truck through the night to Ho Chi Minh City to the Australian Embassy. They would escort her safely to the plane – Tran could not touch her with the diplomats around her. But she could not travel before giving birth. She was too weak, the child would not have lived. She worried for her son, not herself.'

'Could she not have telephoned the Embassy?'

'We advised against it. The *Tinh Bao* would have listened to all calls to the Embassy.'

'Surely a message could have been delivered to the Embassy?'

Sammi looked at him. 'You do not understand our country. It is not the same as yours. She was safe here among friends. But in Hanoi too many people thought of little else but the money Tran Van Luc offered.'

The figure of Mei-Li appeared at the rear of the houses and called to Sammi. Sammi did not even notice. Her eyes were glazed as she recalled the events of the previous year. Mei-Li disappeared indoors again. It was becoming quite dark now.

'The baby was born three weeks premature. He fought for life for two days, then died. She named him Paris.'

Sammi rose and brushed the grass from her pants. 'Shall we walk?' she said. Her voice was low and filled with emotion.

'She made me promise to tell no one of the child lest Tran would hear of it. It was to be his punishment never to know what had become of his heir. She hoped it might drive him mad to think that somewhere on the face of the earth was his issue, yet he would never know where. That would be his karma.'

'Why did she not return to Australia after the death of the child, as she'd planned before?'

'Because she wished Tran to believe she and the child were still in Vietnam - still so close. As each month passed, he redoubled his efforts to find her. We knew that from the gossip on the mainland. So she traveled with Diem to Khe Sanh, and crossed the border into Laos on the Highway 9 border post at Lao Bao. It is a popular smuggling route where money buys most things. She hung below the truck as it crossed into Laos.'

The wind had ceased and the temperature had risen once more. The night air was still, the silence broken only by the distant laughter of the children in the village.

'I traveled with her to the crossing. I had to see her safe. The last time I saw her, she was walking down the road to Tchepone. She waved at me and smiled. Then we returned to Lao Bao.'

'Why didn't you come back here?'

'She asked me to help her.'

'By watching Tran?'

'There was a man. He came to the My Guy often while I worked there. He had always asked for me. He was a Dutchman. He flew the plane of Tran Van Luc. I found him at the club one night. I told him I had a small sister. Could he bring back from Australia a souvenir next time he flew there. I would save the money, and pay him nearer the time. That way we would learn accurately when he would leave.'

'It was Venice's intention to kill Tran. You knew that?'

'Yes, I knew.'

'Why? Was it revenge?'

'In some ways, yes. Not for the way he had treated her, but because he was responsible for the death of her son. Also because of what he had done to me. I begged her to let go. Her child was dead, I would survive, these things were past. But it ate away at her soul. She wished him to die believing he had fathered a son that he would never have seen. That was her reason.'

32.

25th May.

They set off on the return trip to Hanoi at first light. The whole village had dined together the previous evening on a wide terrace facing the sea. It was a mark of respect for Venice. Mei-Li prepared a seafood feast of crabs, steamed fish and salt-fried prawns. Sammi remained subdued. Possibly she regretted her involvement in the conspiracy to kill Tran – he had lived, while others had died, and she felt culpable. Equally possibly she did not – she was merely grieving for a friend.

McCann bade farewell to Wing as the Chinese guided the barque towards the mainland boat jetty, pressing a bundle of dollars into his hand. Initially the fisherman was embarrassed, refusing the money with a dignified smile. Then McCann asked Sammi to explain to him that it was a gift for all the children of the village. Perhaps Wing could buy them some treats. He bowed, accepting gratefully on behalf of the little ones, the *nguoi con*.

Diem was waiting at the quayside, his face wreathed in smiles. It amazed McCann that men such as Diem not only had the stamina to drive the terrible roads for ten hours at a time, but also were never short of good humor. The big Ywat truck was standing in the street, the whole chassis throbbing as ever.

'I shall not be returning with you,' said Sammi. 'I'm staying on the island for a while. I had forgotten the meaning of peace and love among friends.'

McCann was at a loss to know how to thank her. She had risked her newly regained tranquility to help strangers, solely because they were friends of Venice's father. There was no question of making her a gift of money, she would have been insulted. Perhaps there would be some way of helping her financially at some later time.

'Thank you Sammi,' he said simply. She smiled, then walked back to Wing.

The return drive was slower than the race from Hanoi. Diem had picked up a full load of sapodilla fruit outside Troi. The rusty Russian workhorse strained up each hill, thundering down into every valley. Diem had the disconcerting habit of free-wheeling out of gear down the hills to save fuel, and changing into top gear to overtake as though under the impression that top was the most powerful.

At Hai Phong they stopped to unload produce, then sped on at a faster pace northwest towards Hanoi.

As they barrelled through Hai Duong, McCann tapped Diem on the arm and gestured towards the rear of the truck. Maybe this was the time for him to hide again among the vegetables. Diem pulled a face and shook his head as if to say that, as far as he was concerned, it wasn't necessary. McCann put the *non* on his head and draped the orange cloth again around his shoulders.

It was just past two o'clock when they reached the outskirts of Hanoi. Diem swung the truck right off Giai Phong into Thruong Dinh Street. The traffic was once again a snail-like solid mass. Diem wove his way slowly forwards, his fist on the horn. The heat in the cab must have been over a hundred and thirty, yet Diem was hardly sweating. McCann was drenched.

At the major intersection at Dai Co Viet Street, a uniformed traffic policeman held up a hand just as Diem had got up a good head of steam. Nevertheless Diem stood hard on the brakes, and the truck skidded to a halt two meters into the intersection, dust swirling around the hood and front wheels. The policeman stared hard at Diem, waving him back aggressively with his baton, annoyed that the truckie hadn't been paying sufficient attention.

McCann glanced across at Diem, lifting his *non* briefly to wipe away the sweat that was literally running down his face in rivulets. Diem was muttering some obscenity, rebuking himself for his own stupidity. He looked apprehensive. The *Camh Sat*, the local beat police, had wide arbitrary powers. They could make life extremely difficult for truck drivers if they chose to. It was quite routine for long-distance truckies to be stopped four or five times on the road between Ho Chi Minh City and Hanoi for what the *Camh Sat* euphemistically categorized as 'technical infringements'. These were pretexts for collecting handouts to swell the policemen's pitiful remuneration into living wages.

Diem backed up the Ywat as far as was possible. It proved only to be a matter of three inches – another truck laden with hogs was right up his backside. He then smiled submissively at the traffic cop, shrugging his shoulders. However, the policeman continued to stare hard at Diem as he waved the traffic on across the Ywat's nose.

Diem looked down at his lap in an attempt to escape the cop's glare. McCann pulled his conical hat down as far as looked natural to conceal the fact that he was a westerner. It was then that he accidentally made eye contact with the policeman. Immediately he looked elsewhere, but he could tell the cop was still staring at him inquisitively. A few seconds later he was beckoning another policeman from across the street.

McCann glanced across again at Diem. The Vietnamese now looked positively scared. His hands clutched the wheel tight as a vice and his knuckles were white with tension. His right foot was revving the accelerator. He was sweating. It was now a full three minutes since they'd been stopped, and still the cop was waving the traffic across their nose.

Two more men dressed in dark shirts had now joined the two *Camh Sat* in the center of the intersection. One was pointing at McCann, while the other was on a cellular phone. Then the two men in mufti began to walk over to Diem's side of the truck and it all suddenly began.

Diem slammed his foot hard down on the gas pedal as he engaged the gears, and the Ywat shot forward across the intersection. He swerved to avoid the rear fender of a bus but caught the last two inches, shearing them off in an explosion of metal. Everyone close dived for cover. The two policemen in the center of the road leapt aside as the Ywat careened past them on two wheels, missing them by inches. McCann could hear infuriated shouting from behind, and the piercing sound of police whistles.

Grabbing Diem's arm, McCann yelled at him to stop, but the man's face was set in an expression of panic. He was now on the wrong side of the road, his left hand hard on the horn, pressing continuously as the oncoming trucks braked, swerved, and skidded into the right-hand ditch as they attempted to avoid the runaway heading towards them.

McCann continued screaming at Diem to stop, then dived across the driver's bench seat to grab at Diem's right leg, attempting to wrench it off the accelerator. In his panic, the Vietnamese had clearly forgotten about the children in the back, who were being tossed around like peas in a pod. In the wide rear-view mirror McCann could see a Toyota four-wheel drive plunging after them through the dust kicked up by the Ywat's wheels. On all sides, people were diving for cover, cars were colliding with each other, and scooters were running off the road into the ditch.

McCann felt for the muscle in Diem's thigh, stabbing hard at it with his fingers. Immediately he felt the leg spasm and it lifted off the accelerator. As it did, McCann just had time to see a massive container truck thundering towards them. It clearly didn't have the capacity to stop. Diem wrenched frantically at the wheel, pulling the Ywat to the right, at the same time standing hard on the brake. A second later the Ywat smashed into a telegraph pole at the side of the street and McCann lost consciousness.

As his mind began to clear, McCann became aware of voices close by. He was lying beside the truck, his head on the pavement, his body in the road. A crowd of close to a hundred had surrounded the accident peering open-mouthed at the steaming vehicle. One of the two men in dark shirts he'd seen before at the intersection was standing near his head. Between his legs he could see the broken windscreen of the Ywat truck. The second dark shirt was inside the cab pulling Diem from behind the wheel. Blood was running down the side of his friend's face from a gash at his temple, but it was clear Diem was alive. He was shouting, frantically gesturing to the back of the truck. Immediately, McCann's thoughts turned to the children, and he jumped up. As he did so, a third man, grabbed him round the chest, trying to restrain him. McCann pulled roughly away, elbowing the man in the solar plexus with a short sharp jab. The man went down like a sack of potatoes. Seconds later McCann was at the rear of the truck, pulling up the canvas to reveal the two children, lying face up among the fruit. The were unhurt, but terrified.

'*Cha!*' the eldest screamed at McCann, as he leapt down and ran towards the cab of the Ywat, frightened that his poppa might be badly injured.

McCann lifted the younger boy down. Then he felt a white burning light in his brain, as his head exploded with pain. He slumped down unconscious on the roadway, one of the blue shirted men standing over him, a short black wooden truncheon at his side.

When McCann regained consciousness, he was in the wide rear seat of a small van, his forehead pushed against the seat in front. His hands had been handcuffed behind his back, and he could feel his feet had been secured together with a length of nylon rope. The two men in dark shirts were on either side of him. The van was travelling at speed down the narrow lanes of the Old Quarter.

McCann craned his head round, eyeballing the man on his left. He opened his mouth to speak, but the Vietnamese barked at him to be quiet. Over the man's shoulder, McCann could see the buildings flashing by. Even though his head was pounding with an intense lancing pain from the blow to the base of his neck, it was vitally important to keep a sense of orientation.

The unmistakable rumble of the Unification Express above them as they roared through the underpass at Hang Ga Street told McCann he was heading north. A left turn and he knew he would be heading towards Ho Chi Minh's Mausoleum. As the massive ramparts of the third century Co Loa Citadel flashed by, he knew he was right.

McCann made a show of appearing to be in great pain, breathing hard and keeping his eyes the smallest slits, so that the men on either side wouldn't notice he was continuously glancing left and right over their shoulders for clues to where they were heading.

The van slammed into a pothole and McCann caught the briefest glimpse of a street sign as they made a turn half right. Hunh Vuong. By his calculations they were now again heading directly north. If he'd been accurate, they'd be about to reach the southern edge of Ho Tay Lake.

At that precise moment the succession of two storey buildings gave way to blue sky, and McCann could smell the water. He'd been right. It was Ho Tay - West Lake.

As the van sped north, McCann made a quick assessment of the logic behind his kidnapping. The Immigration Police were south of the city center on Tran Hung. The Ministry of the Interior was again south on Hang Bai. These men weren't the *Tinh Bao*. They were Tran's men. They were taking him to their master.

33.

25th May

Tran Van Luc's mansion stood on five acres of the most valuable real estate in Vietnam, the four kilometer stretch directly behind the main flood dyke at the northern end of Ho Tay Lake, often called the Lake of the Mist. This was the Bel Air of Hanoi. The average luxury house in Hanoi stood on two blocks. Tran Van Luc's residence stood on fifteen.

Where once had been the home to Hanoi's flower-growing villages, now stood exclusive neo-Franco villas, replete with gabled roofs, lavish stucco embellishments, ornate metal lace balconies, French-style wooden shutters and satellite dishes.

Pride of place was given to 'Nha Mau Trang' – 'The White House', so nicknamed by the Hanoi gossipmongers. It stood apart from all other buildings; a series of colonnades in front, gardens leading gently down to the lake at the rear. At each corner of the structure soared a fifty feet tower, topped by spires that seemed to reach up to touch the clouds. The Vietnamese national flag flew from each.

McCann felt the van slow marginally as it turned left off the lake road. Then it came briefly to a halt.

As it picked up speed again, he caught a glimpse of elaborate wrought iron gates that had been opened to allow the van entry. The sound of the tires on gravel rather than a road surface suggested to him that he'd arrived at a private estate. Twenty-five seconds later the van stopped, and he heard the driver's door open and close. The side door was slid open and he was pulled from the van. The man who had been sitting to his left bent down and untied the nylon rope that bound his feet. The men then took an arm each and frog-marched McCann across the gravel driveway, up the wide stone steps that led to the main entrance, and through the doors into the palatial residence.

The interior of the main hall would have done justice to a nineteenth century Italian palazzo. The floor was of the palest, ice pink, Carrara marble. Four giant columns reached to the ceiling, and a twin staircase swirled left and right upwards to the floor above. Two exaggerated crystal chandeliers hung from the high ceiling.

An athletic man in a black suit stood by double doors at the far end of the hall. As McCann and his minders approached, the man pushed the doors open and McCann was dragged through.

As they halted in the center of the huge reception room, one of the men slipped a key into the handcuffs, snapping them open. Abruptly, both men released him and walked back through the main doors.

McCann looked around him. Floor to ceiling windows looked out across gardens and lawns to Ho Tay Lake.

The furniture was possibly the most beautiful he'd seen outside of the Palace of Versailles. A massive Louis Quinze rosewood marquetry *table de salon* had pride of place in the center of the room, surrounded by six gilt French Regency *chaises cannée*. Two *chiffonnier éscritoires* were set in recesses on either side of the French windows.

Opposite the window, under a richly ornate gilt regency mirror, was the fireplace, surrounded by a blush pink period marble mantelpiece.

As McCann took a couple of paces towards the central table, the doors behind him re-opened and a manservant entered. He was carrying a silver tray upon which were a Sèvres teapot, milk jug, two cups and saucers and a plate of petits fours. He put down the tray, and without looking at McCann turned on his heel and left the room.

McCann ignored the refreshments, walking to the window. His head still ached unbearably, both from the battering caused by the accident, and the blow administered to the base of his skull.

The minutes passed in silence as McCann stared out at the lake across the flowerbeds and lawns, debating what course of action to take.

He was about to turn towards the door, when he caught sight of a figure emerging from a copse of jacaranda trees, and begin to cross the lawn towards the French windows. The man was walking with the aid of a cane, and was dressed in a midnight blue Indian shot silk achkan, closed at the neck, the jacket falling well below the knees over the pleated churibar pajama pants. On his feet were soft black leather jootis.

Though he walked with a pronounced limp, the man held his broad shoulders back, and his head high. He was a couple of inches over six feet tall, with short wavy jet hair, flecked with gray at the temples. His waist was slim. With the exception of his right leg, which was marginally shorter than his left, his limbs were long and graceful. He waved cheerily as he caught sight of McCann through the French windows, as if greeting a weekend guest.

'Good afternoon, Mr. McCann,' he said, stepping into the reception room. 'I'm so sorry to have kept you waiting, it was quite unavoidable. My name is Tran Van Luc. I hope you helped yourself to some tea.'

Sammi had not been exaggerating. Tran was a strikingly handsome man – *trés distingué*, the French would have said. Though McCann couldn't remember exactly whether Tran was in his very late fifties or early sixties, age had dealt kindly with him. His deep olive skin was practically unblemished. His features were sharply defined, the cheekbones high, the nose straight. A thin black moustache delineated his upper lip, and his chin was strong. The eyes were a smoky gray, the lips expressive. The first general impression was of a man of great charm and abundant charisma. Tran could easily have passed for a maharaja. The Cham features were unmistakable – he could almost have been a throwback to the ninth century.

'I fear an apology is in order,' Tran continued as he approached McCann. He spoke in the manner of a 1930's British tea plantation owner in Ceylon. Either he'd benefited from a private education in England, or it was pure affectation. Either way, McCann found his easy manner highly offensive.

Tran held out a hand, which McCann ignored. He let it drop.

'You see, I tried to reach you yesterday, without success. You were off somewhere or other on a trip. So I let it be known that I wished to speak to you, and I'm afraid to say two of my staff members became somewhat carried away. Oh, by the way,' he said, reaching into his breast pocket and pulling out an envelope, 'a friend of yours asked me to return this to you. It's from Tony Vargas.' He paused, looking McCann directly in the eye. 'How are you holding up?' he said, his expression changing to one of solicitation. 'I believe you were involved in a traffic accident. Perhaps I might offer you some pain relief?'

'What do you want from me?' asked McCann.

'No tea, Mr. McCann?' Tran said by way of a reply, leaning on a polished silver and ebony stick.

McCann remained silent.

'Then please excuse me while I take a little. Please be seated,' he said drawing up one of the gilt cane chairs. McCann remained standing across the table from Tran.

'What is your interest in me, Tran?'

'It's *Mr.* Tran, Mr. McCann. And I might ask you the very same thing. It would appear you have been prying into my business affairs around the globe for the past few days,' Tran replied, slipping a wedge of fresh lemon into his teacup.

'I am presently employed by Maynard Buchanan's daughter. You can't have forgotten Maynard, surely. You engineered the theft of close to two hundred million dollars from his petrochemical plant at Telok Anson.'

Tran looked up from his tea with a look of total astonishment. 'I did nothing of the kind,' he replied, then shook his head sadly as he poured himself another cup of tea. 'And I wouldn't repeat that kind of slander in public if I were you.'

'Then you arranged to have Christopher Palmer and Phillip Boydell murdered,' McCann continued, as though Tran had not spoken.

Tran resumed sipping his tea, staring at McCann, quite unfazed. 'Astonishing,' he muttered to himself. 'Quite astonishing.'

'Incidentally,' McCann cut in, 'I gather your paid assassin, Brokov – the man who tried to kill me in Hong Kong – is now under FBI guard in New York. I wouldn't be surprised if he decides to turn state's evidence.'

'*I* would, Mr. McCann,' replied Tran affably, without a hint of annoyance. 'It would surprise *me* greatly.' He reached out a perfectly manicured hand for a pastry.

It was the smile that was the giveaway. He could have brazened it out, denying everything, but Tran just couldn't resist. His arrogance was just too insurmountable. He truly believed himself invulnerable.

McCann felt the blood in his veins beginning to pump at an accelerated rate. He would gladly have given a year of his life to be able to yield to the temptation to tear the smug Vietnamese limb from limb.

'There's no way you can close this thing down,' McCann continued after a second or two. 'Brokov will have no alternative but to talk, as will Bradley Radcliffe. As, incidentally, will I. I'd also imagine Sir Henry Trevor and Francis Greville would be considering their positions.'

Tran put down his cup and leant back in his chair. 'I really don't have the least interest in your theories regarding people I have only the smallest connection with. As will be amply proved at a later stage. I have no knowledge of the man you refer to as Brocnov,' Tran said, deliberately mispronouncing the name, 'nor Palmer, nor the man called Boydell. As for Sir Henry Trevor, he is the chairman of a major bank in Jersey. We do business together. As far as I can recall, I have had no association whatsoever with Bradley Radcliffe. He may very well have dealt with one of my companies. However, we have never spoken - let alone met.'

Perhaps sensing McCann's ever-growing antipathy, Tran rose from the chair, pressing a button recessed in the side of the inlaid table. Instantly the main doors opened and two bodyguards entered the room. One closed the door, remaining by the door, while the other walked across towards them, taking up a position midway between his employer and McCann.

'Enough of this nonsense, Mr. McCann,' continued Tran prosaically. 'I wish to talk of your interest in Venice Messon. I believe she was the reason you came to my country?' The sentence was couched as a question. McCann didn't feel like obliging.

'You're not about to tell me you hardly knew *her* either, are you, Tran? Or that 'the association' was a purely business one?' said McCann.

'Quite the contrary,' replied Tran easily, not about to rise to the gibe. 'I have been telling the truth up till now. Why should I choose to lie now? I encountered Venice Messon in Sydney. We had an affair. It was as simple as that. I should never have allowed the romance to blossom. I am to blame.' He caught sight of a fleck of dust on his cuff as he spoke, brushing it away with the flat of his hand. 'But it was something that could not last. I explained that to her when she came to visit me last year.'

McCann stared at Tran in total disbelief, amazed that the man could lie with such consummate ease, and with such conviction that it appeared he almost believed his own words.

'However, how this could be any of your, or Miss Buchanan's, business is beyond me,' he continued, walking to the window, then turning to face McCann. 'It was a personal matter between Venice and myself.'

'When Venice detonated the explosive in Sydney, three men died with her, one of whom, as you know, was your brother. At that point it shifted into the public domain. Miss Buchanan wished to know what had driven the girl to do what she did. It now seems quite clear that you were her torturer, and thus the catalyst.'

'Torturer? How melodramatic,' Tran replied with a smirk. 'I cannot be held responsible for the vagaries of a young girl's romanticized vision of life. Nor do I care to discuss the matter with you. However, the issue of Sammi Chung's involvement in all this is something I would like to investigate further. Here you can help. Vargas informs me you met with Sammi the night before last.'

McCann merely stared back into Tran's smoky gray eyes.

'Mr. McCann, you choose to involve yourself in affairs that are none of your business,' Tran continued after a few moments. 'I am asking you a civil question. Sammi is a friend of mine. I wish to contact her.'

'I believe the last time you contacted her you chose to throw acid in her face.'

Tran's face darkened. 'If Sammi has suggested this, you are a fool to believe it. Her former boyfriend scarred her face, not I.' The urbane tone to his conversation had suddenly vanished, replaced by a hard edge.

'Kien Khanh?'

'The same,' he said, returning to his chair and sitting. He looked down at the marble floor, taking a couple of deep breaths. It seemed to McCann that for a moment Tran had teetered on the brink of losing his façade of genteel equilibrium. It had been a struggle to regain it, but regain it he had.

'The man whose throat you cut,' McCann shot back immediately, sensing he had the man emotionally on the ropes.

The Vietnamese's gray eyes narrowed. 'I shall fence with you no further, McCann,' Tran replied, cold as ice, all pretence of politeness and good manners thrown suddenly to the wind. 'Venice Messon bore a child. My issue. She then returned to Australia alone, effectively deserting the infant. The Australian immigration records are quite clear on that matter. As the child's father, I am deeply concerned for its welfare. It's quite apparent that Miss Chung has fed you a tissue of lies concerning my part in all this. Be that as it may, I believe Miss Chung has known the whereabouts of the child from the start. It was a grave error on my part to have believed otherwise.'

Tran rose, his crippled foot snagging momentarily on the chair leg, then moved across to McCann. His minder moved closer to the pair, in case it crossed McCann's mind to initiate some violence towards his master.

'Where is my child, Mr. McCann? I wish to know. I *will* know.'

They locked eyes for a few moments, then McCann smiled. 'That, Mr. Tran, is none of my business. It is, as you rightly state, your personal affair. Why don't you get on with it, I have other things to do.'

'You *will* tell me,' said Tran, adding softly, 'Given time.'

'You plan to hold me a prisoner as you did Venice Messon?'

Tran snapped his fingers. The minder at the door immediately walked forwards to stand directly behind McCann.

'If I choose,' said Tran matter-of-factly.

McCann stared at Tran, his eyes sparkling with the thought of initiating some terrible violence to the man before him - Tran was so temptingly close to him. But his Hereford SAS training cautioned restraint. Though the two minders in the room would present no problem, how many others were in the house? Many would almost certainly be carrying weapons. And if he managed to break through into the streets of Hanoi, how far would he get before he was picked up by the *Tinh Bao* and imprisoned for causing grievous bodily harm to one of their most prominent citizens.

'To hold me against my will would be a mistake,' replied McCann. 'I make two calls a day to the American Embassy at specified times. If I fail to do so they will come knocking on your door.' It was a hoary old bluff, yet one Tran would be foolish to ignore.

'Your Embassy does not concern me.'

'It really should, Mr. Tran. I've recently been working with a major international financial criminal task force, and they're of the view that your position right now is less than tenable to say the least. You may or may not also be aware that I work for the British Government. They, also, would be less than pleased if advised you were keeping me a hostage.' McCann paused to let the thrust of his words sink in. 'An international diplomatic incident? I'd imagine that would strain even your cozy relationship with the Party here in Hanoi.'

Tran's face was a mirror of darkness.

'I would have said you're in enough trouble without adding the US and the United Kingdom into the equation. I'd concentrate on Constantin Khamovnikakh if I were you.'

Though Tran's expression hardly changed, McCann could see the mention of the Muscovite Mafia *capo* had stuck a fundamental chord in the psyche of the Vietnamese.

'I shall find my son, McCann. Be assured of that,' said Tran with venom.

'A son?' McCann teased. From what Sammi had told him, the man had no idea whether the child had been a son or a daughter.

The walking stick clicked on the marble floor as Tran walked crab-like towards the door, never taking his eyes off McCann.

'Sadly I cannot guarantee your safety outside this house,' Tran said with some satisfaction.

'I'd make sure I did just that. I wouldn't upset your government buddies here in Hanoi, if I were you. They'll shortly be the only friends you have. You'll need them onside to knock back the extradition requests.

'You will be shown out,' said Tran, his white knuckles gripping the ebony stick as if he were toying with the idea of taking a swing at McCann. 'I'd take care, if I were you,' he added, then limped from the room.

34.

25th May.

McCann felt as though his head would explode. The fury he'd had to contain during his interview with Tran Van Luc had set the blood pounding through his temples, resulting in an unbelievable migraine. Now he was being escorted by four of Tran's people down the long graveled driveway to the front gates, and each step was a pistol shot through his brain.

The air was still, and the combination of the temperature in the high eighties and the near hundred per cent humidity would have been enough to have steamed a salmon.

There were another two men on the gates, one of them quite openly carrying a machine pistol. His partner opened a smaller door to the left of the gatehouse and waved McCann through. As it closed behind him, McCann was left standing by the side of Nghi Tam Street, the road that ringed the lake.

It was close to four-fifteen, and the rush hour traffic was building to its most frenetic.

McCann felt in his pocket for the envelope that Tran had returned to him. At least the money would be useful. His wallet had earlier gone missing at the site of the accident and he doubted very much it had fallen accidentally from his pocket while he was unconscious.

As he pulled out the smallest bill, a cyclo drew up on his left, the driver calling out to him. McCann stepped up into the seat and pointed in the direction of the Pullman.

They'd only traveled about fifty feet when McCann happened to look to his right. Through the crush of pedestrians on the footpath, he could still clearly see the twelve-foot walls that guarded the sides of the mansion. Tran obviously took the matter of security seriously. Then, as a party of young schoolgirls, all dressed in snow-white *ao dai*, blue flowers threaded into their hair, crossed his field of vision, McCann's gaze drifted further right.

At first he thought he'd imagined it - the face was so similar. But surely it was out of the question, not here in Hanoi. The man was standing by the wall, looking up at the sun, then scanning the roof of Tran's mansion. But for some unexplained reason a voice within McCann sent a message to his brain that this was no chance encounter.

McCann fought to clear the fog in his pounding head. He searched the sidewalk again for a second sighting, but the man was gone.

Could it conceivably have been the man he thought he'd seen? Despite the throbbing pain in his temples, he sat bolt upright in the cyclo, closing his eyes tightly then opening them to sharpen his vision, searching over and around the mass of pedestrians in the direction he'd last seen the face. But there were just a thousand unfamiliar Vietnamese faces criss-crossing in front of him. He leant back in the chair of the cyclo. He must have been mistaken.

The cyclo continued forwards at little more than a walking pace as trucks, scooters, and bicycles jammed the main artery that fed back into the center of the city. McCann leant to the left so he could continue studying the crowd on the sidewalk.

A scooter flashed by on the inside at a dangerous speed, practically taking McCann's elbow with it, and his head whipped round to the front instinctively, following the path of the bike. It was then that he saw him again; a face in the crowd, crossing the street thirty feet ahead. This time there was no mistake.

It was Alan Messon.

McCann thrust the money he held in his hand up to the driver and sprang from the cyclo, shouting loudly to Messon to stop. But the bedlam of the traffic was so loud his voice scarcely reached further than ten feet.

To keep Messon sighted through the crush of people was practically impossible. Fortunately the old man was several inches taller than the average Vietnamese, and was one of a very few hatless white faces in a sea of straw *non*.

McCann ran down the center of the road, ducking and weaving left and right in among the traffic, taking advantage of the smallest spaces between the cars and scooters. All the time he was calling Messon's name out loudly to attract his attention, praying he wouldn't lose him in the crowd.

As he leapt on to the flagstones at the far side of the road, he could clearly see Messon up ahead; now only a matter of twenty feet away. The old man looked to be in a great hurry, elbowing his way roughly through the crowds; the Vietnamese around him abusing him for his loutish behavior.

McCann was maybe ten feet from Messon, when the old man's head turned sharply towards him. It must have been the first time he'd heard McCann's calls. Their eyes locked for an instant. McCann called out yet again, waving his arms, but Messon's reaction was both startling and unexpected. For some reason that McCann couldn't fathom, Messon's expression was that of a child caught at the cookie jar. Whereas before he'd been merely hurrying, now he broke into a run, barging through the crowd into the street, running helter-skelter through the rush-hour traffic like a bag snatcher cornered by the cops.

McCann leapt over a pile of trash in the gutter, side-stepping a scooter that was coming up fast on his right. Messon was two car lengths away, glancing over his shoulder every couple of seconds with a look of panic, as though pursued by savage dogs. Truckies were sounding their horns, fists bunched out of the window, braking and swerving to avoid hitting the old man.

As the mad race continued, Messon and McCann were now drawing the attention of the crowds on the sidewalk. Many had stopped, and were pointing at the old man as he ran suicidally in and out of the articulated trucks and buses.

McCann was practically within an arm's reach of Messon when a Honda scooter, carrying a man, woman, a small child, and a monkey, clipped the panicked man on the hip, and sent him crashing into the gutter.

Within seconds McCann was kneeling beside him, cradling his head, feeling his carotid artery for a pulse. The crowd immediately pressed round in a tight suffocating circle.

Messon was breathing erratically, gasping for air, his eyes rolling. McCann yelled at the crowd, waving them back to give Messon air. Quickly he looked for telltale signs of blood in the nose, ears and mouth. There were none yet – a good sign. Then Messon opened his eyes and stared at McCann, twitching both legs. Another promising sign.

'Shit,' Messon murmured, smiling grimly. 'Thought I could outrun you. Stupid old bugger, aren't I?'

McCann had to hand it to the man. At his age, to have sprinted through the traffic in the heart of the Hanoi rush hour was the equivalent of running round the Arc de Triomphe in Paris against the flow of traffic. Perhaps the old guy was in better shape than he'd imagined.

'Give me a hand up, will you,' Messon said, sitting up, at the same time wincing and massaging his hip where he'd been hit by the Honda.

McCann helped him to his feet. 'Why the hell run from me, Alan? Is this your idea of fun, for Christ's sake?' he said, trying to make light of it.

He had one arm round Messon's shoulders, while he held up the other, searching for a cyclo to get them away. 'Where are you staying, Alan. We'd better get you back to your hotel – have a doctor take a look at you.'

A flash of anger crossed Messon's face. 'Who the hell are you to tell me what to do?' he snapped. 'I'm going nowhere. I'll do what I came here for, thank you very much.'

Two cyclos had now stopped at the side of the road near them, blocking one of the traffic lanes, and both drivers were shouting at McCann, pointing at their tricycles. The traffic behind quickly backed up fifty feet, and everyone was leaning on their horns. The only saving grace was that the crowd was beginning to disperse – there were no dead bodies, so it was hardly worth standing around.

'If you've come all this way to confront Tran Van Luc, forget it Alan,' McCann shouted over the roar of the traffic and the abusive shouts of the cyclo drivers. 'You won't get further than the gates. The place is like a fortress. He's got more goons that the President's got Secret Service people.'

The muscles in Messon's jaw twitched with determination, his eyes fixed on the wall of Tran's compound. 'I haven't come all this way to walk away now. I'll have it out with him, or die in the attempt.'

McCann knew he had to somehow dissuade Messon from his fixed purpose. God alone knew how Tran would react to the old guy's tirade.

'Believe me, Alan. It's just not possible. I've just been kicked out myself. He's in no mood to discuss his affairs with you.'

Messon's eyes snapped round to meet McCann's. 'You've been in there?'

'I have. Just now.'

'The man's at home? You actually spoke to him?'

'Yes,' McCann replied wearily, anything to get Messon to come with him. He didn't know how long he could suffer the continuous bleating of the two cyclo drivers, and the deafening din of the car horns around him. He had to get some strong painkillers into his system quickly. 'Look, Alan. Come with me to my hotel right now and I'll tell you everything he said. We talked of Venice.'

At the mention of his daughter, Messon's expression changed at once. 'Deal,' he replied quickly.

McCann helped Messon into the front cyclo, then climbed in the second, shouting the name of his hotel to both drivers, who for the first time in several minutes stopped braying at him.

Messon sat in stunned silence as McCann told him of his daughter's friendship with Sammi and their house in Ha Long Bay. He told Messon of how Venice had arrived in Hanoi, and how Tran Van Luc had rejected her. He chose not to mention that Tran had kept her prisoner, nor that she'd been drugged by Kien Khanh – there was little point it inflaming the man again, causing him unnecessary suffering. However, he felt Messon had a right to know of the child, even though it might cause him heartache. After all, it had been for his sake that

Sammi had risked her life taking McCann to Ha Long. To keep it from him now would be to defeat Sammi's purpose.

He told Messon of the depth of feeling and respect the Wing family and all those on the island had felt towards his daughter, and of the small grave among the tamarind trees. Finally he explained that Venice had determined to keep the fact of her son's death a secret from Tran so as to punish him, adding that during the conversation he'd had with the Vietnamese at his mansion, her retribution seemed to be paying dividends.

They sat in silence for the best part of fifteen minutes; Messon slumped in an armchair, McCann sitting on the edge of the bed. Messon looked empty, desolate and broken. At length he spoke.

'How can I forgive a man who treated my daughter in such a cruel way?'

McCann merely shrugged. He had done his best to calm his friend and keep him from any precipitous action, yet there was no way he was about to extenuate Tran's monstrous behavior.

'Do you seriously think there's the slightest chance of the man being brought to book, Leo,' Messon asked.

'I would like to think so, yes. If the man who attempted to kill Bradley Radcliffe in New York lives to incriminate Tran, I'd imagine the US State Department will move heaven and earth to have him extradited. And if they don't succeed, the Moscow Mafia will take a shot at him sometime in the near future.'

Messon looked away, deep in his own private thoughts. 'But the damage is done, isn't it? My girl is dead.'

'There's nothing to be gained by confronting the man, Alan – he's too powerful, and anything you do might rebound on Sammi. She was like a sister to Venice. She could be in danger from Tran if you stir him up further.'

Messon looked up at McCann. 'Don't worry, Leo. I can see you're right. I'll leave things as they are. There's no bringing Venice back, and we owe it to Sammi,' he said, then suddenly held his head with both hands, as though gripped by some terrible pain.

McCann crouched down beside him. 'Are you all right, Alan? Would you like some more pills?'

When they'd reached the hotel half an hour earlier, McCann had insisted that Messon see the hotel doctor, Herr Kreissmann, a friendly German who billed like a Swiss. Messon had grudgingly agreed. However, apart from quite a few substantial bruises, Kreissmann had judged that Messon was in surprisingly good shape for a man of his age who'd just been struck by a motor scooter. Now this fresh onset of searing pain was worrying.

Messon declined McCann's offer of more painkillers, saying he thought he might see if the Pullman had any rooms left. He felt exhausted, his body was bruised, his head was pounding, and he felt he could use some sleep.

'Look, Alan, I have to get over to the Embassy to speak to Larry Wycoff. Why not take a nap here. I'll be out for a good hour.' It was a lie, but he was concerned for the old man's health – he looked as though he would barely be able to stand if he tried.

McCann watched Messon debate the matter briefly, then he agreed to the idea, shuffling his way towards the large bed, and dropping like a stone on the bedspread.

McCann's first stop was the hotel bar for a couple of stiff belts of Scotch. Thankfully, the strong painkillers the German had given him were beginning to take effect, and he felt practically human again.

Next stop was the telephone booth to the left of the reception.

A few moments later he was put through to Larry Wycoff at the US Embassy. Fortunately the American CIA man was working late, a state department agricultural delegation was due to arrive in two days, and last minute security arrangements were Wycoff's responsibility.

He told Wycoff the details of his discussion with Tran at Ho Tay, apologizing for having lied about his link with the Embassy.

'To be frank, Leo, I'd think seriously about moving ass,' Wycoff said candidly. 'Tran's not a man to fool around with. He's connected at the highest level. If he had it in his mind to make you disappear, he'd only have to call it to the wind. Fact of the matter is, I can't guarantee your safety here either.'

'I understand, Larry. I'll make arrangements to leave first thing tomorrow. I'll call you from the airport. If by any chance you don't hear from me by nine, be a friend and crank up the diplomatic pressure. If I'm dead it's too bad for me, but at least it'll stir up the bastard.'

'It'll be a pleasure. Sorry I couldn't have been more help,' Wycoff said, then rang off.

The concierge couldn't have been more helpful. Two seats were booked on the early morning flight to Hong Kong. There were no direct flights to Australia, and the arrival time in Sydney was marginally earlier through Hong Kong than via Ho Chi Minh City. McCann then booked Messon into the hotel – a room had become available, and was presently being cleaned. McCann then returned to the bar so as to give Messon a good couple of hour's sleep before waking him.

McCann sat at the bar nursing a whisky. He was in the eye of the hurricane, travelling fast towards the other side – he just didn't know it.

35.

New York
24th.

The Buchanan jet touched down at Los Angeles at 11.15 a.m. for re-fuelling. The plane was in the air again an hour and twenty minutes later. Touch down at JFK was 8.35 p.m. local time. The trip from Hanoi had taken close to twenty-three hours.

Theodore Radcliffe had arranged VIP facilities at the airport over and above those accorded to private flights. He was awaiting her arrival in the VIP lounge – alone. Though obviously doing his best to appear otherwise, he looked tired and grim. He hugged Rosalind to him.

Two cars were waiting outside the terminal. Three fit young FBI agents stood by the door to the building as Radcliffe Snr and Rosalind stepped out onto the concourse, flanking them as they walked to the front limousine.

During the ride into the city Theo held Rosalind's hand; whether to comfort her, or to draw some comfort for himself, was debatable. Either way, Rosalind found it an endearing gesture.

Bradley's condition had improved dramatically. He could now speak for short periods. However, Theo felt his son's interests were best served now by allowing him to sleep through the night – the family had been with him all day. Bradley's system was still in post shock trauma, and required stabilization.

Theo again apologized for suggesting Rosalind not visit Bradley that evening - Martha and Blanche had thought it best. Rosalind noted with interest that Theo had referred to Martha first, and Blanche, Bradley's mother, second. There'd be no question about who would be making the decisions.

The media circus was still camped outside Radcliffe Snr's apartment on Fifth Avenue. The three FBI agents fought to provide Rosalind and Theo a passage to the entrance through the milling television crews and press hounds on the sidewalk.

'The media were, as you'd expect, like ravening dogs,' said Theo some minutes later in the quiet of his library. 'The shooting was a gift from God.'

'You know who was responsible?' Rosalind asked. The question was couched to mask the fact she was leading on to a secondary.

'I believe so,' Theo replied carefully, studying Rosalind. 'If what you're really asking me is whether Bradley spoke to me about your encounter with Dieter Fischer, the answer is yes. He did.'

'I don't quite know how to ask this question, Theo, but I wonder how frank Bradley was with you?'

'He told me everything. That's my belief, anyway. I can't imagine there could be more. He rang me the night before the shooting.'

Theo was about to continue, when Rosalind cut in. 'If you'd prefer not to go into the details right now, I understand, Theo.'

Radcliffe shook his head. He wanted to talk.

'It was well past eleven at night when Bradley called me. He said he had an urgent matter to discuss, one he felt could not wait until the morning. I knew he'd never been prone to theatrics or exaggeration, so naturally I called for the car to drive me over.'

'Why didn't he come over here?'

'Brad said he didn't want to worry his mother. He was concerned she might either overhear the conversation, or wish to be included in the discussion.'

Bradley had talked for close to an hour, while his father listened – Theo's heart turned to ice, his life turned upside down.

'He told me it all began without his knowledge - like an invasion of white ants,' Theo continued. 'As campaign funds manager, he should have been more careful. But back then in early January money had been hard to find. That's when the checks had first started to roll in. None were of such a significant amount as to set any alarm bells ringing. As a matter of course, the authors of all funds were routinely scrutinized, then the checks were banked.

'It was the last week of February, just after our stunning victory in New Hampshire, that Brad received the first call. A lawyer representing the Fortress Hill Investment Bank in Hong Kong called to make an appointment. Brad's secretary told him he was unavailable, but the man was persistent. He called personally at the campaign headquarters the following day, calmly walked into Brad's office and informed Bradley that his immediate superior had urgent matters to discuss; it was imperative that Bradley fly to Hong Kong immediately.

'Naturally, Bradley again deferred – the campaign allowed him no time for other matters. It was only then, as the emissary from Fortress Hill began to spell out some facts concerning the campaign funds, that Bradley realized the serious position in which he'd unwittingly placed himself. Since January, money had been flowing into the campaign coffers, money whose true origin he could never allow to be made public. You see, when added together, well over five million US dollars had been injected into my campaign fund. Ostensibly its source was a myriad of small innocuous companies. However, the lawyer made it abundantly clear that in actual fact these innocuous companies were fronts; shell companies that masked the true identities of those that controlled them – gaming syndicate bosses, dubious property speculators, mob-linked identities and the like. In short, the funds came directly from people of questionable morals, and unquestionable criminality.'

'What possessed Brad to keep these matters from you?'

'Arrogance?' Theo replied sadly. 'He always had a deal of that. Be that as it may, he chose to attempt to sort it out himself. He reckoned that if he turned the lawyer down flat, the man from Fortress Hill could arrange for enough dirt to be thrown to sink my campaign without trace. He was probably right, though I in no way condone the decision he made.

'At a clandestine meeting arranged in Macau, Bradley met with a Vietnamese businessman. Contrary to Bradley's expectations, the Asian was affable, charming and highly intelligent. He apologized to Bradley for his under-handedness. He explained that he in no way wished to 'lean' on Bradley or myself. Rather, he merely hoped that by donating to the campaign fund now, that perhaps at a later stage he might appeal to the good nature of the man who, in the Asian's opinion, would undoubtedly become the next President of the United States. Brad said the man had the disconcerting habit of talking in these somewhat obvious euphemisms. The Asian said it undoubtedly made sound business sense. He and I would both be winners.'

'Were you so short of campaign funds at the time?'

'It was a difficult period, put it that way. Here was the instant answer. Brad was a man of easy answers. In short, Bradley made the fundamental mistake of dealing with him, agreeing to use his 'best efforts' to persuade me to 'look kindly' on the Asian's business affairs in the United States, should I win the Presidency. There would, of course, never be any question of criminality. In return, the Asian would inject a further seven million dollars into the fund, this time through reputable agencies. And Bradley's most important proviso was that all negotiations should pass through him as a conduit – I would never be approached directly, either then or at any later stage. I was never to know.

'From that moment of insanity, the die was cast. As the dollars flowed in, Bradley sank deeper and deeper into the Asian's pocket. The hook was all the way down Bradley's throat, and little by little, as the weeks passed, the Asian pulled the line tight. There was no question of backing out. The Asian, a man named Tran Van Luc, made it quite clear that it would spell the end to the campaign once a few details were leaked to the press.

'If it hadn't been for several unconnected matters pulling together at the same time, maybe all of this would never have come to a head. Who knows? Brad could have ended up part of the administration, engineering sweet deals for that man, without my having the smallest inkling of the corruption involved.'

'Was Dieter Fischer the trigger?' asked Rosalind.

'Yes. Brad suddenly found himself caught up in the internecine warfare between Tran in Asia, and the Russian Mafia here in New York and in Moscow. He knew that if he refused to co-operate with either of the factions he was a dead man; and he couldn't do both.'

'A pity that remorse showed no part in all this,' said Rosalind coldly. Half an hour previously, Bradley's involvement in the events that inevitably had contributed to her father's death had been conjecture. Leo had been sure of his guilt, yet she had still clung to some unrealistic hope that there had been some mistake. Perhaps even some obscure reason existed that could explain and justify his actions. Something. Anything. Now she'd listened to the second hand account of Brad's confession from his father, and it had evoked little sympathy from her. His behavior smacked more of an arrogant high flyer, grasping at the main chance, rather than the patsy at the mercy of a stronger man.

'He told me he had no knowledge of the Telok Anson fraud perpetrated on your father,' said Theo.

'I find that impossible to believe. Either way, he betrayed my father's trust, and by so doing he betrayed me. But that's all a thing of the past now. How are you going to move on all this, Theo?'

'I have to withdraw from the race. That much is certain. It's a moral imperative. I've discussed it with Sheila Pasca, and the whole team's in agreement. Needless to say, Martha is the sole voice of dissent.' No mention was made of Blanche or Conrad.

'To some extent I agree with her,' said Rosalind. 'You played absolutely no part in this. This is your whole life, Theo. Why should you have to take the fall for your son?'

'Because he *is* my son, I suppose. We have to accept responsibility somewhere down the line. Either way, I have to step aside, let the people know the facts. They will decide what's best for the party, and ultimately what's best for the people – not me.'

'Have the police been informed?'

'I met with the Attorney General at ten this morning. I plan to hold a press conference tomorrow at eight-thirty. At that time I'll announce I'm quitting the race, giving my reasons. Dan has agreed to hold off releasing any more police statements regarding the shooting till then. At that time, he'll be serving an arrest warrant on Bradley; not that he'll be able to move from the hospital for some time.'

'Brad knows of your plans?'

'He does. It's what he wanted. They're his as much as mine.'

The silence of the room was broken only by the pendulum of the ormolu clock on the mantelpiece.

'Could you understand if I told you that I couldn't see Brad at present?' Rosalind said after a few moments.

Radcliffe nodded his head as he stared at the clock. 'I'd understand, yes. I'm sure Bradley would too. But I'd hate to think that at some time in the future you'll wish you had.'

Rosalind could see he desperately wanted her to at least visit his son before she flew home. Theo had been a fine friend to her father and to herself through the years.

Through no fault of his, his world had collapsed. What did he have to look forward to now? She owed it to Theo.

Rosalind felt that Martha sensed her mood as they briefly met in the corridor outside Bradley's room at Mount Sinai. Though her face smiled, Rosalind felt the matriarch's heart held something back. No one would ever be good enough for her grandson, regardless of his faults. That much was sure.

His room was mercifully uncluttered by flowers. Bradley was on his back, a central line inserted in his chest to give him fluids. His eyes followed Rosalind from the door to the side of his bed. His skin looked pale and drawn, and his eyes had a haunted quality.

Rosalind drew up the chair that Martha had just vacated, pulling it close to the bed. It felt warm. Bradley watched her as she took his right hand in both of hers and held it, a beseeching look in his eyes.

They held each other's gaze in silence for some time. Then Bradley parted his lips to speak. 'I am so very sorry,' he whispered, barely audibly.

Rosalind held his hand even tighter. 'I know you are, Brad,' she replied with as much warmth as she could muster. She could think of nothing else to say. It was too early for compassion. The blood of too many people still clung to her memory.

She remained at his bedside until he fell asleep. Two hours later, Rosalind was flying back to Sydney.

36.

Hanoi.
25th May.

In McCann's dream he was strapped to a chair in the center of a massive empty room. Before him in the semi-darkness was the silhouette of a thin man. One leg was shorter by several inches than the other. The man was balancing on the longer leg, the shorter simply hanging in space, the foot twisted in towards the other. The face was shrouded in blackness, with the exception of the white teeth, which were positively incandescent. The lips were drawn back in a rictus. A deranged laughter echoed off the walls as McCann's heart pounded like a jackhammer.

'Excuse me, sir,' the bellhop said softly at McCann's side, tapping his shoulder.

McCann felt as though a lightning bolt had struck him. His eyes snapped open, and his entire body coiled like a spring. Then with a rush of consciousness he realized where he was.

He looked up at the young hotel employee, seriously embarrassed.

'Yes? What is it?'

'Mr. Messon's room is now available, sir. I'm sorry to have woken you, I didn't realize.'

'Don't worry,' McCann replied, tipping the bellhop. McCann looked at his watch. He'd been out cold for over an hour. It was time to wake Messon.

Even before he turned the key in the door to his room, McCann had an uneasy feeling. As he stepped into the room, he saw at once that Messon was gone.

McCann was downstairs in the lobby within seconds. There was little doubt that the old man would be bent on revenge. If he was on his way to Ho Tay, he had to be stopped before he got himself into serious trouble.

'I've got to get across town fast. Which is quicker – cab or cyclo?' he shouted to the receptionist as he sped past the front desk.

'This time of day, cyclo,' the concierge called back to him.

'What's Vietnamese for "hurry"?'

The receptionist called out the translation as McCann ran for the door.

'Ho Tay. Nghi Tam Street,' he shouted at the cyclo driver, handing him a twenty dollar note, adding 'Vôi vàng!'

The driver grinned broadly as he pocketed what amounted to the best part of a week's wages. The tricycle then shot forward into the traffic. This driver meant business.

Overtaking in Hanoi's main streets at rush hour is impossible. Nevertheless, the driver would have done justice to any Formula One cyclo team, snaking in and out of the traffic, finding the smallest openings, accelerating, then standing on the brakes, as he raced through the back alleys towards Ho Tay. To him it was a challenge, and he smelled a big tip at journey's end.

As they flew up Hung Vuong Street, McCann could see the sun beginning to set blood red to his left, the lower section of the lake sparkling as the reflections danced on the rippled water. How long had Messon been gone? If he'd said he needed sleep merely as a ruse to get rid of him, then he could easily have been gone forty minutes. If so, he might already have tried the main gates and been thrown out by the goons. He may even have attempted to scale the walls somewhere, and been seized and beaten. McCann hoped to God he'd arrive in time.

At the juncture of Thanh Nien and Nghi Tam Street, he held up the money to the driver and jumped down into the street, running alongside Tran's compound walls, ducking in and out of the pedestrians as he scanned the crowd for Messon.

It was then he heard the engines for the first time.

At first it was just the vaguest of buzzing sounds, blending into the roar of the traffic. Little by little, as he ran towards the entrance to Tran's mansion, the noise became louder and louder. Still McCann scanned the faces in the crowd. Any second now he was certain he'd see Messon in front of him, and the race would be on once again.

It was the look on an elderly woman's face that stopped him dead in his tracks. She was standing by the wall, looking back over her shoulder, pointing up into the sky, her eyes filled with terror, her mouth gaping. The look on her wrinkled face was one McCann had only seen once before – during the Gulf War on the faces of the Iraqis as they looked up at the American strike aircraft racing towards them over the desert.

McCann spun round, looking up in the direction to which all heads were turned. More and more people in the crowd around him had stopped and were staring, transfixed, up into the sky towards the southern end of the lake.

The plane was descending at a steep angle over the buildings at the far end of Ho Tay. The twin wasp radials were screaming loudly as it leveled out at less than twenty feet above the surface of the lake, the prop wash whipping the lake up into a fury of water behind it. Judging by the shrill whine of the engines, the C-47 was now accelerating to full speed rather than slowing, as it skimmed the surface of the lake heading north across the water.

All around him, women and children were screaming; their faces painted with terror, running wildly in all directions. Some tripped and fell as they ran blindly for safety. Others were trampled by the panicked crowd. Mothers snatched small children and ran for cover, while some crouched in the gutters, pressing themselves flat to the ground, offering the small protection of their bodies to their children.

As the drivers in the busy street began to comprehend what was happening above them, the madness became still worse. As those at the controls of trucks, buses and scooters looked skywards at the plane that headed in towards them, collision followed collision, the vehicles slamming into each other in a deafening amalgam of twisted metal and human cries. Panic had gripped everyone.

McCann raced forward down the street, leaping over the bodies of those couched for cover. It was Messon. He must have left for the airport the second he'd been left to his own devices. McCann cursed himself for not having thought of the C-47. He'd taken it for granted that the man had taken a commercial flight from Sydney. Now it was too late. Messon's intention was clear, there was no stopping him now. The C-47 was on a bombing run, directed squarely at the southern face of Tran's house. McCann could only watch with a dreadful churning in the pit of his stomach as Effie barreled past him doing close to two hundred and twenty knots, fifty feet out into the lake from where he stood, now less than fifteen feet above the water.

As the plane flashed by, McCann followed the plane with his eyes. The room where he'd stood just over an hour ago talking to Tran was seconds away from total devastation.

Messon eased the stick forward, and the nose of the C-47 dipped further still. If he'd been lying on the wing, he could practically have touched the water's surface. The adrenalin was now rushing through every vein in his body like a succession of tidal waves. It was the most exhilarating feeling he'd ever experienced - fighting to keep Effie level and straight at a height of barely ten feet above the lake. His dead reckoning had been pinpoint accurate. He felt as though his head would burst with the pressure, it felt so wonderful.

He glanced at the fuel gauge. Both main tanks and the auxiliaries registered full. He grinned with satisfaction. Six hundred and sixty imperial gallons of Avgas would be more than enough.

But as his eyes flicked back from the instruments to the windscreen, his heart stopped still. Before him was the faintest of reflections in the glass. He knew it couldn't possibly have been his own – the angle of the windscreen precluded it. But as he stared at the obscure contours, an apparition began to form, like pictures painted by clouds in a stormy sky. Had he gone quite mad? The outline was unmistakably of his daughter. Venice! Her eyes were wide, her mouth open in terror. Then the phantom features swirled and were lost, fading almost as quickly as they had appeared. At that instant Messon's brain registered disaster.

With a shattering implosion, a wild lake bird reduced the left-hand windscreen to tiny fragments. Messon's head was jack-knifed to the left by the blast, his mouth immediately twisted into the appearance of a ghostly smile.

The plane continued to hurtle forwards, the hurricane force of the wind pushing Messon's eyes back into their sockets, his cheeks full spinnakers as the windbast tore through the shattered windscreen, pressing his feeble body back into the seat.

Effie roared on across the lake, dead level, Messon's fingers like white talons on the stick.

The plane was now less than a hundred feet from the house. McCann watched as the French windows opened and a figure supporting himself with a cane, stepped out onto the manicured lawns. One second later the C-47 slammed head-on at two hundred and twenty knots into the bowed windows of the white building.

Even at a distance of half a mile, the blast had the power and ferocity of an Exorcet missile. McCann felt the tremendous concussion as the plane impacted into the White House, the massive shockwave rippling across the lake with the speed of sound. A moment later the C-47's fuel tanks blew, and the entire house erupted in a fireball that leapt hundreds of feet into the air.

37.

Sydney
August 2nd.

It was possibly the best day they'd had all winter. Blue sky, soft breeze around eighteen knots, temperature in the mid seventies. Perfect easy harbor sailing weather. Yet here he was, confined in his office at the Priory, listening as the CEO of a large light industrial company outlined his requirements for a superannuation fund.

Life had been remarkably quiet over the past two months. He hadn't seen Rosalind since his return to Sydney from Hanoi. They'd talked many times on the phone, but a lunch or dinner had been impossible. She'd had to leave for Malaysia the day he arrived home. Her visit to Kuala Lumpur was immediately followed by a business trip to Laos. Rosalind was taking over close executive control of Buchanan Construction from McKintosh and Zeltis, and it was proving a full-on task.

She told McCann that she'd invited Sammi to visit her in Sydney and had arranged a ticket. Sammi had been initially overwhelmed, but had accepted.

Task Force Acorn had been disbanded. The conclusion had been drawn that the explosion at the Savoy could not be linked to any particular group; nor, as the Major Investigation Plan rules stated, was it "part of an on-going conspiracy that might cause particular concern to the government or the public at large." Torrance had thanked McCann for his great input.

Late each afternoon McCann drove down to the State Library in Macquarie Street to scan the world press for developments in Vietnam, Hong Kong, Malaysia, the United Kingdom, and the States. Piece by piece the news filtered through.

Brokov had cut a deal with the FBI to avoid the death penalty. He sang like the proverbial canary, implicating Sir Henry Trevor and Francis Greville, among others. Trevor was arrested in St Helier, Jersey, and released on half a million pounds bail. He promptly disappeared without trace. Greville attempted to do the same, but was intercepted in Macau by Inspector Tsui of the People's Liberation Army.

Osip Shirayev and his consiglière Dieter Fischer were indicted on seventy-nine counts of corporate fraud, money laundering and tax evasion. They were both refused bail, their trials marked down for the end of the year.

Constantin Khamovnikakh allied himself with the political bedfellows of Vladimir Zhiranovski, and stood for a seat in the Russian parliament. He was duly elected.

The umbrella task force, Mainstream, of which Lotus was one arm, continued its investigations.

McCann rented an apartment in Macleay Street, Potts Point, with a view that looked right out through the heads to the Pacific. If he couldn't sail, he'd watch others doing so.

On his return from Vietnam, McCann had called Boesel at Task Force Lotus. The FinCEN man told him he'd been shocked to the core to hear of the catastrophe in Hanoi on the news. But generally Boesel's tone had been cool. Perhaps the violent death of Tran Van Luc had taken all the fun out of a couple of years of hard work.

There would be no triumphant serving of papers, no extradition, no satisfaction of a trial.

McCann returned several times to the burnt out house in McCarr's Creek searching for Cyclops. He'd always been an incurable romantic, and the one-eyed bird had become a friend and a part of his life. On the fifth visit, he found her. She flew into a tree above his head. McCann swore she knew him. He arranged for a neighbor to continue regular feeding.

As the door closed behind the last client of the day, the phone rang on his desk.

'McCann,' he said, returning to his desk.

'Leo McCann?' It was the one woman he'd hoped might call.

'That's me,' he replied, rising to her humor.

'I'd like to see you as soon as possible.'

He remembered their first conversation, thinking then that when this woman spoke, she took it as a matter of course that others would listen. He smiled – he didn't mind in the least being classified among such people.

'Rosie! It's good to hear your voice. Tell me you're in town.'

'You guessed it was me,' Rosalind said, laughing. 'Damn! Yes, I'm in town. What are you up to right this second?'

'Absolutely nothing. Why?'

'I'm at the CYC. See you down here in fifteen minutes. Okay with you?'

'They'd have to fight me if they tried to stop me.'

Nine minutes later, McCann pulled off New Beach Road into the Cruising Yacht Club car park. He stuck his head round the door of the office, but there was no sign of Rosalind. As he began walking down the ramp towards the marina, one of the staff called out after him.

'Mr. McCann?'

'That's me,' he called back, turning.

'Miss Buchanan's up the end of 'B' arm. Number 56. She asked me to tell you.'

McCann thanked him, continuing down the marina.

As he made the final left turn he saw her.

Rosalind was standing facing him thirty feet down at the end of the walkway. She had her arms crossed, and was wearing blue jeans, a white Aran sweater, and the widest grin McCann had ever seen.

'Hello,' she said. 'It's very good of you to see me at such short notice. I'm Rosalind Buchanan.'

McCann laughed. They were the first words she'd ever spoken to him face to face, that first night at the Regent Club bar.

'Feel like a twilight sail?' she asked.

'Sure. In what?'

'Why don't we take this beauty,' she replied, stepping to one side, and gesturing behind her.

Moored to the end of the jetty was a late 40's, forty foot, carvil hull, old style gaff cutter. It had teak decks, a six-foot bowsprit, and ox-blood red canvas sails tied to the boom.

McCann stared in awe for a few seconds. 'She's very, very fine, Rosie,' he said, taking in the classic lines of the boat.

'She's yours,' said Rosalind. 'Her name's Tahuna.'

McCann switched his gaze from the cutter to Rosalind. 'Sounds pretty, but you paid me already, Rosie.'

'The company paid you. This is from me. You like her?'

'She's the finest damn boat I ever saw.'

'Glad you like her. Can you handle her by yourself?'

McCann's reply was a mixture of a shrug and a smile. 'Might need a bit of help. By the time she's carrying a jack yard topsail, a main, and a couple of jibs she'll be a handful. You sail?'

'No.'

'Then I'll just have to teach you.'

She walked towards him, gave him a hug, then looked up at him. 'That was always part of the deal.'

FOOTNOTE.

If you enjoyed my novel, and I hope you did as it is my favourite, then why not try another? See the rear cover for details. Or visit my web site http:// www.shanebriant.com

I wrote this book with a vision in my head for a film starring Cate Blanchett as Rosalind and Russell Crowe as McCann. They'd make a great team. I still live in hope that one day it will be made.

ABOUT THE AUTHOR

Shane Briant began his career in Dublin playing Hamlet aged twenty-one. The following year he was nominated for the London West End Theatre Critics 'Best Newcomer' award for his portrayal of Robin in the play "Children of the Wolf" opposite Yvonne Mitchell. He has made 34 films to date and had seven thrillers and his autobiography published. His novels have been published in the United States, Europe and Australia and New Zealand.